A Text Book of

ESSENTIALS OF NETWORKING

FOR
M.C.A. : MANAGEMENT : SEMESTER - II
SUBJECT CODE : IT24

**AS PER NEW REVISED SYLLABUS FOR
M.C.A. (PART II) FROM ACADEMIC YEAR 2015-2016**

A. V. DHAYGUDE
B.E. (Computer)
Dept. of Computer Engineering
Bharati Vidyapeeth's College of Engineering for Women, Pune.

A. V. DHUMANE
M.E. (Computer)
Vishwakarma Institute of Information Technology,
Kondhwa (Bk), Pune.

R. PATIL
M.C.S.
Lecturer and Head of Computer Science Dept.,
N.D.M.V.P. Samaj's K.T.H.M. College, Nasik.

NIRALI PRAKASHAN
ADVANCEMENT OF KNOWLEDGE

N3189

Essentials of Networking
ISBN 978-93-5164-99-08

First Edition : **January 2016**

© : **Authors**

The text of this publication, or any part thereof, should not be reproduced or transmitted in any form or stored in any computer storage system or device for distribution including photocopy, recording, taping or information retrieval system or reproduced on any disc, tape, perforated media or other information storage device etc., without the written permission of Authors with whom the rights are reserved. Breach of this condition is liable for legal action.

Every effort has been made to avoid errors or omissions in this publication. In spite of this, errors may have crept in. Any mistake, error or discrepancy so noted and shall be brought to our notice shall be taken care of in the next edition. It is notified that neither the publisher nor the authors or seller shall be responsible for any damage or loss of action to any one, of any kind, in any manner, therefrom.

Published By :

NIRALI PRAKASHAN

Abhyudaya Pragati, 1312, Shivaji Nagar

Off J.M. Road, PUNE – 411005

Tel - (020) 25512336/37/39, Fax - (020) 25511379

Email : niralipune@pragationline.com

☞ **DISTRIBUTION CENTRES**

PUNE

Nirali Prakashan : 119, Budhwar Peth, Jogeshwari Mandir Lane, Pune 411002, Maharashtra
Tel : (020) 2445 2044, 66022708, Fax : (020) 2445 1538
Email : bookorder@pragationline.com, niralilocal@pragationline.com

Nirali Prakashan : S. No. 28/27, Dhyari, Near Pari Company, Pune 411041
Tel : (020) 24690204 Fax : (020) 24690316
Email : dhyari@pragationline.com, bookorder@pragationline.com

MUMBAI

Nirali Prakashan : 385, S.V.P. Road, Rasdhara Co-op. Hsg. Society Ltd.,
Girgaum, Mumbai 400004, Maharashtra
Tel : (022) 2385 6339 / 2386 9976, Fax : (022) 2386 9976
Email : niralimumbai@pragationline.com

☞ **DISTRIBUTION BRANCHES**

JALGAON

Nirali Prakashan : 34, V. V. Golani Market, Navi Peth, Jalgaon 425001,
Maharashtra, Tel : (0257) 222 0395, Mob : 94234 91860

KOLHAPUR

Nirali Prakashan : New Mahadvar Road, Kedar Plaza, 1st Floor Opp. IDBI Bank
Kolhapur 416 012, Maharashtra. Mob : 9850046155

NAGPUR

Pratibha Book Distributors : Above Maratha Mandir, Shop No. 3, First Floor,
Rani Jhanshi Square, Sitabuldi, Nagpur 440012, Maharashtra
Tel : (0712) 254 7129

DELHI

Nirali Prakashan : 4593/21, Basement, Aggarwal Lane 15, Ansari Road, Daryaganj
Near Times of India Building, New Delhi 110002
Mob : 08505972553

BENGALURU

Pragati Book House : House No. 1, Sanjeevappa Lane, Avenue Road Cross,
Opp. Rice Church, Bengaluru – 560002.
Tel : (080) 64513344, 64513355,Mob : 9880582331, 9845021552
Email:bharatsavla@yahoo.com

CHENNAI

Pragati Books : 9/1, Montieth Road, Behind Taas Mahal, Egmore,
Chennai 600008 Tamil Nadu, Tel : (044) 6518 3535,
Mob : 94440 01782 / 98450 21552 / 98805 82331,
Email : bharatsavla@yahoo.com

niralipune@pragationline.com | www.pragationline.com

Also find us on ⓕ www.facebook.com/niralibooks

PREFACE

There has been significant development in recent years in the field of Computer Science. The book is a perfect blend of technology which has been a field of dramatic revolution; this subject focuses on different technologies of it.

It gives us great pleasure in presenting this book **"Essentials of Networking"** designed to serve as a textbook for students of the Second Semester of Master of Computer Application (M.C.A.). The book is organized in such a way that it mirrors the revised syllabus. The book will be found useful by a wide section of readers, teachers and students of Business, Technology and Computer Management courses in Indian Universities. The entire book is freshly written as per the revised syllabus.

The book has its own unique features. It brings out the subject in a very simple and lucid manner for easy and comprehensive understanding of the basic concepts, its intricacies, procedures and practices. This book will help the readers to have a broader view on Networking Concepts. The language used in this book is easy and will help students to improve their vocabulary of Technical terms and understand the matter in a better and happier way.

Particular attention has been paid to making this book stimulating and highly readable. The result is a text which is clear, focused and designed to capture student interest. This text is equally suitable for courses directed at undergraduates and postgraduates.

We have given our best inputs for this book. Any suggestions towards the improvement of this book and sincere comments are most welcome on niralipune@pragationline.com.

Authors

ACKNOWLEDGEMENT

We sincerely thank Shri. Dineshbhai Furia and Shri. Jignesh Furia, the publishers, for the confidence reposed in us and giving us this opportunity to reach out to the students of management studies.

We thank Prof. Gautam Bapat for the friendly manner in which he reviewed my script and suggested improvements from time to time, We must say he has done the editing, exceptionally well for our book.

We thank Mrs. Anita Panajkar and Mrs. Aabha Athavale for their important inputs time to time. Mrs. Prachi Sawant painstakingly attended to all the details to make this book appear good.

We also thank Mr. Ravindra Walodare, Mr. Sachin Shinde, Nikunj Joshi, Nilesh Deshmukh, Ashok Bodke, Moshin Sayyed and Nitin Thorat.

We am also grateful to all the staff members of Nirali Prakashan, who were involved in the publication of this book.

Authors

SYLLABUS

1. **Introduction** (12 M, 5 Hrs.)

   What is a Computer communication, communication system, Signal and Data, Channel Characteristics, Transmission Modes, Synchronous and asynchronous transmission. Transmission Media:

   a) Guided Media : Twisted Pair, Coaxial and Fiber-optic cables,

   b) Unguided Media: Radio, VHF, Micro Waves and Satellite

   Multichannel Data Communication: Circuits, channels and multichanneling

   Multiplexing: FDM, TDM, CDM and WDM

2. **Common Network Architecture** (13 M, 5 Hrs.)

   Connection oriented N/Ws vs Connectionless N/Ws, Peer to peer networks, X.25 networks, Ethernet (Standard and Fast): frame format and specifications, Wireless LANs - 802.11(Architecture, issues, features etc.), 802.11x.

3. **The OSI Reference Model** (13 M, 5 Hrs.)

   Protocol Layering, ISO/OSI reference Model, TCP/IP Model, OSI vs.TCP/IP

4. **Local Area Networks** (7 M, 3 Hrs.)

   Components & Technology, Access Technique, Transmission Protocol & Media

5. **Broad Band Networks** (10 M, 4 Hrs.)

   Integrated Service Digital Networks (ISDN), Broad Band ISDN, ATM and ATM Traffic Management, Very Small Aperture Terminal (VSAT)

6. **IP Addressing & Routing** (25 M, 10 Hrs.)

   IP addresses – Network part and Host Part, Network Masks, Network addresses and

   Broadcast addresses, Address Classes, Loopback address, IP routing concepts, Routing Tables, Stream & Packets, Sliding Windows, Role and Features of IP, TCP, TCP Connections, types and working. IPV6: The next generation Protocol

7. **Application Layer** (20 M, 8 Hrs.)

   Domain Name System (DNS) and DNS servers, Electronic Mail: Architecture and services, Message Formats, MIME, message transfer, SMTP, Mail Gateways, Relays, Configuring Mail Servers, File Transfer Protocol, General Model, commands, World Wide Web: Introduction, Architectural overview, static and dynamic web pages, WWW pages and Browsing, HTTP.

CONTENTS

1. **Introduction**   **1.1 – 1.58**

2. **Common Network Architecture**   **2.1 – 2.28**

3. **The OSI Reference Model**   **3.1 – 3.18**

4. **Local Area Networks**   **4.1 – 4.22**

5. **Broad Band Networks**   **5.1 – 5.24**

6. **IP Addressing & Routing**   **6.1 – 6.62**

7. **Application Layer**   **7.1 – 7.64**

Chapter 1 ...

INTRODUCTION

Contents ...

1.1 Introduction

    1.1.1 What is a Computer Communication?

    1.1.2 Communication System

    1.1.3 Signal and Data

    1.1.4 Channel Characteristics

    1.1.5 Transmission Modes

    1.1.6 Synchronous and Asynchronous Transmission

1.2 Transmission Media

    1.2.1 Guided Media – Twisted Pair, Coaxial and Fiber-optic Cables

    1.2.3 Unguided Media: Radio, VHF, Micro Waves and Satellite

1.3 Multichannel Data Communication

    1.3.1 Circuits

    1.3.2 Channels and Multichanneling

1.4 Multiplexing

    1.4.1 FDM

    1.4.2 TDM

    1.4.3 WDM

    1.4.4 CDM

    • Practice Questions

1.1 Introduction

Computer networks are now business critical in all modern organizations and business enterprises. They are important in everyday life. This subject introduces students to the fundamental issues in modern data communications and computer networks. This is essential knowledge for all users of IT, IT professionals and those who wish to specialize in computer networking.

1.1.1 What is a Computer Communication?

Communication is the conveyance of a message from one entity, called the source or transmitter, to another, called the destination or receiver, using a communication channel.

Communication is defined as transfer of information, such as thoughts and messages between two entities. The invention of telegraph, radio, telephone, and television made possible instantaneous communication over long distances.

To give a very basic example of such a communication system is conversation; people commonly exchange verbal messages, with the channel consisting of waves of compressed air molecules at frequencies, which are audible to the human ear. This is depicted in Fig. 1.1.

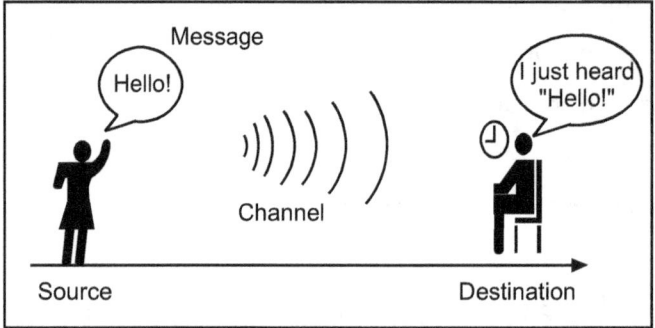

Fig. 1.1: Basic communication model

The conveyance of a message could be followed by a reciprocal response message from the original destination (now a source) to the original source (now a destination) to complete one cycle in a dialogue between corresponding entities. Depending on the application or need for the information exchange, either atomic one-way transactions or a two-way dialogue could be appropriate.

The only way that a message source can be certain that the destination properly received the message is by some kind of acknowledgment response from the destination.

Fig. 1.2 shows communication between one computer (sender/source) sending a message to another computer (receiver/destinations) over a wire.

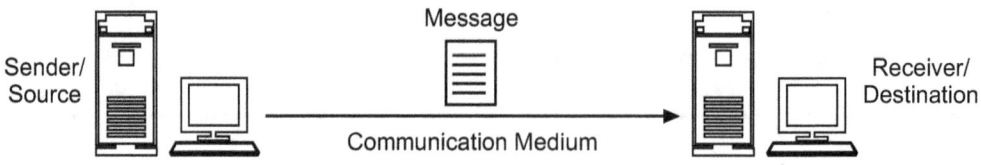

Fig. 1.2: Communication between two computers

1.1.2 Communication System

Data is a collection of facts in raw forms that become information after processing.This is the transfer of data or information between a sources to a destination. The source transmits the data and the receiver receives it. In case of computer networks this exchange is done between two devices over a transmission medium.

The purpose of data communications is to provide the rules and regulations that allow computers with different disk operating systems, languages, cabling and locations to share resources. The rules and regulations are called protocols and standards in data communication.

The main objective of data communication and networking is to enable seamless exchange of data between any two points in the world. This exchange of data takes place over a computer network.

When we communicate, we are sharing information. This sharing can be local or remote. Data communications through the telephone network can reach any point in the world. The volume of overseas fax transmissions is increasing constantly, and computer networks that link thousands of businesses, governments and universities are pervasive.

In data communication, information comes in different forms such as text, images, audio, video and numbers.

1. **Text** is represented as a bit pattern. The sequence of bits is 0's or 1's. It consists of number of bit patterns. They represent text symbols. Each set of bit patterns is called as a code and process of representing symbols is called as coding.

2. **Images** are also represented by bit patterns. Image is composed of a matrix of pixels.

3. **Audio** refers to the recording or broadcasting of sound. Audio is continuous, not discrete. It is by nature different from text, numbers, images.

4. **Video** refers to recording or broadcasting of a picture or movie. Video can be combination of images, each a discrete entity arranged to convey the idea of the motion.

5. **Numbers** are represented by bit patterns.

A Computer Communication Network system containing any combination of computers, computer terminals, printers, audio or visual display devices, or telephones interconnected by telecommunications equipment or cables: used to transmit or receive information.

Components of Data Communication :

The main purpose of communication system is to exchange data between two points by electric means.

Fig. 1.3 shows exchange of the data between workstation and server on telephone lines.

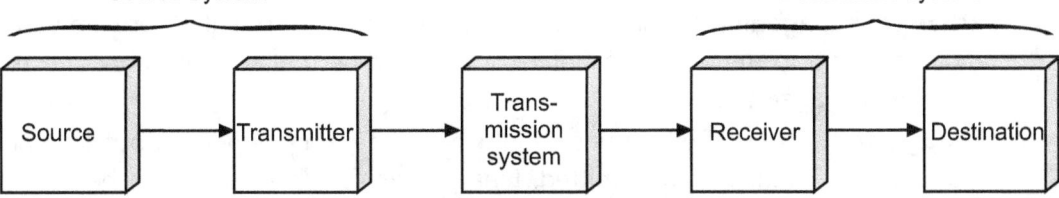

Fig. 1.3: Components of data communication

Following are the different blocks of communication system.

1. **Source:** Source generates the data which is to be transmitted. Examples of sources are telephone and personal computers.

    Examples: (a) Terminal, (b) Computer, (c) Mainframe.

2. **Transmitter:** Data from the source are not transmitted in the same form which are generated by source, transmitter converts and encodes the data so as to produce electromagnetic signals. Modem is used to convert incoming data stream into analog signals that can be handled by telephone network.

3. **Transmission system:** It is a single transmission line or network connecting source and destination.

    Examples: (a) Cabling, (b) Microwave, (c) Fiber optics.

4. **Receiver:** Function of the receiver is to accept the information from transmission line or network and converting it into digital data in the form of stream so that destination computer can handle the data.

    Example: Printer terminal.

5. **Destination:** Destination is a device like computer that receives the data.

Characteristics of Data Communication System :

Characteristics of data communication system are listed below:

1. **Delivery:** The data or information should be delivered to correct destination.

2. **Timeliness:** For video and audio data the system should deliver the data or information in a timely manner i.e. without any time delay.

3. **Accuracy:** The communication system should be deliver data accurately i.e. without any error.

4. **Transmission system utilization:** It is a measure of use of transmission facilities that are shared among the number of communicating devices. Various multiplexing techniques are used to share total capacity of transmission medium with number of users.

5. **Synchronization:** Receiver must be able to detect when transmission begins and when it ends. Synchronization between receiver and transmitter should be achieved using handshaking signals.

6. **Error detection and Correction:** Transmitted signal may get distorted when it travels long distance through medium. For example, a file from one computer can be transmitted to other should be accompanied by error detection code.

7. **Exchange management:** Besides the nature and timing of signals, there are various requirement for communication between two parties that comes under the term exchange management.

8. **Message formatting:** Two parties should have some agreement about format of data to be exchanged or transmitted. Binary code for characters is to be adopted universally.

1.1.3 Signal and Data

Information that is stored within computer systems and transferred over a computer network can be divided into two categories: data and signals. Data are entities that convey meaning within a computer or computer system. If you want to transfer this data from one point to another, either by using a physical wire or by using radio waves, the data has to be converted into a signal. Signals are the electric or electromagnetic encoding of data and are used to transmit data.

Converting Data into Signals :

Like data, signals can be analog or digital. Typically, digital signals convey digital data, and analog signals convey analog data. However, you can use analog signals to convey digital data and digital signals to convey analog data. The choice of using either analog or digital signals often depends on the transmission equipment that is used and the environment in which the signals must travel. There are four combinations of data and signals: digital data transmitted using digital signals, digital data transmitted using analog signals, analog data transmitted using analog signals, and analog data transmitted using digital signals.

Table 1.1 : Four combinations of data and signals

Data	Signal	Encoding or Conversion Technique	Common Devices	Common Systems
Analog	Analog	Amplitude modulation Frequency modulation	TV tuner Radio tuner	Telephone AM and FM radio Broadcast TV Cable TV
Digital	Digital	NRZ-L NRZI Manchester Differential Manchester Bipolar-AMI 4B/5B	Digital encoder	Local area networks Telephone systems
Digital	(Discrete) Analog	Amplitude shift keying Frequency shift keying Phase shift keying	Modem	Dial-up Internet access DSL Cable modems Digital Broadcast TV
Analog	Digital	Pulse code modulation Delta modulaiton	Code	Telephone systems Music systems

1.1.4 Channel Characteristics

In computer networking, a communication channel or channel, refers either to a physical transmission medium such as a wire, or to a logical connection over a multiplexed medium such as a radio channel. A channel is used to convey an information signal, for example a digital bit stream, from one or several senders (or transmitters) to one or several receivers. A channel has a certain capacity for transmitting information, often measured by its bandwidth in Hz or its data rate in bits per second.

Communicating data from one location to another requires some form of r medium. These medium called communication channels, use two types of media: cable (twisted-pair wire, cable, and fiber-optic cable) and broadcast (microwave, satellite, radio, and infrared). Cable or wire line media use physical wires of cables to transmit data and information. Twisted-pair wire and coaxial cables are made of copper, and fiber-optic cable is made of glass.

Propagation time (channel latency): It is the amount of time required to propagate information from source to destination through the channel. It depends on media characteristics, signal propagation speed and transmission distance.

Throughput: It defined as the number of bits, characters or blocks passing through a data communication system over a period of time.

Throughput = Packet length in bits = Packet length in bits/(transmission time + propagation on time).

Bandwidth of a Signal:

Bandwidth of a signal is defined as the portion of the electromagnetic spectrum occupied by a signal. We can also define the bandwidth as "the frequency range over which an information signal is transmitted".

Bandwidth of analog and digital signals are calculated in separate ways; analog signal bandwidth is measured in terms of its frequency (Hz) but digital signal bandwidth is measured in terms of bit rate (bits per second, (bps)).

The bandwidth is the difference between the upper and lower frequency limits of the signal. Each of these signals (voice, music etc. signals) will have its own frequency range and this frequency range of a signal is known as its bandwidth.

The range of voice signal is 300 Hz to 3400 kHz as shown in Fig. 1.4.

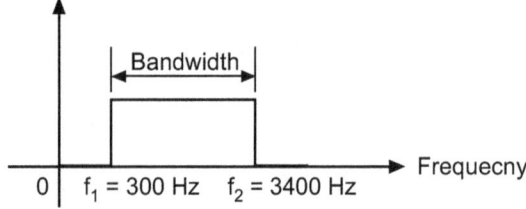

Fig. 1.4: Bandwidth of voice signal

Therefore, BW (Bandwidth) $\quad = f_2 - f_1$

$$= 3400 - 300$$

$$= 3100 \text{ Hz.}$$

Table 1.2 shows bandwidth of different signals.

Table 1.2: Bandwidths of different signals

Sr. No.	Signal types	Frequency range	Bandwidth
1.	Voice signal for telephony	300 – 3400 Hz	3,100 Hz
2.	TV signals (picture)	0 – 5 MHz	5 MHz
3.	Digital data	* 300 – 3400	3,100
4.	Music signal	20 – 15000 Hz	14,980 Hz

1. Frequency Spectrum:

It is the representation of a signal in the frequency domain. Frequency spectrum can be obtained by using either Fourier series or Fourier transform.

Frequency spectrum consists of the amplitude and phase spectrum of the signal and indicates the amplitude and phase of various frequency components present in the given signal. It enables us to analyze and synthesize a signal.

2. Effect of Pulse Width of data on the Bandwidth:

When data is to be transmitted then the bandwidth depends on the pulse width of data. As the width of the data pulses which are to be transmitted reduces the bandwidth requirement increases according to the time scaling property of Fourier transform, (See, Fig. 1.5).

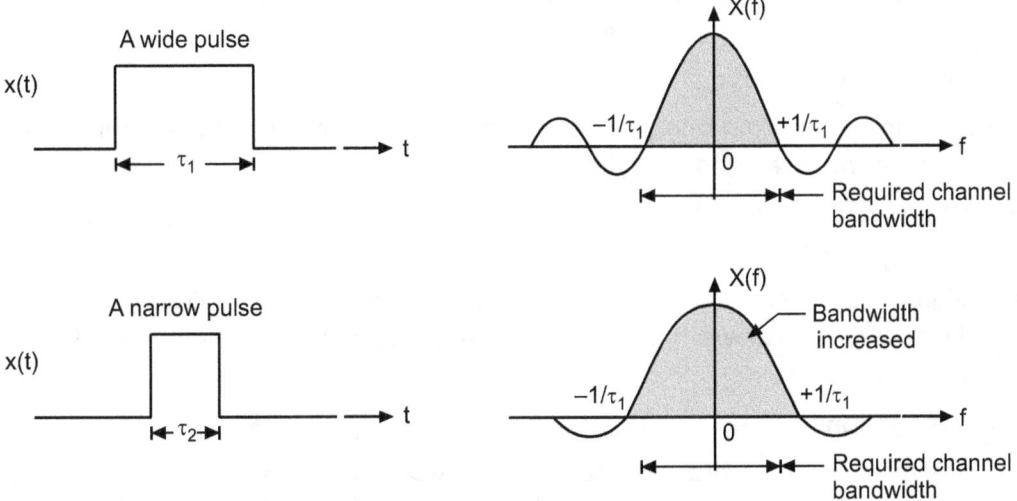

Fig. 1.5: Effect of data pulse width on bandwidth

Bandwidth of a Medium :

Bandwidth of a medium also known as channel bandwidth. A channel is the medium through which the signal carrying information will be passed. The channel bandwidth determines the type of signal to be transmitted i.e. analog or digital.

Bandwidth of a medium is defined as the maximum frequency it can allow to pass through it without attenuating it and without distorting the shape of the signal.

When the medium has less bandwidth than required, then signal distortion will take place as shown in Fig. 1.6. Channel or medium bandwidth is used to describe the range of frequencies required to transmit the desired information.

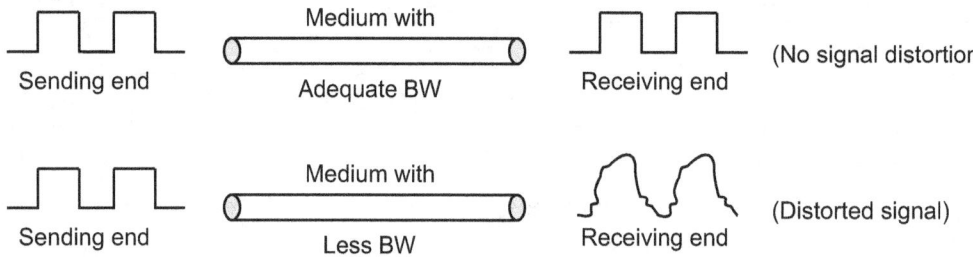

Fig. 1.6 : Distortion in signal

Terms related to Bandwidth:

1. **Amplitude:** The maximum value of an AC quantity is called as amplitude. It is measured in volts, amperes or watt depending on the type of signal.

2. **Frequency:** It is defined as the number of cycles completed by an AC quantity in one second. Its unit is Hz (Hertz).

3. **Phase:** Phase describes the position of the waveform with respect to time zero.

4. **Time period:** It is defined as the time taken in seconds by the waveforms of an AC quantity to complete one cycle.

Analog and Digital Signals :

Data is transmitted from one point to another point by means of electrical signals that may be in digital and analog form.

- **Analog data** refers to information that is continuous; For example, sounds made by a human voice.

- **Digital data** refers to information that has discrete states. Digital data take on discrete values. For example, data are stored in computer memory in the form of 0's and 1's.

Signal Propagation:

Movement of signal through the channel wired or wireless is called as signal propagation. Fig. 1.7 shows a signal source, a communication channel and the destination of signal receiver.

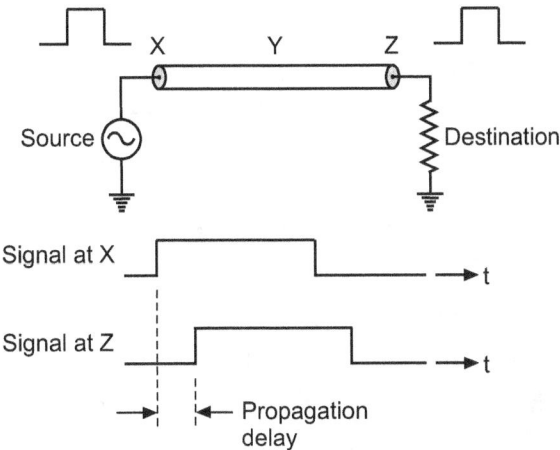

Fig. 1.7: Signal Propagation

The signal containing the data or information is in the electric form and it is applied at point X of the conducting medium. The electrons in the conducting medium will transfer the charge to the adjacent electrons and the signal at point X gets transferred to Y and then to Z which is the receiving point (See Fig. 1.7). The shape of the signal at the receiver i.e. point Z is almost same as that at the source i.e. point X, but the signal reaches point Z after a finite delay called **propagation delay**.

The signal in the Fig. 1.7 producing source can be a person talking on the computer producing a data signal. If we apply a signal at one end of the conducting medium then eventually this signal gets propagated to the other end of the medium. Signals which repeat itself after a fixed time period are called periodic signals. Signals which do not repeat itself after a fixed time period are called non-periodic signals.

Analog Signal :

An analog signal is a continuous wave form that changes smoothly over time which is usually represented by sine wave. This signal can take on any value in a specified range of values. As the wave moves from value A to B, it passes through and includes an infinite number of values along its path.

A simple example is Alternating Current (AC), which continually varies between about +110 volts and −110 volts in a sine wave fashion 60 times per second.

A more complex example of an analog signal is the time-varying electrical voltage generated when a person speaks into a dynamic microphone or telephone.

Analog signals are usually specified as a continuously varying voltage over time and can be displayed on a device known as an oscilloscope. The maximum voltage displacement of a periodic (repeating) analog signal is called its amplitude, and the shortest distance between crests of a periodic analog wave is called its **wavelength**.

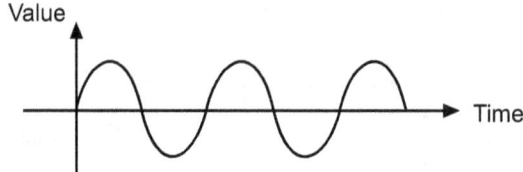

Fig. 1.8: Analog Signal

Advantages of Analog Signal:

1. The main advantage is the fine definition of the analog signal which has the potential for an infinite amount of signal resolution.

2. Compared to digital signals, analog signals are of higher density.

3. Processing of analog signals may be achieved more simply than with the digital equivalent. An analog signal may be processed directly by analog components, though some processes are not available except in digital form.

4. Best suited for of audio and video transmission.

5. Consumes less bandwidth than digital signals to carry the same information.

6. Analog signal is less susceptible to noise.

Disadvantages of Analog Signal:

1. The primary disadvantage of analog signaling is that any system has noise – i.e., random unwanted variation.

2. The effects of noise create signal loss and distortion.

3. Most of the analog systems also suffer from generation loss.

Analog Transmission :

Analog (or analogue) transmission is a transmission method of conveying voice, data, image, signal or video information using a continuous signal which varies in amplitude, phase, or some other property in proportion to that of a variable. It could be the transfer of an analog source signal, using an analog modulation method such as Frequency Modulation (FM) or Amplitude Modulation (AM) etc.

Analogue data transmission consists of sending information over a physical transmission medium in the form of a wave.

Data is transmitted via a carrier wave, a simple wave whose only purpose is to transport data by modification of one of its characteristics (amplitude, frequency or phase), and for this reason analogue transmission is generally called carrier wave modulation transmission.

Three types of analogue transmission are defined depending on which parameter of the carrier wave is being varied:

- Transmission by amplitude modulation of the carrier wave.
- Transmission by frequency modulation of the carrier wave.
- Transmission by phase modulation of the carrier wave.

This type of transmission refers to a scheme in which the data to be transmitted are already in analogue form. So, to transmit this signal, the DCTE (Data Circuit Terminating Equipment) must continuously convolve the signal to be transmitted and the carrier wave. In the case, of transmission by amplitude modulation, it occurs as shown in Fig. 1.9.

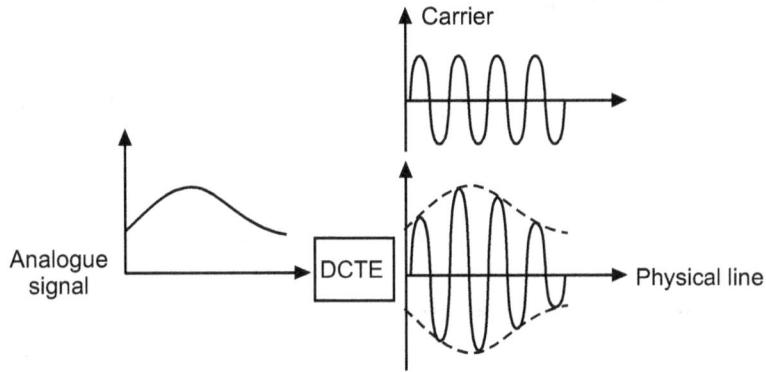

Fig. 1.9 : Transmission by amplitude modulation

Digital Signal :

A digital signal is discrete in nature. Transmission of signals that vary discretely with time between two values of some physical quantity, one value representing the binary number **0** and the other representing 1.

With copper cabling, the variable quantity is typically the voltage or the electrical potential. With fiber-optic cabling or wireless communication, variation in intensity or some other physical quantity is used.

Digital signals use discrete values for the transmission of binary information over a communication medium such as a network cable or a telecommunications link. On a serial transmission line, a digital signal is transmitted 1-bit at a time.

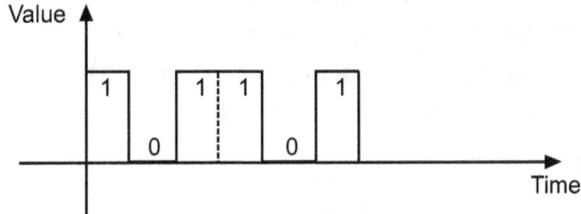

Fig. 1.10: Digital signal

Advantages of Digital Signal:

1. Digital signals are more secure – it is easier to encrypt digital signals making internet shopping less risky for example.

2. Digital signals suffer less from noise because any errors can be detected and corrected using regenerators.

3. Optical fibres can transmit digital signals and optical fibres are cheap.

4. Digital signals can be compressed so more channels can be transmitted along the same fibre.

5. Can connect several different users to the same line - such as video conferencing.

Disadvantages of Digital Signal:

1. Digital signals need more bandwidth to transmit the same information.

2. The transmitter and receiver have to synchronise very carefully so that the information makes sense.

Digital Transmission :

Digital transmission means of transmitting both digital and analog signals. Usually assume the signal is carrying digital (or digitized) data. This transmission can be propagated a limited distance before reduction distorts the signal and compromises the data integrity. A repeater retrieves the (digital) signal; recovers the (digital) data, e.g., a pattern of 1's and 0's; retransmits a new signal.

A similar technique used for the analog signal where we assume that the data is digital or digitized; repeater recovers the (digital or digitized) data and amplifies only the data and retransmits. Fig. 1.11 shows digital transmission by a repeater.

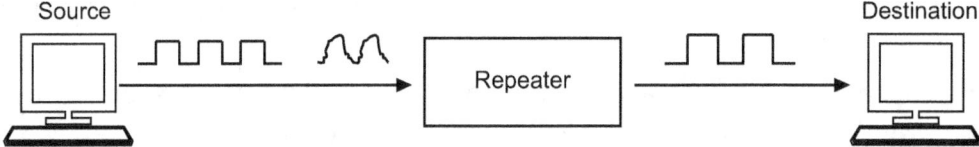

Fig. 1.11: Digital transmission

Digital Signal to Analog Transmission

For the problem of how to send digital signal over an analog network, Modems are required to convert to digital signal to analog signal in telephone networks. Modem stands for modulator and demodulator. A modulator uses some coding scheme and converts a digital signal into an analog signal and demodulator converts the analog signal back into the digital signal. Fig. 1.12 shows role of modem.

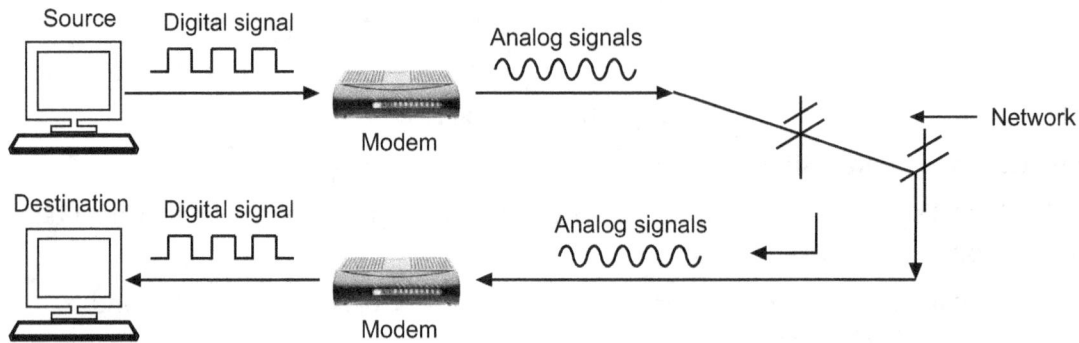

Fig. 1.12: Digital to analog transmission using a modem

When data from one computer is sent to another via some analog carrier, it is first converted into analog signals. Analog signals are modified to reflect digital data, i.e. binary data. An analog is characterized by its amplitude, frequency and phase. There are three kinds of digital-to-analog conversions possible as given below:

Amplitude Shift Keying (ASK):

In this conversion technique, the amplitude of analog carrier signal is modified to reflect binary data, (See Fig. 1.13).

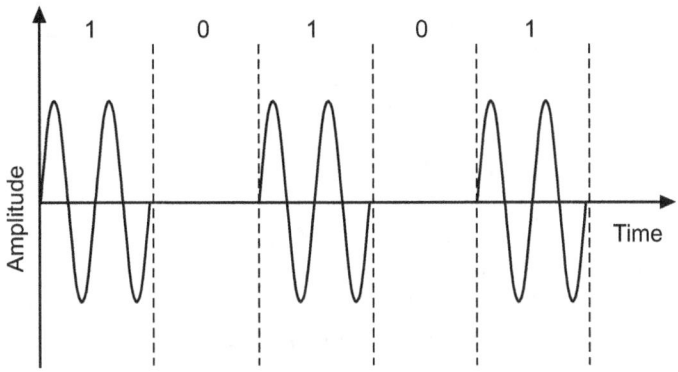

Fig. 1.13 : Amplitude Shift Keying

When binary data represents digit 1, the amplitude is held otherwise it is set to 0. Both frequency and phase remain same as in the original carrier signal.

Frequency Shift Keying (FSK):

In this conversion technique, the frequency of the analog carrier signal is modified to reflect binary data, (See Fig. 1.14).

FSK technique uses two frequencies, f1 and f2. One of them, for example f1, is chosen to represent binary digit 1 and the other one is used to represent binary digit 0. Both amplitude and phase of the carrier wave are kept intact.

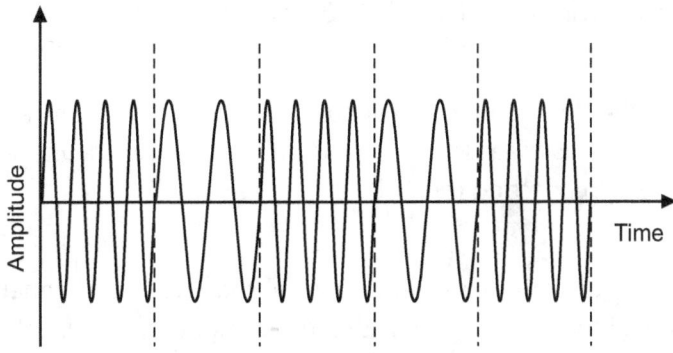

Fig. 1.14 : Frequency Shift Keying

3. Phase Shift Keying (PSK):

In this conversion scheme, the phase of the original carrier signal is altered to reflect the binary data, (See Fig. 1.15).

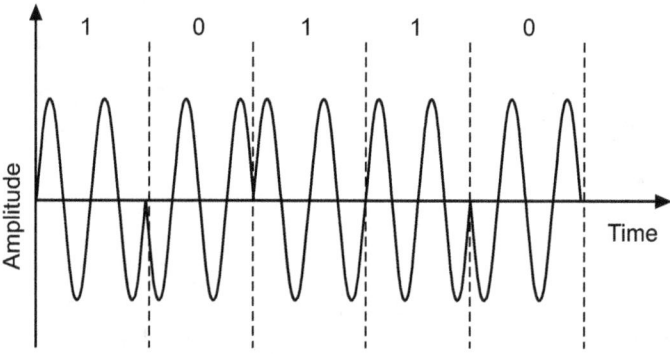

Fig. 1.15 : Phase Shift Keying

When a new binary symbol is encountered, the phase of the signal is altered. Amplitude and frequency of the original carrier signal is kept intact.

Baud Rate and Bits per Second :

Bit rate:

Bit rate is the number of bits transmitted in one second i.e. bits per second (bps).

Relation between bit rate and bit interval can be as follows,

$$\text{Bit rate} = 1/\text{Bit interval}$$

It is expressed as bits per second (bps).

Other units used to express bit rate are Kbps, Mbps and Gbps.

1 kilobit per second (Kbps) = 1,000 bits per second.

1 Megabit per second (Mbps) = 1,000,000 bits per second.

1 Gigabit per second (Gbps) = 1,000,000,000 bits per second.

Bit interval:

The bit interval is the time required to send one single bit. The bit rate is the number of bit intervals per second. This means that the bit rate is number of bits sent in one second, usually expressed in bits per second (bps).

Baud rate:

Baud rate is the number of times the signal level changes in a channel per second. Baud rate is less than or equal to the bit rate. It is the rate of signal speed, i.e. the rate at which the signal changes. A digital signal with two levels '0' and '1' will have the same baud rate and bit rate. Fig. 1.16 shows bit rate and interval.

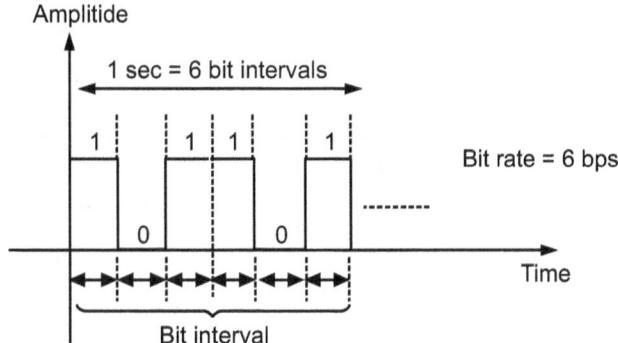

Fig. 1.16: Bit rate and bit interval

Example 1: A signal carries three bits in each signal element. If 1200 signal elements are sent per second, find the baud rate and the bit rate.

Solution: Baud rate = Number of signal elements

= 1200 bps

Bit rate = baud rate × Number of bits per signal element

= 1200 × 3

= **3600 bps.**

Example 2: The bit rate of a signal is 2000. If each signal element carries five bits, what is the baud rate ?

Solution: Baud rate = Bit rate / Number of bits per signal element

= 2000 / 5

= **400 bps.**

Comparison of Analog and Digital Signals:

Analog and digital signals are used to transmit information.

Table 1.3 : Difference between analog and digital signals

Terms	Analog signal	Digital signal
Signal:	Analog signal is a continuous signal which represents physical measurements.	Digital signals are discrete time signals generated by digital modulation.
Waves:	Denoted by sine waves:	Denoted by square waves:

Representation:	Uses continuous range of values to represent information.	Uses discrete or discontinuous values to represent information.
Example:	Human voice in air, analog electronic devices.	Computers, CDs, DVDs, and other digital electronic devices.
Flexibility:	Analog hardware is not flexible.	Digital hardware is flexible in implementation.
Uses:	Can be used in analog devices only. Best suited for audio and video transmission.	Best suited for Computing and digital electronics.
Applications:	Thermometer	PCs, PDAs
Power:	Analog instrument draws large power.	Digital instrument draws only negligible power.
Cost:	Low cost and portable.	Cost is high and not easily portable.
Impedance:	Low.	High order of 100 Mega Ohm.

1.1.5 Transmission Modes

There are three ways or modes of data transmission i.e., Simplex, Half duplex (HDX), Full duplex (FDX) as shown in Fig. 1.17.

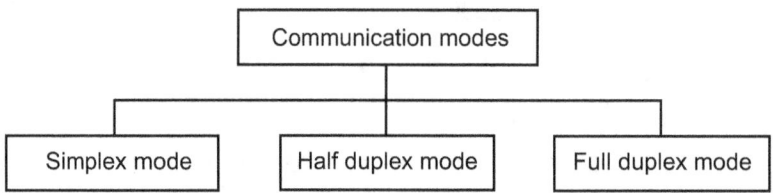

Fig. 1.17: Data Transmission Modes

Simplex Mode

In Simplex Mode, the communication can take place in only one direction(uni-directional). That means that a terminal can only send data and cannot receive it or it can only receive data but cannot send it.

Today, Simplex Mode of data communication is not popular, because most of the modem communications require two-way exchange of data. However, simplex mode of communication is used in business field at certain point-of-sale terminals in which sales data is entered without a corresponding reply. The other examples of simplex communication modes are Radio and T.V transmissions.

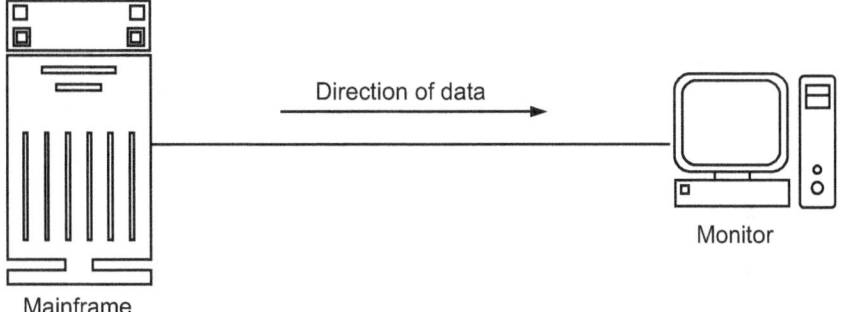

Fig. 1.18: Simplex communication mode

In computer system, the keyboard, monitor and printer are examples of simplex devices. The keyboard can only be used to enter data into computer, while monitor and printer can only accept (display/print) output.

Advantages:

1. Very simple and easy communication method.

2. Cheaper in cost.

Disadvantages:

1. Only allows for communication in one direction.

2. Simplex transmission are not often used because it is not possible to send back error to the transmit end.

Half-Duplex Mode

In Half-duplex mode, the communication can take place in both directions, but only in one direction at a time. In this mode, data is sent and received alternatively. It is like a one-lane bridge where two-way traffic must give way in order to cross the other. At a time only one end transmits data while other end receives. In addition, it is possible to perform error detection and request the sender to re-transmit information.

The Internet browsing is an example of half duplex mode. A walkie-talkie operates in half duplex mode. It can only send or receive a transmission at any given time. It cannot do both at the same time. When we issue a request to download a web document, then that document is downloaded and displayed before we issue another request.

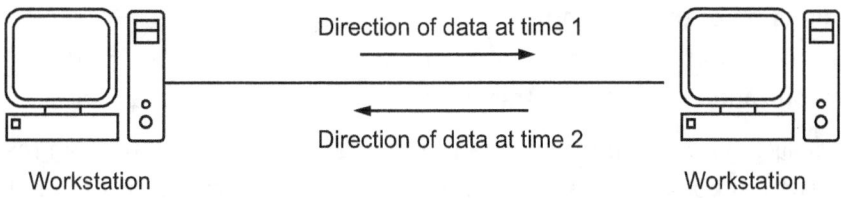

Fig. 1.19: Half-duplex communication mode

Advantages:

1. Enable to two way communication.

2. Low cost than full duplex communication mode.

Disadvantages:

1. Only one device can transmit at a time.

2. High cost than simplex mode.

Full-Duplex Mode

In Full-duplex mode, the communication can take place in both directions simultaneously, i.e. at the same time on the same channel. Full-duplex mode type of communication is similar to automobile traffic on a two-lane road. Full-duplex mode is the fastest directional mode of communication. The telephone communication system is an example of full-duplex communication mode.

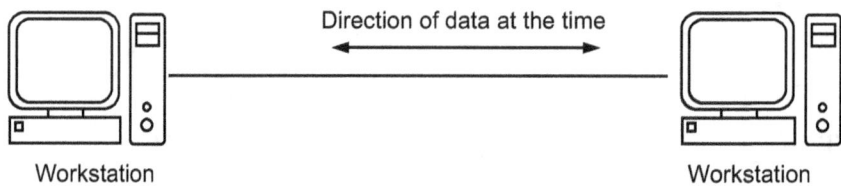

Direction of data at the time

Workstation   Workstation

Fig. 1.20: Full-duplex communication mode

Advantages:

1. Enables two-way communication simultaneously.

2. Fastest method of data communication.

Disadvantages:

1. More expensive and complex method.

2. Two bandwidth channels are required for data transmission.

Types of data transmission modes :

Data transmission means transferring of data or information from one computer to another computer using a transmission medium. This can occur in several different ways.

The transmission is characterized by:

- The direction of the exchanges,
- The transmission mode: the number of bits sent simultaneously, and
- Synchronization between the transmitter and receiver.

By Multiplexing different message signals can share a single transmission media (guided or unguided) such as coaxial cable, fiber-optic etc. Fig. 1.21 shows types of data transmission modes.

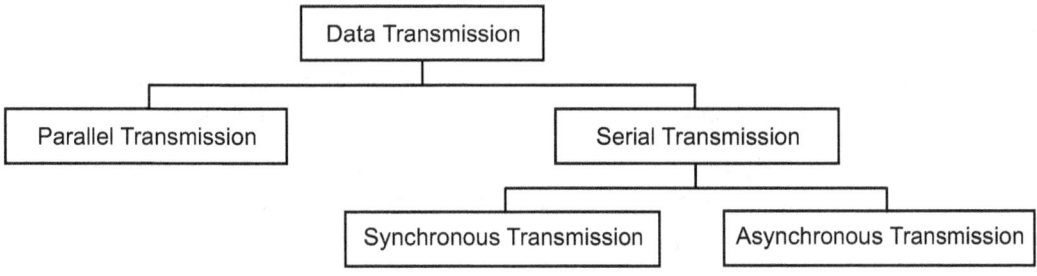

Fig. 1.21 : Data transmission modes

Parallel Transmission :

In Parallel Transmission, all the bits of data are transmitted simultaneously on separate communication lines. This transmission is used for short distance communication. The automobile traffic on a multi-lane highway is an example of parallel transmission. Parallel transmission is very fast data transmission mode.

Inside the computer binary data flows from one unit to another using parallel mode. If the computer uses 32-bk internal structure, all the 32-bits of data are transferred simultaneously on 32-lane connections. Similarly, parallel transmission is commonly used to transfer data from computer to printer. The printer is connected to the parallel port of computer and parallel cable that has many wires is used to connect the printer to computer.

In parallel transmission all the bits of a byte are transmitted simultaneously on separate wires. Parallel transmission is shown in Fig. 1.22.

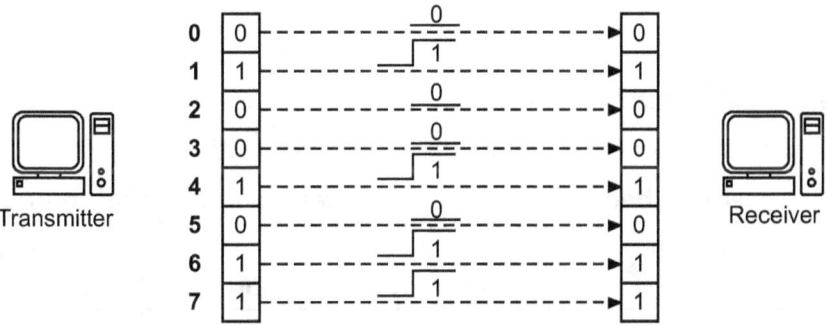

Fig. 1.22: Parallel data communication

Advantages:

1. Fastest method for data transmission because of the data bits will be transmitted simultaneously.
2. It does not require high frequency for operation.

Disadvantages:

1. Cost is high.
2. Requires separate lines for each bit of word.
3. It uses more wires causing transmitted signals to become distorted and the data unreliable when communicating over long distances.

Serial Transmission

In serial data transmission, bits of data flow in sequential order through single communication line. This transmission is used for long distance communication.

Serial transmission is typically slower than parallel transmission, because data is sent sequentially in a bit-by-bit fashion. Usually the Least Significant Bit (LSB) has been transmitted first. This requires only one circuit interconnecting two devices. Suitable for Transmission over Long distance.

Examples:

- Serial mouse uses serial transmission mode in computer.

- The flow of traffic on one-lane residential street.

Serial data transmission is shown in Fig. 1.23.

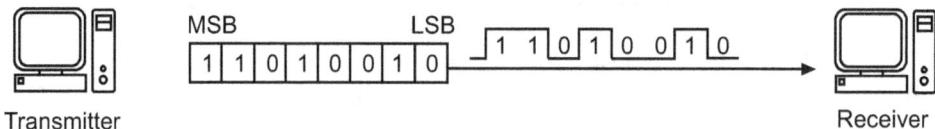

Fig. 1.23: Serial data transmission

Advantages:

1. Only one communication wire required.

2. Cheaper than parallel data transmission.

Disadvantages:

1. Speed of data transfer is slow.

2. It requires high frequency for data transmission operations.

Table 1.4 : Difference between serial communication and parallel communication

Sr. No.	Factors	Serial communication	Parallel communication
1.	Number of bits transmitted at one clock pulse.	One bit	n bits
2.	Number of lines required to transmit n bits.	One line	n lines
3.	Speed of data transfer.	Slow	Fast
4.	Cost of transmission.	Low as one line is required.	Higher as n lines are required.
5.	Application	Long distance communication between two computers.	Short distance communication like computer to printer.

There are two types of serial transmission-synchronous and asynchronous both these transmissions use 'Bit synchronization'. Bit Synchronization is a function that is required to determine when the beginning and end of the data transmission occurs.

1.1.6 Synchronus and Asynchronus Transmission

Synchronous Transmission

In this type of transmission, data is transmitted block by block or word by word simultaneously. Each block in this transmission may contain several bytes of data. A special communication device known as synchronized clock is required to schedule the transmission of information. In a synchronous mode, the transmitter and the receiver use the same clock.

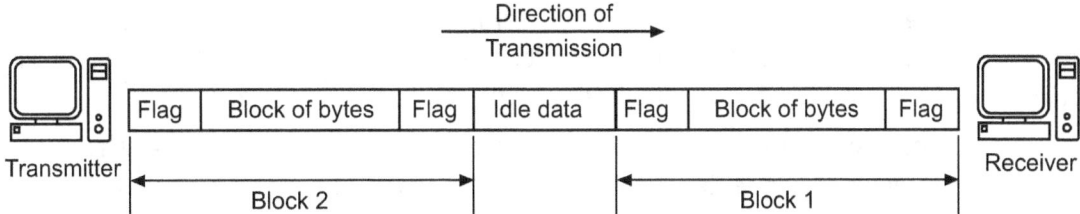

Fig. 1.24: Synchronous data transmission

Synchronous transmission does not use start and stop bits. In this method bit stream is combined into longer frames that may contain multiple bytes. There is no gap between the various bytes in the data stream, (see Fig. 1.25)

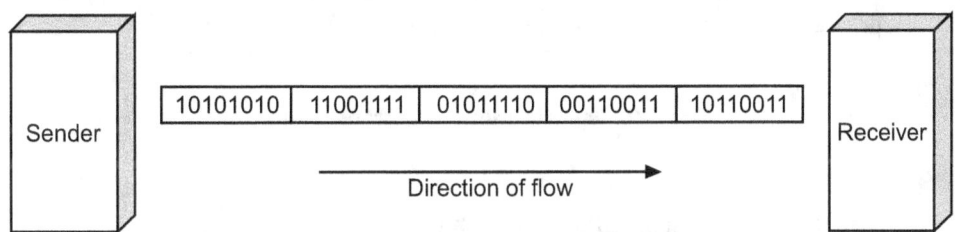

Fig. 1.25: Synchronous transmission

In the absence of start and stop bits, bit synchronization is established between sender and receiver by 'timing' the transmission of each bit.Since, the various bytes are placed on the link without any gap, it is the responsibility of receiver to separate the bit stream into bytes so as to reconstruct the original information. In order to receive the data error free, the receiver and sender operates at the same clock frequency.

Synchronous transmission is used for high speed communication between computers.

Advantages:

1. Speed of data transmission is very high.
2. Lower overhead and thus greater throughput.

Disadvantages:

1. Expensive and complex data transmission method.

2. Requires proper synchronization.

Asynchronous Transmission

In Asynchronous Data Transmission, data is transmitted one byte at a 'time'. Asynchronous Transmission sends only one character at a time where a character is either a letter of the alphabet or number or control character i.e. it sends one byte of data at a time.

An asynchronous line that is idle (not being used) is identified with a value 1, also known as 'Mark' state. This value is used by the communication devices to find whether the line is idle or disconnected. When a character (or byte) is about to be transmitted, a start bit is sent. A start bit has a value of 0, also called a space state. Thus, when the line switches from a value of 1 to a value of 0, the receiver is alerted that a character is coming.

This type of transmission is most commonly used by Microcomputers. The data is transmitted character-by-character as the user types it on a keyboard.

Asynchronous transmission is best suited to Internet traffic in which information is transmitted in short bursts. This type of transmission is used by modems.

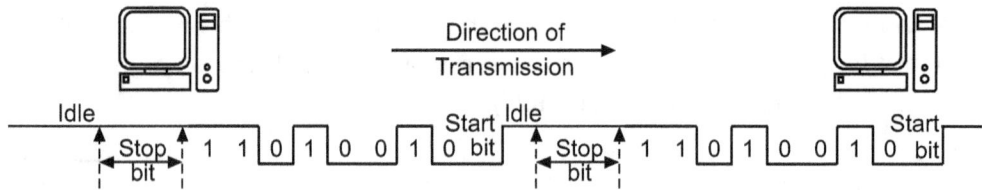

Fig. 1.26: Asynchronous data transmission

Advantages:

1. Does not require synchronization of both communication side.

2. Easy to implement.

3. Cheaper in cost.

4. Set-up is very fast, so well suited for applications where messages are generated at irregular intervals.

5. It is possible to transmit signals from sources having different bit rates.

6. The transmission can start as soon as data byte to be transmitted becomes available.

Disadvantages:

1. Data transmission is slow.

2. Large overheads.

3. Requires additional bits (start and stop).

Table 1.5 : Comparison between Synchronous and Asynchronous Data Communications

Sr. No.	Factors	Asynchronous communication	Synchronous communication
1.	Data sent at one time:	Usually 1 byte	Multiple bytes
2.	Start and stop bit:	Used	Not used
3.	Gap between data units:	present	Not present
4.	Data transmission speed:	Slow	Fast
5.	Cost:	Low	High

Isochronous Data transfer system

An Isochronous Data transfer system combines the features of an asynchronous and synchronous data transfer system. This system sends blocks of data asynchronously, in other words, the data stream can be transferred at random intervals.

Each transmission begins with a start packet. When the start packet is transmitted, the data must be delivered with a guaranteed bandwidth.

Isochronous data transfer is commonly used for where data must be delivered within certain time constraints, like streaming video.

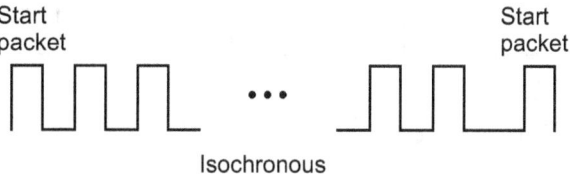

Fig. 1.27: Isochronous communication

Isochronous systems do not have an error detection mechanism (acknowledgment of receipt of packet) because if an error were detected, time constraints would make it impossible to resend the data.

1.2 Transmission Media

Transmission media means a communication signal is carried from one computer system to another.

Definition of Transmission Media:

Transmission media are the physical pathways that connect computers, other devices, in a computer network.

OR

We can define transmission medium as "the physical path between transmitter and receiver in a data transmission system."

Fig. 1.28 (a) shows transmission of data from sender to receive through a medium.

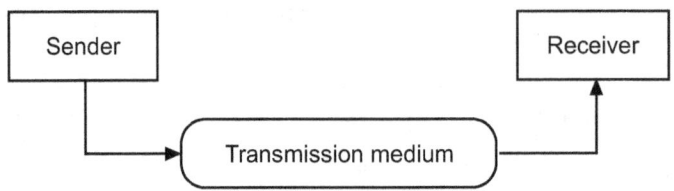

Fig. 1.28 (a) : Transmission of data through medium

Fig. 1.28 (b) shows categories of transmission media.

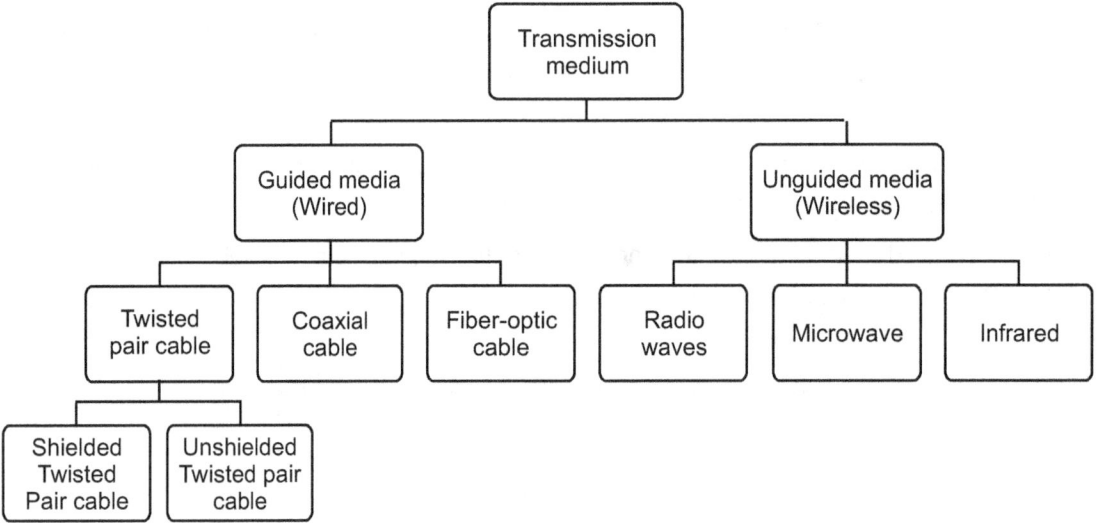

Fig. 1.28 (b) : Transmission Media

1.2.1 Guided Media

Guided transmission media uses a cabling system that guides the data signals along a specific path. This media uses a "cabling" system that guides the data signals along a specific path. Guided media is also known as bound media or wired media.

There three basic types of guided media as shown in Table 1.6.

Cable Characteristics :

For guided media, electromagnetic waves are guided along a solid medium.

The characteristics and quality of a data transmission are determined by the characteristics and the quality of the medium and the characteristics of the signal.

Table 1.6 : Point-to-point transmission characteristics of guided media

Transmission medium	Total data rate	Bandwidth	Repeater spacing
Twisted pair	4 Mbps	3 MHz	2 to 10 km
Coaxial cable	500 Mbps	350 MHz	1 to 10 km
Optical fiber cable	2 Gbps	2 GHz	10 to 100 km

Note:

Mbps: Mega bits per second = 10^6 bps,   Gbps: Giga bits per second = 10^9 bps

MHz: Mega Hertz per second = 10^6 Hz,   GHz: Giga Hertz per second = 10^9 Hz

In the design of data transmission systems, there are two areas of concern. They are data rate and distance. The greater the data rate, the distance is better. A number of design factors determine the data rate and distance. They are:

1. **Bandwidth:** All other factors remaining constant, the greater the bandwidth of a signal, the higher the data rate that can be achieved.

2. **Transmission impairment:** Impairments, such as attenuation, limit the distance. For guided media, twisted pair generally suffers more impairment than coaxial cable, which in turn suffers more than optical fiber.

3. **Interference:** Interference from competing signals in overlapping frequency bands can distort or wipe out a signal. Interference is of particular concern for unguided media but it is also a problem with guided media. (For example, emanations from nearby cables.)

4. **Number of receivers:** A guided medium can be used to construct a point-to-point link or a shared link with multiple attachments. In the latter case, each attachment introduces some attenuation and distortion on the line, limiting distance and/or data rate.

Twisted-Pair (TP) Cable :

Twisted pair cable is the most common type of cable used in computer networks. It is reliable, flexible and cost effective. The wires in twisted pair cabling are twisted together in pairs. Each pair would consist of a wire used for the negative data signal and a wire used for the negative data signal.

Twisted pair cables are most effectively used in systems that use a balanced line method of transmission such as polar line coding (Manchester Encoding) as opposed to unipolar line coding (TTL logic). Frequency range of TP cable is 100 Hz to 5 MHz. Transmission time is measured in minutes and hours – not milliseconds.

Transmission Characteristics:

1. Requires amplifiers every 5-6 km for analog signals.

2. Requires repeaters every 2-3 km for digital signals.

3. Attenuation is a strong function of frequency.

4. Higher frequency implies higher attenuation.

5. Susceptible to interference and noise.

6. Improvement possibilities.

7. Shielding with metallic braids or sheathing reduces interference.

8. Twisting reduces low frequency interference.

9. Different twist length in adjacent pairs reduces crosstalk.

Physical Description:

Fig. 1.29 shows physical description of twisted pair cable.

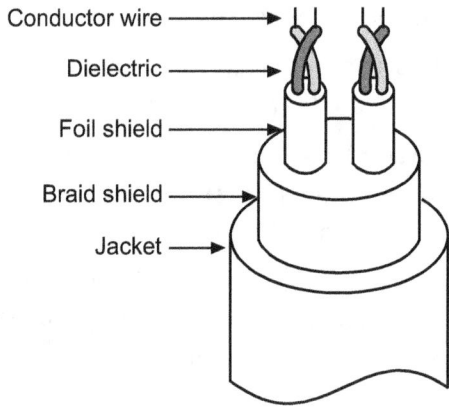

Fig. 1.29: Twisted pair cable

1. **Conductor wire:** Made of copper, copper treated with tin or silver, or aluminium or steel covered with copper.

2. **Dielectric :** Nonconductive material (such as Polyethylene or Teflon)

3. **Foil Shield:** Made of Polypropylene or Polyester tape coated with aluminum on both sides (STP only).

4. **Braid Shield:** Flexible conductive wire braided around the dielectric. Braid may be made of aluminium or bare or treated copper.

5. **Jacket :** Made of Polyvinylchloride or Polyethylene for nonplenum made of Teflon or Kynar for plenum cable.

There are two main categories of twisted pair cable i.e. Unshielded Twisted Pair (UTP) Cable, and Shielded Twisted Pair (STP) Cable.

(a) Unshielded Twisted Pair (UTP) Cable:

UTP can be either voice grade or data grade depending on the condition. UTP cable normally has an impedance of 100 ohm. Unshielded Twisted Pair (UTP), illustrated in Fig. 1.30, is the copper media inherited from telephony that is being used for increasingly higher data rates.

A twisted pair is a pair of copper wires with diameters of 0.4 to 0.8 mm that are twisted together and protected by a thin Polyvinyl-Chloride (PVC) or Teflon jacket. The amount of twist per inch for each cable pair has been scientifically determined and must be strictly observed because it serves a purpose. The twisting increases the electrical noise immunity and reduces crosstalk as well as the Bit Error Rate (BER) of the data transmission. UTP is a very flexible, low-cost media and can be used for either voice or data communications.

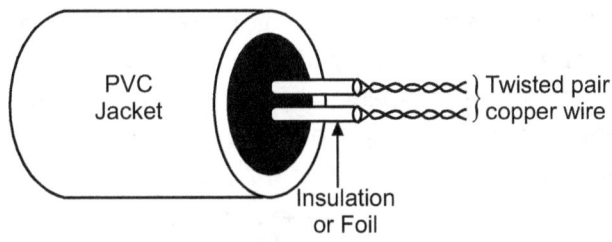

Fig. 1.30 : UTP cable

Table 1.7 : Table of categories of UTP cable

Category	Specified Data Rate	Application
CAT 1	Less than 1 Mbps	Telephone wiring (only audio signals, not for data)
CAT 2	4 Mbps	4 Mbps Token Ring
CAT 3	16 Mbps	10BaseT Ethernet
CAT 4	20 Mbps	16 Mbps Token Ring
CAT 5	100 Mbps	100BaseT Ethernet 155 Mbps ATM
CAT 5E	100 Mbps	100BaseT Ethenet 155 Mbps ATM
CAT 6	250 Mbps	1000BaseT Broadband
CAT 7	600 Mbps	Broadband – over 1 GHz bandwidth per pair

Advantages of UTP:

1. Easy installation and setup.
2. Capable of high speed for LAN.

3. Low cost.

4. UTP is very flexible.

Disadvantages of UTP:

1. Short distance due to attenuation.

2. Limited bandwidth.

(b) Shielded Twisted Pair (STP) Cable:

It is similar to UTP but has a mesh shielding that's protects it from EMI which allows for higher transmission rate. Shielded Twisted Pair (STP), depicted in Fig. 2.15 is a 150 Ω cable composed of two copper pairs. Each copper pair is wrapped in metal foil and then sheathed in an additional braided metal shield and an outer PVC jacket. The shielding absorbs radiation and reduces the EMI. As a result, STP can handle higher data speeds than UTP.

Foil Twisted Pair (FTP) or Screened Twisted Pair (ScTP) are variations of the original STP. They are thinner and less expensive, as they use a relatively thin overall outer shield. STP is used extensively by the telephone company for moving digitized information over distances of 2 km between repeaters, to span the distance of several miles between telephone company switching stations.

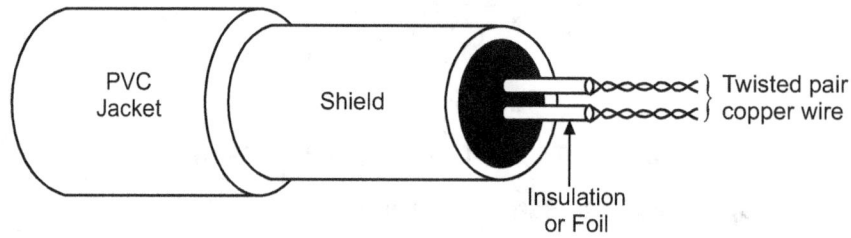

Fig. 1.31 : STP cable

Table 1.8 : Table of categories of STP cable

Category	Description
IBM Type 1	Token Ring transmissions on AWG #22 wire up to 20 Mbps.
IBM Type 1A	Fiber Distributed Data Interface (FDDI), Copper Distributed Data Interface (CDDI), and Asynchronous Transfer Mode (ATM) transmission up to 300 Mbps.
IBM Type 2A	Hybrid combination of STP data cable and CAT3 voice cable in one jacket.
IBM Type 6A	AWG #26 patch cables.

Advantages of STP:

1. STP reduces interference.

2. Faster than UTP and coaxial cable.

3. Better performance at higher data rates.

Disadvantages of STP:

1. More expensive than UTP and coaxial cable.

2. More difficult installation and setup.

3. High attenuation rate.

4. High cost.

Table 1.9 : Comparison of unshielded and shielded twisted pair cables

Sr. No.	Unshielded Twisted Pair (UTP) Cable	Shielded Twisted Pair (STP) Cable
1.	Ordinary telephone wire.	Shielded with a metallic braid or sheath.
2.	Subject to external electromagnetic interference.	Reduces interference.
3.	Low performance at higher data rates.	Better performance at higher data rates.
4.	Less expensive.	More expensive and difficult to work compared to UTP.
5.	Cheaper in cost.	Cost is more.
6.	Easy to install.	Difficult to install.
7.	Flexible.	Not flexible.

Applications:

1. TP cables are used in telephone lines to provide voice and data channels.

2. The line that connects subscribers to the central telephone office is most commonly UTP cable.

3. The DSL lines that are used by the telephone companies to provide high data rate connections also use high bandwidth capability UTP cable.

4. Local Area Network (LAN) also uses twisted-pair cable.

Coaxial Cable

Coaxial cable was invented in 1929 and first used commercially in 1941. The name "coax" comes from its two-conductor construction in which the conductors run concentrically with each other along the axis of the cable. Coaxial cabling has been largely replaced by twisted-pair cabling for Local Area Network (LAN) installations within buildings, and by fiber-optic cabling for high-speed network backbones.

It has been largely replaced by twisted-pair cabling for Local Area Network (LAN) installations within buildings, and by fiber-optic cabling for high-speed network backbones. Frequency ranges of coaxial cable is 100 kHz to 500 MHz. Coaxial cable (or coax) carries signals of higher frequency ranges than twisted-pair cable.

Transmission Characteristics:

1. Used to transmit both analog and digital signals.

2. Superior frequency characteristics compared to twisted pair.

3. Can support higher frequencies and data rates.

4. Shielded concentric construction makes it less susceptible to interference and crosstalk than twisted pair.

5. Constraints on performance are attenuation, thermal noise, and intermediation noise.

6. Requires amplifiers every few kilometers for long distance transmission.

7. Usable spectrum for analog signaling up to 500 MHz.

8. Requires repeaters every few kilometers for digital transmission.

9. For both analog and digital transmission, closer spacing is necessary for higher frequencies/data rates.

Physical Description:

Fig. 1.32 shows construction of coaxial cable.

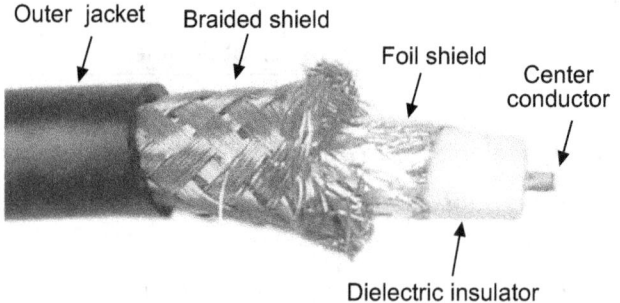

(a) Actual coaxial cable

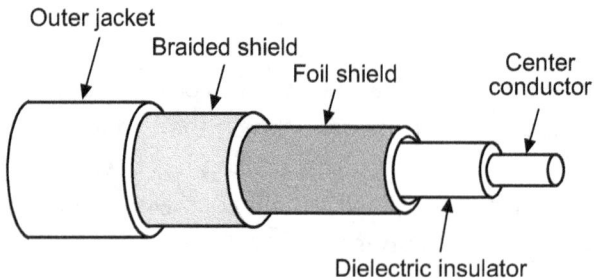

(b) Diagrammatically representation of coaxial cable

Fig. 1.32 : Construction of Co-axial cable

Each of these components in Fig. 1.32 plays a specific role. Let's take a look at each in more detail:

1. **Center Conductor:** At the heart of a coaxial cable is a center conductor. Typically constructed of either pure copper (in higher-end cables) or copper-coated steel or aluminium (in less-expensive cables), the center conductor is responsible for transmitting the cable's signal.

2. **Dielectric Insulator:** The dielectric insulator's purpose is two-fold; first, it acts as an insulator between the center conductors and the outer braided / foil shielding. Second, it helps physically hold the center conductor in the center of the cable. This is important, as signal loss can occur if the centre conductor strays too close to the outer area of the cable. Various materials are commonly used for the dielectric. A few of the more common materials, in order of quality (from best to worst), are Foamed Polyethylene (FPE), Teflon, Polyethylene (PE), Polypropylene (PP), and Polyvinylchloride (PVC).

3. **Braided Shield:** Interference tends to come in two different types: electromagnetic interference (known as EMI) and radio frequency interference (RFI). EMI interference is often caused by heavy power lines, cell phone signals, etc. A braided shield protects the signal from EMI interference. When looking at cable specs, the braided shield will often be expressed in a percent coverage, which often ranges anywhere from 30% to 95% coverage. Higher the coverage, the better the protection.

4. **Foil Shield:** Although not always present on coaxial cables, the Foil Shield serves to protect from RFI interference. Foil shields are almost always made out of aluminium foil, and simply wrap around the inner parts of the cable. Unlike braided shields, which have a percent coverage, foil shields always cover 100%.

5. **Outer Jacket:** The Outer Jacket is generally made out of flexible PVC (polyvinyl chloride) and serves primarily to hold the cable together and protect it from the elements.

Advantages of Coaxial Cable:

1. Low cost due to less total footage of cable, hubs not needed.
2. Lower attenuation than twisted pair.
3. Good immunity to EMI/RFI / highly insensitive to EMI.
4. Supports high bandwidths.
5. Heavier types of coax are sturdy and can withstand harsh environments.
6. Represents a mature technology that is well understood and consistently applied among vendors.

Disadvantages of Coaxial Cable:

1. Limited in network speed.
2. Limited in size of network.
3. One bad connector can take down entire network.

4. Although fairly insensitive to EMI, coax remains vulnerable to EMI in harsh conditions such as factories.

5. Coax can be bulky.

6. Coax is among the most expensive types of wire cables.

Applications of Coaxial Cable:

1. The use of coaxial cable started in analog telephone networks where a single coaxial network could carry 10,000 voice signals.

2. Later it was used in digital telephone networks where a single coaxial cable could carry digital data up to 600 Mbps.

3. Most common use is in cable TV.

4. Coaxial cabling is often used in heavy industrial environments where motors and generators produce a lot of electromagnetic interference (EMI), and where more expensive fiber-optic cabling is unnecessary because of the slow data rates needed.

5. Another common application of coaxial cable is in traditional Ethernet LANs.

Fiber-Optic Cable

Fiber-optic is a glass cabling media that sends network signals using light. Fiber-optic cabling has higher bandwidth capacity than copper cabling, and is used mainly for high-speed network, Asynchronous Transfer Mode (ATM) or Fiber Distributed Data Interface (FDDI) backbones, long cable runs, and connections to high-performance workstations.

Light is a form of electromagnetic energy. It travels at its fastest in a vacuum: 3, 00,000 kilometers/sec. The speed of light depends on the density of the medium through which it is traveling, (the higher the density, the slower the speed). Light travels in a straight line as long as it is moving through a single uniform substance. If a ray of light traveling through one substance suddenly enters another (more or less dense), the ray changes direction.

Data transmission over optical fiber has greatly increased over the last few years, although fiber to the desktop has not really caught on as expected.

Transmission Characteristics:

1. Fiber optic cabling can provide extremely high bandwidths in the range from 100 mbps to 2 gigabits because light has a much higher frequency than electricity.

2. The number of nodes which a fiber optic can support does not depend on its length but on the hub or hubs that connect cables together.

3. Fiber optic cable has much lower attenuation and can carry signal to longer distances without using amplifiers and repeaters in between.

4. Fiber optic cable is not attached by EMI effects and can be used in areas where high voltages are passing by.

5. The cost of fiber optic cable is more compared to twisted pair and co-axial cable.

6. The installation of fiber optic cables is difficult and tedious.

Construction of Fiber-Optic Cable:

Optical fiber cable carries light signals instead of electric signal.

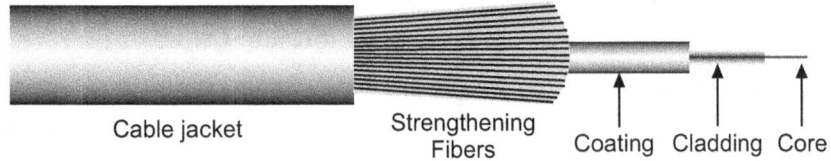

Fig. 1.33: Construction of fiber optic cable

Fig. 1.33 shows following parts of fiber-optic cable:

1. **Core:** This is the physical medium that transports optical data signals from an attached light source to a receiving device. The core is a single continuous strand of glass or plastic that's measured in microns (μ) by the size of its outer diameter. The larger the core, the more light the cable can carry. All fibre optic cable is sized according to its core's outer diameter. The three multimode sizes most commonly available are 50, 62.5, and 100 microns. Single-mode cores are generally less than 9 microns.

2. **Cladding:** This is the thin layer that surrounds the fibre core and serves as a boundary that contains the light waves and causes the refraction, enabling data to travel throughout the length of the fibre segment.

3. **Coating:** This is a layer of plastic that surrounds the core and cladding to reinforce and protect the fibre core. Coatings are measured in microns and can range from 250 to 900 microns.

4. **Strengthening fibres:** These components help protect the core against crushing forces and excessive tension during installation.

5. **Cable jacket:** This is the outer layer of any cable. Most fibre optic cables have an orange jacket, although some types can have black or yellow jackets.

Propagation Modes:

An optical fiber guides light waves in distinct patterns called modes. Mode describes the distribution of light energy across the fiber. Current network technology supports two modes i.e. multimode and single mode for propagating light along optical channels, each requiring fiber with different physical characteristics. Multi mode can be implemented in two forms i.e. step index or graded-index.

1. **Multimode:** Multimode means multiple beams from a light source move through the core in different paths.

   Multimode step index fiber, the density of the core remains constant from the center to the edges. A beam of light moves through this constant density in a straight line until it reaches the interface of the core and the cladding. At the interface, there is an abrupt change due to a lower density; this alters the angle of the beam's motion.

(i) The term **step index** refers to the suddenness of this change, which contributes to the distortion of the signal as it passes through the fiber.

(ii) A **graded index** fiber therefore is one with varying densities. Density is higher at the center of the core and decreases gradually to its lowest at the edge.

2. **Single Mode:** Single mode uses step index fiber and a highly focused source of light that limits beams to a small range of angles, all close to the horizontal.

Fig. 1.34 shows various modes of fiber optic cable.

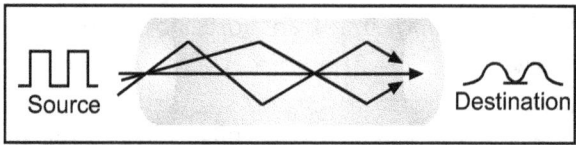

(a) Multimode, step index

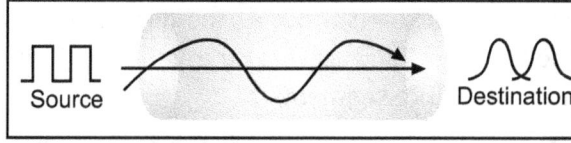

(b) Multimode, graded index

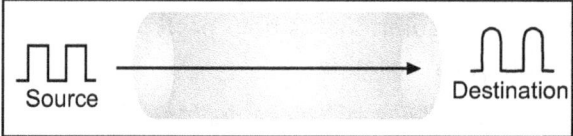

(c) Single mode

Fig. 1.34 : Modes of Fiber Optic Cable

Advantages of fiber optic cable:

1. Higher data rate than TP and coaxial cable.
2. Less signal attenuation.
3. Noise resistance.
4. Light weight.
5. More immune to tapping (or Security).
7. More Reliability.
8. Long distance.

Disadvantages of fiber optic cable:

1. Installation and maintenance need expertise that is not yet available everywhere.
2. Propagation of light is unidirectional.
3. Fiber-optic cable is more expensive.
4. Limited physical arc of cable of cable.

Table 1.10 : Characteristics comparison of guided media

Twisted Pair	Coaxial Cable	Fiber Optic Cable
1. It uses electrical signal for transmission.	It uses electrical signal for transmission.	It uses optical signal for transmission.
2. Affected by EMI and noise.	Less affected by EMI and noise.	Not affected by EMI and noise.
3. Bandwidth is low which is 3 to 4 MHz.	Bandwidth is high which is 300 to 400 MHz.	Bandwidth is very high which is 2 to 3 GHz.
4. Used for analog and digital transmission.	Used for analog and digital transmission.	Used for analog and digital transmission.
5. Supports low data rates upto 4 Mbps.	Supports high data rates upto 400 to 500 Mbps.	Supports very high data rates upto 3 Gbps.
6. Cost is very less.	Cost is moderate.	More costly.
7. For long distance communication repeaters are required after every 2 km distance.	For long distance communication repeaters are required after every 1 km distance.	For long distance communication repeaters are required after every 10 km distance.
8. Signal attenuation is more.	Signal attenuation is moderate.	Signal attenuation is least.
9. Installation is easiest.	Installation is easy.	Installation is difficult.
10. Signal to noise ratio is less.	Signal to noise ratio is moderate.	Signal to noise ratio is very high.
11. Crosstalk is more.	Crosstalk is moderate.	No crosstalk is present.
12. Losses like copper losses and radiation losses are present.	Losses like copper losses and radiation losses are present.	Losses like microbending and macrobending losses are present.

1.2.3 Unguided Media

Unguided transmission media consists of a means for the data signals to travel but nothing to guide them along a specific path. The data signals are not bound to a cabling media.

Unguided media transport data without using a physical conductor. This type of communication is often referred to as wireless communication. It uses wireless electromagnetic signals to send data. The media used in wireless communications are air, vacuum and even water. Air is the most commonly used medium. Signals are normally broadcasted through air and are available to anyone who has a device capable of receiving them.

Before understanding the different types of wireless transmission medium, let us first understand the ways in which wireless signals travel. These signals can be sent or propagated in the following three ways i.e. Ground-wave propagation, Sky-wave propagation, and Line-of-sight propagation.

1. Ground-wave Propagation:

Ground-wave Propagation follows the curvature of the Earth. These waves have carrier frequencies up to 2 MHz. AM radio is an example of ground wave propagation. Ionospheric propagation bounces off of the Earth's ionospheric layer in the upper atmosphere.

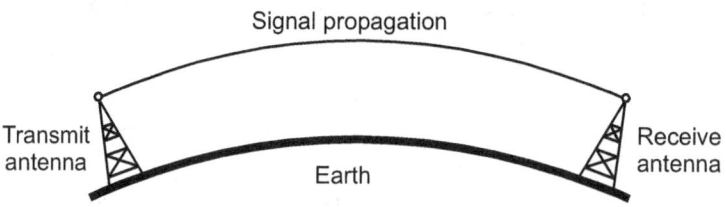

Fig. 1.35: Ground Propagation of waves

2. Sky-wave Propagation:

In this propagation, signal reflected from ionized layer of atmosphere back down to earth. Signal can travel a number of hops, back and forth between ionosphere and earth's surface.

Examples : Amateur radio, and CB radio.

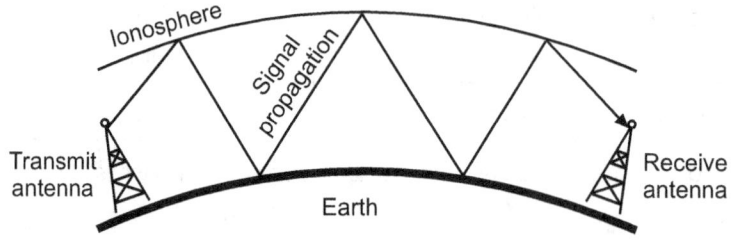

Fig. 1.36 : Sky- wave Propagation

3. Line-of-sight Propagation:

Line of sight propagation transmits exactly in the line of sight. The receive station must be in the view of the transmit station. It is sometimes called space waves or tropospheric propagation. It is limited by the curvature of the Earth for ground-based stations (100 km, from horizon to horizon). Reflected waves can cause problems.

Examples of line of sight propagation : FM radio, Microwave and Satellite.

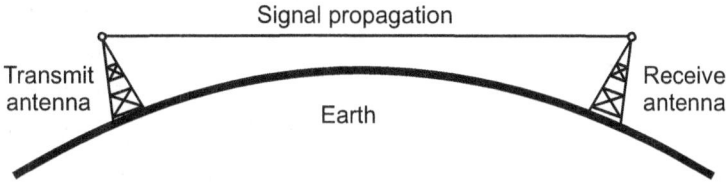

Fig. 1.37 : Line of sight propagation of waves

Electromagnetic Spectrum:

Signals are broadcast through the air and are available to anyone who has a device capable of receiving them. In wireless communication, transmission and reception are achieved using an antenna. Transmitter sends out the electromagnetic signal into the medium. Receiver picks up the signal from the surrounding medium.

Electromagnetic energy, a combination of electrical and magnetic fields vibrating in relation to each other includes power, voice, radio waves, infrared light, visible light, ultraviolet light, and X, gamma, and cosmic rays.

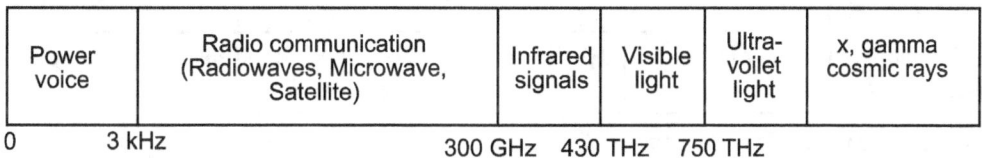

Fig. 1.38 : Electromagnetic spectrum

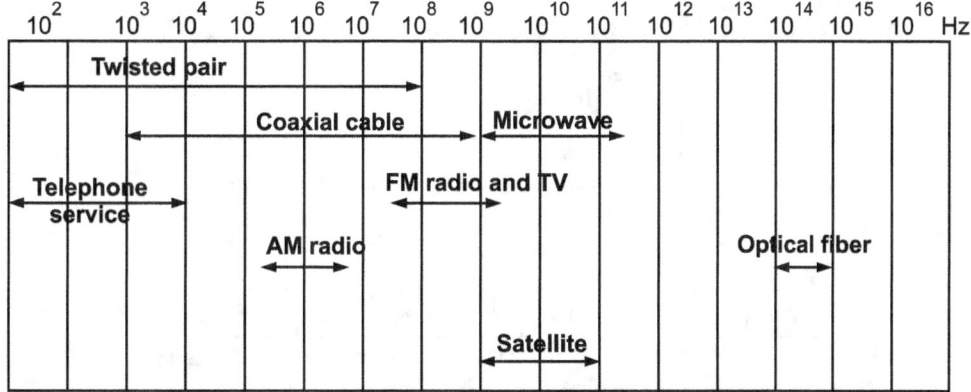

Fig. 1.39 : Electromagnetic spectrum with frequency ranges

Table 1.11 : Table of frequency band and wavelength

Frequency band	Wavelength	Applications
30 Hz – 300 Hz : Extremely Low Frequencies (ELF).	10^4 km to 10^3 km	Used in power transmission.
300 Hz – 3 kHz : Voice Frequencies (VF)	10^3 km to 100 km	Used in audio applications.
3 kHz – 30 kHz : Very Low Frequencies (VLF)	100 km to 10 km	Used in submarine communications and Navy, Military communications.
20 kHz – 300 kHz : Low Frequencies (LF)	10 km to 1 km Long waves	Used in aeronautical and marine, navigation.
300 kHz – 30 MHz : Medium Frequencies (MF)	1 km to 100 m Medium waves	Used in AM radio broadcast, Marine and aeronautical communications.
3 MHz – 30 MHz : High Frequencies (HF)	100 m to 10 m Short waves	Used in shortwave transmission, Amateur and CB communication.
30 MHz – 300 MHz : Very High Frequencies (VHF)	10 m to 1 m	Used in TV broadcasting and FM broadcasting.
300 MHz – 3 GHz : Ultra High Frequencies (UHF)	1 m to 10 cm Microwaves	Used in TV channels, Cellular phone, Military applications.
3 GHz – 30 GHz : Super High Frequencies (SHF)	10^{-1} m to 10^{-2} m	Used in satellite communication and Radar.
30 – 300 GHz : Extremely High Frequencies (EHF)	10^{-2} m to 10^{-3} m	Used in satellites and specialized radars.

Types of Communication Bands

Unguided media, also called as wireless communication, transport electromagnetic waves without using a physical conductor. The signals propagate through air.

The communication band for unguided media is as shown in Fig. 1.40.

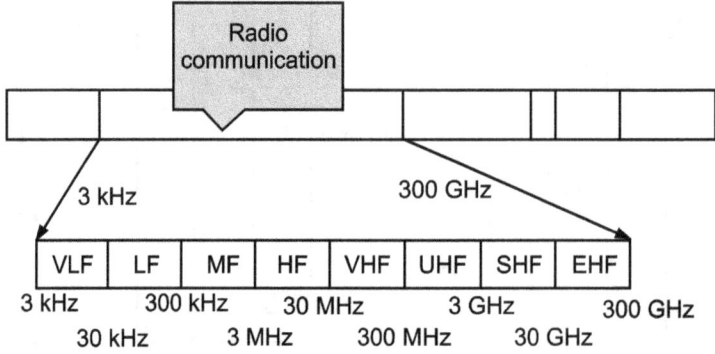

Fig. 1.40 : Radio communications band

1. **Very Low Frequency (VLF):** VLF waves propagate as surface waves, usually through air, but sometimes also through water. VLF waves are usually used for long-range radio navigation and submarine communication.

2. **Low Frequency (LF):** LF waves also propagate as surface waves. These waves are used for long-range radio navigation or navigation locators.

3. **Middle Frequency (MF):** MF waves rely on line-of-sight antennas to increase and control absorption problems. These waves are used for AM radio, radio direction finding and emergency frequencies.

4. **High Frequency (HF):** HF waves are used for amateur radio, citizen's band radio, international broadcasting, military communication, telephone, telegraph and facsimile communication.

5. **Very High Frequency (VHF):** VHF waves use line-of-sight propagation and are used for VHF television, FM radio, aircraft AM radio and aircraft navigation.

6. **Ultra High Frequency (UHF):** UFH waves use line-of-sight propagation. They are used for television. mobile phone, cellular radio, paging and microwave links.

7. **Super High Frequency (SHF):** SHF waves are transmitted as either line-of-sight or into the space. They are used for terrestrial and satellite microwave and radar communication.

8. **Extremely High Frequency (EHF):** EHF waves are transmitted into space and are used for scientific applications such as radar, satellite and experimental communication.

Microwave Communication

Electromagnetic waves having frequencies between 1 GHz to 300 GHz are called Microwaves. Microwaves are unidirectional; when an antenna transmits microwaves they can be narrowly focused. This means that the sending and receiving antennas need to be aligned. This communication is widely used for long distance telephone communication, cellular telephones, television distribution and other uses that a severe shortage of spectrum has developed.

Electromagnetic radiation beyond the frequency range of radio and television can be used to transport information. Microwave transmission is usually point-to-point using directional antenna with a clear path between transmitter and receiver. Fig. 1.42 shows typical example of microwave link using dish antenna and satellite.

A parabolic dish antenna can be used to focus the transmitted power into a narrow beam to give a high signal to noise ratio, and before the advent of optical fiber, some long distance telephone transmission systems were heavily dependent on the use of a series of microwave towers.

Because microwaves travel in a straight line, the curvature of the earth limits the maximum distance over which microwave towers can transmit. So repeaters are needed to compensate for this limitation.

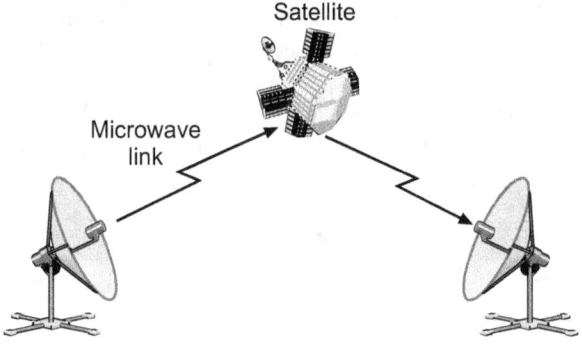

Fig. 1.41 : Microwave Link

Microwave transmission is line of sight transmission. The Transmitter station must be in visible contact with the receiver station. This sets a limit on the distance between stations depending on the local geography.

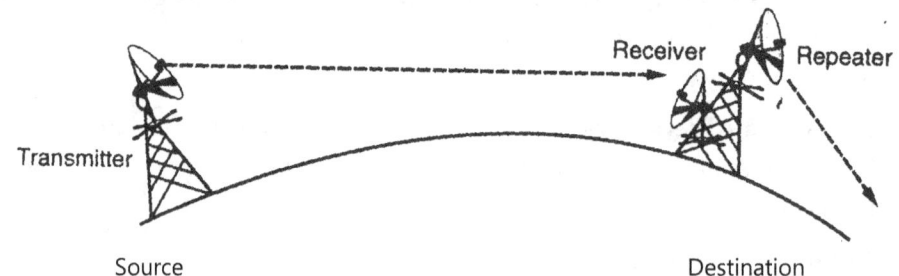

Fig. 1.42 : Example of Microwave transmission

Typically the line of sight due to the Earth's curvature is only 50 km to the horizon. Repeater stations must be placed so the data signal can hop, skip and jump across the country.

Microwaves operate at high operating frequencies of 3 to 10 GHz. This allows them to carry large quantities of data due to the large bandwidth.

Advantages of Microwave:

1. They require no right of way acquisition between towers.

2. They can carry high quantities of information due to their high operating frequencies.

3. Low cost land purchase: each tower occupies small area.

4. High frequency/short wavelength signals require small antenna.

Disadvantages of Microwave:

1. Microwave signals can be affected by weather, especially rain and other objects as birds, fog, snow.

2. Reflected from flat surfaces like water and metal.

3. Diffracted (split) around solid objects.

4. Refracted by atmosphere, thus causing beam to be projected away from receiver.

There are two types of Microwave data Communication systems: Terrestrial Microwave Communication and Satellite Microwave Communication.

1. Terrestrial Microwave Transmission:

Terrestrial Microwave Transmission systems transmit tightly focused beams of radio frequencies from one ground-based microwave antenna to another. These microwave systems typically use directional parabolic antennas to send and receive signals in the lower Gigahertz (GHz) range.

The signals are highly focused and the physical path must be line-of-sight. Relay towers are used to extend signals. Terrestrial microwave systems are typically used when using cabling is cost-prohibitive.

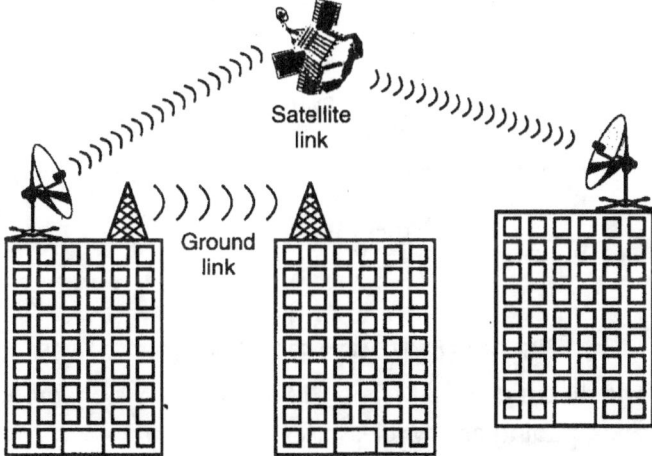

Fig. 1.43: Example of terrestrial and satellite microwave links

Advantages:

1. High data rates.
2. Low cost land purchase for towers.
3. High frequency / short wavelengths require short distant antennas.

Disadvantages:

1. Attenuation.
2. Reflected from flat surface, metal etc.
3. Line of sight is required.

2. Satellite Microwave Transmission:

In satellite microwave, the signals are transmitted from a ground station to a satellite and then after amplifying, from the satellite to some other ground station. It covers large geographical areas than terrestrial microwaves.

Radio Wave Communication

Radio wave is the transmission of signals through free space by modulation of electromagnetic waves with frequencies below those of visible light. These waves have frequencies between 3 kHz to 1GHz. Radio waves are omnidirectional i.e. they travel in all the directions from the source. Because of this property, transmitter and receiver need not to be aligned.

Radio waves can penetrate buildings easily, so they are widely use for communication both indoors and outdoors communications. The properties of radio waves are frequency dependent at low frequencies, radio waves pass through obstacles. The power falls off sharply with distance (r) from sources, roughly as $1/r^2$ in air. At high frequencies, radio waves tends to travel in straight line and bounces off the obstacles. These are also absorbed by rain. At all frequencies, radio waves are subject to interference from motors and other electrical equipments. In VLF, LF and MF bands, radio waves follow the ground.

In HF and VHF bands, ground waves are absorbed by earth. In these bands or frequencies, radio waves are radiated upward into ionosphere where they are reflected back to earth as shown in the Fig. 1.44.

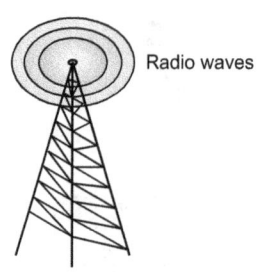

Fig. 1.44 : Radio wave communication

Radio waves are widely used for AM and FM radio, television broadcasting, cordless telephone, cellular phones, paging and wireless LAN.

Fig. 1.45 shows Radio Transmission using ground wave propagation.

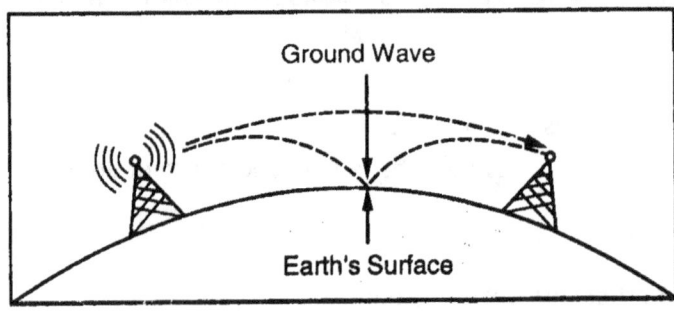

Fig. 1.45 : Radio transmission

RF is used in many standard as well as proprietary wireless communication systems. It has long been used for radio and TV broadcasting, wireless local loop, mobile communications, and amateur radio.

High (HF) and very high (VHF) frequency radio waves that reach the ionosphere is a layer of charged particles approximately 100-500 km above the earth's surface. These are refracted by it and sent back to earth. These bands are used by amateur radio operators to talk over long distances, and are also used for military radio communications.

Radio waves have virtually no distance limitations. However, the radio waves are government regulated, expensive, and can be tapped into. This can be used across continents.

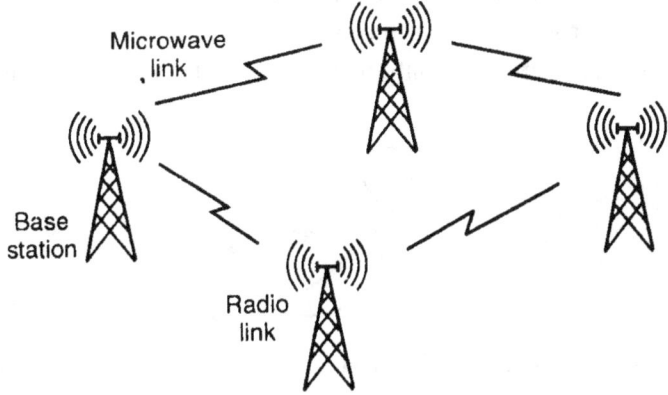

Fig. 1.46: Radio waves radiated by a base station's antenna

Fig. 1.47 shows examples of radio wave communications

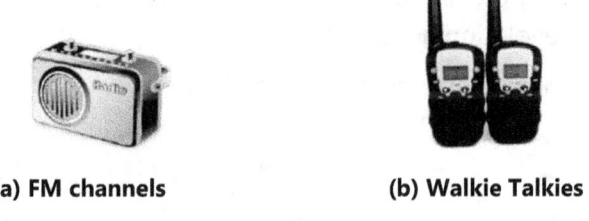

       (a) FM channels   **(b) Walkie Talkies**

Fig. 1.47 : Examples of Radio wave communications

Advantages:
1. Simpler than for Microwaves.
2. Cheap and No licenses needed.
3. High speed/bandwidth and covers large areas.

Disadvantages:
1. Travel in a straight line, so repeater stations may be needed.
2. Limited number of free frequency bands.
3. Shielding is difficult.
4. Greater power consumption.
5. Limited spectrum of frequency.

Satellite Communication

A satellite is a body that revolves around the earth just in same way earth revolves around the sun. It can be artificial/manmade (created by human). Satellites are widely being used for communication purposes as they cover maximum area on the earth for a particular transmission. The paths in which satellites move are called orbits. The orbit can be equatorial, inclined or polar. The period of a satellite, i.e. the time required for a satellite to make a complete trip around the earth, is determined by Kepler's law. Kepler's law defines the period as a function of the distance of the satellite from the center of the earth.

Satellites process microwaves with bi-directional antennas (line-of-sight). Therefore, the signal from a satellite is normally aimed at a specific area called the footprint. The signal power at the center of footprint is maximum. The power decreases as we move out from the footprint center. A communication satellite acts as a big microwave repeater in the sky.

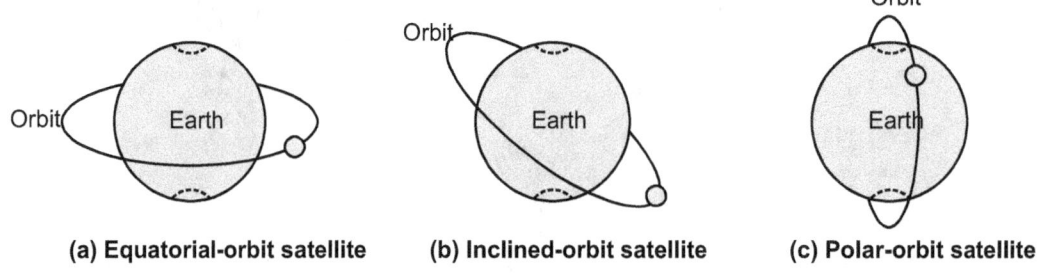

(a) Equatorial-orbit satellite   **(b) Inclined-orbit satellite**   **(c) Polar-orbit satellite**

Fig. 1.48 : Orbits of communication satellites

Satellite communication makes use of geostationary satellites. A geostationary satellite is a satellite that is placed approximately 36,000 km above the equator and take exactly 24 hours to complete one revolution around the earth.

Fig. 1.49 shows typical Satellite communication system.

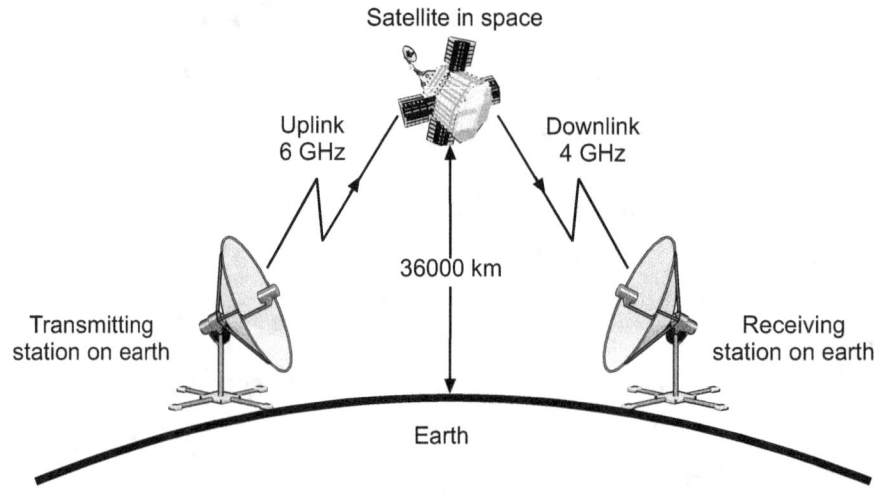

Fig. 1.49 : Satellite communication system

A geostationary satellite contains several transponders. The transponder receives signal from one earth station, amplifies it and sends the signal back to other earth stations. A typical satellite has 12-20 transponders each with 36-50 GHz bandwidth.

In case of satellite communication two different frequencies are used as carrier frequencies to avoid interference between incoming and outgoing signals. The signal which is being transmitted upwards to the satellite is called as the uplink. Thus uplink frequency is the frequency used to transmit signal from earth station to satellite. The signal which is being transmitted back to the receiving earth station is called as the downlink. Thus, downlink frequency is the frequency used to transmit the signal from satellite to earth station. Uplink and downlink frequencies are always different so as to avoid interference between them. There are three different bands of frequencies where satellites can operate:

1. C band, also called 6/4 GHz band, is one of the oldest and most widely in use.

2. Ku band, also called 11/14 GHz band.

3. Ka band, called 20/30 GHz band.

Advantages of Satellite Communication:

1. **Availability:** The biggest advantage of satellite Internet access is its availability compared to other Internet connection types.

2. **Speed:** Satellite Internet access is much faster than dial-up, with entry-level service tiers typically providing approximately 1 mbps download speeds--nearly 18 times faster than a dial-up modem.

3. **Latency:** Satellite Internet connections are high-latency, meaning that a great deal of time is required for packets of information to travel to the satellite and back.

Disadvantages of Satellite Communication:

1. Communication through satellite is highly costly.

2. Security measures are required to prevent the unauthorized tapping of information.

Infrared Communication :

Electromagnetic waves having frequencies from 300 GHz to 400 THz are called IR waves or Infrared waves. These waves are used for short range communication and use line-of-sight propagation. Infrared waves cannot pass through solid objects, like walls and can be easily contained in a room. Because of this property, IR waves can be used with much reduced interference. It is also possible to reuse same frequency bands in different rooms. This communication is cheap, easy to build and do not require any government license to use them.

Security system of IR systems against eavesdropping is better than that of radiowaves as they cannot pass through walls. The most common application of IR waves is remote controls used for TV, DVD players and stereo system.

Working:

- IR wireless is used for short and medium-range communications and security control.
- For IR communication to work, the systems mostly operate in line-of-sight mode which means that there must be no obstruction between the transmitter (source) and receiver (destination).
- Infrared is used in television remote controls and security systems.
- In the electromagnetic spectrum, infrared radiation lies between microwaves and visible light, therefore, they can be used as a source of communication.
- Fig. 1.50 shows uses of infrared communication.

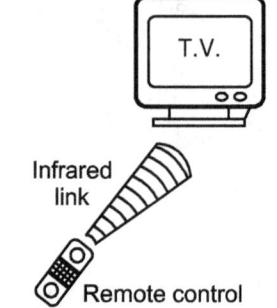

Fig. 1.50 (a): TV remote control uses infrared

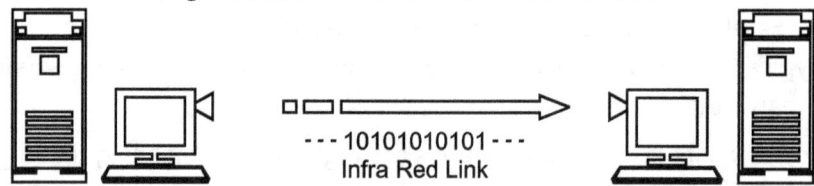

Fig. 1.50 (b): Computer communication uses infrared

Fig. 1.51 shows devices communicate using infrared.

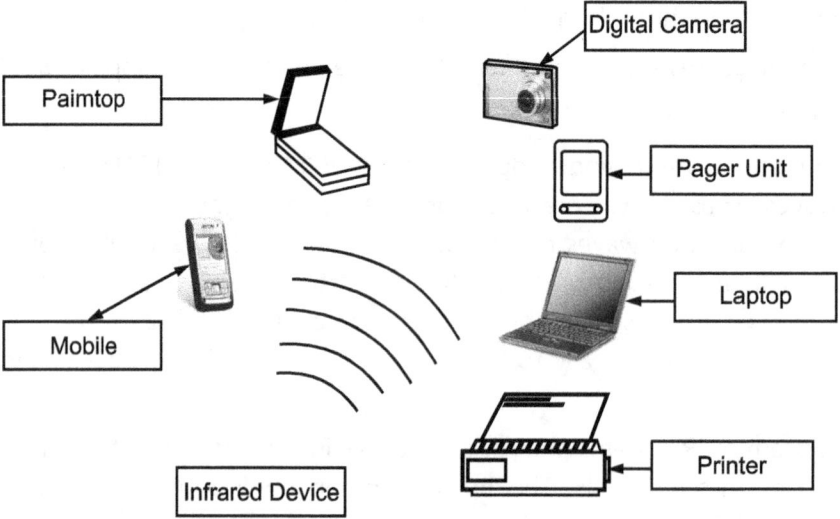

Fig. 1.51: Devices communicate using infrared

Advantages :

1. Simple circuit and cheap in cost.
2. Low power consumption.
3. No licenses needed.
4. Higher security and simple shielding.
5. Portable.

Disadvantages:

1. Works only on Line-Of-Sight (LOS) mode.
2. Short range.
3. Blocked by common materials: people, walls, etc.
4. Low bandwidth.
5. Speed is comparatively slow.

Table 1.12 : Comparison between Guided Media and Unguided Media

Guided Media	**Unguided Media**
1. Guided media also called bounded or wired media.	1. Unguided media also called unbounded or wireless media.
2. Twisted pair wires, coaxial cable, optical fiber cables are the examples of wired media.	2. Microwave, satellite and mobile communication are the examples of unguided media.
3. Additional transmission capacity can be obtained by adding more wires.	3. It is not possible to obtain additional capacity.
4. Wired media lead to discrete network topologies.	4. Wireless media leads to continuous network topologies.
5. Installation is costly, time-consuming and complicated.	5. Installation needs less time and money.
6. Attenuation depends exponentially on the distance.	6. Attenuation is proportional to square of the distance.
7. The signal energy is contained and guided within a solid medium.	7. The signal energy propagates in the form of unguided electromagnetic waves.
8. Used for point-to-point communication.	8. Used for radio broadcasting in all directions.

1.3 Multi-Channel Data Communication

Let's see the technologies related to multiplexing.

1.3.1 Circuits

A circuit is defined as a path over which data, voice or other signals can pass between two computers or between terminal and computer.

The circuit may be a physical path consisting of one or more wires. It may also be wireless. A network which may be wired or wireless is an arrangement of circuits consisting of a number of intermediate switches. A circuit maybe classified based upon its uses. In case of dial up connection it is reserved for the user only for a limited period, the period 'for which the connection is invoked. On the other hand, leased line arrangement, a circuit is reserved in advance and can only be used by the owner of the circuit.

Further, connection between two or more points may be established virtually unlike the connection made by dial up and leased line as physical in nature. Therefore, circuit maybe defined as Virtual Circuit (VC) based upon the type and nature of the connection. A virtual circuit may be defined as logical path between two or more points. It is selected out of many possible physical paths available between those points. However, the connection is not definite. Therefore, it seems like a fixed physical path. A permanent connection is ensured using Permanent Virtual Circuit (PVC) which provides a definite connection between two or more points when needed without having to reserve or commit to a specific physical path in advance. A Switched Virtual Circuit (SVC) is similar to a permanent virtual circuit, but allows users to dial in to the network of virtual circuits.

1.3.2 Channels and Multichanneling

A Channel is defined as a connection between initiating and terminating nodes of a circuit. A single path provided by a transmission medium through either physical such as by multi pair cable or electrical separation, such as by frequency or time division multiplexing. A channel may be furnished by wire, fiber optics, radio or a combination thereof.

When a signal transmits through the channel, channel inherently added some noise to the signal. This noise is known as thermal noise. Noise means any undesirable effect on the signal of interest which results in attenuation, degradation or corruption of the signal. The noise generated by the components is categorized as thermal noise that is also known as additive noise. The effect of the noise on the signal can be reduced by increasing the power in the transmitted signal but which results in lesser battery life i.e. more power consumption. There is one more limitation that is available channel bandwidth. Because of these two limitations of the channel, we have to design our communication system such that we can transmit as much data as possible with out getting corrupted i.e. these constraints make us to derive new algorithms or techniques for reliable transmission of information over channel with high data rates.

Types and Characteristics of Channels:

There are many types of Channels. Here ,we will just discuss their operating frequencies.

Wire line channels: operates at frequency few kHz to several hundreds of kHz

1. Fiber Optical Channels: provides bandwidth in the magnitude several times higher than that of wire line channel

2. Wireless Electromagnetic Channels: operates in the range of 10kHz to =~ 100 GHz, this is further categorized as long wave radio, short wave radio, microwave radio as they operates in radio frequency they are also known as 'radio' or 'radio channel'.

3. Under Water Acoustic Channels: operated at extremely low frequencies.

4. Storage Channels: like magnetic tapes, magnetic disks etc.

Multichanneling : When the capacity or bandwidth of the media is separated into multiple channels is known as multi channeling. It is the passage of multiple signals over the signal media. Mainly it is used for broadband services where the entire media bandwidth is separated into multiple channels. Each channel carries the different signal.

Multichannel communication is used in transmitting telephone or telegraph messages, telemetry data, remote control signals, television and facsimile images, computer data, and signals of automatic control systems over cables or radio relay or satellite communications lines. Multichannel communication systems combined with switching systems are the most important components of an integrated automatic communication system. The principle of multiplexing of communication lines is the basis for the design of multichannel communication systems.

1.4 Multiplexing

Multiplexing is a technique by which different analog and digital streams of transmission can be simultaneously processed over a shared link. Multiplexing divides the high capacity medium into low capacity logical medium which is then shared by different streams.

Multiplexing also known as MUX. The sending of multiple signals or streams of information on a carrier at the same time is known as multiplexing. It is in the form of a single, complex signal. Fig. 1.52 recapturing the separate signals at the end the receiver. The opposite process of multiplexing is called demultiplexing.

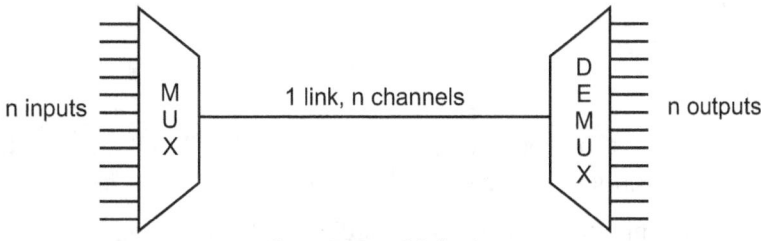

Fig. 1.52: Multiplexing

Demultiplex (DEMUX) combines multiple unrelated analog or digital signals into one signal over a single shared medium, such as a single conductor of copper wire or fiber optic cable.

Technical terms used in Multiplexing:

1. **Multiplexer:** A device that can combine and transmit several signals over a single line.

2. **DeMultiplexer:** A device that decode the single line signal into multiple signals.

3. **Multilevel:** Used when the data rate of the input links are multiples of each other.

4. **Multislot:** Used when there is a GCD between the data rates. The higher bit rate channels are allocated more slots per frame, and the output frame rate is a multiple of each input link.

5. **Pulse Stuffing:** Used when there is no GCD between the links. The slowest speed link will be brought up to the speed of the other links by bit insertion, this is called Pulse Stuffing.

Multiplexing are of following forms:

1. **Frequency Division Multiplexing (FDM):** FDM is an analog multiplexing technique that combines analog signals.

2. **Time Division Multiplexing (TDM):** TDM is a digital multiplexing technique for combining several low-rate digital channels into one high-rate one.

3. **Wavelength Division Multiplexing (WDM):** WDM is an analog multiplexing technique to combine optical signals.

4. **Code Division Multiplexing (CDM).:** ode division multiplexing (CDM) is a networking technique in which multiple data signals are combined for simultaneous transmission over a common frequency band

Advantages of Multiplexing:

1. Simple and easy.

2. Large capacities and scalable.

3. Inexpensive and signals may have varying speed.

Disadvantages of Multiplexing:

1. Complexity.

2. Bandwidth is wasted.

Types of Multiplexing :

Multiplexing is the set of techniques that allows the simultaneous transmission of multiple signals across a single data link.

Whenever, the transmission capacity of a medium linking two devices is greater than the transmission needs of the devices, the link can be shared in order to maximize the utilization of the link, such as one cable can carry a hundred channels of TV.

Fig. 1.53 shows types of multiplexing.

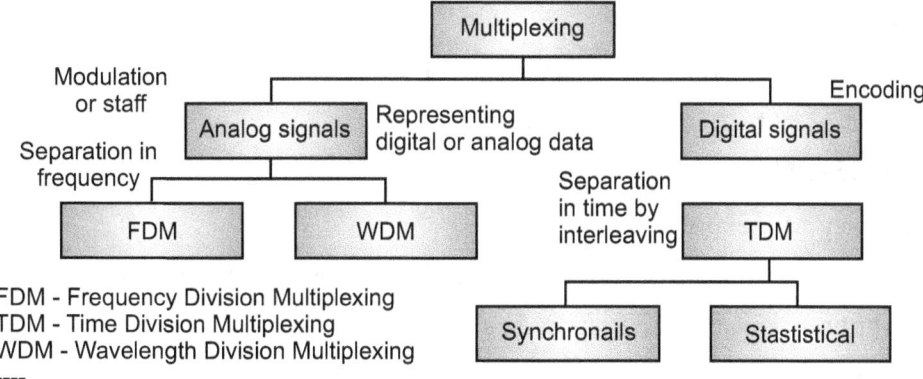

Fig. 1.53: Types of Multiplexing

1.4.1 Frequency Division Multiplexing (FDM)

In FDM, signals generated by each sending device modulate different carrier frequencies. These modulated signals are then combined into a single composite signal that can be transported by the link. The carrier frequencies have to be different enough to accommodate the modulation and demodulation signals.

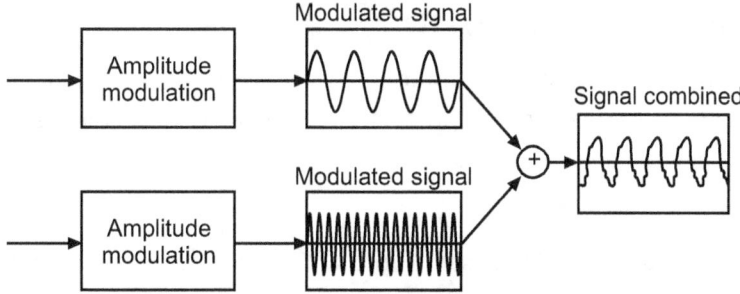

Fig. 1.54 (a): Frequency Division Multiplexing

FDM used with analog signals. Perhaps its most common use is in television and radio transmission. It accept signals from multiple sources. It has a specified bandwidth, the signals are combined into another, more complex signal with large bandwidth. MUX extracts and separates the individual components that carries frequencies.

Fig. 1.54 (b) shows medium is divided into number of channels.

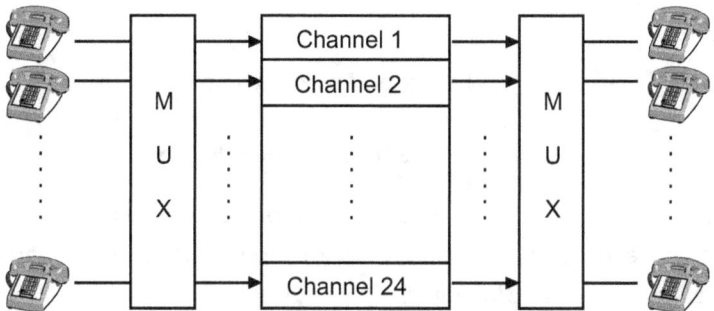

Fig. 1.54 (b) : Division of medium into channels

Applications of FDM:

1. FDM is used for A.M. Radio and Radio broacasting.

2. FDM is used for T.V. broadcasting.

Advantages of FDM:

1. Simple and inexpensive.

2. All the receivers, cellular telephones, need not to be at the same location

3. It is not sensitive to propagation delays.

4. It allows maximum transmission link usage.

Disadvantages of FDM:

1. In FDM there is need of filters, which are very expensive and complicated to construct and design.

2. Analog signal only having limited frequency range.

3. Sometimes, it is necessary to use more complex linear amplifiers in FDM systems.

1.4.2 Time Division Multiplexing (TDM)

In the Time-Division Multiplexing, multiple transmissions can occupy a single link by subdividing them and interleaving the portions. TDM can be implemented in two ways i.e. synchronous TDM and asynchronous TDM.

Synchronous TDM:

The multiplexer allocates exactly the same time slot to each device at all times, whether or not a device has anything to transmit. Time slots are grouped into frames. A frame consists of one complete cycle of time slots. For example, Time slot 1 is assigned to device 1 alone and cannot be used by any other device as shown in the Fig. 1.55.

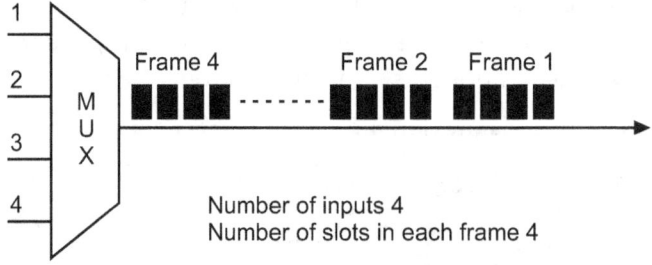

Fig. 1.55 : Time Division Multiplexing

Frames : In Synchronous TDM, a frame consists of one complete cycle of time slots. Thus the number of slots in frame is equal to the number of inputs. Fig. 1.56 (a) and (b) below are an example of how/the synchronous TDM works.

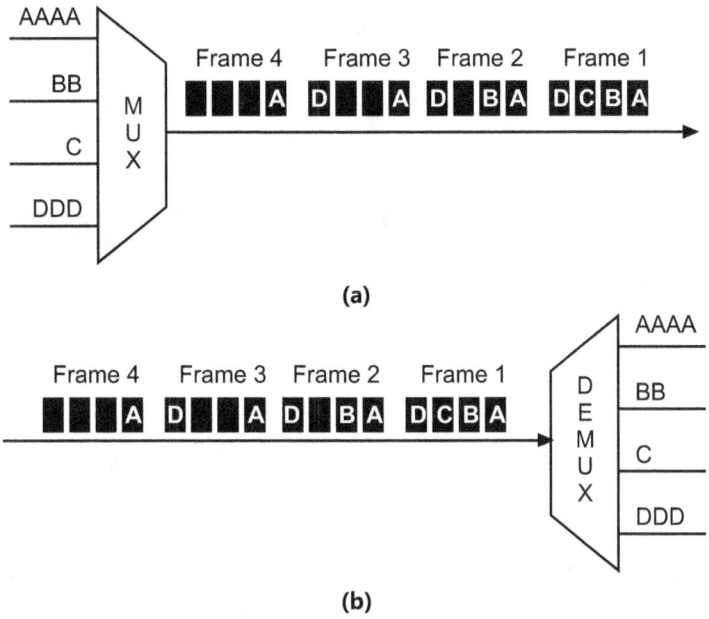

Fig. 1.56 : Working of Synchronus TDM

Advantages of synchronous TDM:

(i)   Relatively simple, and

(ii) Commonly used with ISDN (Integrated Services Digital Network).

Disadvantages of synchronous TDM:

(i)   Wastage of bandwidth.

Asynchronous (statistical) TDM:

In asynchronous TDM, each slot in a frame is not dedicated to the fix device. Each slot contains an index of the device to be sent to and a message. Thus, the number of slots in a frame is not necessary to be equal to the number of input devices. More than one slot in a frame can be allocated for an input device Asynchronous TDM allows maximization the link. It allows a number of lower speed input lines to be multiplexed to a single higher speed line, (See Fig. 1.57).

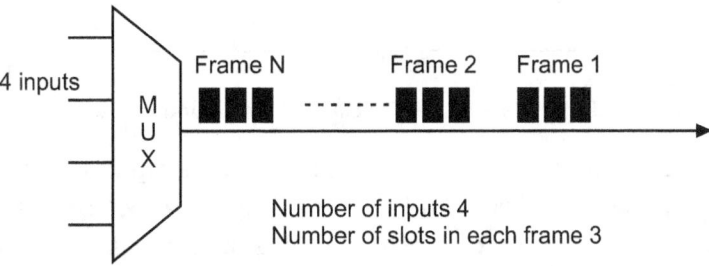

Fig. 1.57 : Asynchronous TDM

Frames : Asynchronous TDM also called as statistical time division multiplexing.In asynchronous TDM, a frame contains a fix number of time slots. Each slot has an index of which device to receive. Fig. 1.58 (a) and (b) are examples of how asynchronous TDM works.

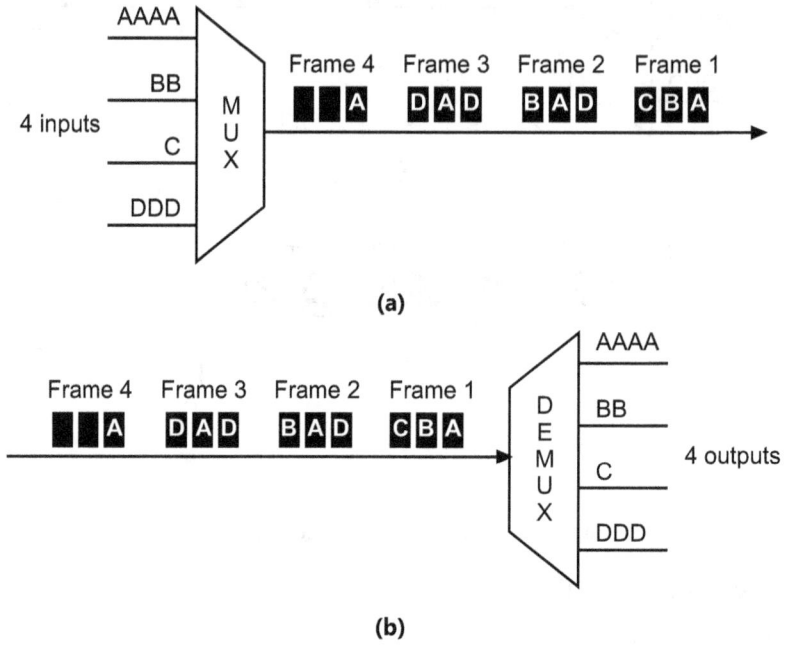

(a)

(b)

Fig. 1.58 : Working of Asynchronous TDM

1.4.3 Wavelength Division Multiplexing (WDM)

This a type of multiplexing developed for use on optical fiber. WDM modulates each of several data streams onto a different part of the light spectrum. WDM is the optical equivalent of FDM.

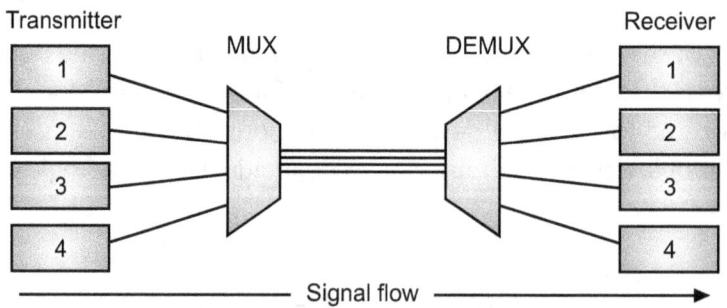

Fig 1.59 : Wavelength Division Multiplexing (WDM)

Wavelength division multiplexing systems can combine signals with multiplexing and split them apart with a demultiplexer. And with the proper fiber cable, the two can be done simultaneously; moreover, these two devices can also function as an add/drop multiplexer (ADM), i.e. simultaneously adding light beams while dropping other light beams and rerouting them to other destinations and devices.

As of 2011, WDM systems can handle 160 signals, which will expand a 10 Gbit/second system with a single fiber optic pair of conductors to more than 1.6 Tbit/second (i.e. 1,600 Gbit/s).

Typical WDM systems use single-mode optical fiber (SMF); this is optical fiber for only a single ray of light and having a core diameter of 9 millionths of a meter (9 μm). Other systems with multi-mode fiber cables (MM Fiber; also called premises cables) have core diameters of about 50 μm. Standardization and extensive research have brought down system costs significantly.

WDM systems are divided according to wavelength categories, coarse WDM (CWDM) and dense WDM (DWDM). CWDM operates with 8 channels (i.e., 8 fiber optic cables) in what is known as the "C-Band" or "erbium window" with wavelengths about 1550 nm (nanometers or billionths of a meter, i.e. 1550 x 10-9 meters). DWDM also operates in the C-Band but with 40 channels at 100 GHz spacing or 80 channels at 50 GHz spacing.

DWDM System Advantages :

1. Less fiber cores to transmit and receive high capacity data.

2. A single core fiber cable could divide into multiple channels instead of using 12 fiber core.

3. Easy network expansion, especially for limited fiber resource, no need extra fiber but add wavelength,

4. Low cost for expansion, because no need to replace many components such as optical amplifiers, can move to STM-64 when economics improve.

5. DWDM systems capable of longer span lengths, TDM approach using STM-64 is more costly and more susceptible to chromatic and polarization mode dispersion.

DWDM Disadvantages :

1. Not cost-effective for low channels, low channel recommend CWDM.

2. Complicated transmitters and receivers.

3. Wide-band channel, CAPEX and OPEX high.

4. The frequency domain involved in the network design and management, increase the difficulty for implementation.

1.4.4 Code Division Multiplexing (CDM)

CDM is widely used in second-generation (2G) and third-generation (3G) wireless communications. The technology is used in ultra-high-frequency (UHF) cellular telephone systems in the 800-MHz and 1.9-GHz bands. This is a combination of analog-to-digital conversion and spread spectrum technology.

In the Code division Multiplexing (CDM) data transmission from different stations are multiplied by different channel codes and sent on a common channel. Each different transmissions use the same frequency. Each user separated by spreading code. The receivers of the transmissions have their respective transmitter's code word. At the receiving end, these codes are removed from the desired signal. For the receiver the signals of all other users appear as noise.

A disadvantage of CDM is that each user's transmitted bandwidth is enlarged than the digital data rate of the source. The result is an occupied bandwidth approximately equal to the coded rate. Therefore, CDM and spread spectrum are used interchangeably. The transmitter and receiver require a complex electronic circuitry.

The main advantage of CDM is protection from interference and tapping because only the sender, the receiver knows the spreading code.

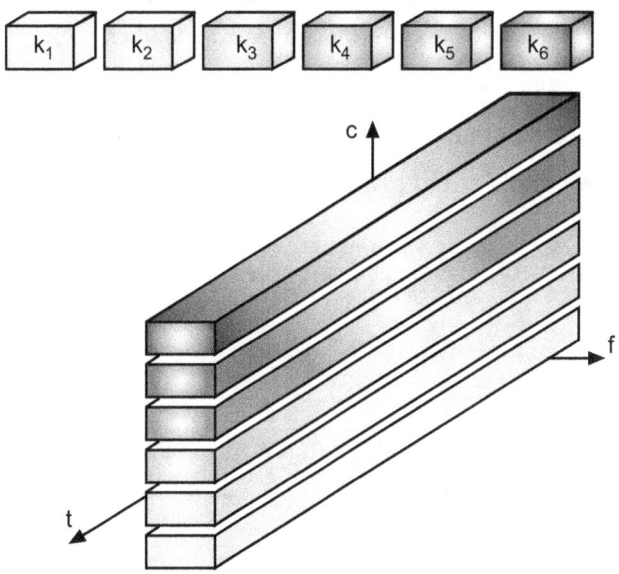

Fig. 1.60 : Code Division Multiplexing (CDM)

Demultiplexing :

Demultiplexing is the process of separating multiplexed data channels at the destination. Demultiplex (DEMUX) is the reverse of the multiplex (MUX) process combining multiple unrelated analog or digital signal streams into one signal over a single shared medium, such as a single conductor of copper wire or fiber optic cable. Thus, demultiplex is reconverting a signal containing multiple analog or digital signal streams back into the original separate and unrelated signals.

In demultiplexing process, we use filters to decompose the multiplexed signal into its constituent component signals. Then each signal is passed to an amplitude demodulation process to separate the carrier signal from the message signal. Then, the message signal is sent to the waiting receiver.

The process of demultiplexing is shown in the Fig. 1.61.

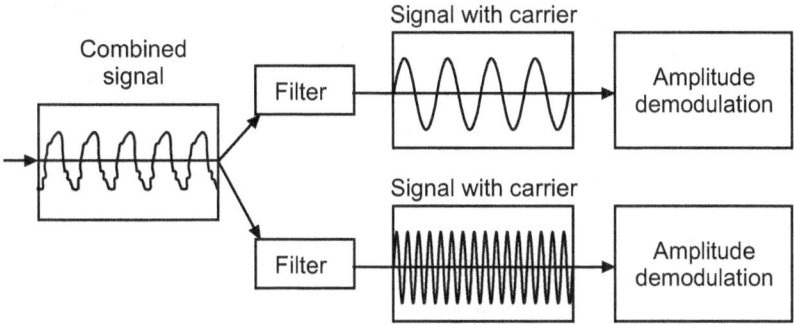

Fig. 1.61 : Demultiplexing

Table 1.13: Difference between TDM vs FDM

Sr. No.	TDM	FDM
1.	TDM stands for Time Division Multiplexing.	FDM stands for Frequency Division Multiplexing.
2.	TDM divides a channel by allocating a time period for each channel.	FDM divides the channel into multiple, but smaller frequency ranges to accommodate more users.
3.	TDM provides much better flexibility compared to FDM.	FDM provides much less flexibility compared to TDM.
4.	In FDM spectrum is divided into frequency.	TDM divided into time slot.
5.	FDM is used in 1st generation analog system.	TDM is used in 2nd generation analog system.
6.	Difficult to install.	Easy and simpler to install.
7.	TDM imply partitioning the bandwidth of the channel connecting two nodes into finite set of time slots.	In FDM the signals multiplexed come from different sources/transmitters.
8.	TDM is sensitive to propagation delays.	FDM is not sensitive to propagation delays.

A basic advantage of multichannel communication systems with frequency-division multiplexing and single-side band modulation is the economical use of the frequency spectrum. Among the essential disadvantages of such systems are the accumulation of interference noise originating at repeater stations and the resulting low noise immunity. Systems with time-division multiplexing and pulse-code modulation do not have the latter disadvantage. In designing multichannel communication systems of high capacity in terms of the number of channels) there is a trend toward simultaneous use of frequency-division and time-division multiplexing methods.

Practice Questions

1. What is Computer Communication?

2. Name two major categories of Transmission media.

3. How do guided media differs from Unguided media?

4. Write a short note on Coaxial cable.

5. Write a short note on Fiber optic Cable.

6. Which are data Transmission Modes?

7. Give a use for each class of Guided Media.

8. What is meaning of Multiplexing? Explain its types.

9. Write definition : circuit, channel, signal.

10. Write the advantages of Satellite media.

Chapter 2...

COMMON NETWORK ARCHITECTURE

Contents ...

2.1 Connection Oriented N/Ws vs Connectionless N/Ws

2.2 X.25 Networks

2.3 Peer to Peer Networks

2.4 Ethernet (Standard and Fast)

2.5 Wireless LANs

    2.5.1 802.11(Architecture, Issues, Features etc.)

    2.5.2 802.11x

    • Practice Questions

2.1 Connection Oriented N/Ws vs Connectionless N/Ws

Connection Oriented Networks (CO)

Network architecture is a method of describing the logical design of a network of computers and how they interact. Connection-oriented and Connectionless networks are two different type of networks are used in Data communication.

Connection-oriented networks are sometimes called switched networks. These networks are in which connection setup is performed prior to information transfer. However, information about the connections in CO networks helps in providing service guarantees and furthermore. This makes it possible to use network resources (e.g., bandwidth) most efficiently by "switching" them to appropriate connections.

With this goal of providing users service guarantees and service providers, improved bandwidth utilization that there is an interest in carrying IP traffic over various CO networks.

Examples of CO networks are: Asynchronous Transfer Mode (ATM) networks, Multi Protocol Label Switching (MPLS), Synchronous Optical Network/Synchronous Digital Hierarchy (SONET/SDH) and Wavelength Division Multiplexed (WDM) networks.

Fig. 2.1 shows various Communication Networks.

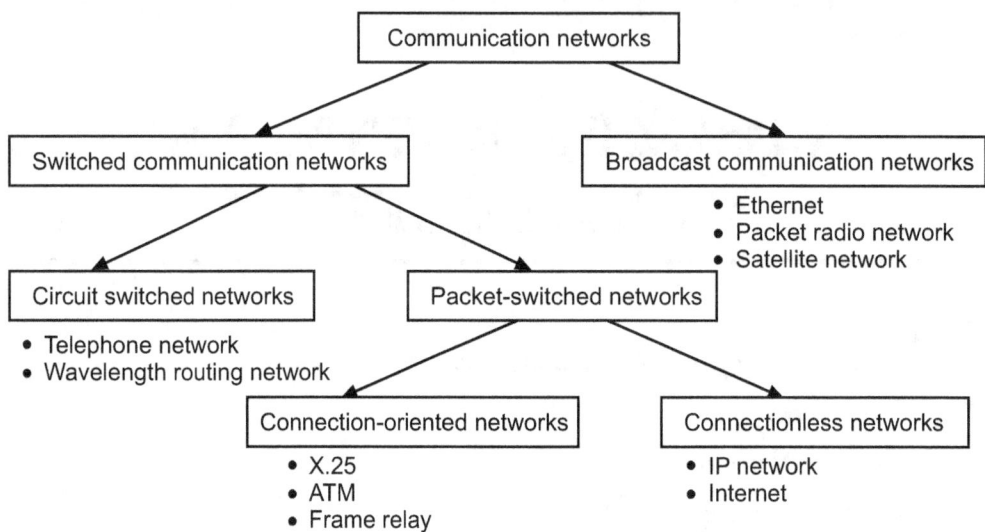

Fig. 2.1 : Communication Networks

Connection oriented networks can be packet-switched or circuit-switched. The switching mode of a network indicates whether the network nodes are circuit switches or packet switches. Where is description of "Connection less network". Connection oriented vs connection less.

Circuit switches are "position-based," in that bits arriving in a certain "position" are switched to a different "position," with the position being determined by a combination of one or more of three dimensions: space (interface number), time and wavelength. Packet switches are "label-based," in that they use information in packet headers (labels) to decide how to switch a packet.

Connectionless Network :

Connectionless networks are often called as router based networks. In connectionless (CL) networks, no explicit connection setup actions are executed prior to transmitting data; instead, data packets are routed to their destinations based on information in their headers. CL networks do not suffer the delay and processing overhead associated with connection setup.

1. IP Network:

An internet protocol-based network (an IP Network) is a group of hosts that share a common physical connection and that use internet protocol for network layer communication. Network provides communication between computing devices. All computer (hosts) on a network need to use the same communication protocols to communicate properly. An internet protocol network is a network of computer using internet protocol for their communication protocol.

All computers within an IP network must have an IP address that uniquely identifies that individual host. The IP addresses in an IP network are contiguous, that is, one address follows right after the other with no gaps.

Within a given range of IP addresses used in every IP network are special addresses reserved for:

- Host Addresses.
- Network Addresses.
- Broadcast Addresses.

In addition, IP network has a subnet mask. The subnet mask is a value stored at each computer that allows that computer to identify which IP addresses are within the network to which they are attached, and which IP addresses are on an outside network.

(i) Host Address:

A host's IP address is the address of a specific host on an IP network. All hosts on a network must have a unique IP address. This IP address is usually not the first or the last IP address in the range of network IP addresses as the first IP address and last IP address in the range of IP addresses are reserved for special functions. The host addresses are all the addresses in the IP network range of IP addresses except the first and last IP addresses. Host IP addresses allow network hosts to establish one-to-one direct communication. This one-to-one communication is referred to as unicast communication.

All host IP addresses can be split into two parts: a network part and a host part. The network part of the IP addresses identifies the IP Network, the host is a member of. The host part uniquely identifies and individual host.

(ii) Network Address:

The network address is the first IP address in the range of IP addresses. To be more precise, the network address is the address in which all binary bits in the host portion of the IP address are set to zero. The purpose of the network address is to allow hosts that provide special network services to communicate. In practice, the network address is rarely used for communication.

(iii) Broadcast Address:

The broadcast IP address is the last IP address in the range of IP addresses. To be more precise, the broadcast address is the IP address in which all binary bits in the host portion of the IP address are set to one. The broadcast address is reserved and allows a single host to make an announcement to all hosts on the network. This is called broadcast communication and the last address in a network is used for broadcasting to all hosts because it is the address where the host portion is all ones. This special address also sometimes called the all hosts' address. Some vendors allow you to set an address other than the last address as the broadcast address.

2. Internet:

Internet is the extensive, worldwide computer network available to the public. An internet is a more general term for any set of interconnected computer networks that are connected by internetworking. It is made up of thousands of smaller commercial, academic, and government networks. It is a network of networks in which users at any one computer can, in case they have permission, get information from any other computer.

It was realized by the Advanced Research Projects Agency (ARPA) of the U.S. government in 1969, it was known as the ARPA Net. The originally a network created that would allow users of a research computer at one university to be able to communicate research computers at other universities.

Internet carries various information and services, such as electronic mail, on-line chat and the interlinked web pages and other documents of the World Wide Web. Hypertext is viewed using a program called a web browser which retrieves pieces of information, called "documents" or "web pages", from web servers and displays them, typically on a computer monitor.

One can then follow hyperlinks on each page to other documents or even send information back to the server to interact with it.

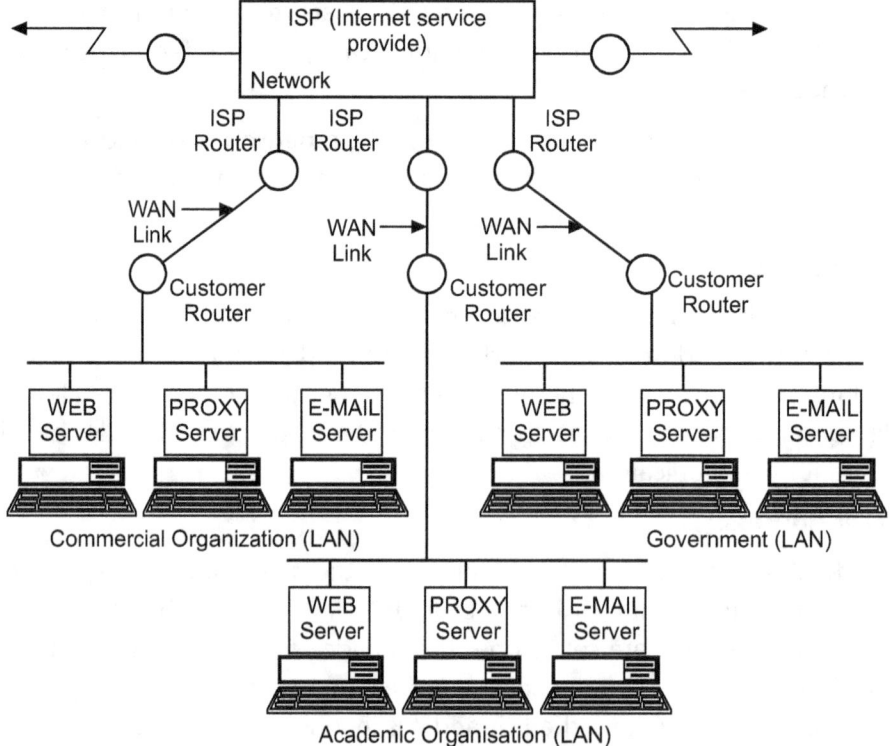

Fig. 2.2: Typical internet connection components

The act of following hyperlinks is often called "surfing" or "browsing" the web. Web pages are often arranged in collections of related material called "web sites."

An internet contains following components:

- Web Server (LAN components),
- Proxy Server (LAN components),
- Email Server (LAN components),
- Customers (Orgonization's) router,
- WAN links,
- ISP Routers, and
- ISP (Internet Service Provider).

E-mail server is used to provide different E-mail accounts for E-mail transactions. Thus, routers are used to interconnect different LANs to form Internet. Organization's router and ISP's router are interconnected to form Internet.

- Customer router to ISP router link
- Dial-up-line
- Leased line
- ISDN line, etc.
- LAN Technology can be of:
- Ethernet (802.3 or CSMA/CD) Technology
- Token Ring (802.5) Technology
- Token Bus (802.4) Technology

Internet consists of the following groups of networks:

1. **Backbones:** Large networks that exist primarily to interconnect other networks.

2. **Regional networks:** Connecting for example, Universities and colleges.

3. **Commercial Networks:** Providing access to the backbones to subscribers and networks owned by commercial organizations for internal use that also have connections to the Internet.

4. **Local Networks,** such as campus – wide university networks.

Connectionless communication is usually achieved by transmitting information in one direction, from source to destination without checking to see if the destination is still there, or if it is prepared to receive the information. When there is little interference, and plenty of speed available, these systems work fine. In environments where there is difficulty transmitting to the destination, information may have to be re-transmitted several times before the complete message is received.

Walkie-talkies, or Citizens Band radios are a good examples of connectionless communication. You speak into the mike, and the radio transmitter sends out your signal. If the person receiving you doesn't understand you, there's nothing his radio can do to correct things, the receiver must send you a message back to repeat your last message.

IP, UDP (User Datagram Protoco), ICMP (Internet Control Message Protocol), DNS, TFTP and SNMP (Simple Network Management Protocol) are examples of connectionless protocols in use on the Internet –

Table 2.1 : Comparison between Connection-oriented and Connectionless Communication

Feature	Connectionless	Connection-oriented
How is data sent?	one packet at a time	As continuous stream of packets.
Do packets follow same route?	No	Virtual circuit: Yes Without virtual circuit: No
Are resources reserved in network?	No	Virtual circuit: Yes
Are resources reserved in communicating hosts?	No	Yes
Can data sent can experience variable latency?	Yes	Yes
Is connection establishment done?	No	Yes
Is state information stored at network nodes?	No	Virtual circuit: Yes Without virtual circuit: No
What is impact of node/switch crash?	Only packets at node are lost.	All virtual circuits through node fail.
What addressing information is needed on each packet?	Full source and destination address.	Virtual circuit: A virtual circuit number. Without virtual circuit: Full source and destination address.
Is it possible to adapt sending rate to network congestion?	Hard to do.	Virtual circuit: Easy if sufficient buffers allocated. Without virtual circuit: Harder to do.

2.2 X.25 Networks

X.25 is a standard suite of protocols used for packet switching across computer networks. The X.25 protocols work at the physical, data link, and network layers (Layers 1 to 3) of the OSI model. X.25 is an ITU-T (International Telecommunication Union-Telecommunication) standard protocol suite for packet switched wide area network (WAN) communication that defines how connections between user devices and network devices are established and maintained.

The general concept of X.25 was to create a universal and global packet-switched network. Much of the X.25 system is a description of the rigorous error correction needed to achieve this, as well as more efficient sharing of capital-intensive physical resources. It is designed to operate effectively regardless of the type of systems connected to the network. Typically used in the Packet-Switched Networks (PSNs) of common carriers, such as the telephone companies. Subscribers are charged based on their use of the network.

The development of the X.25 standard was initiated by the common carriers in the 1970s. At that time, there was a need for WAN protocols capable of providing connectivity across Public Data Networks (PDNs).X.25 is now administered as an international standard by the ITU-T.

1. X.25 Devices and Protocol Operation:

X.25 network devices fall into three general categories: Data Terminal Equipment (DTE), Data Circuit-terminating Equipment (DCE), and Packet-Switching Exchange (PSE). **Data terminal equipment** devices are end systems that communicate across the X.25 network. They are usually terminals, personal computers, or network hosts, and are located on the premises of individual subscribers. DCE devices are communications devices, such as modems and packet switches, that provide the interface between DTE devices and a PSE, and are generally located in the carrier's facilities. PSEs are switches that compose the bulk of the carrier's network. They transfer data from one DTE device to another through the X.25 PSN.

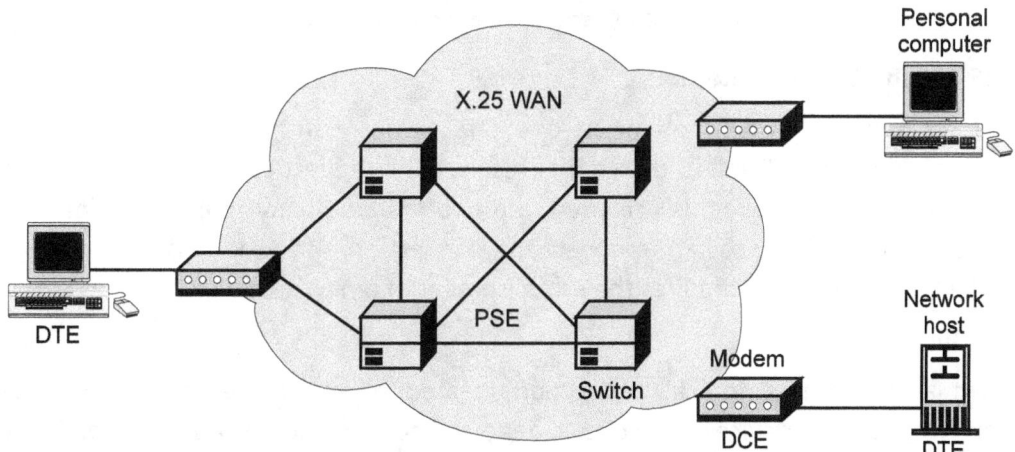

Fig. 2.3 : DTEs, DCEs, and PSEs make up an X.25 network

2. Packet Assembler/Dissembler (PAD)

The Packet Assembler/Disassembler (PAD) is a device commonly found in X.25 networks. PADs are used when a DTE device, such as a character-mode terminal, is too simple to implement the full X.25 functionality.

The PAD is located between a DTE device and a DCE device, and it performs three primary functions: buffering (storing data until a device is ready to process it), packet assembly, and packet disassembly. The PAD buffers data sent to or from the DTE device. It also assembles outgoing data into packets and forwards them to the DCE device. (This includes adding an X.25 header.) Finally, the PAD disassembles incoming packets before forwarding the data to the DTE. (This includes removing the X.25 header.).

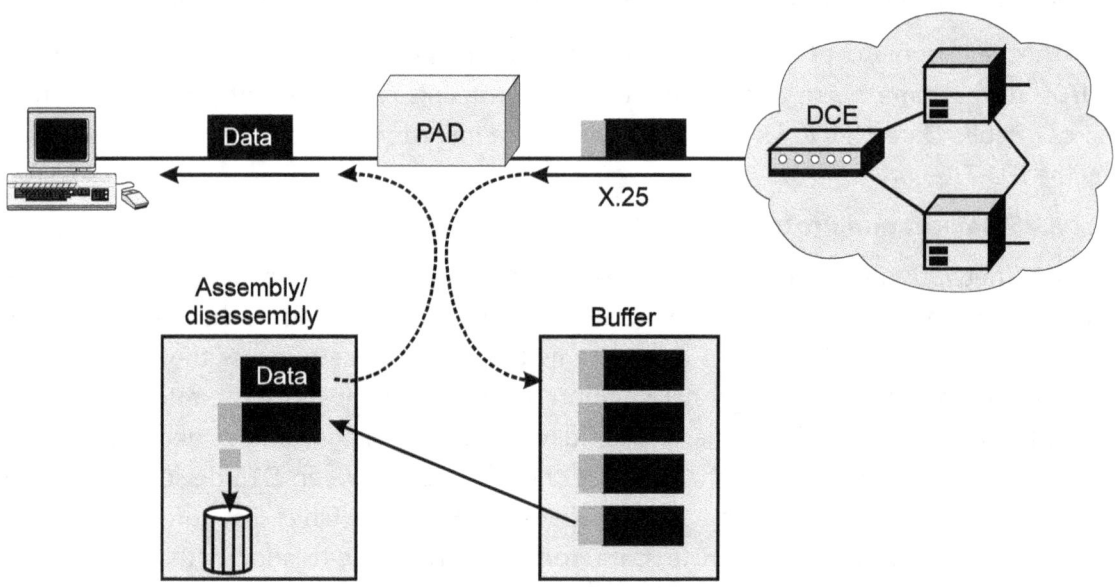

Fig. 2.4 : The packet assemblers/disassembles

3. X.25 Session Establishment:

X.25 sessions are established when one DTE device contacts another to request a communication session. The DTE device that receives the request can either accept or refuse the connection. If the request is accepted, the two systems begin full-duplex information transfer. Either of DTE device can terminate the connection. After the session is terminated, any further communication requires the establishment of a new session.

4. X.25 Virtual Circuits:

A virtual circuit is a logical connection created to ensure reliable communication between two network devices. This circuit denotes the existence of a logical, bidirectional path from one DTE device to another across an X.25 network.

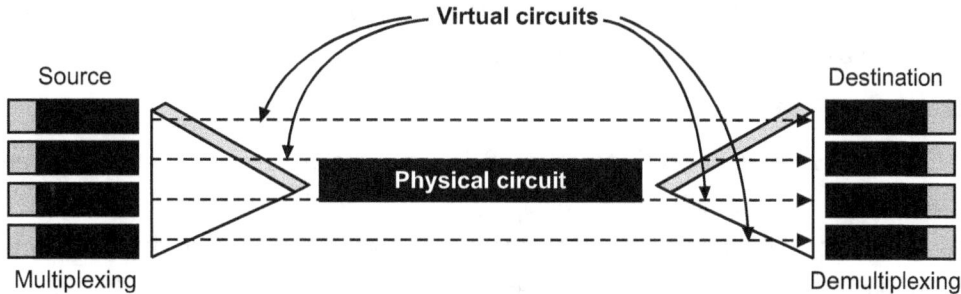

Fig. 2.5 : Virtual circuits can be multiplexed onto a single physical circuit

Physically, the connection can pass through any number of intermediate nodes, such as DCE devices and PSEs. Multiple virtual circuits (logical connections) can be multiplexed onto a single physical circuit (a physical connection).

Virtual circuits are demultiplexed at the remote end, and data is sent to the appropriate destinations. Two types of X.25 virtual circuits exist: switched and permanent.

Switched virtual circuits (SVCs) are temporary connections used for sporadic data transfers. They require that two DTE devices establish, maintain, and terminate a session each time the devices need to communicate.

Permanent virtual circuits (PVCs) are permanently established connections used for frequent and consistent data transfers. PVCs do not require that sessions be established and terminated. Therefore, DTEs can begin transferring data whenever necessary because the session is always active.

The basic operation of an X.25 virtual circuit begins when the source DTE device specifies the virtual circuit to be used (in the packet headers) and then sends the packets to a locally connected DCE device.

At this point, the local DCE device examines the packet headers to determine which virtual circuit to use and then sends the packets to the closest PSE in the path of that virtual circuit. Then PSEs (switches) pass the traffic to the next intermediate node in the path, which may be another switch or the remote DCE device.

When the traffic arrives at the remote DCE device, the packet headers are examined and the destination address is determined. The packets are then sent to the destination DTE device. If communication occurs over an SVC and neither device has additional data to transfer, the virtual circuit is terminated.

5. The X.25 Protocol Suite:

The X.25 protocol suite maps to the lowest three layers of the OSI reference model. The following protocols are typically used in X.25 implementations: Packet-Layer Protocol (PLP),

Link Access Procedure Balanced (LAPB), and those among other physical-layer serial interfaces (such as EIA/TIA-232, EIA/TIA-449, EIA-530, and G.703).

(i) Packet-Layer Protocol (PLP) :

PLP is the X.25 network layer protocol. PLP manages packet exchanges between DTE devices across virtual circuits. PLPs also can run over Logical Link Control 2 (LLC2) implementations on LANs and over Integrated Services Digital Network (ISDN) interfaces running Link Access Procedure on the D channel (LAPD).

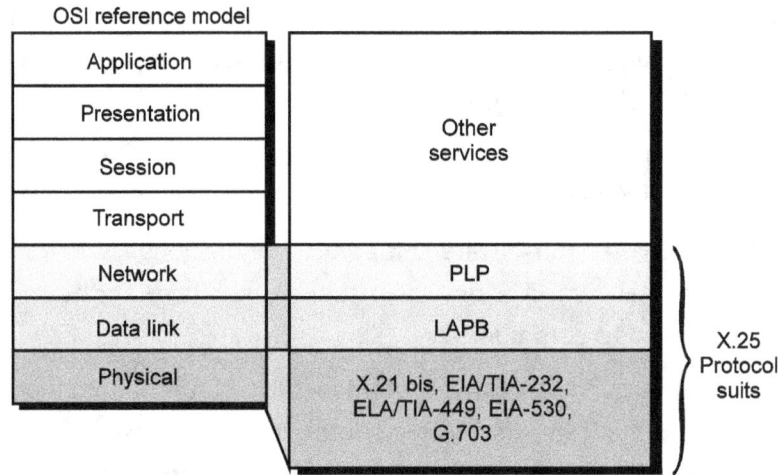

Fig. 2.6 : Key X.25 Protocols map to the three lower layers of the OSI reference model

The PLP operates in five distinct modes: Call Setup, Data transfer, Idle, Call clearing, and Restarting.

- **Call setup mode** is used to establish SVCs between DTE devices. A PLP uses the X.121 addressing scheme to set up the virtual circuit. The call setup mode is executed on a per-virtual-circuit basis, which means that one virtual circuit can be in call setup mode while another is in data transfer mode. This mode is used only with SVCs, not with PVCs.

- **Data transfer mode** is used for transferring data between two DTE devices across a virtual circuit. In this mode, PLP handles segmentation and reassembly, bit padding, and error and flow control. This mode is executed on a per-virtual-circuit basis and is used with both PVCs and SVCs.

- **Idle mode** is used when a virtual circuit is established but data transfer is not occurring. It is executed on a per-virtual-circuit basis and is used only with SVCs.

- **Call clearing mode** is used to end communication sessions between DTE devices and to terminate SVCs. This mode is executed on a per-virtual-circuit basis and is used only with SVCs.

- **Restarting mode** is used to synchronize transmission between a DTE device and a locally connected DCE device. This mode is not executed on a per-virtual-circuit basis. It affects all the DTE device's established virtual circuits.

Four types of PLP packet fields exist, they are:

1. **General Format Identifier (GFI):** Identifies packet parameters, such as whether the packet carries user data or control information, what kind of windowing is being used, and whether delivery confirmation is required.

2. **Logical Channel Identifier (LCI):** Identifies the virtual circuit across the local DTE/DCE interface.

3. **Packet Type Identifier (PTI):** Identifies the packet as one of 17 different PLP packet types.

4. **User Data:** Contains encapsulated upper-layer information. This field is present only in data packets. Otherwise, additional fields containing control information are added.

(ii) Link Access Procedure, Balanced (LAPB):

LAPB is a data link layer protocol that manages communication and packet framing between DTE and DCE devices. LAPB, a bit-oriented protocol, ensures that frames are correctly ordered and error-free.

Three types of LAPB frames exist: information, supervisory, and unnumbered.

- The **Information Frame (I-frame)** carries upper-layer information and some control information. I-frame functions include sequencing, flow control, and error detection and recovery. I-frames carry send and receive-sequence numbers.

- The **Supervisory Frame (S-frame)** carries control information. S-frame functions include requesting and suspending transmissions, reporting on status, and acknowledging the receipt of I-frames. S-frames carry only receive-sequence numbers.

- The **Unnumbered Frame (U frame)** carries control information. U-frame functions include link setup and disconnection, as well as error reporting. U frames carry no sequence numbers.

LAPB Frame Format:

LAPB frames include a header, encapsulated data, and a trailer.

Flag: Delimits the beginning and end of the LAPB frame. Bit stuffing is used to ensure that the flag pattern does not occur within the body of the frame.

Address: Indicates whether the frame carries a command or a response.

Control: Qualifies command and response frames and indicates whether the frame is an I-frame, an S-frame, or a U-frame. In addition, this field contains the frame's sequence number and its function (for example, whether receiver-ready or disconnect). Control frames vary in length depending on the frame type.

Data: Contains upper-layer data in the form of an encapsulated PLP packet.

FCS: Handles error checking and ensures the integrity of the transmitted data.

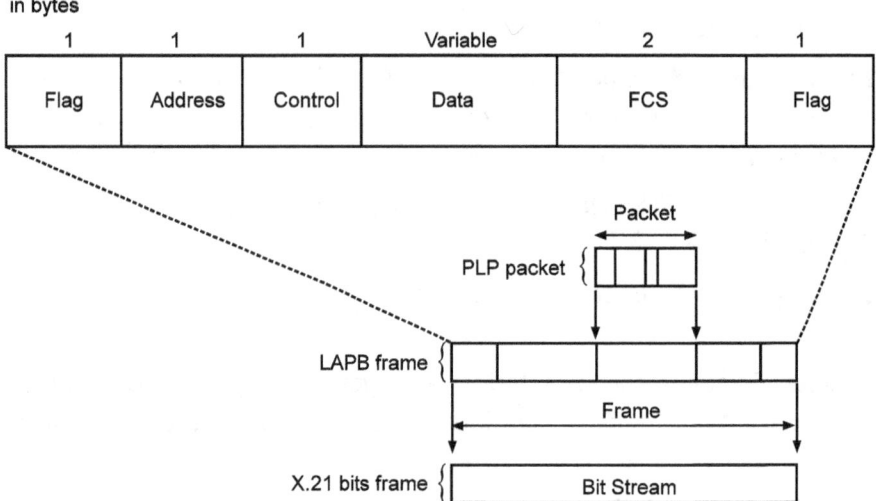

Fig. 2.7: An LAPB frame includes a header, a trailer, and encapsulated data

(iii) The X.21bis Protocol:

X.21bis is a physical layer protocol used in X.25 that defines the electrical and mechanical procedures for using the physical medium. X.21bis handles the activation and deactivation of the physical medium connecting DTE and DCE devices. It supports point-to-point connections, speeds up to 19.2 kbps, and synchronous, full-duplex transmission over four-wire media.

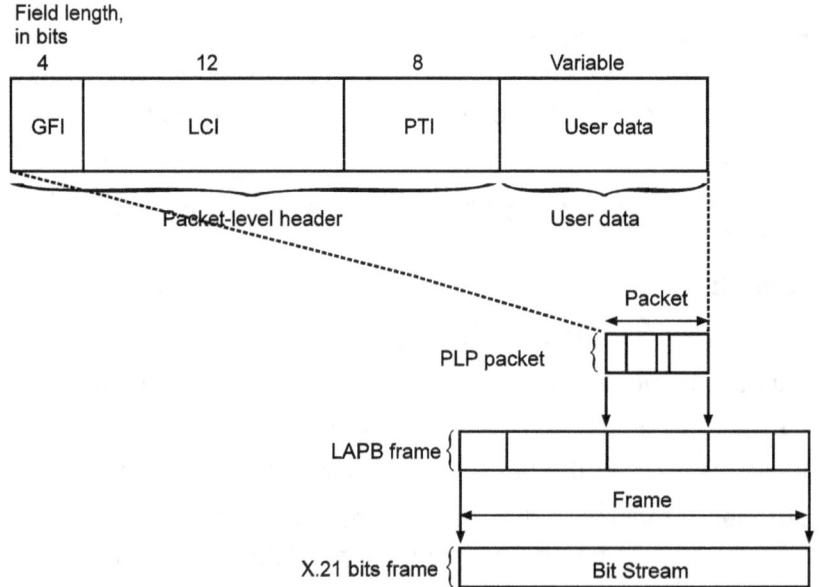

Fig. 2.8: The PLP packet Is encapsulated within the LAPB frame and the X.21bis frame

Uses of X.25 Network :

- X.25 is a mechanism for transferring transparent data. Standards exist for encapsulation of higher-level data such as TCP/IP or SNA traffic over X.25. One of the largest uses of X.25 is the transfer of asynchronous data streams such as those produced by simple terminals like credit card readers. These devices connect to a Packet Assembler/ Disassembler (PAD) that organizes the asynch data streams into X.25 packets for transmission across the network. PAD design is based on ITU standards X.28, X.29 and X.3.

- By the year 2000, use of X.25 for general networking such as SNA support, ATM connectivity and data transfer was in decline, replaced by TCP/IP based systems. X.25 remains important in Point-of-Sale credit card and debit card authorization. However, there is an huge investment in X.25 infrastructure throughout the world, and in some regions, it continues to expand. Thus X.25 will remain important for years to come.

Characteristics of X.25 Network :

- Maximum packet sizes vary from 64 bytes to 4096 bytes, with 128 bytes being a default on most networks. Both maximum packet size and packet level windowing may be negotiated between DTE's on call set up.

- X.25 is optimized for what today would be considered quite low speed lines: 100kbps and below. At line speeds above 100 kbps the effects of latency, small packet sizes and small window sizes are such that the bandwidth cannot be efficiently utilized.

- X.25 has been around since the mid 1970's and so is pretty well debugged and stable. There are literally no data errors on modern X.25 networks.

- The major technical drawback of X.25 today is the inherent delay caused by the store-and-forward mechanism, which in turn restricts the useful data transmission rate. Frame Relay andATM, for instance, have no inter-node error or flow control, so end-to-end latency is minimal.

- X.25 has been the basis of the development of other packet switched protocols like TCP/IP and ATM. These protocols also have the ability to handle one-to-many connections and the ability to match DTE's having different line speeds, both characteristics of X.25.

2.3 Peer to Peer Networks (P2P Network)

Network's architecture can be described in two ways : **Peer-to-Peer**, and **Client-Server**. A peer-to-peer network is a grouping of personal computers that all share information between each other. Peer to Peer network is decentralized communication architecture. This is a different way of approaching a network for communication. Peer means device. So the term 'Peer to Peer' means the devices which are connected to the network which is fulfilling it's queries by communicating with other equivalent peers in the network.

There is no master or controller or central server in this network and computers join hands to share files, printers and Internet access.

It is practical for workgroups of a dozen or less computers making it common environments, where each personal computer acts as an independent workstation. Each workstation maintains its own security that stores data on its own disk but which can share it with all other PCs on the network. Software for Peer-to-Peer network is included with most modern desktop operating systems such as Windows and Mac OS.

Peer to Peer relationship is suitable for small networks having less than 10 computers on a single LAN.

In a Peer to Peer network, each computer can not act as both a server and a client.

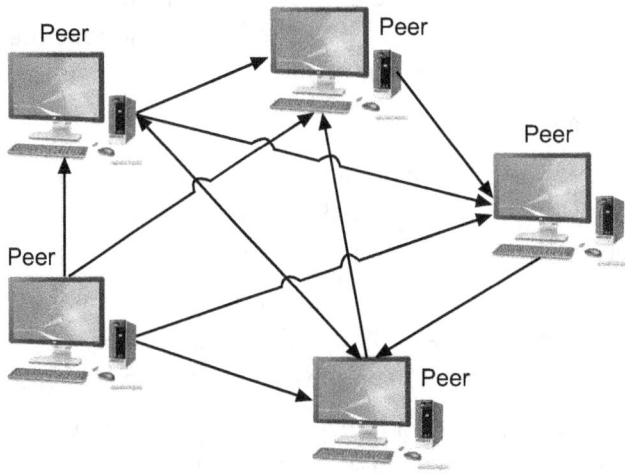

Fig. 2.9 : Peer to Peer network

Advantages of Peer to Peer Network :

Peer to Peer network have following advantages:

1. Peer to peer networks are easy to set up and maintain as each computer manages itself.

2. It eliminates extra cost required in setting up the server.

3. Since each device is master of its own, they are not dependent on other computers for their operations.

Disadvantages of Peer to Peer Networks:

1. In Peer-to-Peer network, the absence of centralized server make it difficult to backup data as data is located on different workstations.

2. Peer-to-Peer networks are very susceptible to hackers and other malicious users because there is no solid security policy enforced.

3. There is no central point of data storage for file archiving.

2.4 Ethernet (Standard & Fast)

Ethernet (pronounced "eether net") is a local area network, connecting computers together with cables so the computers can share information. Within each main branch of the network, Ethernet can connect up to 1,024 personal computers and workstations.

All the devices (Servers, Workstations, Printers, Scanners etc) connected in an Ethernet network share a common transmission medium. Ethernet uses Carrier Sense Multiple Access/Collision Detection (CSMA/CD) for determining when a computer is free to transmit data on to the access medium. Using Carrier Sense Multiple Access/Collision Detection (CSMA/CD), all computers monitor the transmission medium and wait until the medium is free before transmitting. If two computers try to transmit at the same time, a collision occurs. The computers then stop, wait for a random time interval, and attempt to transmit again. Collisions were common in Ethernet network (when used in a shared media) and network infrastructure devices like Ethernet Hubs usually have a small light on their front panel, that blink when collisions happen in your network. Presently, all the business networks are installed and connected using Ethernet Switches instead of Ethernet Hubs. There is no collision when devices are connected using Ethernet Switches.

The maximum data rate of the original Ethernet technology carries 10 Mbps , but a second generation FAST ETHERNET carries 100 Mbps, and the latest version called GIGABIT ETHERNET works at 1000 Mbps. SWITCHED ETHERNET involves adding switches so that each workstation can have its own dedicated 10 Mbps connection rather than sharing the medium, which can improve network throughput - it has the advantage over rival switched technologies such as ASYNCHRONOUS TRANSFER MODE that it employs the same low-level protocols, cheap cabling and NETWORK INTERFACE CARDS as ordinary Ethernet.

Ethernet, Fast Ethernet and Gigabit Ethernet are the LAN technologies most commonly used today. Ethernet Version 1 was developed by Xerox Corporation during the early 1970s. Later in 1982 Xerox, Intel and DEC (Digital Equipment Corporation) together released Ethernet Version 2. Since then, Ethernet is the most popular LAN technology used in networking. The network topology on which all the latest Ethernet technologies built is Star Topology. Advantages of Ethernet are :

- Low cost components
- Easy to install
- Easy to troubleshoot

Ethernet networks typically operate at baseband speeds of either 100Mbps (Fast Ethernet), 1000Mbps (Gigabit Ethernet). Fast Ethernet (100 Mbps) or Gigabit Ethernet (1000 Mbps) cannot operate on network infrastructure devices like Ethernet Hubs, Ethernet Switches and network cards designed for a 10Mbps Ethernet network. Many latest network infrastructure devices likeEthernet Switches and Ethernet network cards are capable to operate at speed of 10 Mbps or 100 Mbps or 1000 Mbps. (10/100/100). Even a faster version of Gigabit Ethernet, 10 Gigabit Ethernet is now available. 10 Gigabit Ethernet works well with both fiber optic and copper media.

IEEE 802.3 Frame Format

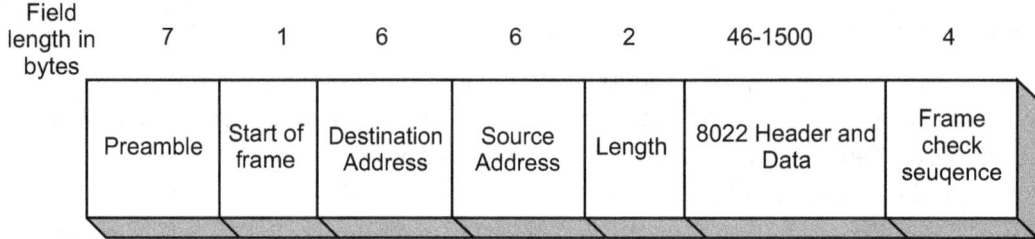

Fig. 2.10 : IEEE 802.3 frame format

Preamble : The alternating pattern of ones and zeros tells receiving stations that a frame is coming (Ethernet or IEEE 802.3). The Ethernet frame includes an additional byte that is the equivalent of the Start of Frame (SOF) field specified in the IEEE 802.3 frame.

Start-of-Frame (SOF) : The IEEE 802.3 delimiter byte ends with two consecutive 1 bits, which serve to synchronize the frame-reception portions of all stations on the LAN. SOF is explicitly specified in Ethernet.

Destination and Source Addresses : The first 3 bytes of the addresses are specified by the IEEE on a vendor-dependent basis. The last 3 bytes are specified by the Ethernet or IEEE 802.3 vendor. The source address is always a unicast (single-node) address. The destination address can be unicast, multicast (group), or broadcast (all nodes).

Length (IEEE 802.3) : The length indicates the number of bytes of data that follows this field.

Data (IEEE 802.3) ; After Physical-layer and Link-layer processing is complete, the data is sent to an upper-layer protocol, which must be defined within the data portion of the frame, if at all. If data in the frame is insufficient to fill the frame to its minimum 64-byte size, padding bytes are inserted to ensure at least a 64-byte frame.

Frame Check Sequence (FCS) : This sequence contains a 4-byte cyclic redundancy check (CRC) value, which is created by the sending device and is recalculated by the receiving device to check for damaged frames.

IEEE 802.2 LLC Header

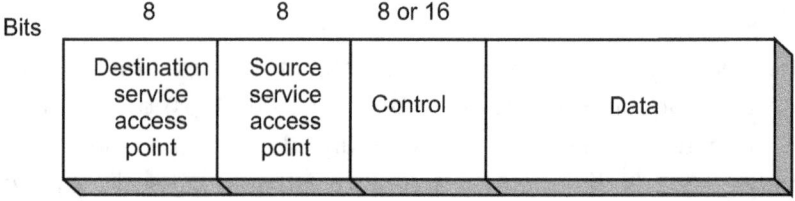

Fig. 2.11 : IEEE 802.2 LLC Header

Destination Service Access Point (DSAP) : A seven bit address with an eighth bit indicating if it is a specific address (0) or a broadcast address (1). The DSAP is not a station or MAC address; it designates the service control point where the message should be routed.

Source Service Access Point (SSAP) : Also a seven bit address; the eighth bit is used to determine if the massage is a command (0) or a response (1). Like the DSAP, the SSAP designates a control point from which the message originated.

Control : This field can be 8 or 16 bits long. Length is indicated by the first two bits. The 16 bit fields are used to exchange sequence numbers; the 8 bit fields are used for unsequenced information.

Data : The frame's payload. This field contains the encapsulated protocol.

2.5 Wireless LAN

A Wireless LAN or WLAN is a Wireless Local Area Network, which is the linking of two or more computers without using wires. This type of LAN utilizes spread-spectrum technology based on radio waves to enable communication between devices in a limited area, also known as the basic service set. This gives users the mobility to move around within a broad coverage area and still be connected to the network.

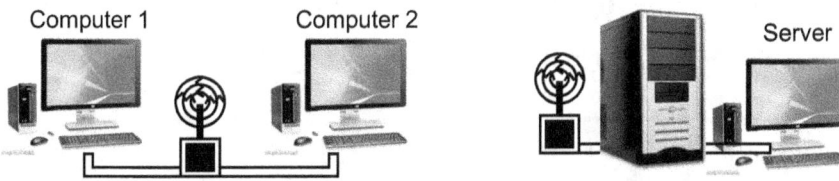

Fig. 2.12 : Wireless LAN

A WLAN gives users the mobility to move around within a local coverage area and still be connected to the network. Most modern WLANs are based on IEEE 802.11 standards, marketed under the Wi-Fi brand name.

Wireless LAN or WiFi is divided into three main modes on which its whole working depends and all of its applications also depend on these modes. These modes are as follows:

1. Infrastructure network mode: Any kind of machine that can communicate with every type of work station of wireless LAN or WiFi with the help of access points is called as infra structure network mode.

2. Ad-hoc network mode: A type of network in which all the work stations are linked together with other work stations without any obstacle is referred to as ad-hoc network mode.

3. Mixed network mode: It is of network which is developed by mixing infra structure and ad hoc network and the work stations can work simultaneously in it, is known as mixed network mode.

Architecture of Wireless LAN:

Components of WAN architecture are listed below:

Station: All components that can connect into a wireless medium in a network are referred to as stations. All stations are equipped with Wireless Network Interface Cards (WNICs). Wireless stations fall into one of two categories: access points and clients.

Access points: Access Points (APs) are base stations for the wireless network. They transmit and receive radio frequencies for wireless enabled devices to communicate with them.

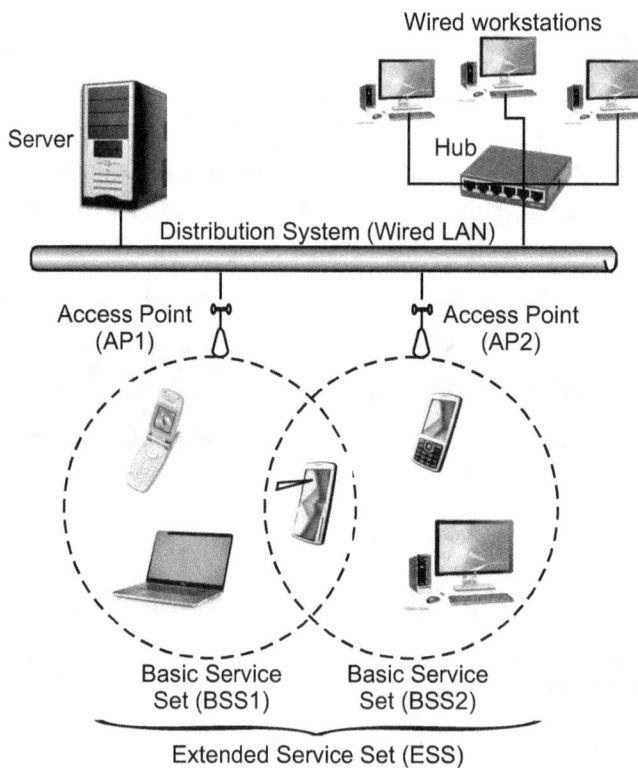

Fig. 2.13 : Architecture of WLAN

Clients: Wireless clients can be mobile devices such as laptops, personal digital assistants, IP phones, or fixed devices such as desktops and workstations that are equipped with a wireless network interface cards.

Basic Service Set: The basic Service Set (BSS) is a set of all stations that can communicate with each other. There are two types of BSS: independent BSS and infrastructure BSS. Every BSS has an identification (ID) called the BSSID, which is the MAC address of the access point servicing the BSS.

o **Independent basic service set:** An independent BSS is an ad-hoc network that contains no access points, which means they can not connect to any other basic service set.

o **Infrastructure basic service set:** An infrastructure BSS can communicate with other stations not in the same basic service set by communicating through access points.

Extended service set: An Extended Service Set (ESS) is a set of connected BSS. Access points in an ESS are connected by a distribution system. Each ESS has an ID called the SSID which is a 32-byte (maximum) character string. For example, "linksys" is the default SSID for Linksys routers.

Distribution system: A distribution system connects access points in an extended service set. A distribution system is usually a wired LAN but can be a wireless LAN.

Design Goals of Wireless LAN:

1. **Global operation:** LAN equipment may be carried from one country to another and this operation should be legal, (frequency regulations national and international).

2. **Low power:** Take into account that devices communicating via WLAN are typically running on battery power. Special power saving modes and power management functions.

3. **Protection of investment:** A lot of money has been invested for wired LANs, WLANs should be able to interoperate with existing network (same data type and services).

4. **Safety and security:** Safe to operate. Encryption mechanism, do not allow roaming profiles for tracking people (privacy)

5. **Transparency for applications:** Existing applications should continue to work.

6. **Simplified spontaneous co-operation:** No complicated setup routines but operate spontaneously after power.

7. **Easy to use:** WLANs are made for simple users, they should not require complex management but rather work on a plug-and-play basis.

Benefits of WLAN:

1. **Convenience:** The wireless nature of such networks allows users to access network resources from nearly any convenient location within their primary networking environment (home or office).

2. **Mobility:** With the emergence of public wireless networks, users can access the internet even outside their normal work environment. Most chain coffee shops, for example, offer their customers a wireless connection to the internet at little or no cost.

3. **Productivity:** Users connected to a wireless network can maintain a nearly constant affiliation with their desired network as they move from place to place. For a business, this implies that an employee can potentially be more productive as his or the work can be accomplished from any convenient location.

4. **Deployment:** Initial setup of an infrastructure-based wireless network requires little more than a single access point. Wired networks, on the other hand, have the additional cost and complexity of actual physical cables being run to numerous locations (which can even be impossible for hard-to-reach locations within a building).

5. **Expandability:** Wireless networks can serve a suddenly-increased number of clients with the existing equipment. In a wired network, additional clients would require additional wiring.

6. **Cost:** Wireless networking hardware is at worst a modest increase from wired counterparts. This potentially increased cost is almost always more than outweighed by the savings in cost and labor associated to running physical cables.

Disadvantages:

1. **Security:** WLAN is not so secured. Security is more difficult to guarantee and requires configuration.

2. **Range:** The typical range of a common 802.11g network with standard equipment is on the order of tens of meters. While sufficient for a typical home, it will be insufficient in a larger structure.

3. **Reliability:** Like any radio frequency transmission, wireless networking signals are subject to a wide variety of interference, as well as complex propagation effects (such as multipath, or especially in this case Rician fading) that are beyond the control of the network administrator.

4. **Speed:** The speed on most wireless networks (typically 1-54 mbps) is reasonably slow compared to the slowest common wired networks (100 Mbps up to several Gbps).

2.5.1 IEEE Standard 802.11 (WLAN)

IEEE has defined the specifications for wireless LAN, named IEEE 802.11, which covers both physical and data link layers. Fig. 2.14 shows various components of WLAN which described below:

Architecture of 802.11 (WLAN):

Each computer, mobile which is portable or fixed, is referred to as a station in 802.11 wireless networks. When two or more stations come together to communicate with each other, they form a Basic Service Set (BSS).

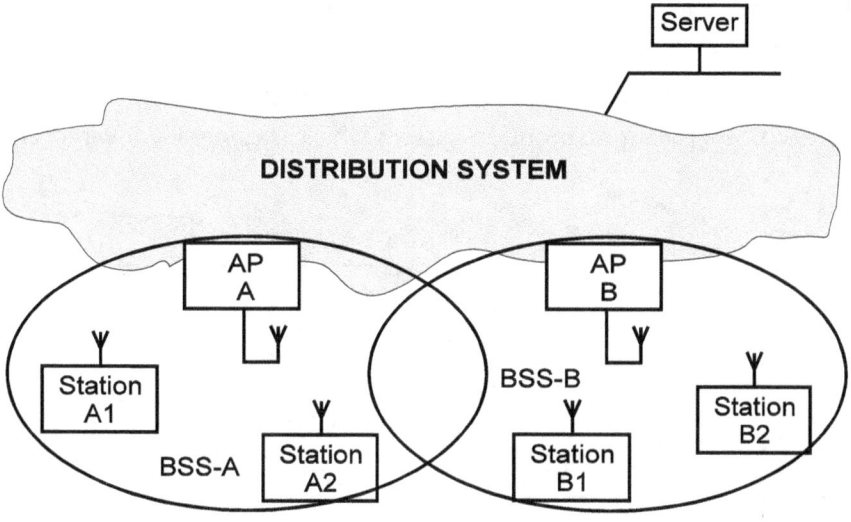

Fig. : 2.14 : Components of WLAN

The minimum BSS consists of two stations. 802.11 LANs use the BSS as the standard building block. The BSS without AP cannot send data to another BSS. So it is called as standalone or ad-hoc network. Two or more BSSs are interconnected using a Distribution System or DS. This concept of DS increases network coverage, which can be either wired or wireless.

The BSS can be either without AP (Access Point) or with AP which is as shown in Fig. 2.15.

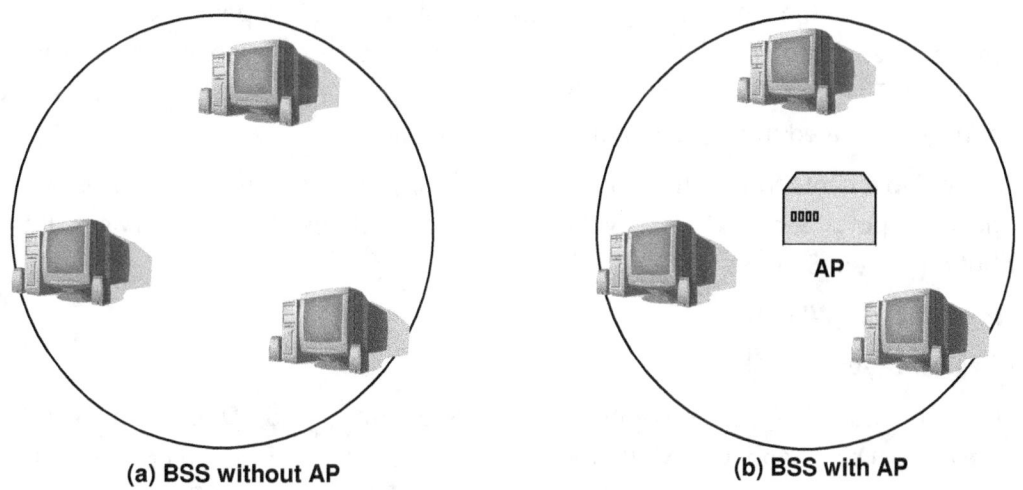

(a) BSS without AP   **(b) BSS with AP**

Fig. 2.15 : Types of BSS

With the use of access points, entry to the DS is accomplished. Data moves between the BSS and the DS with the help of these access points because an access point is a station which is addressable. So create large and complex networks using BSSs and DSs leads us to the next level of hierarchy, the Extended Service Set or ESS.

An Extended Service set contains two or more BSS with APs. The BSSs in the system are connected to each other via a distribution system which is generally a wired LAN as shown in Fig. 2.16.

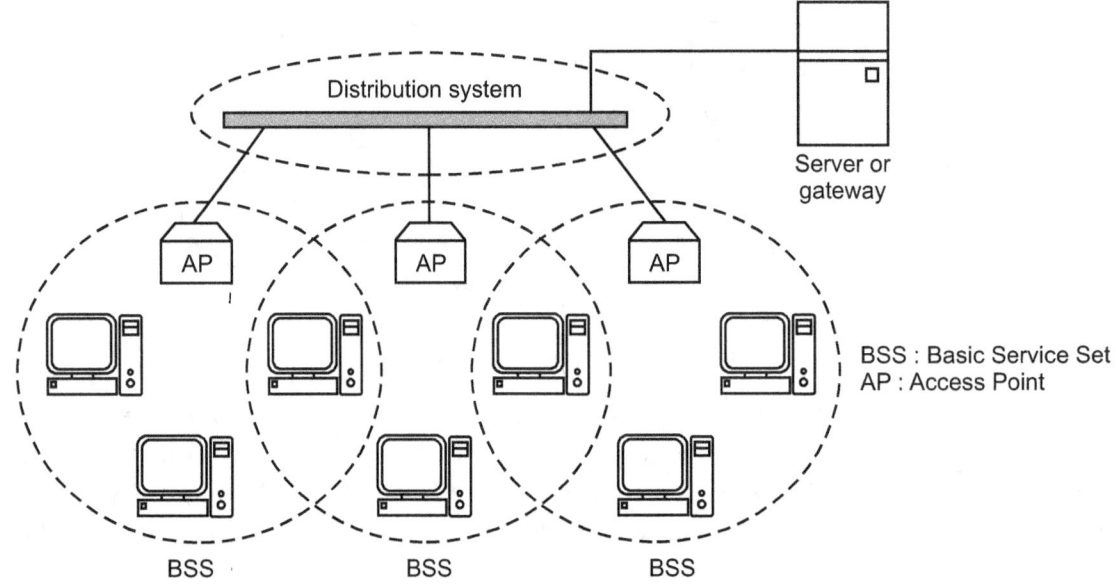

Fig. 2.16 : Extended service set (ESS)

The structure of the ESS is the entire network looks like an independent basic service set. This means that stations within the ESS can communicate or even more between BSSs transparently. The implementation of the DS is not specified by 802.11. So a distribution system may be created from existing or new technologies.

As the implementation for the DS is not specified, 802.11 specify the services, which the DS must support. Services are divided into two sections, Station Services (SS) and Distribution System Services (DSS).

Layers of 802.11 (WLAN):

1. Physical Layer:

802.11 provides Frequency Hopping Spread Spectrum (FHSS), Direct Sequence Spread Spectrum (DSSS) and OFDM (Orthogonal Frequency Division Multiplexing), physical definitions which supports 1 and 2 Mbps data transfer rates and of DM.

Frequency Hopping Spread Spectrum (FHSS):

Frequency Hopping Spread Spectrum (FHSS) uses a narrowband carrier that changes frequency in a pattern known to both transmitter and receiver. Properly synchronized, the net effect is to maintain a single logical channel. To an unintended receiver, FHSS appears to be short-duration impulse noise.

FHSS is a method of transmitting radio signals by rapidly switching a carrier among many frequency channels, using a pseudorandom sequence known to both transmitter and receiver.

Fig. 2.17 shows frame format of FHSS.

80 bit preample	SFD 16 bits	LENGTH 12 bits	PSF 4 bits	CRC 16 bits	CRC 16 bits
PLCP Preample		PLCP Header			Payload MPDU
PPDU					

Fig. 2.17 : FHSS frame format

- The 80 bit preample has a 0101 sync format and is used for signal detection.
- The SFD stands for Start of Frame Delimiter
- The LENGTH field indicates the Payload length in bytes.
- The PSF stands for Payload Signaling Field and indicates the rate used and some bits for future use.

The hopping rules say that there are 79 hopping channels and that the minimum hop should be 6 channels. The transmitter should settle on the new channel within 224 microseconds.

(ii) Direct Sequence Spread Spectrum (DSSS):

DSSS generates a redundant bit pattern for each bit to be transmitted. This bit pattern is called a chip (or chipping code). The longer the chip, the greater the probability that the original data can be recovered and, of course, the more bandwidth required. Each bit is transmitted as 11 chips using a Barker Sequence. Even if one or more bits in the chip are damaged during transmission, statistical techniques embedded in the radio can recover the original data without the need for retransmission. To an unintended receiver, DSSS appears as low power wideband noise and is rejected (ignored) by most narrowband receivers.

With direct sequence spread spectrum the transmission signal is spread over an allowed band. A random binary string is used to modulate the transmitted signal. This random string is called the spreading code. The data bits are mapped to a pattern of chips and mapped back into a bit at the destination.

The number of chips that represent a bit is the spreading ratio. The higher the spreading ratio, the more the signal is resistant to interference. The lower the spreading ratio, the more bandwidth is available to the user.

The FCC dictates that the spreading ratio must be more than 10. IEEE 802.11 standard requires a spreading ratio of 11.

Fig. 2.18 shows frame format of DSSS.

128 bit preample	SFD 16 bits	SIGNAL 8 bits	SERVICE 8 bits	LENGTH 16 bits	CRC 16 bits	
PLCP Preample		PLCP Header				Payload MPDU
PPDU						

Fig. 2.18 : DSSS frame format

- The 128 bit preample is used for signal detection.
- The SFD stands for Start of Frame Delimiter
- The SIGNAL field indicates the speed used.
- The SERVICE field is reserved for future use and now contains 00.
- The LENGTH field indicates the Payload length in bytes.

(iii) OFDM:

OFDM stands for Orthogonal Frequency Division Multiplexing. OFDM is multicarrier spread spectrum technique. In OFDM, high rate serial data stream divided into numerous parallel low-rate data streams that are modulated by a set of subcarriers.

In OFDM subcarriers are orthogonal with overlapping spectra. It uses 5GHz ISM band for its operation. The basic working of OFDM is same as that of FDM but the main difference is that all the frequency sub bands are used by one source at a given time.

2. MAC Layer:

IEEE 802.11 defines two MAC sublayers i.e. the Distributed Coordination Function (DCF) and Point Coordination Function (PCF). MAC provides a reliable delivery mechanism for user data over noisy, unreliable wireless medium. Before transmitting frames, a station must first gain access to the medium, which is a radio channel that stations share.

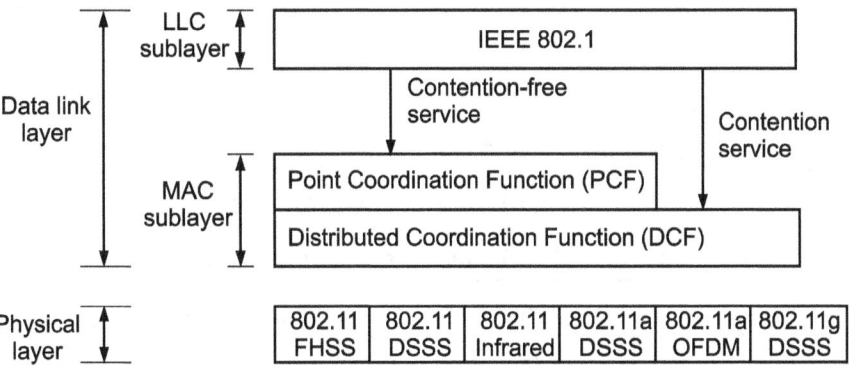

Fig. 2.19 : MAC layer

Fig. 2.19 shows the relationship between the two MAC sublayers, the LLC sublayer and the physical layer. CSMA/CA is the protocol used to access method defined by IEEE at the MAC sublayer is called the distributed coordination function. The Point Coordination Function (PCF) is an optional access method which is implemented in an infrastructure network and not in ad-hoc network. It is implemented on top of the DCF and is used for time sensitive transmission. The 802.11 standard defines two forms of medium access, Distributed Coordination Function (DCF) and Point Coordination Function (PCF).DCF is the fundamental, required contention-based access service for all networks.PCF is an optical contention-free service, used for non-QoS STAs.

The MAC layer consists of nine fields as shown in Fig. 2.20.

2 bytes	2 bytes	6 bytes	6 bytes	6 bytes	2 bytes	6 bytes	0 to 2312 bytes	4 bytes
FC	D	Address 1	Address 2	Address 3	SC	Address 4	Frame Body	FCS

Protocol version	Type	Subtype	To DS	From DS	More flag	Retry	Pwr Mgt	More Data	WEP	Rsvd
2 bits	2 bits	4 bits	1 bit	1 bit	1 bit	1 bit	1 bit	1 bit	1 bit	1 bit

Fig. 2.20 : Frame format

Frame Control (FC): The FC field is 2 bytes long and defines the type of frame and some control information.

Table 2.3 : Table of subfields in FC fields

Field	Explanation
Version	Current version is 0.
Type	Type of information: Management (00), Control (01), or Data (10).

Subtype	Subtype (RTS, CTS, ACK).
TO DS	Shown in Table 2.4.
From DS	Shown in Table 2.4.
More flag	When set to 1, means more fragments.
Retry	When set to 1 means retransmitted frame.
Power management	When set to 1 means station is in power management made.
More data	When set to 1, means station has more data to send.
WEP	Wired equivalence privacy.
Rsvd	Reserved.

- **D:** In all frames, this field defines the duration of the transmission that is used to set the value of NAV.

- **Addresses:** There are four address fields, each 6 bytes long. The meaning of each address field depends on the value of the TO DS and From DS subfields.

- **Sequence Control:** This field defines the sequence number of the frame to be used in flow control.

- **Frame Body:** This field between 0 to 2312 bytes contains information based on the type and the subtype defined in the FC field.

- **FCS:** This field is used for error detection.

Table 2.4 : Address in frame control

To DS	From DS	Address 1	Address 2	Address 3	Address 4
0	0	Destination	Source	BSS ID	N/A
0	1	Destination	Sending AP	Source	N/A
1	0	Receiving AP	Source	Destination	N/A
1	1	Receiving AP	Sending AP	Destination	Source

2.5.2 IEEE Standard 802.11x

802.11x refers to a group of evolving Wireless Local Area Network (WLAN) standards that are under development as elements of the IEEE 802.11 family of specifications, but that have not yet been formally approved or deployed.

As of August 2004, these incomplete standards included the following:

1. **802.11e:** Adds Quality of Service (QoS) features to exiting 802.11 family specifications.

2. **802.11f:** Adds Access Point Interoperability to existing 802.11 family specifications.

3. **802.11h:** Resolves interference issues with existing 802.11 family specification.

4. **802.11j:** Japanese regulatory extensions to 802.11 family specifications.

5. **80211k:** Radio resource measurement for 802.11 specifications so that a wireless network can be used more efficiently.

6. **802.11m:** Enhanced maintenance features, improvements, and amendments to existing 802.11 family specifications.

7. **802.11n:** Next generation of 802.11 family specifications, with throughput in excess of 100 Mbps.

Above standards are being developed with the goal that they support all the 802.11 family specifications in current use. 802.11x is also sometimes used as a generic term for any existing or proposed standard of the 802.11 family.

Security issues of the IEEE 802.11b wireless LAN

Wireless security is a major demand in the secure data transferring services. Security challenges such as identity theft, international credit card fraud, communications fraud and corporate fraud are some of the main barriers preventing wireless technologies from growing and over taking the wired technology position. The 802.11b wireless LAN includes a protocol called wired equivalent privacy (WEP) which is meant to protect the wireless network. We have been able to find some major flaws in this protocol which lead the whole system to be insecure and thus unreliable. For example, the cryptographic technique used in the WEP protocol.

IEEE 802.11 Features:

Specific features of the 802.11 standard include the following:

- Support of asynchronous and time-bounded delivery service.
- Continuity of service within extended areas via a Distribution System, such as Ethernet.
- Accommodation of transmission rates of 1 and 2 Mbps
- Support of most market applications
- Multicast (including broadcast) services
- Network management services
- Registration and authentication services

Like all IEEE 802 standards, the 802.11 standards focus on the bottom two levels of the ISO model, the physical layer and data link layer . Any LAN application, network operating system, or protocol, including TCP/IP and Novell NetWare, will run on an 802.11-compliant WLAN as easily as they run over Ethernet.

Practice Questions

1. Write the difference between Connection-oriented network and Connectionless network.

2. What is Peer to Peer network?

3. Write a short note on X.25 network.

4. Explain frame format of Ethernet.

5. Which are types of wireless LANs?

6. Explain architecture of 802.11 and 802.11x LAN.

7. Which are layers used in 802.11 LAN?

8. Define terms: WLAN, IP network

9. What is Switched virtual circuits?

10. Explain Packet Layer Protocol?

Chapter 3...

THE OSI REFERENCE MODEL

Contents ...

3.1   Protocol Layering

3.2   ISO/OSI reference Model

3.3   TCP/IP Model

3.4   OSI vs.TCP/IP

- Practice Questions

3.1 Protocol Layering

A network protocol defines rules and conventions for communication between network devices. A protocol is a set of rules that governs the communications between computers on a network. These rules include guidelines that regulate the following characteristics of a network:

- Access method
- Allowed physical topologies
- Types of cabling
- Speed of data transfer.

Protocol layering is a common technique to simplify networking designs by dividing them into functional layers, and assigning protocols to perform each layer's task.

For example, it is common to separate the functions of data delivery and connection management into separate layers, and therefore separate protocols. Thus, one protocol is designed to perform data delivery, and another protocol, layered above the first, performs connection management. The connection management protocol is also fairly simple, since it doesn't need to concern itself with data delivery.

Protocol layering produces simple protocols, each with a few well-defined tasks. These protocols can then be assembled into a useful whole. Individual protocols can also be removed or replaced as needed for particular applications. The most important layered protocol designs are the Internet's original DoD (Department of Defence) model, and the OSI Seven Layer Model. The modern Internet represents a fusion of both models.

Layered protocols are designed so that the layer N at the destination receives exactly the same object sent by layer N at the source. Developers only need focus on one layer at a time and focus on the messages needed to be passed to get its job done.

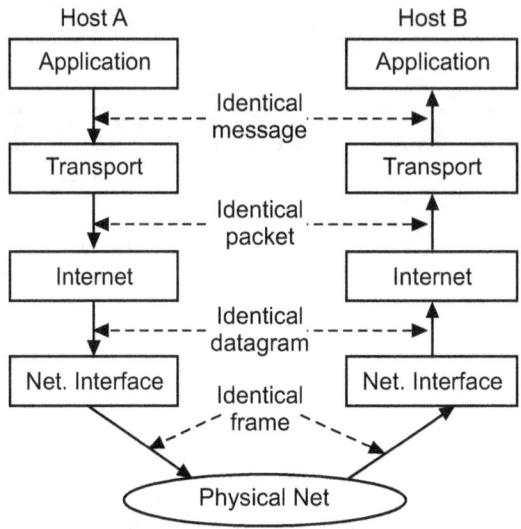

Fig. 3.1 : Protocol layering

Application and Transport layers deal with end-to-end issues and are designed so the software at the source communicates with it's peer at the final destination. Internet and Network-Interface layers view an end-to-end connection as the each pair of links in the network.

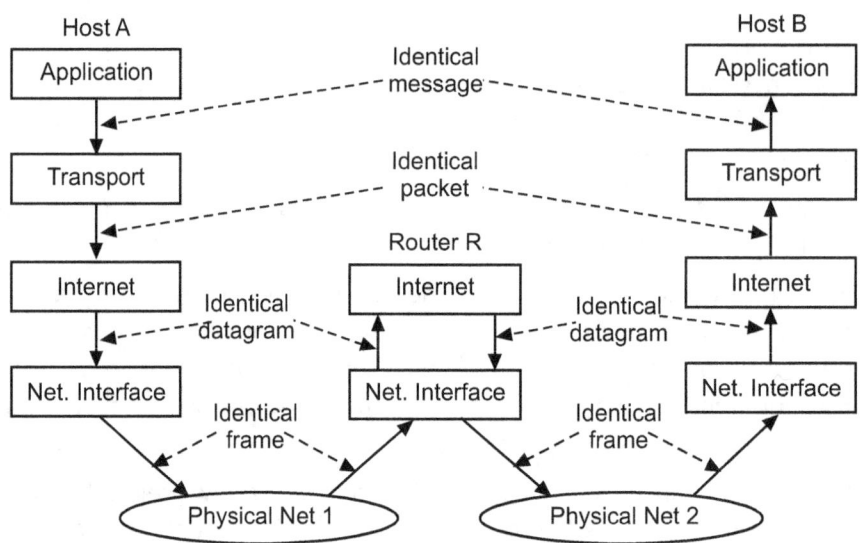

Fig. 3.2 : Protocol layering on multiple network

The layered approach to network communications provides the following benefits:

1. Improved teaching and learning.
2. Accelerated evolution.
3. Reduced complexity.
4. Modular engineering.

5. Standard interfaces.

6. Interoperable technology.

Encapsulation

Fig. 3.3 reveals another aspect of data communication in the OSI model i.e. encapsulation. This is the process of taking data from one protocol and translating it into another protocol, so the data can continue across a network. For example, a TCP/IP packet contained within an ATM frame is a form of encapsulation.

A packet (header and data) at level 7 is encapsulated in a packet at level 6. The whole packet at level 6 is encapsulated in a packet at level 5, and so on.

In other words, the data portion of a packet at level N-1 carries the whole packet (data and header and may be trailer) from level N. The concept is called encapsulation.

Level N-1 is not aware of which part of the encapsulated packet is data and which part is the header or trailer. For level N-1, the whole packet coming from level N is treated as one integral unit.

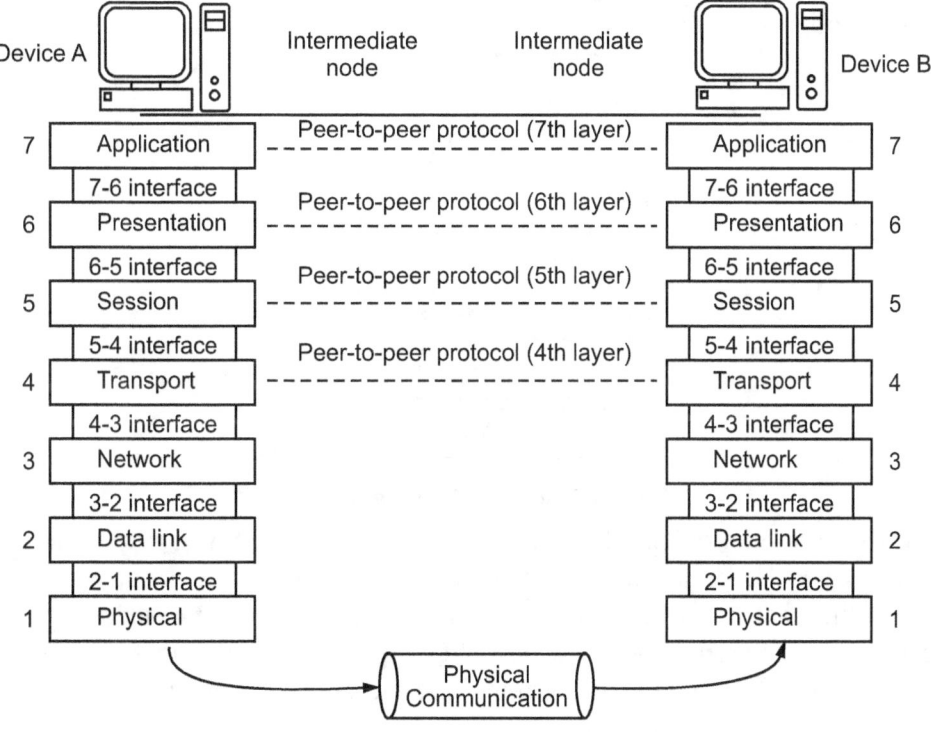

Fig. 3.3 : Encapsulation

3.2 ISO/OSI Reference Model

There are n numbers of users who use computer network and are located over the world. So to ensure national and worldwide data communication systems can be developed and are compatible to each other. ISO has developed Model for this purpose. ISO stands for International organization of Standardization. This is called a model for open system interconnection (OSI) and is normally called as OSI model. In general, ISO-OSI defines standards by which computers can communicate together. ISO-OSI describes the architecture, protocols and services that are needed to achieve this goal. ISO is an organization and ISO-OSI is a model.

The Open System Interconnection (OSI) model is a seven layered framework for the design of network system that allows for communication across all types of computer systems. There are multiple ISO-OSI standards. Some of these are complete, while others are still evolving. The term open system in ISO-OSI defines a computer system that can communicate with another computer system using the OSI protocol.

The foundation of the ISO-OSI architecture is a layering concept, called the ISO-OSI Reference Model. Each layer in the ISO-OSI Reference Model has a name, a number, protocols that provide specific functions, and defined services.

Because the various intended uses of ISO-OSI are very broad, spanning terminals, personal computers, and very large mainframes, different services and protocol options are available at each layer. This range of support can accommodate different connection requirements and environments.

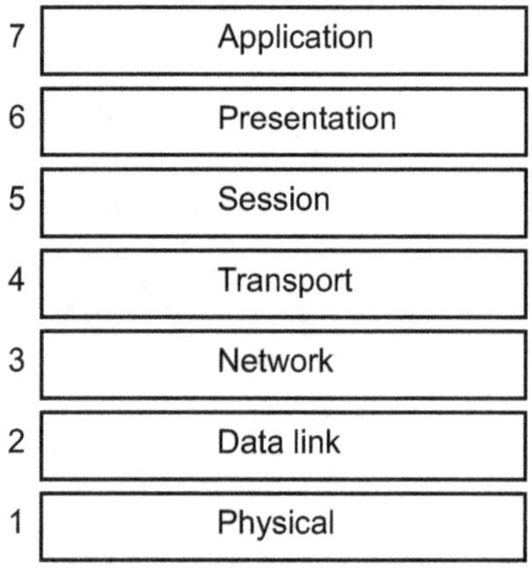

7	Application
6	Presentation
5	Session
4	Transport
3	Network
2	Data link
1	Physical

Fig. 3.4: The ISO-OSI reference model

The reference model defined by ISO-OSI is also an excellent model to understand how networks are work. Although there are many different architectures, standards and models the ISO-OSI Reference Model is mostly used to explain the different functions implemented in protocols from different layers and how these protocols work together. It is a layered framework for the design of network systems that allows for communication across all types of computer systems.

International Standards Organization (ISO) specifications for network architecture, called the Open Systems Interconnect (OSI) model, seven layered model where higher layers have more complex tasks. Each layer provides services for the next higher layer. Each layer communicates logically with its associated layer on the other computer. Packets are sent from one layer to another in the order of the layers, from top to bottom on the sending computer and then in reverse order on the receiving computer. Each layer performs a unique, generic, and well-defined function.

Layer boundaries are designed so that the amount of information flowing between any two adjacent layers is minimized. This is accomplished by having each layer within an open system use the services provided by the layer below. Conversely, each layer provides a sufficient number of services to the layer immediately above it.

Feature of OSI Model :

1. Big picture of network is understandable through this OSI model.
2. We can see how hardware and software work together.
3. We can understand new technologies as they are developed.
4. Troubleshooting is easier by separate networks.
5. Can be used to compare basic functional relationships on different networks.

Layered Architecture of the ISO-OSI Reference Model:

Fig. 3.5 shows layered architecture of the ISO-OSI model. Each interface defines what information and services a layer must provide for the layer above it. Layers 1, 2, and 3 are the network support layers. They deal with physical aspect of moving data from one device to another (such as electrical specification, physical connection). Layer 4 ensures end-to-end reliable data transmission. Layers 5, 6, and 7 are user support layers.

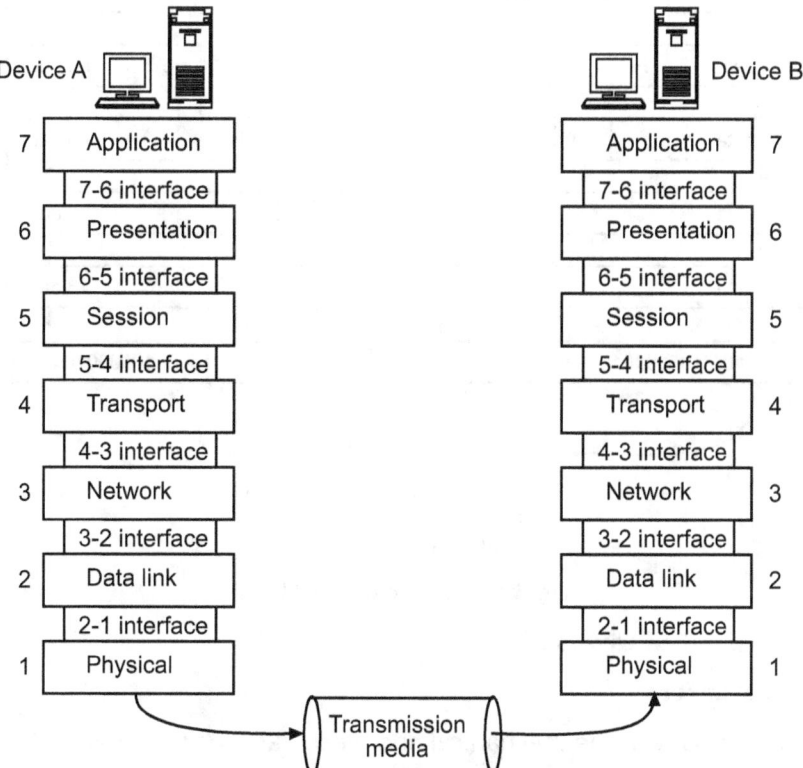

Fig. 3.5 : Layered Architecture of the ISO-OSI Model.

The upper OSI layers are almost always implemented by software; lower layers are a combination of hardware and software, except physical layer, which is mostly hardware. This layered approach was selected as a basis for the OSI reference model to provide flexibility and open-ended capability through defined interfaces.

The interfaces permit some layers to be changed while leaving other layers unchanged. In principle, as long as standard interfaces to the adjacent layers are adhered to, an implementation can still work.

For example, a system implementation could use either HDLC or local area network protocols as the data link layer. Similarly, a particular layer such as the presentation layer, can be implemented as a null layer for the time being.

This means the layer is functionally empty, providing only the mandatory interfaces between the upper and lower layers (application and session layers respectively).

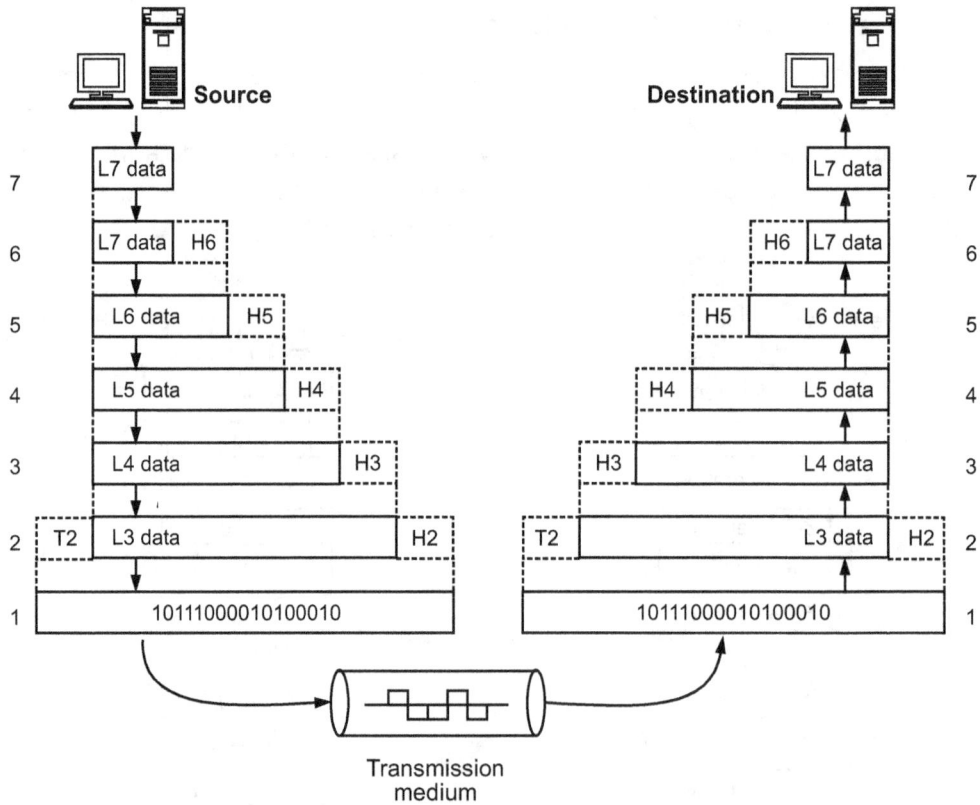

Fig. 3.6: Example of OSI Model

Functions of the ISO-OSI Layers :

Layer 1 : Physical Layer

Physical layer deals with the mechanical and electrical specifications of the interface and transmission medium.

Physical layer:

(a) Transmits the unstructured raw bit stream over a physical medium.
(b) Relates the electrical, optical mechanical and functional interfaces to the cable.
(c) Defines how the cable is attached to the network adapter card.
(d) Defines data encoding and bit synchronization.

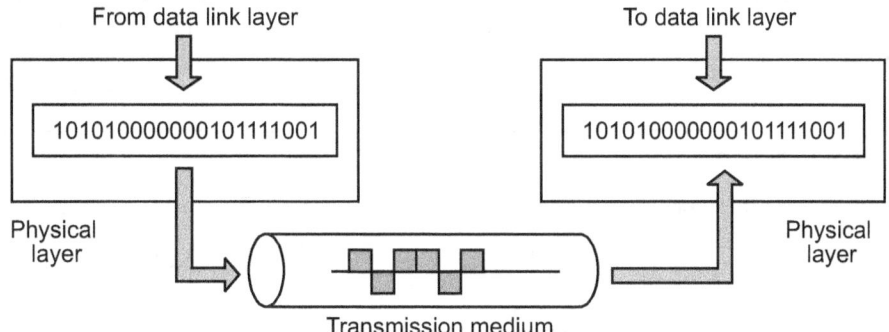

Fig. 3.7: Physical layer

The physical layer concerned with the following Responsibilities or functions:

1. **Physical characteristics of interfaces and media:** Defines type of transmission medium.

2. **Representation of bits:** Data consist of a stream of bits (0's and 1's). To be transmitted, bits must be encoded into signals-electrical or optical. The physical layer defines the type of encoding.

3. **Data rate:** The transmission rate- the number of bits sent per second.

4. **Synchronization of bits:** The sender and receiver clocks must be synchronized.

5. **Physical topology:** It defines how devices are connected to make a network i.e. topologies.
   For example, a star topology (devices are connected through a central device), a ring topology (every device is connected to the next).

6. **Transmission mode:** It defines direction of transmission between two devices: simplex, half-duplex, or full-duplex.

Layer 2 : Data Link Layer

Data link Layer makes the physical layer appear error free to the upper layer.

Data link layer:

(a) Sends data frames from the Network layer to the Physical layer.
(b) Packages raw bits into frames for the Network layer at the receiving end.

(c) Responsible for providing error free transmission of frames through the Physical layer.

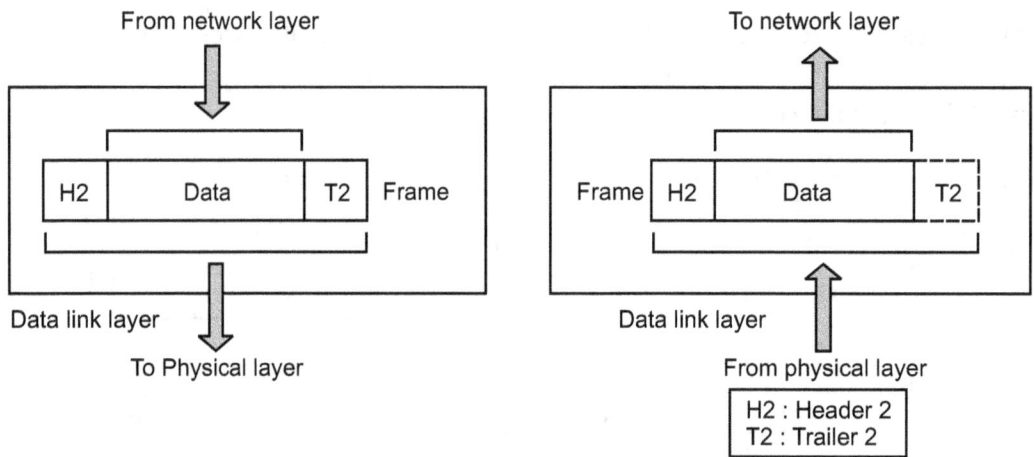

Fig. 3.8: Data link layer packet

Responsibilities or functions of the data link layer are as follows:

1. **Framing:** The data link layer divides the stream of bits received from the network layer into manageable data units called frames.

2. **Physical addressing:** If frames are distributed to different system on the network, the data link layer adds header to the frame to define the physical address of the sender (source address) and receiver address (destination address) of the frame. If the frame is intended for the system outside the sender's network, the receiver address is the address of device that connects one network to the next.

3. **Flow control:** If the rate at which the data are absorbed by receiver is less than the rate produced in the sender, the data link layer imposes a flow control mechanism.

4. **Error control:** It adds reliability to the physical layer by adding mechanism to detect and retransmit damaged or lost frames. It also prevents duplication of frames.

5. **Access control:** When two or more devices are connected to the same link, data link layer protocols determine which device has control over the link at any given time.

Layer 3: Network Layer

The Network Layer is responsible for the source-to-destination delivery of a packet possibly across multiple networks (links). Whereas, the data link layer oversees the delivery of the packet between two systems on the same network (links). If two systems are connected to the same link, there is usually no need for a network layer.

Function of Network layer:

(a) Responsible for addressing messages and translating logical addresses and names into physical addresses.

(b) Determines the route from the source to the destination computer.

(c) Manages traffic such as packet switching, routing and controlling the congestion of data.

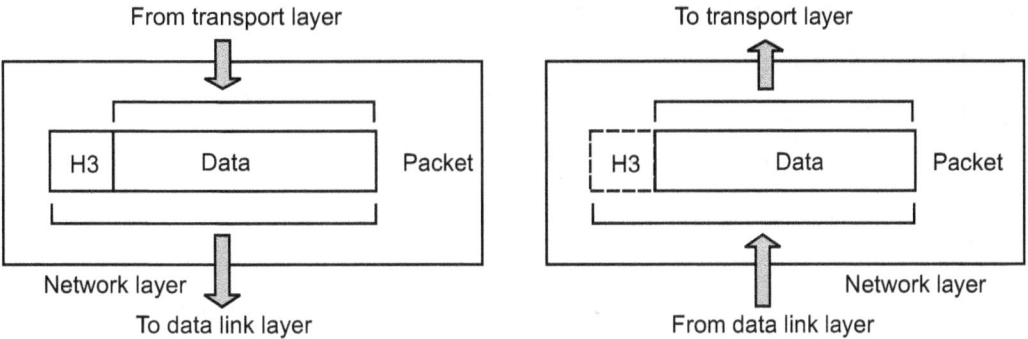

Fig. 3.9: Network layer packet

Responsibilities or functions of Network layer:

1. **Logical addressing:** The physical addressing implemented by the data link layer handles the addressing problem locally. If a packet passes the network boundary, then need of another addressing system to help to distinguish the source and destination systems.

2. **Routing:** When independent networks or links are connected together to create an internetwork (a network of networks), the connecting devices (called router or gateway) route the packets to their final destination.

Layer 4: Transport Layer

The Transport Layer delivers the entire message from source to destination. Transport layer ensures whole message arrives intact and in order, ensuring both error control and flow

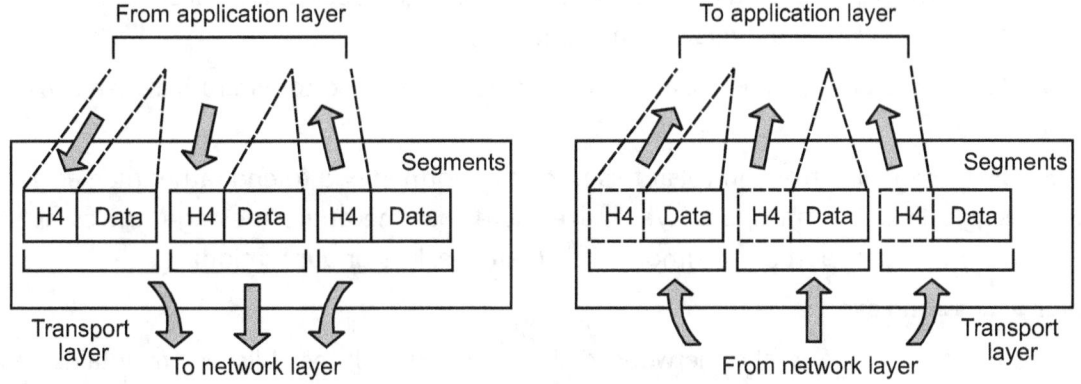

Fig. 3.10: Transport packets

control at the source to destination level. It decides if data transmission should be on parallel path or single path. Transport layer breaks the message (data) into small units (packets) so that they are handled more efficiently by the network layer and ensures that message arrives in order by checking error and flow control.

Functions of Transport layer:

(a) Responsible for packet creation.

(b) Provides an additional connection level beneath the Session layer.

(c) Ensures that packets are delivered error free, in sequence with no losses or duplications.

(d) Unpacks, reassembles and sends receipt of messages at the receiving end.

(e) Provides flow control, error handling and solves transmission problems.

Responsibilities of the transport layer are as follows:

1. **Service-point addressing:** Computers often run multiple programs at the same time. Source-to-destination delivery means delivery not only from one computer to the next but also from a specific process (running program) on the other. The transport layer header therefore must include a type of address called a service-point address (or port address).

   The network layer delivers each packet to the correct destination computer. Then the transport layer delivers the entire message to the correct process on that computer.

2. **Segmentation and Reassembly:** A message is divided into transmittable segments, each segment containing a sequence number. These numbers enable the transport layer to reassemble the message correctly upon arriving at the destination and to identify and replace packets that were lost in the transmission.

3. **Connection control:** It creates a connection between the two end ports. A connection is a single logical path between the source and destination that is associated with all packets in a message.

4. **Flow control:** Flow control at this level is performed end to end rather than across a single link.

5. **Error control:** Error control at this level is performed end to end rather than across a single link. The transport layer makes sure that the entire message arrives at the receiving transport layer without error (damage, loss or duplication).

Layer 5: Session Layer:

The Session Layer is the network dialog controller. It establishes, maintains, and synchronizes the interaction between communicating systems.

Functions of Session Layer:

(a) Allows two applications running on different computers to establish use and end a connection called a Session.

(b) Performs name recognition and security.

(c) Provides synchronization by placing checkpoints in the data stream.

(d) Implements dialog control between communicating processes.

Responsibilities of the Session Layer:

1. **Dialog control:** It allows two systems to enter into a dialog by keeping track of whose turn it is to transmit.

2. **Token management:** Preventing two parties from attempting the same critical operation at the same time.

3. **Synchronization:** It allows a process to add checkpoints (synchronization points) into a stream of data. Use of checkpoints for long transmission that allows them to continue from where they were after a crash.

   For example, if a system sending a file of 2000 pages and process inserts checkpoints after every 100 pages to ensure that each 100-page unit is received and acknowledged independently. If crash happens during transmission of page 545, retransmission begins at page 501; pages 1 to 500 need not be retransmitted.

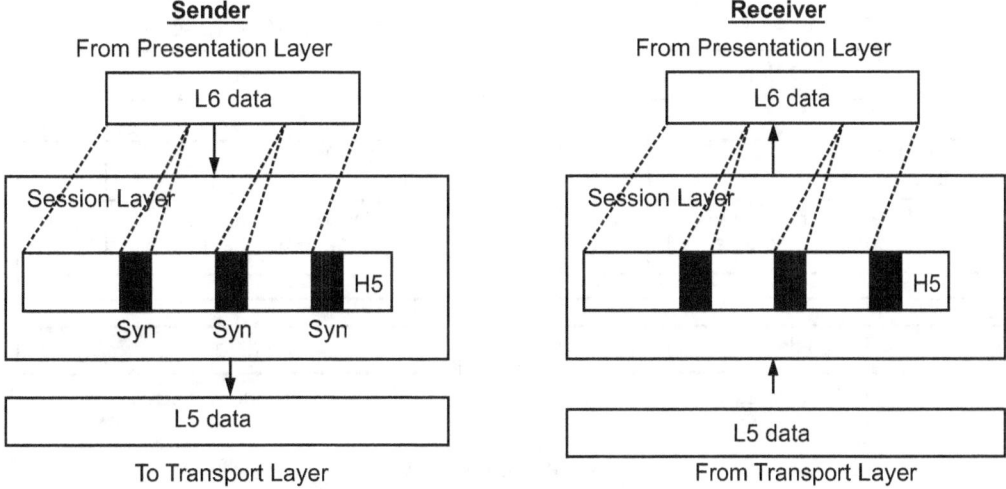

Fig. 3.11: Session Layer

Layer 6: Presentation Layer:

The Presentation Layer is concerned with the syntax and semantics of the information exchanged between two systems. This layer is concerned with the representation of user or system data.

This includes necessary conversions, (For example, printer control characters) and code translation (For example, ASCII to or EBCDIC).

Presentation layer:

(a) Determines the format used to exchange data among the networked computers.

(b) Translates data from a format from the Application layer into an intermediate format.

(c) Responsible for protocol conversion, data translation, data encryption, data compression, character conversion, and graphics expansion.

(d) Redirector operates at this level.

Functions of the Presentation layer:

1. **Translations:** Different computers use different encoding systems, the presentation layer is responsible for interoperability between these different encoding methods. The presentation layer at the sender changes the information from its sender-dependant format into a common format. The presentation layer at the receiving machine changes the common format into its receiver-dependant format.

2. **Encryption:** The process of rendering a message (or data) unusable to all but the intended recipients, who have the ability to decrypt it.

3. **Compression:** Reduces the number of bits to be transmitted. Saves network bandwidth.

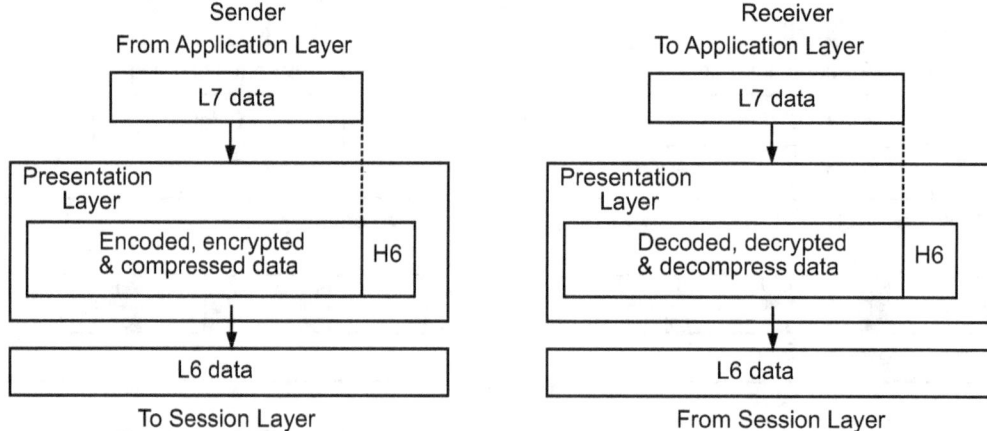

Fig. 3.12: Presentation Layer

Layer 7: Application Layer:

Application layer serves as a window for applications to access network services. This layer handles general network access, flow control and error recovery. This enables the user, whether human or software, to access the network.

Services provided by the Application Layer:

1. **Network virtual terminal:** It allows a user to log on to a remote host.

2. **File Transfer, Access and Management (FTAM):** This application allows a user to access files in remote computer (to make changes or read data), to retrieve files from a remote computer and to manage or control files in a remote computer.

3. **Mail service:** This application provides the basis for e-mail forwarding and storage.

4. **HTTP (HyperText Transfer Protocol):** A standard Internet protocol that specifies the client/server interaction processes between web browsers such as Microsoft Internet Explorer and web servers such as Microsoft Internet Information Services (IIS).

3.3　TCP/IP (Transmission Control Protocol/Internet Protocol) Model

TCP/IP means transmission control protocol and internet protocol. The TCP/IP model is a description framework for computer network protocols created in the 1970s by Department of Defence's Project Research Agency (ARPA, later DARPA). It evolved from ARPANET, which was the world's first wide area network and a predecessor of the Internet. The TCP/IP Model is sometimes called the Internet Model or the DoD Model. The TCP/IP model or Internet Protocol Suite, describes a set of general design guidelines and implementations of specific networking protocols to enable computers to communicate over a network. It provides end-to-end connectivity specifying how data should be formatted, addressed, transmitted, routed and received at the destination. Protocols exist for a variety of different types of communication services between computers.

The TCP/IP model is sometimes called the DoD model because TCP/IP was developed in connection with the ARPANET project of the U.S. Department of Defense. TCP/IP is based on a four-layer reference model. All protocols that belong to the TCP/IP protocol suite are located in the top three layers of this model.

1. Application Layer:

The top layer in the Internet reference model is the Application Layer that provides functions for users or their programs, and it is highly specific to the application being performed. Application layer provides the services that user applications use to communicate over the network, and it is the layer in which user-access network processes reside. These processes include all of those that users interact with directly, as well as other processes of which the users are not aware.

Application layer includes all applications protocols that use the host-to-host transport protocols to deliver data. Other functions that process user data, such as data encryption and decryption and compression and decompression, can also reside at the application layer. The application layer also manages the sessions, (connections) between cooperating applications. The application layer is responsible for standardizing the presentation of data.

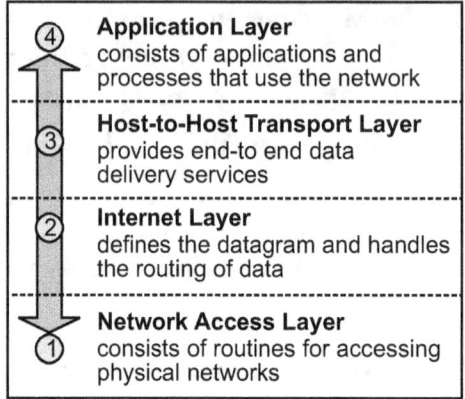

Fig. 3.13: Layers in the TCP/IP Protocol Architecture

2. Host-to-Host Transport Layer:

The Protocol Layer just above the Internet Layer is the Host-to-Host Transport Layer. It is responsible for providing end-to-end data integrity and provides a highly reliable communication service for entities that want to carry out an extended two-way conversation. In addition to the usual transmit and receive functions, this layer uses open and close commands to initiate and terminate the connection. Host-to-host Transport Layer accepts information to be transmitted as a stream of characters, and it returns information to the recipient as a stream.

The service employs the concept of a connection (or virtual circuit). A connection is the state of the host-to-host transport layer between the time that an open command is accepted by the receiving computer and the time that the close command is issued by either computer.

3. Internet Layer:

In the TCP/IP Internet reference model, the layer above the network access layer is called the Internetwork Layer. This layer is responsible for routing messages through internetworks which uses two types of devices. The first device is called a Gateway, which is a computer that has two network adapter cards. This computer accepts network packets from one network on one network card and routes those packets to a different network via the second network adapter card. The second device is a Router, which is a dedicated hardware device that passes packets from one network to a different network.

4. Network Access Layer:

The Network Access Layer is the lowest layer in the Internet reference model. This layer contains the protocols that the computer uses to deliver data to the other computers and devices that are attached to the network. The protocols at network access layer perform three distinct functions:

1. They define how to use the network to transmit a *frame*, which is the data unit passed across the physical connection.

2. They exchange data between the computer and the physical network.

3. They deliver data between two devices on the same network.

TCP/IP protocol suite

All protocols that belong to the TCP/IP protocol suite are located in the top three layers of this model. As shown in the following Fig. 3.14, each layer of the TCP/IP model corresponds to one or more layers of the seven-layer Open Systems Interconnection (OSI) reference model proposed by the International Standards Organization (ISO).

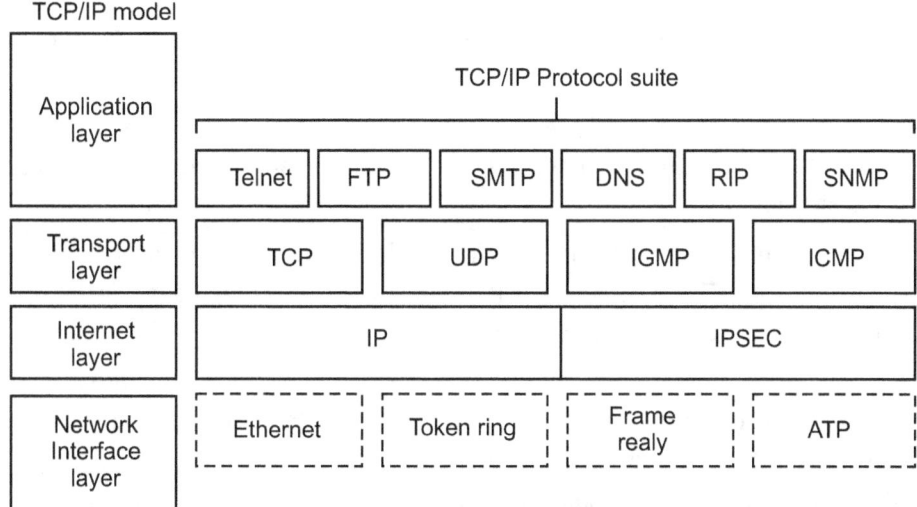

Fig. 3.14 : TCP/IP protocol suite

Table 3.1 : Types of services performed and protocols used at each layer

Layer	Description	Protocols
Application	Defines TCP/IP application protocols and how host programs interface with transport layer services to use the network.	HTTP, Telnet, FTP, TFTP, SNMP, DNS, SMTP, X Windows, other application protocols
Transport	Provides communication session management between host computers. Defines the level of service and status of the connection used when transporting data.	TCP, UDP, RTP
Internet	Packages data into IP datagrams, which contain source and destination address information that is used to forward the datagrams between hosts and across networks. Performs routing of IP datagrams.	IP, ICMP, ARP, RARP

Network interface	Specifies details of how data is physically sent through the network, including how bits are electrically signaled by hardware devices that interface directly with a network medium, such as coaxial cable, optical fiber, or twisted-pair copper wire.	Ethernet, Token Ring, FDDI, X.25, Frame Relay, RS-232, v.35

The TCP/IP protocol suite has two sets of protocols at the Internet layer:

- IPv4, also known as IP, is the Internet layer in common use today on private intranets and the Internet.
- IPv6 is the new Internet layer that will eventually replace the existing IPv4 Internet layer.

HTTP (Hypertext Transfer Protocol) is the protocol that facilitates transfer of data via the "world wide web." Typically, data is transferred in the form of pages, or HTML markup.

HTTPS (Secure HTTP) uses **TCP 443** to securely transfer HTTP data via SSL, or Secure Socket Layer. Sites that require increased security, such as an online merchant, use HTTPS to protect user information.

FTP (File Transfer Protocol) : It is used in simple file transfers from one node to another without any security. **SFTP** (Secure FTP) is a version of FTP that uses SSH to transfer data securely, thus using whichever port SSH uses.

TFTP (Trivial FTP) is a UDP version of FTP is called "trivial" because it is relatively unreliable and inefficient and so is more often used for inter-network communication (along routers) than in real node-to-node file transfers.

Telnet (Telecommunications Network) is used to remotely connect to a node. All communications with telnet are in cleartext (even the password for authentication) and should not be used in sensitive situations. It is called terminal emulation software because the remote terminal is available upon connection.

SSH (Secure Shell) is a secure replacement of Telnet. Telnet transfers information in plain or clear text, but SSH allows terminal emulation in cipher text, which equates to enhanced and increased security.

NNTP (Network News Transfer Protocol) is a protocol used by client and server software to carry USENET (newsgroup) postings back and forth over a TCP/IP network.

LDAP (Lightweight Directory Access Protocol) is a **"Directory Services" protocol** that basically allows a server to act as a central directory for client nodes. A famous implementation of LDAP is **Microsoft's Active Directory** (Domain)..

NTP (Network Time Protocol) allows for synchronizing network time with a server.

POP3 (Post Office Protocol) is the mailbox protocol of the Internet and allows users to download mail from a mail server. The server will hold onto your mail until you access it.

Once you try to access it, your client software will download all of your incoming mail and wipe it from the server.

IMAP4 (The Internet Message Access Protocol) is a slightly better version of the mailbox protocol. IMAP4 allows for server-based repositories of sent mail and other specialized folders. Basically, when using IMAP4 instead of POP3 as your incoming mail protocol, you download very minimal information to your local machine and when you want to access actual incoming mail, you are pulling this directly from the mail server. This allows you to access your mail from virtually anywhere (like yahoo mail)..

SMTP (Simple Mail Transfer Protocol) is the "postman" of the Internet. It allows for mail to be sent. You would use this in conjunction with POP3 or IMAP4 to be able to send/receive mail. If you do not define SMTP (usually is, though), you will only be able to receive mail.

DNS (Domain Name System) : Resolves easy to read domain names such as google.com into computer readable IP addresses such as 72.14.204.147

SNMP (Simple Network Management Protocol) : A protocol for managing devices on IP networks, such as modems, switches, routers, or printers.

3.4 OSI Model Vs. TCP/IP Model

Following are some major differences between OSI Reference Model and TCP/IP Reference Model.

Table 3.2 : OSI model vs TCP/IP Model

S. N.	OSI Reference Model	TCP/IP Model
1.	This is a 7 layer model.	This is a 4 layer model.
2.	OSI model is useful in describing networks, but protocols are too general.	TCP/IP model is weak, but protocols are specific and widely used.
3.	Model is a "Generic protocol independent standard".	TCP/IP protocols are considered to be standards around which the internet has developed.
4.	Model was conceptual; designers didn't know what functionality to put in the layers.	Model is practical, designers know the functionality of each layer and used in real world network.
5.	Model is general, and easier to replace protocols.	Model is not general, and difficult to replace protocols.
6.	Model had to adjust when networks did not match the service specifications (wireless networks, internetworking).	Model need not require to adjust too much in this scenario.

7.	Model describes any type of network.	Model only describes TCP/IP which is not useful for describing any other networks.
8.	Network layer supports both Connection-oriented and Connection-less service.	Network layer supports only Connection-less service.
9.	Transport layers supports only Connection-oriented service.	Transport layers supports both Connection oriented and Connectionless service.

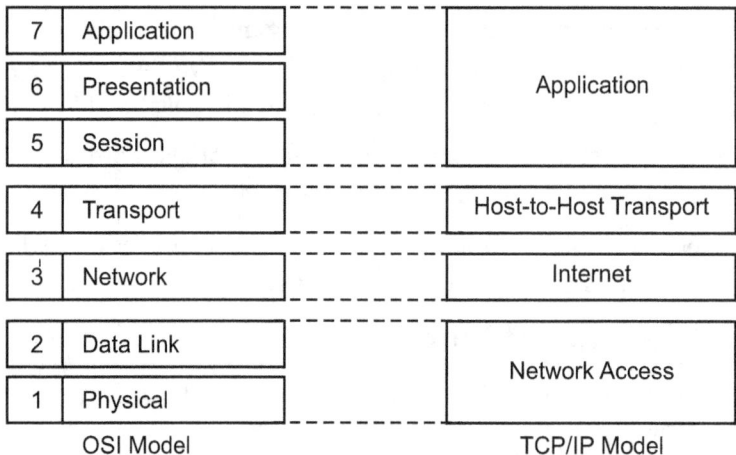

Fig. 3.15 : Comparison of OSI and TCP/IP Model

Practice Questions

1.   Which are benefits provided by the layered approach to network communications?

2.   With neat diagram, describe TCP/IP model.

3.   Explain ISO/OSI reference Model.

4.   What are the features of Data-link layer in OSI Model ?

5.   Write about Application Layer in OSI model.

6.   Write short note on: Protocol layering.

7.   Which are the responsibilities of session layer?

8.   Define terms : Gateway and Router.

9.   Compare TCP/IP and OSI models.

10.   Explain internet layer of TCP/IP protocol model.

Chapter 4...

LOCAL AREA NETWORKS

Contents ...

4.1   Introduction

4.2   Components

4.3   Technology

4.4   Access Technique

4.5   Transmission Protocol

4.6   Transmission Media

- Practice Questions

4.1 Introduction

Local Area Network (LAN) is a privately-owned network that connects computers that covering a limited geographic area i.e. less than 1 km, like a home, office, building or group of buildings (e.g. campus). There are many types of LANs. Ethernet is the most common for PCs. All computers are connected to a central node in star topology. The central node is a special device called a Network Hub. All links are made up of UTP (unshielded twisted pair) cables. The maximum suggested length of a UTP connection in LAN is 100 meters. No computer should be more than 100 meters away from hub.

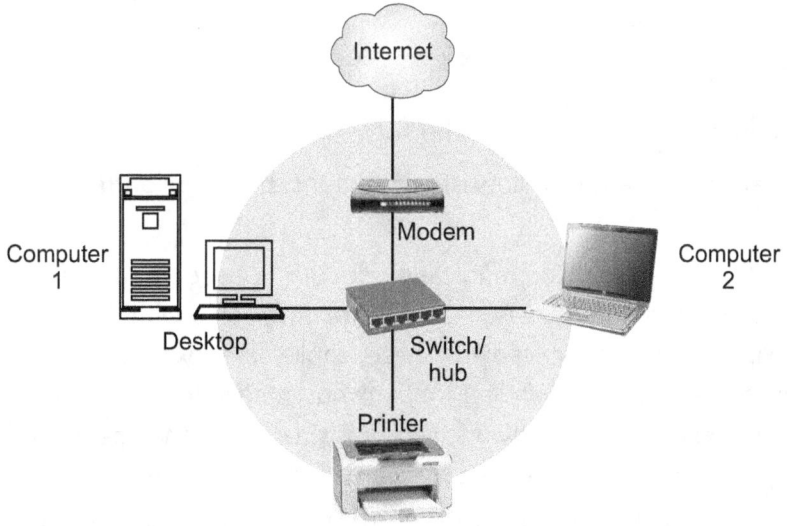

Fig. 4.1 : LAN

(4.1)

All computers in LAN can communicate with each other at a high speed. The speed of communications between any two devices on an Ethernet LAN can be 2 to 1000 millions bits per second (Mbps). LAN can transmit data in a limited distance.

One LAN can be connected to other LANs over any distance via telephone lines and radio waves. A system of LANs connected in this way is called a Wide-Area Network (WAN).

Fig. 4.1 shows the simplest form of LAN is to connect two computers together.

Characteristics of LAN:

1. Every computer has the potential to communicate with any other computers of the network.

2. High degree of interconnection between computers.

3. Easy physical connection of computers in a network.

4. Inexpensive medium of data transmission.

5. High data transmission rate.

The following characteristics differentiate one LAN from another:

- **Topology :** The geometric arrangement of devices on the network. For example, devices can be arranged in a ring or in a straight line.

- **Protocols :** The rules and encoding specifications for sending data. The protocols also determine whether the network uses a peer-to-peer or client/server architecture.

- **Media :** Devices can be connected by twisted-pair wire, coaxial cables, or fiber optic cables. Some networks do without connecting media altogether, communicating instead via radio waves.

4.2 Components

A LAN is a combination of hardware and software.

The Hardware : The hardware consists of stations, transmission media, and connecting devices.

Communication Media : Communication media is used to transfer data from one computer to another computer. Low-cost LANs are connected with twisted wire pair. Many LANs use coaxial or fiber-optic cables. These cables are expensive but provide faster communication. Some LANs use wireless transmission media. It uses infrared or radio waves to connect computers. Wireless networks are easy to setup and maintain. However, they have low transmission rates and limited distance between two communication devices.

NIC: NIC stands for Network Interface Card. It is also known as network adapter. A Network Interface Card is a device that physically connects each computer to a network. It controls the flow of information between the network and the computer. It is a circuit board that fits in expansion slot on motherboard. Some computers contain built-in network cards.

Cabling and Connectors : Each computer must be physically connected by network cable to the other computers in the network. The perfect cabling system able to carry all kinds of electronic transmissions within the building. The selection of a LAN can affeected by the type of cable that already exists in the building where the LAN is to be installed.

Most LANs are built with unshielded twisted-pair (UTP) cable, shielded twisted-pair (STP), or fiber-optic cable. Many LANs use a combination of STP and UTP wire.

Bridge : Bridge is a device that connects two network segments. It is used to connect similar types of networks.

Router : A router is a device that connects multiple networks using similar or different protocols. It manages the best route between two communication networks. Routers are used when several networks are connected together. They can connect networks of different countries. They transfer data in less time.

Gateway : Gateway is a device that connects two or more networks with different types of protocols. Two different types of networks require a gateway to communicate with each other. It receives data from one network and converts it according to the protocol of other network. For example, the computers on a LAN require gateway to access the internet.

PCs/workstation and Servers: A server is a high-powered computer connected to the network that serves a special function for the network.

The Software : There are two primary categories of software, the Operating System, and Application Programs.

Network Operating System (NOS): There needs to be some software at the operating system level that manages the network connection. Most modern operating systems are capable of using the network.

Application Programs: The primary purpose of having a LAN is to allow several application programs to talk to each other.

Advantages of LAN:

1. System resources such as printers can be shared between several people in network.
2. All users of LAN can share one copy of a software and data.
3. It is easy to manage the data stored on a centralized computer in the network.
4. The data is more secure from being copied or destroyed.
5. High rate of data transmission is possible.
6. Less expensive to install.
7. The reliability of network is high because the failure of one computer in the network does not affect the functioning for other computers.

Limitations of LAN:

1. Used for small geographical areas.

2. Limited computers are connected in Local Area Network.

3. Special security measures are needed to stop users from using programs and data that they should not have access to network.

4. Networks are difficult to set up and need to be maintained by skilled technicians.

5. If the file server develops a serious fault, all the users are affected, rather than just one user in the case of a stand-alone.

LAN Transmissions :

Broadband :

A communication medium that can carry a wide range of signal frequencies, from audio to video frequencies. In telecommunications, the significance of a broadband system is that it can carry television and videoconferencing data as well as voice calls. A broadband medium can be made to carry many signals at once by apportioning its total bandwidth into many independent channels. Each channel carries only a specific range of frequencies. In contrast, a BASEBAND can carry only a single channel. ATM, ADSL and Cable TV are all broadband media. There exist two LAN transmission options, Baseband and Broadband. Baseband LANs, is the Single-channel system that supports a single transmission at any given time.

Broadband LANs are based on coaxial cable as the transmission medium, although fiber optic cable is also used. Individual channels offer bandwidth of 1 to 5 Mbps, with 20 to 30 channels typically supported. Aggregate bandwidth is as much as 500 MHz.

Its characteristics are:

- Digital signal modulated onto RF carrier (analog).

- Channel allocation based on FDM (Frequency division multiplexing).

- Head-End for bidirectional transmission.

- Stations connected via RF modems, Le. radio modems accomplish the digital-to-analog conversion process, providing the transmitting device access to an analog channel.

Advantages :

1. Broadband permits data, voice and video to be transmitted simultaneously over the same transmission medium.

2. Greater distances i.e. it covers large area.

3. Greater bandwidth. The data transmission speed is more than 200 kbps.

Disadvantages :

1. Cable design.
2. Complex installation and maintenance.
3. Requires RF modems and amplifiers. So it has high cost.
4. Lack of well-developed standards.

Some broadband LANs are referred to as IOBroadband36 where 10stands for 10Mbps, Broadband for multichannel and 36 for 3600 meters maximum separation between devices.

Baseband :

Baseband LAN is single channel, supporting a single communication at a time. Digital signals are used. Total bandwidth of I to 100Mbps is provided over coaxial cable, UTP, STP, or fiber optic cable. Distance limitations depend on the medium employed and the specifics of the LAN protocol. Baseband LAN physical topologies including Ring, Bus, Tree, and Star.

Baseband LANs are by far the most popular and the most highly standardized. Ethernet, Token Passing, Token Ring and FDDI LANs are all baseband. They are intended only for data, as data communications is, after all, the primary reason for the existence of LANs. The characteristics of this system may be summarized as follows:

- Unmodulated digital signal.
- Entire bandwidth of the cable is consumed by a single signal in a baseband transmission.
- Bidirectional transmission of signal.
- Stations connected, via T connectors.
- No need of modems - low cost installation.

Advantages :

1. Simpler Technology.
2. Less expensive.
3. Easier and quicker to install.
4. High rates.

Disadvantages :

1. Limited capacity and length.
2. Data and voice only.

4.3 Technology

LAN technology refers to the technologies used to create a local area network. These technologies usually consist of servers, clients, data and various applications.

Ethernet :

Ethernet is a popular packet-switching LAN technology. Ethernet was invented at Xerox PARC in early 1970s. The ethernet specified in IEEE 802.3 standard. An Ethernet LAN typically uses coaxial cable or special grades of twisted pair wires. Ethernet is also used in wireless LANs. The most commonly installed Ethernet systems are called 10BASE-T and provide transmission speeds up to 10 Mbps. Devices are connected to the cable and compete for access using a Carrier Sense Multiple Access with Collision Detection (CSMA/CD) protocol.

Fast Ethernet or 100BASE-T provides transmission speeds up to 100 megabits per second. It is typically used for LAN backbone systems and supporting workstations with 10BASE-T cards. Gigabit Ethernet provides an even higher level of backbone support at 1000 megabits per second (1 gigabit or 1 billion bits per second). 10-Gigabit Ethernet provides up to 10 billion bits per second.

Ethernet uses a single coaxial cable as transmission media. A transceiver device is used to establish the connection between a computer and the Ethernet. Fig. 4.2 shows Ethernet using the bus architecture. All the hosts in the Ethernet LAN connect to this, cable.

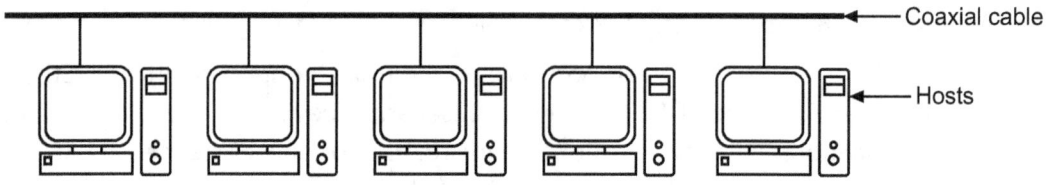

Fig. 4.2 : Bus architecture used in Ethernet

Properties of Ethernet:

1. It is a broadcast networks.
2. Ethernet is a decentralized access control network.

Advantages of Ethernet:

1. The prevalent standard with hundreds of thousands of nodes installed.
2. The protocol is straight forward especially with respect to error handling.
3. Cabling is simple and taps are passive. Nodes can be installed and removed without bringing the network down.
4. High throughput under conditions of light load.

Disadvantages of Ethernet:

1. More complicated engineering because it requires "analog" rather than digital circuits for sensing the carrier and sensing collisions.
2. Minimum frame of 50 bytes — extra overhead for short messages.
3. Non-deterministic can not guarantee access within a defined interval, a problem for real-time applications.
4. No way to prioritize traffic.
5. Limited cable length.

6. Not adaptable to higher data rates.

7. Collisions cause performance to deteriorate rapidly as utilization approaches maximum.

Virtual LAN :

A Virtual Local Area Network (VLAN) is a logical group of workstations, servers and network devices that appear to be on the same LAN despite their geographical distribution. VLAN allows a network of computers and users to communicate in a simulated environment as if they exist in a single LAN and are sharing a single broadcast and multicast domain.

Characteristics of VLAN:

1. Individual VLAN acts as a separate LAN, thus sharing the traffic among VLANs and reducing the congestion.

2. Workstations can be provided with full bandwidth at each port.

3. Relocation of terminals becomes easy.

Fig. 4.3 shows VLAN configuration.

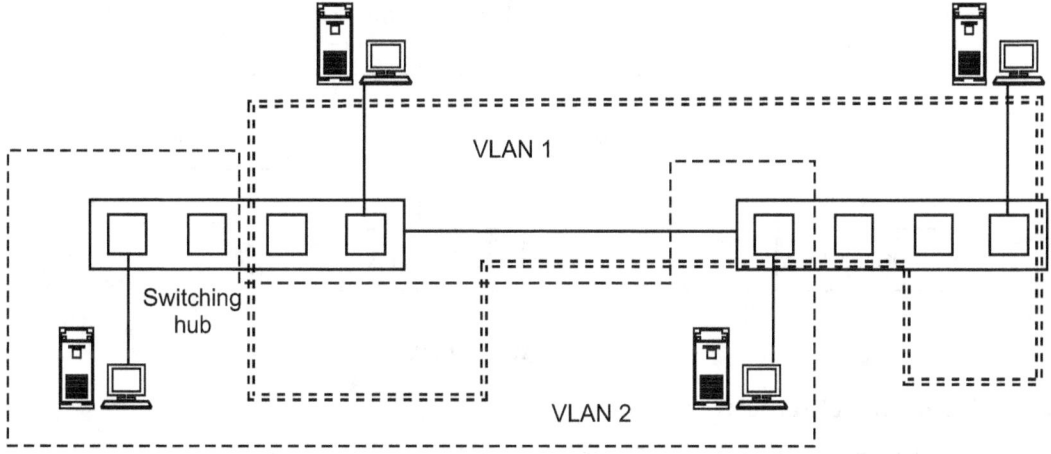

Fig. 4.3 : VLAN Configuration

A router is generally required to establish communication between VLANs.

Benefits:

1. Additional security to network communication.

2. Make expansion and relocation of a network or a network device easier and simpler.

3. Provide flexibility because administrators are able to configure in a centralized environment while the devices might be located in different geographical locations

4. Decrease the latency and traffic load on the network and the network devices, offering increased performance

Disadvantages (Limitations):

1. High risk of virus issues because one infected system may spread a virus through the whole logical network

2. Equipment limitations in very large networks because additional routers might be needed to control the workload

3. More effective at controlling latency than a WAN but less efficient than a LAN.

Fast Ethernet :

Fast Ethernet is a Local Area Network (LAN) transmission standard that provides a data rate of 100 megabits per second. It is also called as 100BaseT. It is a version of Ethernet with a 100 Mbps data rate. Fast Ethernet was designed to compete with LAN protocols such as FDDI or Fiber Channel. IEEE created Fast Ethernet under the name 802.3u.

The frame format and addressing scheme of fast Ethernet is same as that of the traditional Ethernet. It also makes use of 48 bit hexadecimal address. IEEE has designed two categories of Fast Ethernet i.e. 100Base-X and 100BaseT4 as shown in Fig. 4.4.

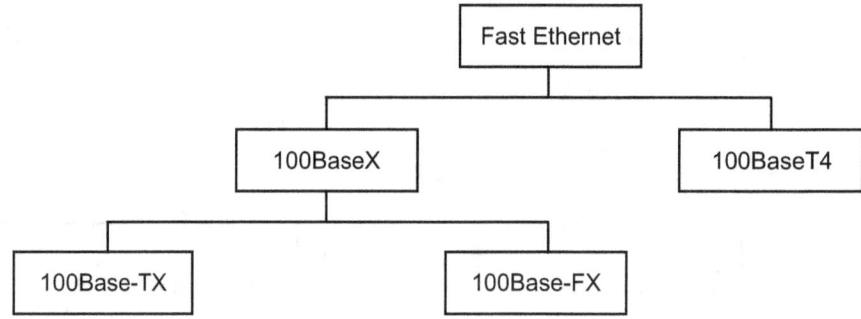

Fig. 4.4 : Fast Ethernet

Advantages of fast Ethernet:

1. Fast Ethernet performance is 10 times more than in traditional Ethernet.

2. It is usually easy and cheap to implement.

3. It is very good for a company wanting fast data transfer.

Limitations of Fast Ethernet:

1. Distance is restricted to 100 meters from node to hub.

2. Shielding may be inadequate for some installations.

3. Intrusion from outsiders may be possible without detection.

Gigabit Ethernet :

Gigabit Ethernet, a transmission technology based on the Ethernet frame format and protocol used in Local Area Networks (LANs). Gigabit Ethernet is defined in the IEEE 802.3 standard and is currently being used as the backbone technology in many enterprise networks.

Gigabit Ethernet is carried primarily on optical fiber (with very short distances possible on copper media). Gigabit Ethernet is part of the family of Ethernet computer networking and communication standards. It provides the data rate of 1 Gbps or 1000 Mbps. IEEE created Gigabit Ethernet under the name 802.3z.

It is compatible with Standard or Fast Ethernet. It also uses similarly 48 bit hexadecimal addressing scheme. The frame format is also similar to standard Ethernet.

In Ethernet, network access by all stations is controlled by the CSMA/CD method. When a station wishes to send data, it "listens" to the line. If no other station is currently transmitting data, it has the opportunity to transmit data itself. If two stations start data transmission at the same time, this is recognized as a collision. Both stations later try to repeat the process at different times.

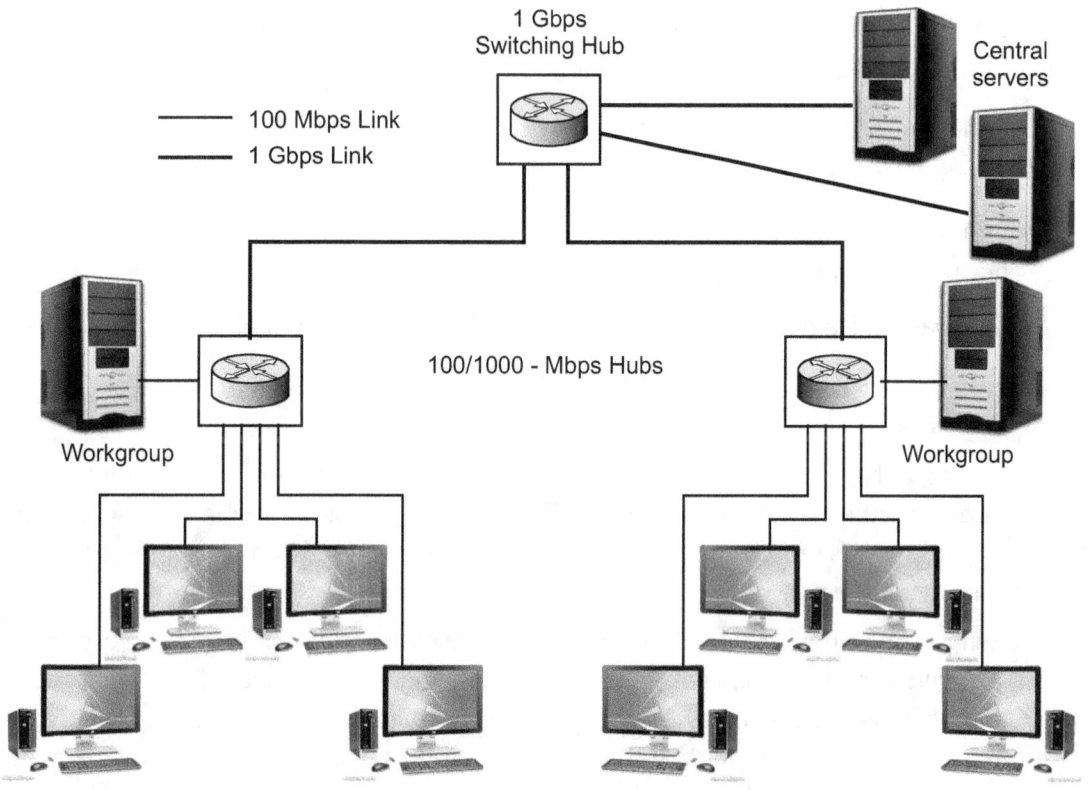

Fig. 4.5 : Gigabit Ethernet Configuration

Initially there were two types of coaxial cable used, which were known as Thick Ethernet and Thin Ethernet. Later, the main type of cable used was the unshielded twisted pair (UTP) copper cable originating from the field of telecommunications. When DEC, Intel and Xerox created what became known as the DIX Ethernet standard in 1980, 10Mbit/s was an enormous bandwidth. As computer technology progressed, however, the demand for more bandwidth in the network grew constantly, leading to the Fast Ethernet standard in the form of IEEE 802.3u in 1995.

Fig. 4.5 A 1-Gbps LAN switch provides backbone connectivity for central servers and high speed workgroup switches. Each workgroup LAN switch supports both 1-Gbps links, to connect to the backbone LAN switch and to support high performance workgroup servers, and 100-Mbps links, to support high performance workstations, servers, and 100-Mbps LAN switches.

Advantages:

1. Same frame format as 10/100 Mbps standards.
2. Full duplex with switching devices (802.x standard).
3. Backwards compatible in shared mode using carrier extension.
4. Extension of a well understood, well characterized network approach.
5. LAN oriented.
6. Wide range of hardware and software available.
7. Highly modular hardware approach.

Disadvantages:

1. Products are not yet available.
2. Gateway device necessary to interface to wide area link protocol.
3. Ethernet does not support time-sensitive data.

Token Ring LAN :

Token Ring LANs use a ring topology, i.e. each station is connected to two other stations which are all together arranged in a loop. Each station can send a signal along the loop after receiving permission to do so. The signal will travel from one station to the other until it reaches its destination.

A token passing ring LAN is a group of computers connected in a loop. The group uses a token passing access mechanism. A computer wishing to send data should first receive permission. When it gets control of the network it may transmit a frame. Each frame transmitted on the ring is transmitted from one computer to the next, until it ultimately returns to the initiator of the transmission.

Token Ring Properties:

1. It supports data rates upto 10 Mbps.
2. The ring in the token ring network consist of a series of STP wires sections that links to their intermediate neighbours.

The Token Passing Ring Network was originally developed by IBM and only Ethernet LANs are more popular. The IEEE 802.5 specification which was modeled after IBM's Token Ring is almost identical and the term Token Ring is used to refer both specifications.

Fig. 4.6 (a) shows a Token Ring Network.

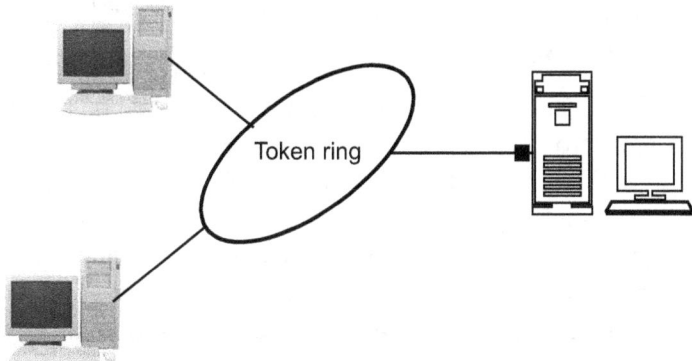

Fig. 4.6 (a) : Token Ring Network

Working of Token Ring:

In token ring the host are arranged to form a circular ring as shown in Fig. 4.6 (b). The sending computer/host transmits a frame which travels across the ring. Each and every host on the ring has to accept it, check the destination address and if it is not meant for it, forward its along.

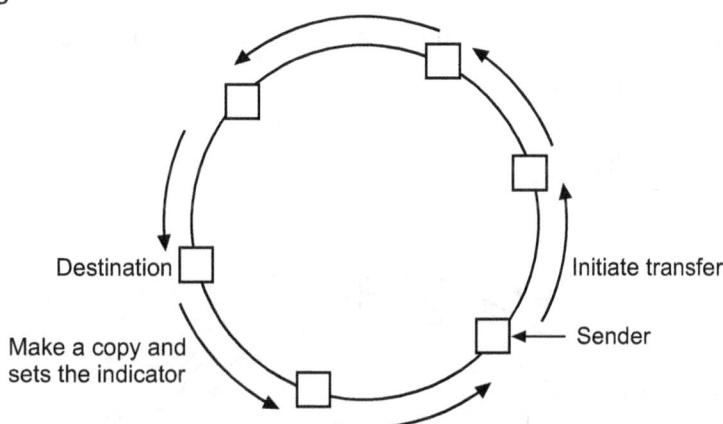

Fig. 4.6 (b) : Working of Token Ring Network

Advantages of Token Ring Network:

1. Simple engineering because it is point-to-point digital — no analog.
2. Standard twisted pair medium is cheap and easy to install.
3. Easy detection and correction of cable failures.
4. Deterministic and traffic can be prioritized.
5. No padding of data required in frame, so frames are short.
6. Excellent performance under conditions of heavy load.

Disadvantages of Token Ring:

1. Necessity of having a monitor function.
2. Under conditions of low load, substantial delay waiting for token to come around, even though network is idle.
3. Can require significantly more wire to be run than a bus architecture.

Fiber Distributed Data Interface.

FDDI stands for Fiber Distributed Data Interface. FDDI is a good choice for medium-sized networks i.e. MANs and large LANs. It is good for networks that require high bandwidth, such as engineering, graphics, and video applications. FDDI provides data speed at 100Mbps which is faster than Token Ring and Ethernet LANs . FDDI comprise two independent, counter-rotating rings : a primary ring and a secondary ring. Data flows in opposite directions on the rings. The counter-rotating ring architecture prevents data loss in the event of a link failure, a node failure, or the failure of both the primary and secondary links between any two nodes. FDDI is a token-based LAN standard developed by the American National Standards Institute.

FDDI uses a ring topology network in which station interfaces are interconnected by optical fiber transmission links operating at 100 Mbps in a ring that spans up to 200 kilometers and accommodates up to 500 stations. FDDI can also operate over twisted-pair cable at lengths of less than 100 meters.

Properties of FDDI:

1. FDDI uses the concept of a token frame to regulate medium access.
2. FDDI uses self healing mechanism.

Working of FDDI:

FDDI operates exactly like token ring except one difference.

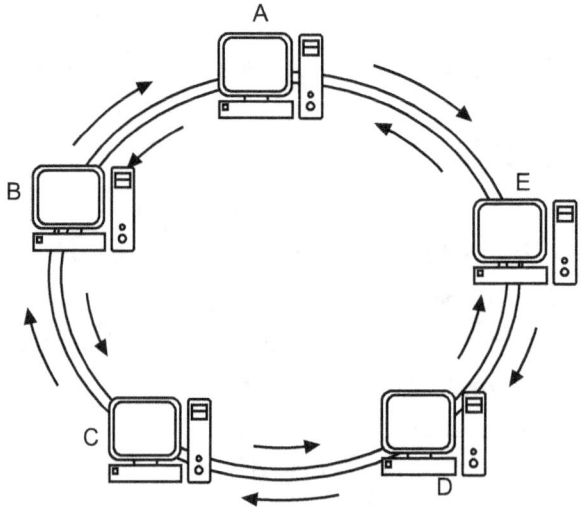

Fig. 4.7 : FDDI token-ring network

Token ring uses single wire through the all hosts, but FDDI uses two wires as shown in Fig. 4.7.

FDDI can be used in the same way as any of the 802 LANs, but with its high bandwidth it is more often used as a backbone network to interconnect various Ethernet LAN sub-networks as shown in Fig. 4.8.

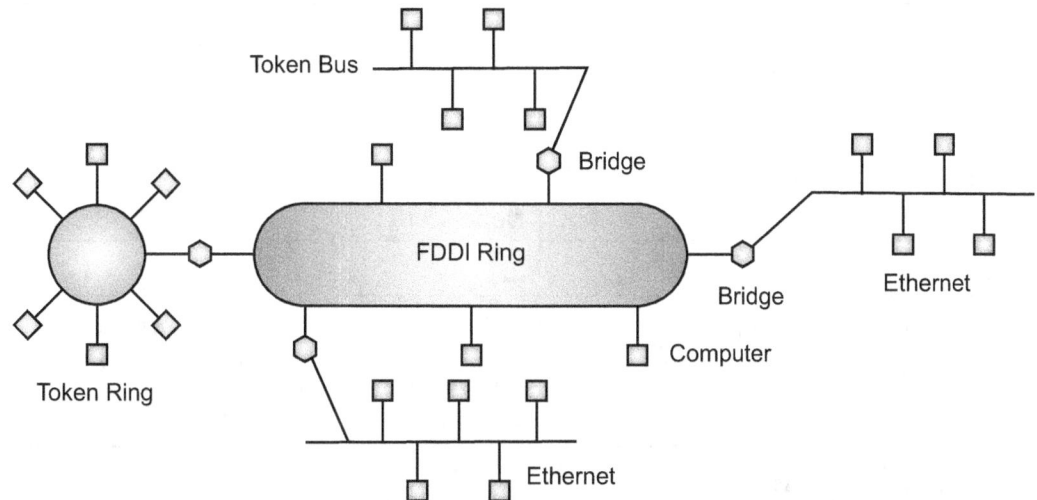

Fig. 4.8: An FDDI ring being used as backbone to connect LANs and computers

Advantages of (Fiber Distributed Data Interface):

1. They provide faster networking to the users with the help of fiber optic and copper cables.
2. Fiber distributed data interface line can tolerate the faults and there is no noise of electromagnetic waves in the transmission
3. Ability to transmit data among long distances with faster speed with the help of different repeaters used in the connection
4. Dual rings technology in the FDDI is really helpful for the users to prevent the distortion.
5. High bandwidth (10 times more than Ethernet).
6. Larger distances between FDDI nodes because of very low attenuation (≤ 0.3 db/km) in fibers.

Disadvantages of Fiber Distributed Data Interface:

1. As always high speed and reliability come with a price. FDDI is relatively expensive to implement, and its distance limitations, though less restrictive than those of other LAN links, make it unsuitable for true WAN communications.
2. High cost of optical components required for transmission/reception of signals (especially for single mode fiber networks).
3. More complex to implement than existing low speed LAN technologies such as IEEE802.3 and IEEE 802.5.

Table 4.1 : Comparison of Ethernet, Token Ring and FDDI

Features	Ethernet	Token Ring	FDDI
Transmission rate	20 MBAUD	8 and 32 MBAUD	125 MBAUD
Data rate	10 MBPS	4 and 16 MBPS	100 MBPS
Signal encoding	Manchester (50 % Efficient)	Differential Manchester (50% Efficient)	4B/5B (80% Efficient)
Maximum coverage	2.5 KM	Configuration Dependent	100 KM
Maximum nodes	1024	250	500
Maximum distance between nodes	2.5 KM	300 M (Recommended 100 M)	2 KM (Multimode fiber) 40 KM (single-mode fiber)

4.4 Access Technique

Media contention occurs when two or more network devices have data to send at the same time. Because multiple devices cannot talk on the network simultaneously, some type of method must be used to allow one device access to the network media at a time. This is done in two main ways: Carrier Sense Multiple Access / Collision Detect (CSMA/CD) and Token Passing.

Because of this type of network contention, the busier a network becomes, the more collisions occur. This is why performance of Ethernet degrades rapidly as the number of devices on a single network increases.

(a) CSMA/CD (Carrier Sense Multiple Access/Collision Detection)

In CSMA/CD (Carrier Sense Multiple Access/Collision Detection) Access Method, every host has equal access to the wire and can place data on the wire when the wire is free from traffic. When a host want to place data on the wire, it will "sense" the wire to find whether there is a signal already on the wire. If there is traffic already in the medium, the host will wait and if there is no traffic, it will place the data in the medium. But, if two systems place data on the medium at the same instance, they will collide with each other, destroying the data. If the data is destroyed during transmission, the data will need to be retransmitted. After collision, each host will wait for a small interval of time and again the data will be retransmitted, to avoid collision again.

In networks using CSMA/CD technology such as Ethernet, network devices contend for the network media. When a device has data to send, it first listens to see if any other device is currently using the network. If not, it starts sending its data. After finishing its transmission, it listens again to see if a collision occurred. A collision occurs when two devices send data simultaneously. When a collision happens, each device waits a random length of time before resending its data. In most cases, a collision will not occur again between the two devices.

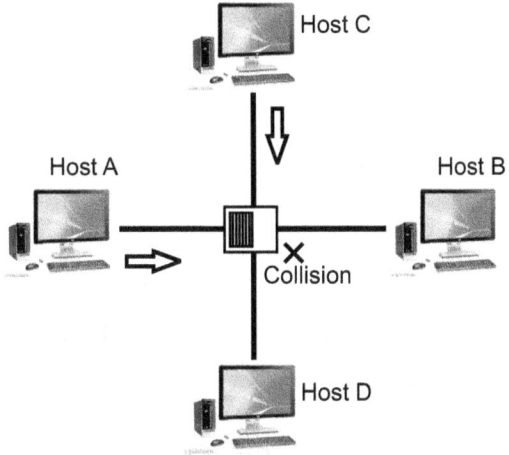

Fig 4.9 : CSMA/CD

(b) CSMA/CA (Carrier Sense Multiple Access/Collision Avoidance)

Carrier sense multiple access with collision avoidance (CSMA/CA) is, perhaps, the least popular of the access methods. In CSMA/CA, before a host sends real data on the wire it will "sense" the wire to check if the wire is free. If the wire is free, it will send a piece of "dummy" data on the wire to see whether it collides with any other data. If it does not collide, the host will assume that the real data also will not collide.

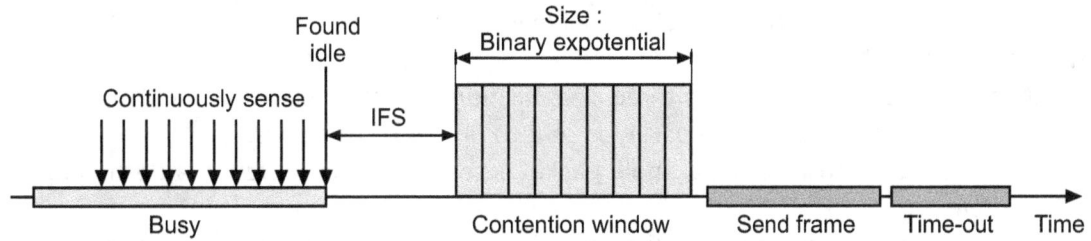

Fig 4.10 : CSMA/CA

Unfortunately, this broadcasting of the intention to transmit data increases the amount of traffic on the cable and slows down network performance. This access method was once a popular method in the Macintosh environment and is now used with Wireless LANs. The additional signaling makes CSMA/CA a slower access technique when compared to the CSMA/CD technique used in Ethernet networking.

Token Passing

In CSMA/CD and CSMA/CA the chances of collisions are there. As the number of hosts in the network increases, the chances of collisions also will become more. In token passing, when a host want to transmit data, it should hold the token, which is an empty packet. The token is circling the network in a very high speed. If any workstation wants to send data, it should wait for the token. When the token has reached the workstation, the workstation can take the token from the network, fill it with data, mark the token as being used and place the token back to the network.

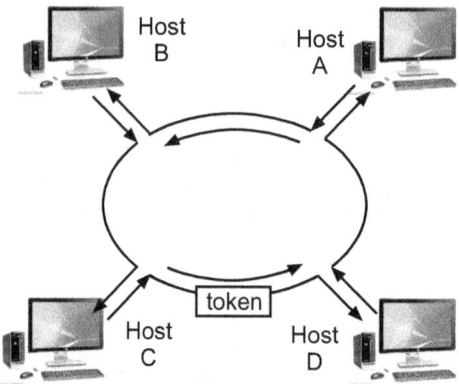

Fig 4.11 : Token Passing

In token-passing networks such as Token Ring and FDDI, a special network frame called a token is passed around the network from device to device. When a device has data to send, it must wait until it has the token and then sends its data. When the data transmission is complete, the token is released so that other devices may use the network media. The main advantage of token-passing networks is that it is easy to calculate the maximum time that will pass before a device has the opportunity to send data. This makes token passing networks popular in some real-time environments such as factories, where machinery must be capable of communicating at a determinable interval.

LAN Transmission Methods :

LAN data transmissions fall into three classifications: unicast, multicast, and broadcast. In each type of transmission, a single packet is sent to one or more nodes.

1. In a **unicast** transmission, a single packet is sent from the source to a destination on a network.
2. A **multicast** transmission consists of a single data packet that is copied and sent to a specific subset of nodes on the network.
3. A **broadcast** transmission consists of a single data packet that is copied and sent to all nodes on the network

4.5 Transmission Protocol

Protocols: Protocols govern the way data is transmitted over a LAN and include the following Transmission Protocols:

TCP/IP: The most basic and common transmission protocol. TCP stands for Transmission Control Protocol. This is responsible for managing the connection between a server (including an Internet ISP) and a client computer. It makes sure that the data which has to be transferred is split into multiplepackets which will then be transmitted to their destination. IP means Internet Protocol, which assigns the unique addresses to computers on the network as Version 4 (IPv4 - 32 bits long) and later Version 6 (IPv6 - 128 bits).

- **IPV4:** IPv4 stands for Internet Protocol version 4. It is the underlying technology that makes it possible for us to connect our devices to the web. Whenever a device access the Internet it is assigned a unique, numerical IP address such as 99.48.227.227. To send data from one computer to another through the web, a data packet must be transferred across the network containing the IP addresses of both devices.

- **IPv6:** IPv6 is the sixth revision to the Internet Protocol and the successor to IPv4. It functions similarly to IPv4 in that it provides the unique, numerical IP addresses necessary for Internet-enabled devices to communicate. It utilizes 128-bit addresses.

PPP: Stands for Point-to-Point Protocol. It is an extension to TCP/IP that adds the ability to transmit TCP/IP over a serial links and has login security. This protocol, which was developed prior to PPPoE provides secure login and traffic metering. It can use authentication, encryption and compression for establishing a connection between two networking nodes, over a large variety of networks, but because of its capabilities it is most often used by ISPs to allow their dial-up and cable users to connect to the Internet. But not DSL users, because they use ethernet, not serial, connectivity.

PPPoE: This stands for Point-to-Point Protocol over Ethernet is a derivative of PPP. It is originally developed by UUNET, Redback Networks and RouterWare. It was specifically designed to bring the security and other benefits of PPP to always-on (i.e. permanently connected) ethernet connections such as DSL. It is used to connect multiple computer users on a local area network ("LAN") to a remote site through common customer location equipment like a DSL modem. PPPoE can be used to have an office, hotel or residential building with multiple users share a common Digital Subscriber Line (DSL), cable modem, or wireless connection to the Internet. The PPP protocol information is encapsulated within an Ethernet frame. It has the advantage that neither the telephone/cable company nor the Internet service provider (ISP) needs to provide any special support. It is also commonly used with PPTP to create VPNs. Usually, it leverages PPP facilities for authenticating the user with a username and password. This is normally done through either the PAP or CHAP protocols.

PAP: Stands for Password Authentication Protocol. It is a networking protocol supported by almost every operating system due to its simplicity. However, because it transmits ASCII passwords in an unencrypted manner, it therefore not secure and not useful for many businesses. PAP is a protocol where both ends of the transmission share a password in advance, which can be either weak or strong, depending upon the difficulty of their computational overhead.

CHAP: Stands for Challenge-Handshake Authentication Protocol. Because this provides better security than PAP (above), it is a more secure protocol. CHAP occasionally and randomly verifies the identity of the client .A variant of CHAP,MS-CHAP, is considered less secure, as it doesn't require both the client and server to know the plain text of the encrypted secret.

Ethernet LAN Standards:

Ethernet LAN standards specify cabling and signaling at both the physical and data link layers of the OSI reference model. Let us see Ethernet LAN standards at the data link layer.

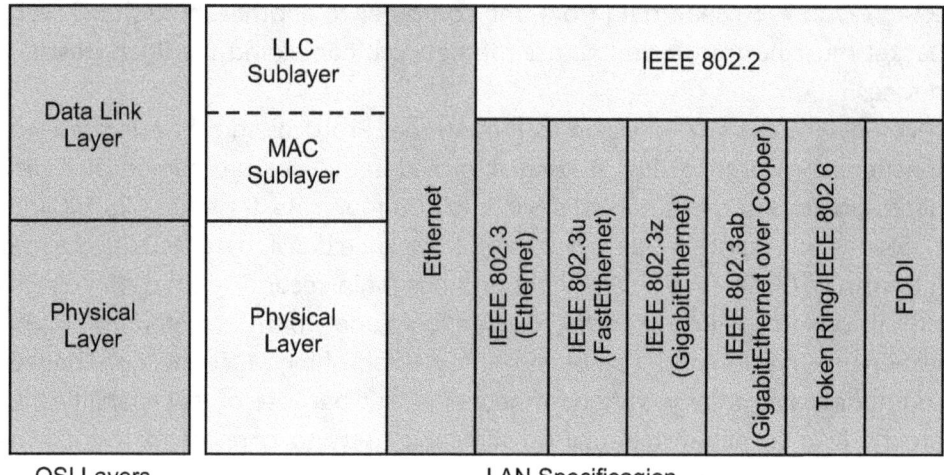

Fig 4.12 : Mapping of LAN protocols to the OSI Reference Model

The IEEE divides the OSI data link layer into two separate sublayers:

- **Logical link control (LLC):** Transitions up to the Network Layer
- **MAC:** Transitions down to the Physical Layer

LAN protocols are based on the IEEE 802 reference model, consisting of three layers.

- **Physical layer:** This layer specifies Encoding/decoding of signals, Preamble generation / removal for synchronization and bit transmission/reception.
- **Medium access control (MAC):** A special protocol is required because a number of nodes share the same medium. This Protocol is known as the medium access control protocol. The MAC sub layer governs access to the LAN transmission medium. It assembles data into frames with addresses and error detection-fields. In Ethernet, the Medium Access protocol is carrier sense multiple access/ collision detection (CSMA/CD).
- **Logical link control (LLC):** LLC performs flow and error control. The data received from the higher level(IP layer) is assembled into frames and error detection and address fields are added at the transmitter and sent to the MAC layer. When MAC sublayer gets a chance to send its data using CSMA/CD protocol, it sends the frame through the physical layer. At the receiver, frames are disassembled, the address is recognized and error detection is carried out. The LLC player provides an interface to higher layers.

The MAC and LLC layers combined make a data link layer. The separation is for the following reasons.

- o Traditional data link layers are not concerned with shared-access medium.
- o Different MAC options may be provided for the same LLC.

4.6 Transmission Media

Transmission Methods and Media

LAN technology centers on three areas:

1. The transmission method and medium used to transmit signals between nodes: coaxial cable versus telephone wire, digital versus analog, and so on.

2. The topology of the network: bus, ring, star, and the tradeoffs between them.

3. The protocols used to transmit data between nodes on the LAN and for medium access control.

For bus networks, medium access control means preventing or handling collisions; for ring networks, it refers to the method used for inserting messages on and removing them from the ring. Two methods are used to transmit signals between nodes: baseband and broadband. See the Baseband and Broadband Signals diagram below. In the context of LANs, broadband refers to analog transmission of digital signals, and baseband refers to digital transmission of digital signals.

Baseband is analogous to a telegraph. 0 voltage levels are modulated onto a constant carrier signal. Transitions from one level to the other indicate a "0" or a "1." Baseband is relatively simple, is less costly than broadband, and yet is still very fast. It is far more widely used than Broadband.

Broadband is analogous to TV cable transmission. Just as many different TV channels can broadcast different programs at the same time, a broadband link can support many independent communications channels. These channels can be used as independent links between nodes, or they can be used in parallel to increase the effective throughput of the link.

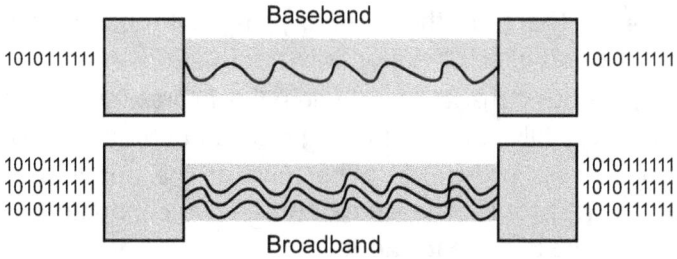

Fig. 4.13 : Baseband and Broadband Signals

Though potentially much faster and able to span longer distances than baseband, broadband requires a modem at each end of a link, increasing the cost of every device attached to the LAN.

There are three major forms of transmission media used for LANs:

- **Twisted Pair:** Two insulated copper wires twisted together in a regular spiral pattern; one pair establishes one communication link; it transmits electromagnetic signals. Twisted pairs are distinguished between shielded and unshielded twisted pairs according to their protection against electromagnetic fields.

Fig. 4. 14 : Twisted pair cable

- **Coaxial Cable:** A single insulated inner wire is surrounded by a cylindrical conductor which is covered with a shield; it transmits electromagnetic signals. Coaxial cable is classified into two categories: baseband (uses digital signals) and broadband (uses analog signals) coaxial cable.

- **Optical Fiber :** It consists of three concentric sections, the core (a fiber conducting optical rays), the cladding (reflecting optical rays) and the jacket (surrounding one or many fibres to protect them); transmits optical signals, which must be transformed to electromagnetic signals

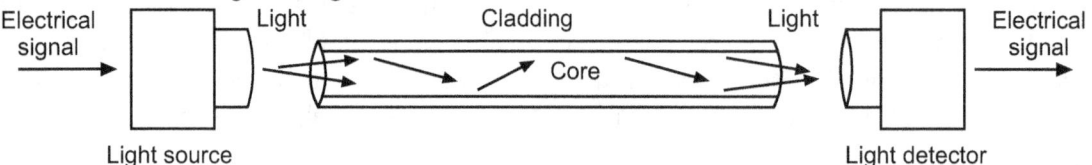

Fig. 4.15 : Optical fiber

Each transmission media has its own advantages and disadvantages. They differ in costs, capacity, possible length, and electromagnetic isolation.

LAN Topologies: LANs can be organized into various different structures. There are two types of topologies : Physical and Logical topologies. The physical topology is how wires are organized. The logical topology is how the network behaves logically.

Devices on the network are referred to as 'nodes.' The most common nodes are computers and peripheral devices. Network topology is illustrated by showing these nodes and their connections using cables.

Physical Topologies: There are three primary physical topologies: Bus, Ring, and Star. The star topology plays a part in combination with a ring.

1. Bus Topology : A bus consists of a single pair of wires (twisted pair) or a wire and a shield (coaxial) which electrically constitute a single circuit (although the bus might be made up of many individual pieces of wire).At either end of the bus is a terminator, which is essentially a resistor. The resistor is connected between two conductors to provide a load for the circuits that attach to the bus in each node.

This topology consists of a Backbone cable connecting all nodes on a network without intervening connectivity devices. The single cable is called Bus and can support only one channel for communication; as a result, every node shares the bus's total capacity. On a Bus Topology network, devices share the responsibility for getting data from one point to another. But only the intended recipient actually receives and processes the transmitted message while a device wants to send the broadcast message to all the devices that connected to the shared cable.

At the ends of each bus network are 50-ohm resistors known as terminators. The terminators stop signals after they have reached the end of the cable. Without these terminators, signals on a bus network would travel endlessly between the two ends of the network; this phenomenon is called signal bounce, and new signals could not get through.

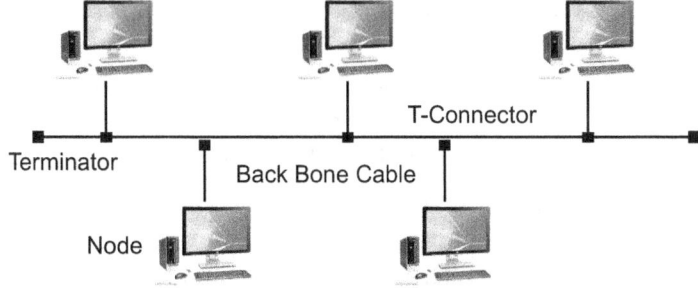

Fig. 4.16 : Bus Topology

Ethernet bus topology is actually easy to install and does not require much cabling and only a main shared cable is used for network communication. 10BASE2 and 10BASE-T are two popular types of the Ethernet cables used in the Bus topology. Also, Bus network works with very limited devices. Performance issues are likely to occur in the Bus topology if more than 12-15 computers are added in a Bus Network. In addition, if the Backbone cable fails then all network becomes useless and communication fails among all the devices.

2. Ring Topology: In ring network, each node is connected to the two nearest nodes so that the entire network forms a circle. In a ring network, all the communication messages are transmitted clockwise in one direction, around the ring. Each workstation accepts and responds to packets addressed to it, and then forwards the other packets to the next workstation in the network. Each workstation just acts as a repeater for the transmission, in other words, all workstations participate in delivery makes the ring topology an active topology. A Ring Topology has no "ends" and transmitted data stops at its destination. Twisted-pair or fiber-optic cabling is commonly used as the physical medium.

Any damage of the cable of any cable or device can result in the breakdown of the whole network. In addition, just as in a bus topology, the more workstations that must participate in data transmission, the slower the response time. Due to these shortcomings, ring topology now has become almost obsolete. FDDI, SONET or Token Ring Technology can be used to implement Ring Technology. Ring topologies can be found in office, school or small buildings.

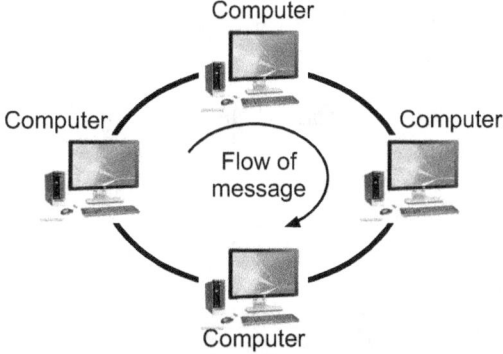

Fig. 4.17 : Ring topology

3. Star Topology : In the computer networking world the most commonly used topology in local area networking is the star topology. Star topologies can be implemented in home, offices or even in a building. All the computers in the star topologies are connected to central devices like hub, switch or router. The functionality of all these devices is different. Computers in a network are usually connected with the hub, switch or router with the unshielded twisted-pair (UTP) or Shielded Twisted-pair cables. Star Topology networks can support a maximum of only 1024 addressable nodes on a logical network.

Star Topology requires more cabling than ring and bus. It also requires more configurations. However, because each node is separately connected to a central connectivity device, they are more fault-tolerant. A single malfunctioning workstation cannot disable an entire star network. A failure in the central connectivity device can take down a local area networking segment. Because they include a centralized connection point, star topology can easily be moved, isolated or interconnected with other networks through hubs, switches to form more complex topologies. Most Ethernet networks are based on the Star Topology.

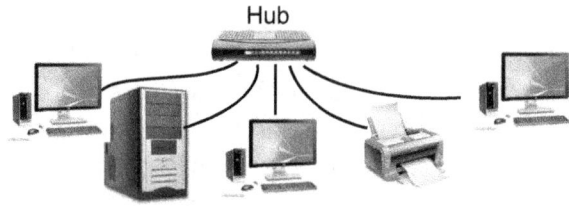

Fig. 4.18 : Star topoloty

In some situations, a wireless LAN, or Wi-Fi, may be preferable to a wired LAN because of its flexibility and cost. Companies are assessing WLANs as a replacement for their wired infrastructures as the number of smartphones, tablets and other mobile devices proliferates.

Practice Questions

1. Describe the concept of Local area network.
2. Which are the components are used in LAN?
3. What are characteristics of LAN?
4. Which are access techniques used for LAN?
5. Explain bus topology of LAN.
6. Write short note on 'Fiber Distributed Data Interface'.
7. Define terms – NIC, Bridge.
8. What is Gigabit Ethernet?
9. Explain Virtual LAN (VLAN) in detail.
10. What is Ethernet?

Chapter 5...

BROAD BAND NETWORKS

Contents ...

5.1   Integrated Service Digital Networks (ISDN)

5.2   ATM and ATM traffic Management

5.3   Very small Aperture Terminal (VSAT)

•   Practice Questions

5.1 Integrated Services Digital Network (ISDN)

ISDN is a design for a completely digital telephone/telecommunications network. It is designed to carry voice, data, images, video, everything you could ever need. It is also designed to provide a single interface (in terms of both hardware and communication protocols) for hooking up phone, fax machine, computer, videophone, video-on-demand system (someday), and microwave systems. ISDN was originally envisioned as a very fast service, but this was a long time ago when it was hoped to have fiber all the way to house. It turned out that running all that fiber would be too expensive, so they designed ISDN to run on the copper wiring that you already have. ISDN has been very slow in future. The standards organizations have taken their time in coming up with the standards. In fact, many people consider them to be out of date already. But on the other side of the coin, the phone companies (especially in the U.S.) have been very slow at designing products and services, or marketing them with ISDN in mind. Things are starting to pick up, but still very slowly. ISDN is available now in many places, but it is not widely used.

How ISDN Works ?

Only single transmission channel for communication is available in analog network or regular telephone lines that are provided to us by telephone companies. Therefore only one service can be carried at time, i.e. voice, data, video at single time. Whereas in ISDN lines there the same pair telephone lines are logically divided into multiple channels, they are normally divided into two channels.

B-Channel is first type of channel. 64Kbps of data can be transferred using B-channel. Normally ISDN lines possess two B channels. One channel is dedicated for voice and the other channel is dedicated for data communication. The data transmission takes place on one pair copper wire.

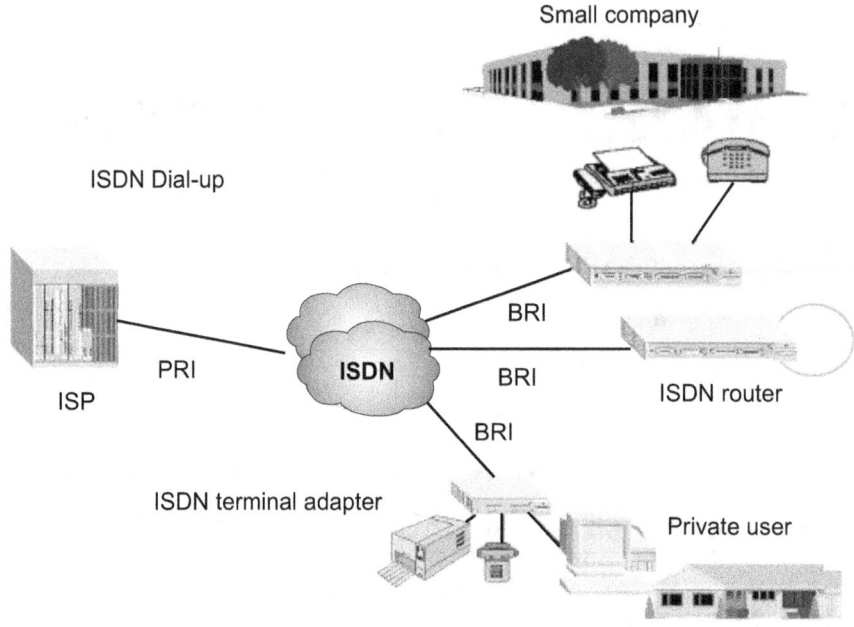

Fig. 5.1 : Working of ISDN

Second type of channel is used for line and calling system setup, is it know as D-channel or delta channel also. Third channel on the other have on 16Kpbs of bandwidth. (See more information in section : ISDN structure)

Advantages of ISDN Lines :

1. Speed Line: Speed is the most obvious advantage of ISDN line, the maximum limit for commonly used dialup connections is 56 kbps and due to many factors this limit reduce to only 45 kbps. Where as ISDN lines possess multiple digital channels which operates simultaneously by using same regular one pair copper wire. If telephone company can provide digital connections then change in speed can occur, this way digital signals can be transmitted through telephone lines rather than analog. The digital signals can provide better transmission rates comparing analog setup.

2. Multiple lines for Multiple Devices : If multiple services are required by consumer for example, fax, video conferencing, telephone etc, separate telephone line will be required for each device, where as ISDN line can handle multiple services at single line. There are eight channels which can be supported by ISDN lines simultaneously. That means one single ISDN line can support telephone, video conferencing, fax, credit card machine and other services together on single line and all these devices can work simultaneously.

3. Connection Time : V.34 or V.90 modems usually takes up to 30 to 60 seconds to make connection to the network whereas ISDN lines takes less than 2 seconds to make connection live to be used.

Disadvantages of ISDN Lines :

There are some disadvantages associated with ISDN lines and they are as follow.

1. ISDN lines are more expensive when compare to the regular landline telephone system.

2. ISDN provider companies and ISDN users are require to have special dedicated line and then can encore at extra cost.

The original version of ISDN employs baseband transmission. Another version, called B-ISDN, uses broadband transmission.

ISDN Structure : ISDN structure includes a central ISDN office. All the users are linked to this office through a digital pipe. This digital pipe may be of different capacities and may have different data transfer rates. These digital pipes between the customers and central office are organized into multiple channels of different size.

ISDN standard defines the following three channel types:

1. B Channel,   2. D Channel,   3. H Channel.

1. B Channel

A Bearer Channel (B Channel) is defined at a rate of 64 kbps.It is the basic user channel and can carry any type of digital information in full duplex mode as long as the required transmission rate does not exceed 64 kbps. It can be used to carry digital data, digital voice and any other low data rate information.

Four kind of connections can be set up over a B channel:

(a) Circuit switched

The user places a call and a current switched connection is established with another network user.

(b) Packet switched

The user is connected to a packet switching mode and data are exchanged with other users via X.25.

(c) Frame mode

The user is connected to a frame relay mode and data are exchanged with other users via LAPF.

(d) Semi-permanent

This is a connection to another user set up by prior arrangement and not requiring-a call establishment protocol. It is equivalent to a leased line.

2. D Channel

A data channel (D channel) carry control signal for bearer channels. This channel does not carry data and can be either 16 or 64 kbps, depending upon the user's need.

In-band signaling, the same cable carries data as well as control signals. In out-of-band signaling (as in ISDN), two different cables carry data and control information.

3. H-Channel

A Hybrid channel (H-channel) is provided for user information at higher bit rates.

There are three types of H-Channels depending on the data rates:

H0 with data rate of 384 kbps

H11 with data rate of 1536 kbps

H12 with data rate of 1920 kbps

Hybrid channels are used for high data rate applications such as video, teleconferencing.

ISDN Interfaces

There are several kinds of access interfaces to the ISDN :

1. Basic Rate Interface (BRI)
2. Primary Rate Interface (PRI)
3. Broadband-ISDN (B-ISDN)

1. Basic Rate Interface (BRI)

Basic Rate Interface service consists of two data-bearing channels ('B' channels) and one signaling channel ('D' channel) to initiate connections. The B channels operate at 64 Kbps maximum.

The D channel operates at a maximum of 16 Kbps. The two channels can operate independently. For example, one channel can be used to send a fax to a remote location, while the other channel is used as a TCP/IP connection to a different location. ISDN service on the iSeries supports basic rate interface (BRI).

The basic rate interface (BRI) specifies a digital pipe consisting of two B channels and 16 Kbps D channel. Two B channels of 64 Kbps each, plus one D channel of 16 Kbps, equal 144 Kbps. In addition, the BRI service itself requires 48 Kbps of operating overhead. BRI therefore requires a digital pipe of 192 Kbps. Conceptually, the BRI service is like a large pipe that contains three smaller pipes, two for the B channels and one for the D channel.

The remainder of the space inside the large pipe carries the overhead bits required for its operation. In the following figure shaded portion of the circle surrounds the Band D channels shows the overhead.

2. Primary Rate Interface (PRI)

Primary Rate Interface service consists of a D channel and either 23 (depending on the country you are in). PRI is not supported on the iSeries. Or 30 B channels.

The usual Primary Rate Interface (PRI) specifies a digital pipe with 23 B channels and one 64 Kbps D channel. Twenty-three B channels of 64 Kbps each, plus one D channel of 64 Kbps equals 1.536 Mbps. In addition, the PRI service itself uses 8 Kbps of overhead.

PRI therefore requires a digital pipe of 1.544 Mbps. Conceptually; the PRI service is like a large pipe containing 24 smaller pipes, 23 for the B channels and 1 for the D channel. The rest of the pipe carries the overhead bits required for its operation. In figure, the shaded portion of the circle surrounding the B and D channels shows the overhead.

3. Broadband-ISDN (B-ISDN)

Two standards exist for ISDN. Narrowband – ISDN (C-ISDN) which is already in operation and Broadband-ISDN (B-ISDN). This B-ISDN is planned to support multimedia applications (Video, audio etc.) because of its high performance.

Broadband Integrated Services Digital Network (B-ISDN) is both a concept and a set of services and developing standards for integrating digital transmission services in a broadband network of fiber optic and radio media. B-ISDN will encompass frame relay service for high-speed data that can be sent in large bursts, the Fiber Distributed-Data Interface (Fiber Distributed-Data Interface), and the Synchronous Optical Network (Synchronous Optical Network). B-ISDN will support transmission from 2 Mbps up to much higher, but as yet unspecified, rates.

A layered structure approach, as used in established ISDN protocols, is also applied to B-ISDN, giving flexibility using different transmission systems for B-ISDN and serving different applications. Asynchronous Transfer Mode (ATM) is the transfer mode for implementing B-ISDN.

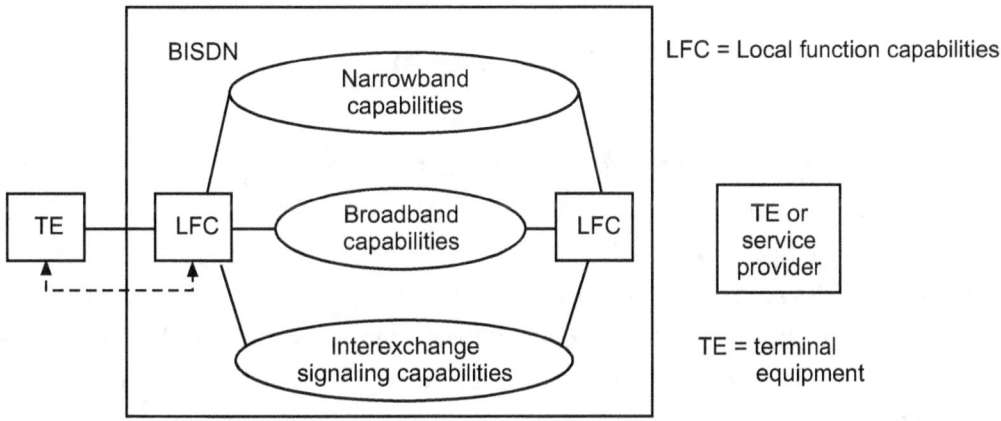

Fig. 5.2 : B-ISDN Architecture

Principles of ISDN

The various principles of ISDN are:

I. To support voice and non-voice applications

The main feature of the ISDN concept is the support of a wide range of voice (for e.g. Telephone calls) & non-voice (for e.g. digital data exchange) applications in the same network.

2. To support switched and non-switched applications

ISDN supports both circuit switching and packet switching. In addition ISDN supports non-switched services in the form of dedicated lines.

3. Reliance on 64-kbps connections

ISDN provides circuit switched and packet switched connections at 64 kbps. This is the fundamental building block of ISDN. This rate was chosen because at the time, it was standard rate for digitized voice.

4. Intelligence in the network

An ISDN is expected to provide sophisticated services beyond the simple setup of circuit switched calls. These services include maintenance and network management functions.

5. Layered protocol architecture

A layered protocol structure should be used for the specification of the access to an ISDN. Such a structure can be mapped into OSI model.

6. Variety of configurations

Several configurations are possible for implementing ISDN. This allows for differences in national policy, in state of technology and in the needs and existing equipment of the customer base.

5.2 ATM and ATM Traffic Management

ATM is a packet oriented transfer mode; it allows multiple logical connections to be multiplexed over a single physical interface. ATM is a connection-oriented, unreliable (does not acknowledge) protocol that can work with either Permanent Virtual Circuits (PVCs) or Switched Virtual Circuits (SVCs). The information flow on each logical connection is organized into fixed-size packets called as cells. By using small, fixed sized cells, the ATM becomes so efficient that it can offer a constant data rate even though it is using a packet switching technique. Similar to frame relay like it does not support link-by-link error control and flow control.

ATM does not provide any error control or flow control at the data link layer. ATM is a fully duplex data transmission system. It is the latest technology for the telephone networks and it has been designed to deliver voice, data and video information.

In ATM, communication between any two hosts takes place through the switch. Each and every ATM switch is in turn connected to many other switches and hosts. It is possible to add new hosts and switches to an ATM network easily. This network is capable of supporting very high data rates i.e. typically upto 155 Mbps.

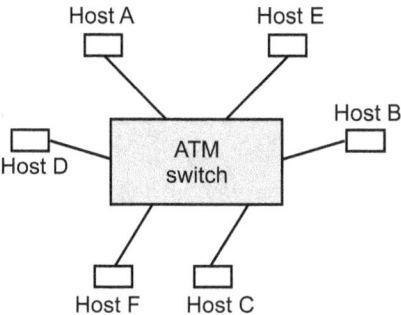

Fig. 5.3 : ATM switch

The transmission medium used for ATM is optical fibers instead of coaxial cables and twisted pair in order to support high data rates.

1. ATM Devices:

An ATM network is made up of an ATM switch and ATM endpoints. An ATM switch is responsible for cell transit through an ATM network. The job of an ATM switch is to accept the incoming cell from an ATM endpoint or another ATM switch.

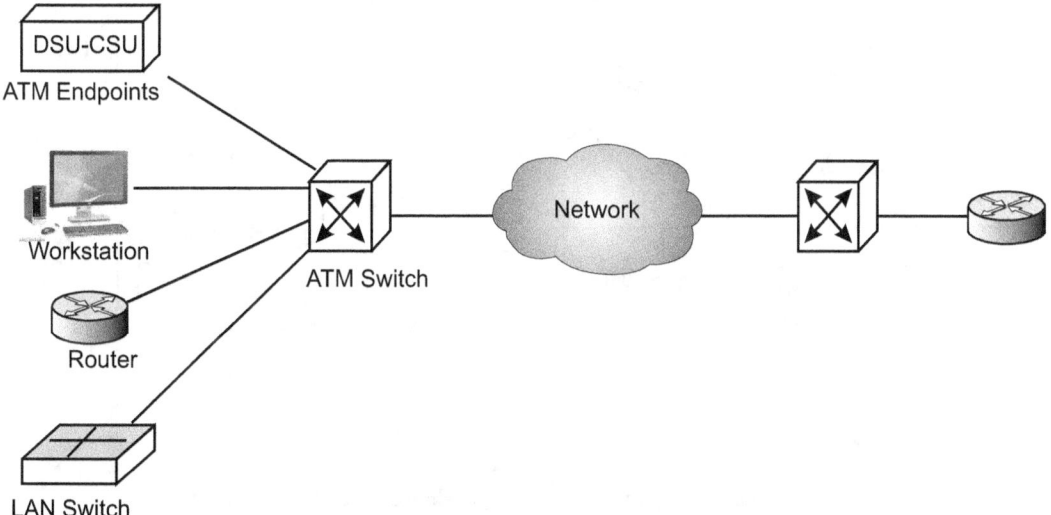

Fig. 5. 4: An ATM network comprises ATM switches and endpoints

Then it reads and updates the cell-header information and quickly switches the cell to an output interface toward its destination.An ATM endpoint contains an ATM network interface adapter.

Examples of ATM endpoints are workstations, routers, Digital Service Units (DSUs), LAN switches, and Video Coder-Decoders (CODECs).

2. ATM Architecture:

As in the case of many large systems, there are a range of components and connections involved in the ATM networks. All connections in the ATM network are Point-to-Point, with traffic being switched through the network by the switching nodes.Two types of networks are included in the ATM architecture, Public networks and Private networks.

Private networks, often referred to as Customer Premises Networks, are typically concerned with end-user connections, or bridging services to other types of networks including circuit switched services, frame relay, and voice sub systems.

The interface between the components in the Private Networks is referred to as the Private User Network Interface (**PUNI**). ATM also extends into the wider area **Public Networks**.

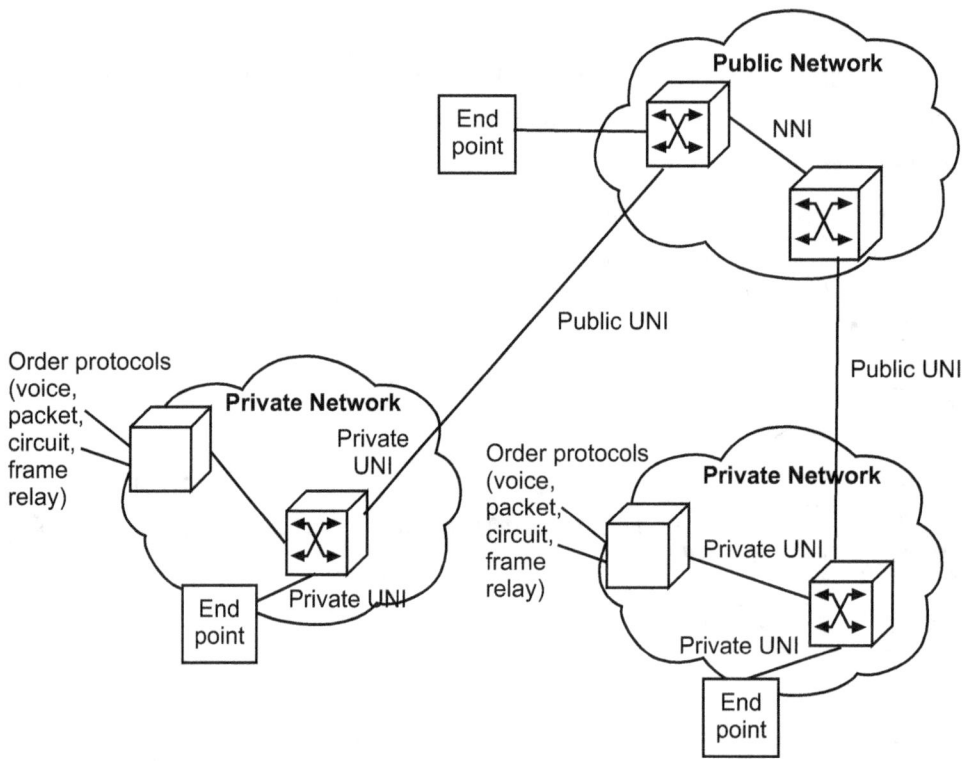

Fig. 5.5 : ATM sample network architecture

Interfaces between the Public and Private network switches conform to the Public UNI. Interfaces between the switches within the Public Network are the Network Node Interface (NNI).

Specifications for both the Public and Private UNI can be found in the ATM Forum's publication "ATM User-Network Interface (UNI) Specification". The private networks often permit the use of lower speed short haul interconnects that are useful in LAN environments, but not of great use in wider area public networks.

Three types of NNI have been developed, NNI-ISSI (Inter Switching System Interface) that connects switches in the same Local Area Transport Area (LATA) the NNI-ICI (Inter

Carrier Interface), that connects ATM networks of different carriers (InterCarrier), and finally, a Private NNI that permits the connection of different switches in a private network.

3. ATM Reference Model:

The ATM architecture uses a logical model to describe the functionality it supports. ATM functionality corresponds to the physical layer and part of the data link layer of the OSI reference model.

The ATM reference model is composed of the following planes, which span all layers:

Control: This plane is responsible for generating and managing signaling requests.

User: This plane is responsible for managing the transfer of data.

Management: This plane contains two components:

- **Layer management** manages layer-specific functions, such as the detection of failures and protocol problems.

- **Plane management** manages and coordinates functions related to the complete system.

Fig. 5.6 illustrates the ATM reference model.

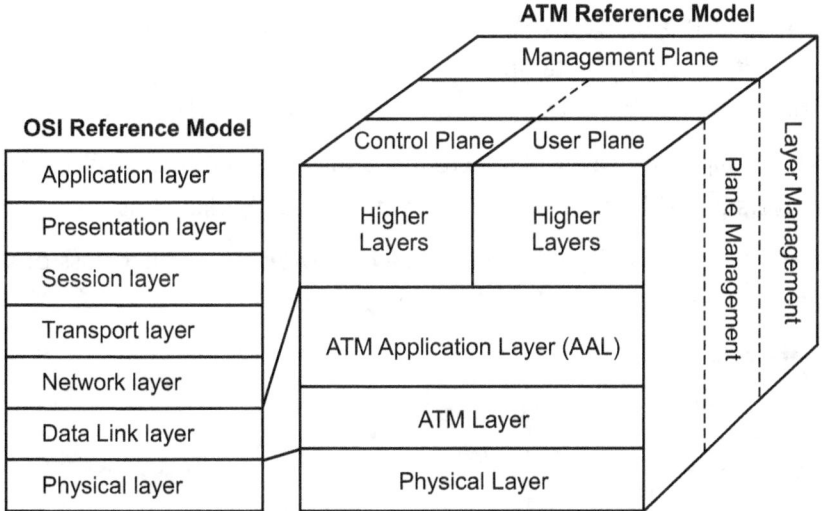

Fig. 5.6 : The ATM reference model relates to the lowest two layers of the OSI reference model

The ATM reference model is composed of the following ATM layers:

(a) Physical layer: Analogous to the physical layer of the OSI reference model, the ATM physical layer manages the medium-dependent transmission. The physical layer helps in the transmission and reception of ATM cells across a physical medium between two ATM devices. This can be a transmission between an ATM endpoint and an ATM switch, or it can be between two ATM switches. The physical layer protocol involves the specifications of a transmission medium and signal encoding scheme.

(b) ATM layer: Combined with the ATM adaptation layer, the ATM layer is roughly analogous to the data link layer of the OSI reference model. The ATM layer is responsible for establishing connections and passing cells through the ATM network. To do this, it uses information in the header of each ATM cell. It regulates cells and cell transport and establishes and releases Virtual Circuits.

The ATM layer provides cell multiplexing, demultiplexing, and VPI/VCI routing functions. The ATM layer also supervises the cell flow to ensure that all connections remain within their negotiated cell throughput limits.

If connections operate outside their negotiated parameters, the ATM layer can take corrective action so the misbehaving connections do not affect connections that are obeying their negotiated connection contract. The ATM layer also maintains the cell sequence from any source.

(c) ATM Adaptation Layer (AAL): Combined with the ATM layer, the AAL is roughly analogous to the data data-link layer of the OSI model. The AAL is responsible for isolating higher-layer protocols from the details of the ATM processes.

The ATM Adaptation Layer (AAL) creates and receives 48-byte payloads through the lower layers of ATM on behalf of different types of applications.

There are five different types of AALs, each providing a distinct class of service. These types are known as AAL1, AAL2, AAL3, AAL4 and AAL5.

AAL Services:

(i)   Handling of transmission errors.

(ii) Segmentation and reassembly.

(iii) Handling of lost and misinserted cell conditions.

(iv) Flow control and timing control.

AAL1 is the basic service structure that handles voice traffic on ATM networks. This structure concerns itself with video transmission service through ATM networks.

The reason we have grouped AAL3 and AAL5 together is that they are both designed to be used with Connection-Oriented Protocols (COP). AAL4 service is a lot different than AAL3 and AAL5. AAL4 is for connectionless transmissions of data.

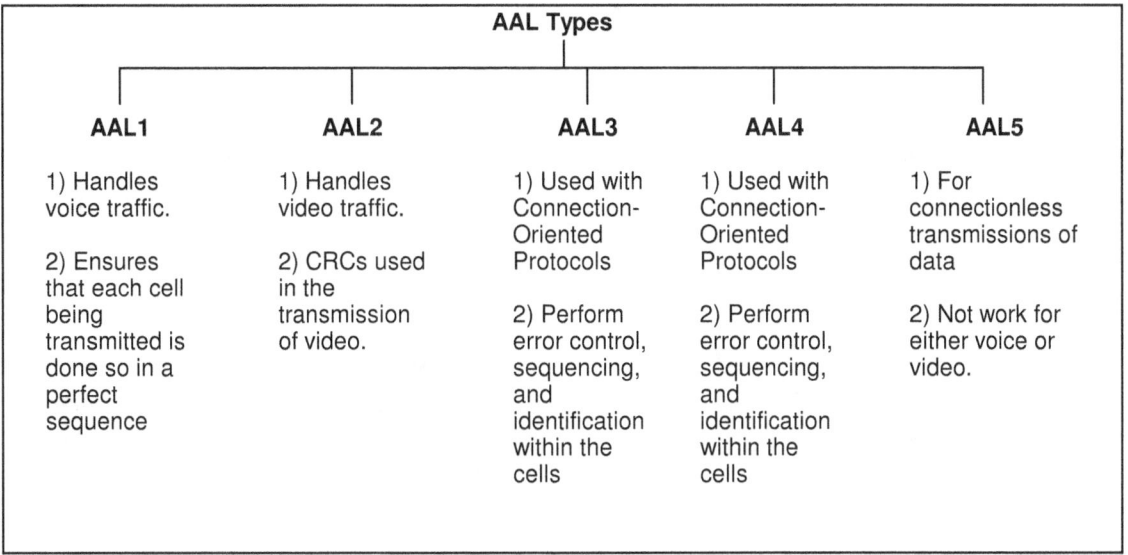

AAL Types				
AAL1	**AAL2**	**AAL3**	**AAL4**	**AAL5**
1) Handles voice traffic.	1) Handles video traffic.	1) Used with Connection-Oriented Protocols	1) Used with Connection-Oriented Protocols	1) For connectionless transmissions of data
2) Ensures that each cell being transmitted is done so in a perfect sequence	2) CRCs used in the transmission of video.	2) Perform error control, sequencing, and identification within the cells	2) Perform error control, sequencing, and identification within the cells	2) Not work for either voice or video.

4. Virtual Channels and Virtual Paths in ATM:

Virtual Channel Connections (VCCs) are the logical connections in the ATM. It is similar to virtual circuit in X.25 or frame relay logical connections. VCC is setup between two end users through the network, and a variable bit rate, full duplex flow of fixed-size cells is exchanged over the connection. These are also used for user-network exchange (control signaling) and network-network exchange (network management and routing).

Refer the following figure. A virtual path connection is a bundle of Virtual channel connections that have the same endpoints. Thus, all of the ATM cells travelling over all of the VCCs in a single VPC are switched together in a same route.

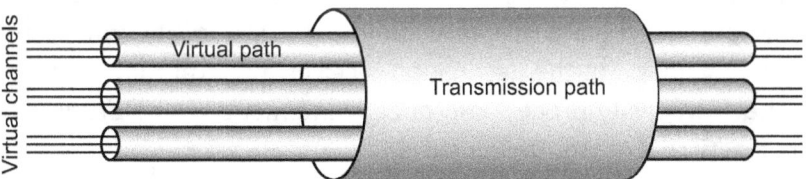

Fig. 5.7 : ATM connections

The virtual path concept comes into existence due to high speed networks, where the control cost of the network is becoming an increasingly higher proportion of overall network cost.The virtual path mechanism helps in reducing the control cost by grouping connections sharing a common path through the network into a single unit.Network management actions can then be applied to a small number of groups of connections rather than large number of individual connections.

Virtual Path Advantages:

1. Simplified network architecture.

2. Increased network performance, reliability.

3. Reduced processing and short connection setup time.

4. Enhanced network services.

Types of ATM Networks Connection:

There are two ways in which ATM connections between endpoints can be distinguished by the Quality of Service parameters and formats of their addressing schemes. The type of ATM is determined by ATM signaling. The signaling components situates at the end station and at the ATM switch. The creation, management and termination of SVCs (switched virtual circuits) are determined by the signaling layer of ATM's software. UNI (User Network Interface) is the ATM standard wire protocol applied by the signaling software. The manner in which an ATM switch signals another ATM switch is composed of a second signaling standard known as NNI (Network Network Interface). ATM has two types:

- Point to Point connections
- Point to Multipoint connections

Point-to-Point Connection:

If an ATM-aware process wants to connect to another process on some other network then it needs to establish an SVC which can be asked from signaling software. The signaling software sends request of creating a SVC by the virtue of ATM adapter and the reserved signaling VC to the ATM switch.

The ATM switches keep forwarding the request until it reaches to its destination. Considering the ATM address for the connection and the internal network database of the switch (routing table), ATM switch has the right to determine which switch to propagate the request next. It is determined by each switch whether the service category and Quality of Service needs of the request are achieved. If the request of virtual circuit is supported by all the switches, the end station of the destination receives a packet that has VC number. From now onwards, the ATM-aware process can directly interact with the destination by sending packets to the VPI/VCI that recognize the specified VC.

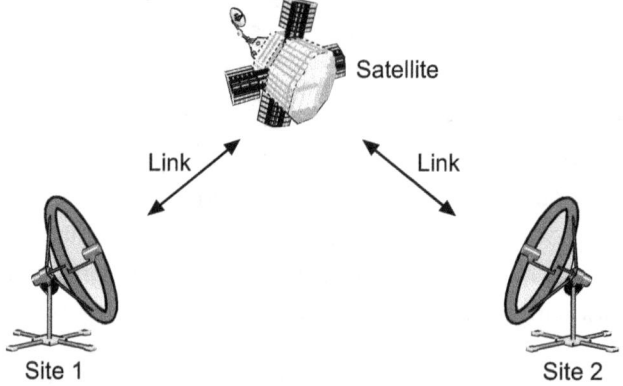

Fig. 5.8 : Point-to- Point network

Point-to-Multipoint Connection (P2MP or PTMP):

Contrary to a LAN environment, ATM has no natural capability to broadcast or multicast packets. It is a connection oriented medium. To make it capable, the sending node can produce a VC to all destinations and send a copy of the data on each virtual circuit. It is highly ineffective. Point to multi point connections is an efficient way to achieve the target. It connects a single source endpoint called root node to multiple destination endpoints called leaves. On splitting into two or more branches, the ATM switches copy cells to multiple destinations. The process is unidirectional. The root can transmit to the leaves but leaves are unable to transmit to the roots or to each other on same connection. Leaf to node and node to leaf transmission needs a unique connection. The reason behind this limitation is AAL5's simplicity and the incapability to interleave cells from multiple payloads on a single connection.

Although complex but they play vital role in boosting networks, ATM is changing the way we communicate and are probably the future of our digital world.

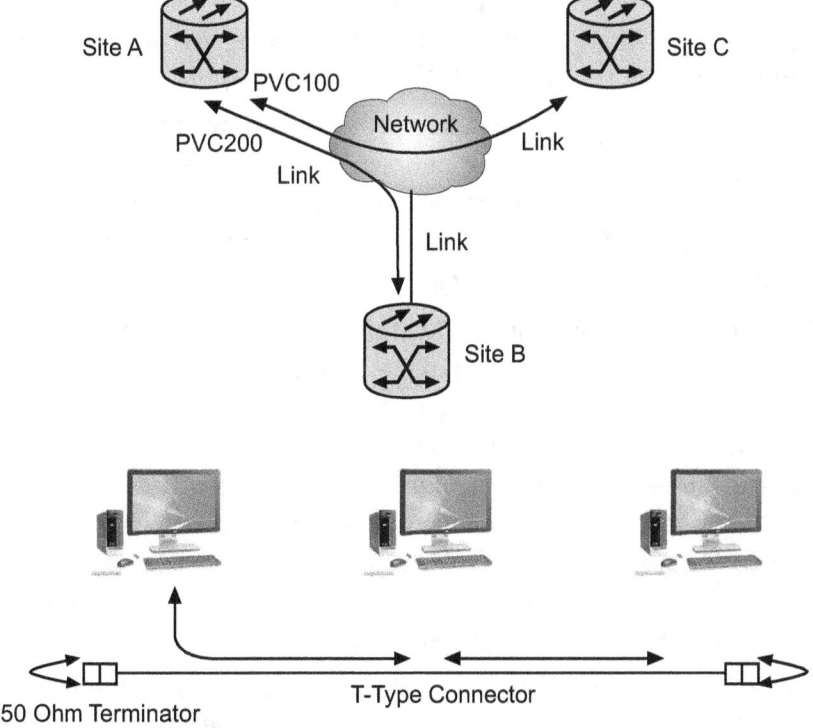

Fig. 5.9 : Point-to-Multipoint Connection

Traffic Management in ATM :

Traffic management is a set of network actions that monitor and control the flow of traffic. It provides each traffic stream its desired level of bandwidth and control over cell loss, cell delay, and delay variation. Traffic management supports differentiated service levels. It prevents different streams from interfering with one another and keeps each stream from consuming more than its contracted share of network resources. And traffic management protects the network and its end systems from congestion.

Network Congestion:

Congestion in a network is a state in which performance degrades due to the saturation of network resources such as communication links, processor cycles, and memory buffers. Network congestion has been well recognized as a resource-sharing problem.

Congestion Control :

Congestion control is concerned with allocating the resources in a network such that it can operate at an acceptable performance level when the demand exceeds or is near the capacity 4 of the network resources (i.e. to prevent it from operating in the congested region for any significant period of time). Without proper congestion control mechanisms, the throughput (or net work) may be reduced considerably under heavy load.

Role of ATM Traffic Management :

ATM technology is intended to support a wide variety of services and applications. The control of ATM network traffic is basically related to the ability of the network to provide properly differentiated Quality of Service (QoS) for network applications.

A primary role of traffic management is to protect the network and the end-system from congestion in order to achieve network performance objectives. An additional role is to promote the efficient use of network resources. Proper traffic management helps ensure efficient and fair operation of networks in spite of constantly varying demand and ensure that users get their desired quality of service.

One of the challenges in designing ATM traffic management was to maintain the QoS for various classes while attempting to make maximal use of network resources. Congestion control deals only with the problem of reducing load during overload. Traffic management deals not only with load reduction under overload but more importantly it tries to ensure that the QoS guarantees are met inspite of varying load conditions. Thus, traffic management is required even if the network is under loaded. The problem is especially difficult during periods of heavy load particularly if the traffic demands cannot be predicted in advance. This is why congestion control, although only a part of the traffic management issues, is the most essential aspect of traffic management.

For each category, a set of parameters is given to describe both the traffic presented to the network, and the Quality of Service (QoS) which is required of the network. A number of traffic control mechanisms are defined, which the network may utilize to meet the QoS objectives.

Quality of Service :

Quality of Service (QOS) parameters include cell loss, the delay and the delay variation incurred by the cells belonging to the connection in an ATM network. QOS parameters can be either specified explicitly by the user or implicitly associated with specific service requests. A limited number of specific QOS classes will be standardised in practice.

ATM QoS Parameters :

Peak Cell Rate (PCR): The maximum instantaneous rate at which cells will be injected by a traffic source Sustained Cell Rate (SCR). The average cell rate when measured over a "long" interval.

Cell Loss Ratio (CLR) : The fraction of cells lost in the network due to transmission errors (typically very small in optical networks) and being dropped because of congestion. The probability of a cell being dropped can be reduced by setting the CLP (Cell loss priority) bit in the cell header to 0.

Cell Transfer Delay (CTD) : The time it takes a cell to traverse the ATM network from entry to exit. It is comprised of propagation delays, queuing delays and actual transmission time.

Cell Delay Variation (CDV) : A measure of the variance of the CTD, the CDV can be measured in various ways. One way is to compute the difference between the x percentile delay (where x > 100) and the minimum delay **Cell Delay Variation Tolerance (CDVT)** The maximum tolerated difference between the nominal interarrival time and the actual interarrival time of arriving cells. (Jain seems to apply this to injected cells) Maximum Burst Size (MBS). The size of the maximum continuous burst of cells that can be sent.

Burst Tolerance (BT) : BT = (MBS 1) (1 / SCR   1 / PCR)

Minimum Cell Rate (MCR) : Minimum rate at which cells will be injected.

ATM Service Categories :

An ATM network can provide Virtual Path (VP) or Virtual Channel (VC) connections with distinct levels of service. The ATM Forum Traffic Management Specification 4.0 defines five service categories:

- **CBR (Constant Bit Rate) :** CBR resembles a leased-line service. It is suited to connections requesting a static amount of bandwidth that is continuously available during the connection lifetime. This bandwidth amount is characterized by a Peak Cell Rate (PCR) value. Typical applications for CBR are videoconferencing, interactive audio (telephony), audio/video distribution (television, distance learning, pay-per-view), and audio/video retrieval (video-on-demand, audio library).

- **VBR-rt (Real-Time Variable Bit Rate) :** VBR-rt is intended for real-time applications — that is, applications requiring tightly constrained delay and delay variation, but not necessarily a fixed transmission rate. VBR-rt connections are characterized in terms of a Peak Cell Rate (PCR), Sustained Cell Rate (SCR), and Maximum Burst Size (MBS). VBR-rt can be used by native ATM voice with bandwidth compression and silence suppression. VBR-rt is also suitable for some types of multimedia communications. VBR-nrt is appropriate for non-real-time bursty applications that require service guarantees from the network.

- **VBR-nrt (Non-Real-Time VBR)** : Like VBR-rt, VBR-nrt connections are characterized in terms of a PCR, SCR, and MBS. Typical applications for this service are data transfers for trans- action-processing applications such as airline reservation, banking transactions, and process monitoring. Frame relay traffic can also use VBR-nrt service.

- **UBR (Unspecified Bit Rate)** : UBR is intended for non-real-time, bursty applications that are tolerant of delay and loss. UBR service does not specify service guarantees and is sometimes referred to as the "best effort" service. It can be used for text/data/image transfers, remote terminal (telecommuting), e-mail, store-and-forward networks, LAN interconnection, LAN emulation, supercomputer applications, remote procedure call, distributed file services, and computer process swapping/paging.

- **ABR (Available Bit Rate)** : ABR is used by applications that can tolerate a Minimum Cell Rate (MCR) but are able to adapt to feedback from the network to take advantage of available bandwidth. On the establishment of an ABR connection, the end-system specifies both a PCR and an MCR. A flow-control mechanism, which supports several types of feedback, fairly allocates the available bandwidth among ABR connections. Application examples for ABR are similar to those for UBR.

The Traffic Contract

An ATM traffic contract specifies the characteristics of a connection, as defined by a Connection Traffic Descriptor and a QoS. The traffic contract is an agreement between an ATM end-system and the ATM network. As long as the end-system sends traffic across the UNI in conformance with the Connection Traffic Descriptor, the network will enforce the negotiated QoS.

The Connection Traffic Descriptor includes two key elements: the Cell Delay Variation Tolerance (CDVT) and the Source Traffic Descriptor.

The Source Traffic Descriptor is a set of parameters that describes the connection's expected bandwidth utilization. These parameters are: Peak Cell Rate (PCR), Sustainable Cell Rate (SCR), Maximum Burst Size (MBS), and Minimum Cell Rate (MCR).

With these parameters, an ATM end-system describes its average and peak bandwidth requirements and its maximum packet size. The network determines whether it can establish the connection and still meet the required QoS level for all connections including the new one. This calculation is referred to as Connection Admission Control (CAC). Conformance is determined by a Usage Parameter Control (UPC) function at the ingress (input edge) to the network.

Traffic Control in ATM Networks :

There are many functions involved in the traffic control of ATM networks which are given as follows.

1. **Connection Admission Control :** This can be defined as the set of actions taken by the network during the call set-up phase to establish whether a VC/VP connection can be made. A connection request for a given call can only be accepted if sufficient network resources are available to establish the end-to-end connection maintaining its required quality of service and not affecting the quality of service of existing connections in the network by this new connection.

   There are two classes of parameters which are to be considered for the connection admission control. They can be described as follows.

   A. Set of parameters that characterize the source traffic i.e. Peak cell rate, Average cell rate, burstiness and peak duration etc.

   B. Another set of parameters to denote the required quality of service class expressed in terms of cell transfer delay, delay jitter, cell loss ratio and burst cell loss etc.

2. **Usage Parameter Control (UPC) and Network Parameter Control (NPC) :** UPC and NPC perform similar functions at User-to-Network Interface and Network-to- Node Interface respectively. They indicate the set of actions performed by the network to monitor and control the traffic on an ATM connection in terms of cell traffic volume and cell routing validity. This function is also known as "Police Function". The main purpose of this function is to protect the network resources from malicious connection and to enforce the compliance of every ATM connection to its negotiated traffic contract.

   An ideal UPC/NPC algorithm meets the following features.

   1. Capability to identify any illegal traffic situation.

   2. Quick response time to parameter violations.

   3. Less complexity and much simplicity of implementation.

3. **Priority Control :** CLP (Cell Loss priority) bit in the header of an ATM cell allows users to generate different priority traffic flows and the low priority cells are discarded to protect the network performance for high priority cells. The two priority classes are treated separately by the network Connection Admission Control and UPC/NPC functions to provide two requested QOS classes.

4. **Network Resource Management :** Virtual Paths can be employed as an important tool of traffic control and Network resource management in ATM networks. They are used to simplify Connection Admission Control (CAC) and Usage/ Network parameter control (UPC/NPC) that can be applied to the aggregate traffic of an entire virtual path. Priority control can also be implemented by separating traffic types requiring different quality of service (QOS) through virtual paths. VPs can also be used to distribute messages efficiently for the operation of particular traffic control schemes like congestion notification. Virtual paths are also used in statistical multiplexing to separate traffic to prevent statistically multiplexed traffic from being interfered with other types of traffic. For example : Guaranteed bit rate traffic.

5. **Traffic Shaping :** Traffic shaping changes the traffic characteristics of a stream of cells on a VPC or VCC by properly spacing the cells of individual ATM connections to decrease the peak cell rate and also to reduce the cell delay variation. Traffic shaping must preserve the cell sequence integrity of an ATM connection. Traffic shaping is an optional function for both network operators and end users. It helps the network operator in dimensioning the network more cost-effectively and it is used to ensure conformance to the negotiated traffic contract across the user-to network interface in the customer premises network.

Usage Parameter Control :

In ATM, excessive reservation of resources by one user affects traffic for other users. So the throughput must be policed at the user-network interface by a Usage Parameter Control (UPC) function in the network to ensure that the negotiated connection parameters per VCC or VPC between network and subscriber is maintained by each other user. Traffic parameters describe the desired throughput and QOS in the contract. The traffic parameters are to be monitored in real time at the arrival of each cell. ITU-T (formerly CCITT) recommends a check of the peak cell rate (PCR) of the high priority cell flow (CLP = 0) and a check of the aggregate cell flow (CLP = 0 and 1), per virtual connection.

Frame discard :

A cell discarded by an ATM switch can cause the loss of an entire packet. Then End-to-end error recovery may be required through packet retransmission by a higher-layer protocol. Mild congestion could results to severe congestion.

To prevent this growth, an ATM switch can discard cells on a frame basis, using Early Packet Discard (EPD) and Partial Packet Discard (PPD) mechanisms. EPD discards an entire incoming packet after detecting that congestion is about to occur. If congestion goes undetected or the EPD action is not drastic enough to mitigate the congestive event, PPD discards all of the remaining cells (with the exception of the End-of-Packet cell) of a packet that has been partially discarded.

EPD and PPD together can significantly reduce partial packet loss and improve overall packet throughput, especially for TCP/IP applications using UBR service. Even better TCP/IP performance can be achieved with the addition of per-VC discard.

EPD/PPD schemes that discard packets indiscriminately may suffer a "global synchronization" problem. This phenomenon is when TCP/IP packets going through a congested switch are discarded at the same time. Related end systems react to packet loss in a synchronous fashion, causing congestion and reduced throughput. Randomizing EPD/PPD actions on VCs can avoid global synchronization.

5.3 Very Small Aperture Terminal (VSAT)

A very small aperture terminal (VSAT) is a small telecommunication earth station that receives and transmits real-time data via satellite.

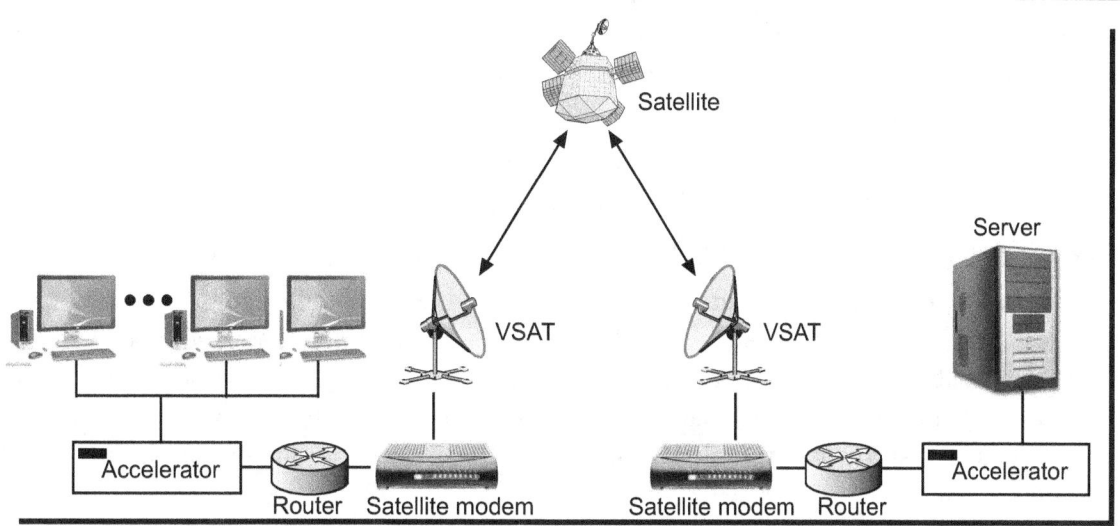

Fig. 5.10 : VSAT

VSAT end users have a box that acts as an interface between the computer and the external antenna or satellite dish transceiver. The satellite transceiver sends data to and receives data from the geostationary satellite in orbit. The satellite sends and receives signals from an earth station, which acts as the hub for the system. Each end user is connected to this hub station through the satellite in a star topology. For one VSAT user to communicate with another, the data has to be sent to the satellite. Then the satellite sends the data to the hub station for further processing. The data is then retransmitted to the other user via a satellite. The majority of VSAT antennas range from 30 inches to 48 inches. Data rates typically range from 56 Kbps up to 4 Mbps.

VSAT applications :

VSATs are most commonly used to transmit:

- Narrowband data : This includes point of sale transactions such as credit card, polling or radio-frequency identification (RFID) data, or supervisory control and data acquisition (SCADA) data.

- Broadband data : For the provision of satellite Internet access to remote locations, Voice over Internet Protocol (VoIP) or video.

VSATs are also used for transportable, on-the-move communications (using phased array antennas) and mobile maritime communications. Possible VSAT applications include: point of sale, Internet access, file distribution, database access, environmental monitoring, police, customs and excise offices.

Capacity is not a problem with both very small to very large networks all viable. Growth is possible in small steps thus keeping costs related to actual use. VSAT systems provide a both data and, if required, voice services. Voice or data services with the possibility of communication between all sites (i.e. in mesh mode connection) requires slightly larger antennas and/or transmitter power amplifiers. Mesh networks may be attractive for telephony applications such as remote industry, hotel chains, exploration, disaster, emergency relief etc.

VSAT systems are attractive where the coverage area is large. In these areas, quick installation is required and terrestrial alternatives are difficult to organise.

Advantages of VSAT Satellite Networks:

- **Access in Remote Locations:** A Satellite in the Geo Synchronous orbit can cover around 33% of the earth's surface and can provide connectivity to any region covered by it. A satellite can also focus on a particular high density region. Multiple satellites can work together to provide global coverage. This is very useful for remote locations (rural areas, ships and coastal regions, hills, etc) where there is limited or no terrestrial connectivity.

  A VSAT network can carry data as well as latency sensitive applications like voice and video. This is the reason why the DTH (Cable TV), Internet Radio and other technologies have found applications in real life situations. IP based Multi-cast applications like audio and video streaming are possible (Eg. Digital Signage applications).

- **Internet Access:** A VSAT Network can provide Internet access in addition to the point to point WAN links. It is all set to create a next major wave in the consumer broadband industry with the launch of satellites. This offers very high throughput, in the non metro regions.

- **Rapid deployment:** Once the Satellite is put in to its orbit, the deployment at the customer premises. It can be done (usually in hours) if the equipment is available, with minimum training. The deployment can be done in any region, irrespective of where it is located.

- **VPN:** Satellites support encryption of all data transmitted between two sites or multiple sites, which make the creation of Virtual Private Networks (VPN) possible. The VSAT networks could find more acceptance in the corporate and Government/ Defense connectivity requirements due to this reason.

- **QoS:** VSAT Networks support QoS (Quality of Service) and Layer 2 prioritization policies to be applied across the WAN link which enables real time applications to be deployed across the network.

- **Mobile Access:** Mobile access has been another traditional strength of a satellite network. For example:

  1. TV broadcasters make broadcasts from anywhere - even when they are on the move.

  2. Mobile Internet access, while on the move.

- **Bandwidth Allocation:** It is possible to allocate bandwidth based on individual applications.

For example:

1. In business communications,

2. In the critical business applications like ERP that always have a certain dedicated bandwidth across the VSAT networks.

- **Scalable:** VSAT networks can be easily and cost effectively be scaled to accommodate multiple locations across the globe. In fact, some of the largest customers of VSAT networks have as many as 10,000 sites on a single network!

- **Cost:** Though the initial investment (service provider perspective) might be high in terms of the cost of satellites and putting them in the orbit, the running cost (end point terminals and on going subscription) is coming down rapidly – That's why applications like Direct To Home (Cable TV) are broadcasted directly from satellites to homes at a reasonable cost to the subscriber.

- **Standards based:** VSAT networks are standards based and support IP (Internet Protocol) and its variants through a protocol called IPoS (Internet Protocol over Satellite – TIA 1008). Since the developments are standards based, it enables the creation of a healthy ecosystem of terminal, hub and ancillary equipment manufacturers and hence new innovations and improvements are faster.

- **Reliable:** Satellite Networks are very reliable (having up-times in the magnitude of 99.5% and above) and have been field tested for many years now. Mission critical applications like Bank ATM's, Navy and Point of Sale appliances use VSAT.

- **Inter-operation with Terrestrial Networks:** An interesting area where the VSAT service providers are getting stronger is the comprehensive network provision and management. For example: MPLS networks in the metro areas and VSAT networks in the rural areas for the same company can inter-operate with each other acting as a single network.

- **Back-up to Terrestrial Networks:** VSAT networks make a good back up network to the terrestrial networks (Leased Lines, MPLS circuits, Broadband DSL Connectivity, Internet Leased Lines, etc) and there are certain customized plans available for backup exclusively with satellite service providers. VSAT networks are not affected by natural calamities like earthquakes, storms etc. Some network routers come with optional VSAT modules for terminating the VSAT links and providing auto fail-over during the failure of terrestrial network links.

- **Single Hop:** Satellite transmissions are single hop (mostly) when compared to the multiple hops that the communications based on terrestrial networks need to take to reach to their destination. Some factors like router performance etc, depends on multiple service providers and hence end to end QoS may not be possible with terrestrial public networks.

- **Cost per connection is independent of the distance:** With a VSAT network, the cost per node is independent on the number of nodes and also distance between the various nodes.
- **Bandwidth on Demand:** VSAT networks support and are better suited for Bandwidth on Demand services than their terrestrial counterparts

Limitations of VSAT Technology:

- **Extremely high initial cost** needed for building and launching satellites in the Geo-Synchronous orbit.
- **Bit Error Rate** is common for satellite based technologies.
- **Rain Attenuation** might affect the performance of VSAT communications under rainy conditions, latencies (>200 ms) are still higher than their terrestrial equivalent technologies (<100 ms).
- **Careful direction** of subscriber side terminals and dish antennas are critical for proper working.
- **Trained man power** is required for installation and maintenance.

  Other competitive technologies (Internet Leased Lines, 3G/HSDPA/4G Cellular technologies etc) offer much higher bandwidth at a lower cost than what is possible by VSAT based networks, the antennas need to be fixed outside the offices or homes hence making them susceptible to damage or theft.

VSAT Resource Access Techniques

The access techniques used in VSAT mainly are

1. SCPC:

The term "Single Channel Per Carrier" or SCPC is widely used term in satellite communication. The satellite transponder will have some bandwidth and it is divided into number of carriers considering bandwidth across each carrier.

For example, C band satellite having total bandwidth of 500MHz is divided among many transponders having 36MHz bandwidth. Each transponder's band is used to carry information in the form of voice or data. This voice or data lines are called as channel.

SCPC means single channel (i.e. either voice channel or data channel) per RF carrier of a satellite transponder. For Star configuration it will have two hops. Information flows from Transmitting VSAT to satellite, satellite to hub station, hub to satellite and further from satellite to receiving VSAT.

SCPC is mainly useful for defense applications requiring dedicated connection from one end to the other with encryption always enabled.

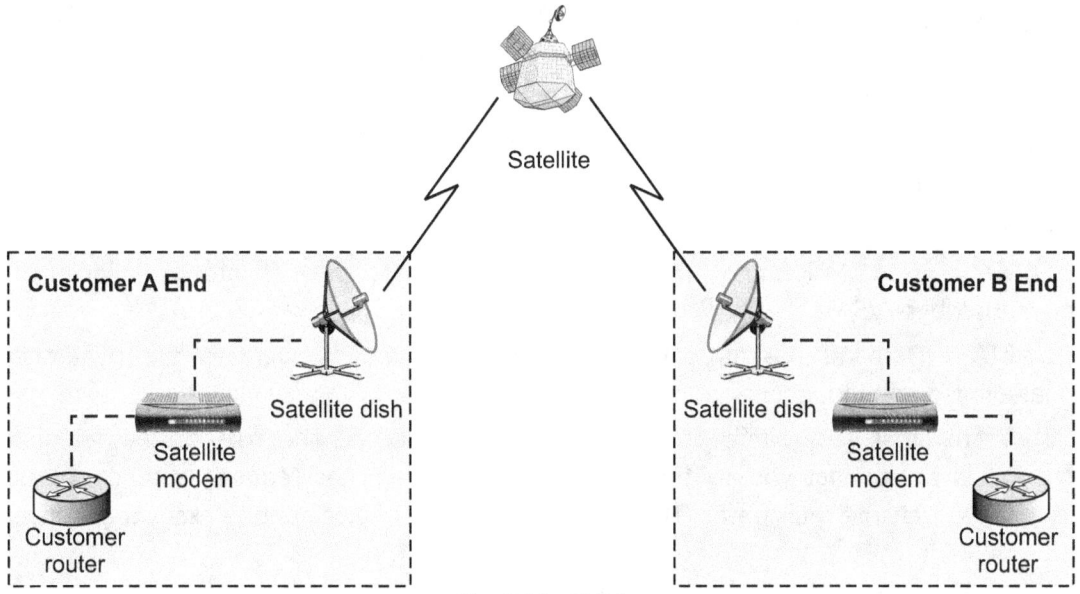

Fig. 5.11 : SCPC

2. MCPC:

The term "multiple channels per carrier" or MCPC is widely used in satellite communication. All the channels are multiplexed before being modulated as shown in the figure. TDM is used for multiplexing information of individual multiple channels into a serial frame of bits.

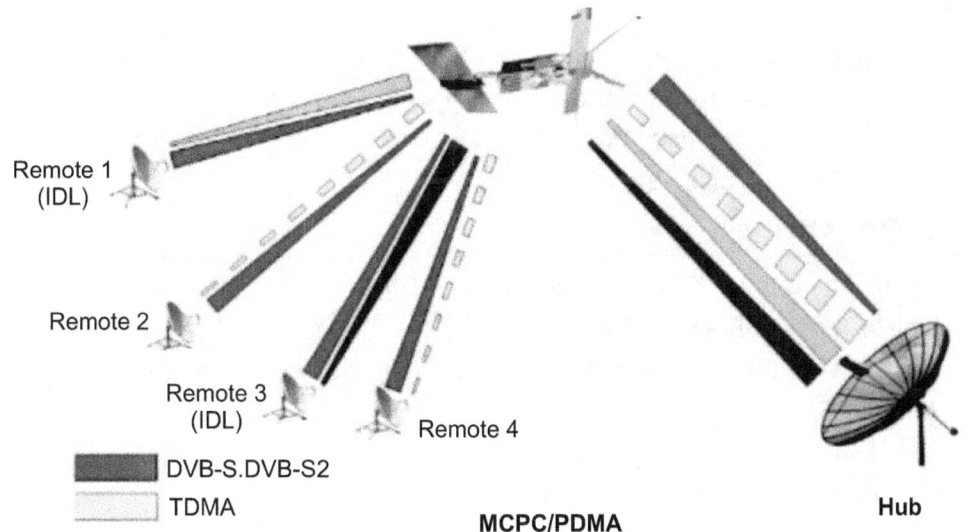

Fig. 5.12 : MCPC/PDMA in satellite access technology

3. FDMA

Frequency Division Multiple Access, here entire band of frequencies is divided into multiple RF channels/carriers. Each carrier is allocated to different users. For example in GSM entire frequency band of 25 MHz is divided into 124 RF carriers of bandwidth 200 KHz each.

In Satellite applications entire transponder band of 500 MHz is divided into 24 channels each of bandwidth 40MHz (36 MHz useful and 4MHz guard band).

There are two main types of FDMA scheme used in satellite network. SCPC (Single channel per carrier) and MCPC (multiple channel per carrier). MCPC uses FDM or TDM as multiplexing scheme.

FDMA Types

FAMA : Fixed Assignment Multiple Access, here frequencies are pre-allocated to users/subscribers/VSATs.

DAMA : Demand Assignment Multiple Access, here frequencies are dynamically allocated based on requests.

The scheme is very similar to a telephone connection. The role of the telephone exchange is to connect you to the desired number. Remotes requires a time slot or a frequency to transmit their traffic. The Hub plays the role of a telephone exchange, between any two VAST's.

- NMS allocates each remote a time slot or a frequency to transmit this traffic.
- The attributed frequency or time slot will not be released until the end of the transmission. The hub plays the role of a telephone exchange, between any two VSAT's.
- The DAMA service addresses point to point voice, fax, and data communication requirements of remote sites.

4. TDMA :

Time Division Multiple Access, here entire bandwidth is shared among different subscribers at fixed predetermined or dynamically assigned time intervals/slots. For example in GSM each RF carrier is used/shared by 8 users at different time instants.

TDMA uses TDM multiplexing technique.

Practice Questions

1. Explain The terms: ISDN and B-ISDN.
2. Explain Terms : BRI and PRI in ISDN.
3. What is ATM network? Write short note on ATM traffic Management.
4. What is VSAT?
5. Which are Access Techniques of VSAT?
6. For which purposes VSATs are used?
7. Explain the term : Quality of Service in network?
8. What is a Traffic Contract in ATM network?
9. Which are types of ISDN?
10. Explain the ATM reference Model.

Chapter 6...

IP ADDRESSING AND ROUTING

Contents ...

6.1   Internet Protocol

6.2   IP Addresses

6.3   Network Masks

6.4   Network and Broadcast addresses

6.5   Address Classes

6.6   Loopback Address

6.7   IP Routing Concepts

6.8   Routing Tables

6.9   Stream & Packets

6.10 Sliding Windows

6.11 Role and Features of IP, TCP/IP

6.12 TCP Connections Types and Working.

6.13 IPV6: The Next Generation Protocol

- Practice Questions

6.1 Internet Protocol

The Internet Protocol (IP) is a network layer (Layer 3) protocol that contains addressing information and some control information that enables packets to be routed. Internet protocol is responsible for routing the data packets between the source machine and destination machine. IP is connectionless internetworking protocol. IP relies on protocols in other layers to establish the connection if connection oriented service is required, as well as to provide error detection and error recovery.

Each IP datagram is handled independently and each one can follow a different route to the destination. So there is always a possibility of receiving the packets out of order at the destination.

IP relies on ICMP (Internet Control Message Protocol) to report errors in the processing of datagrams and provide additional administrative and status message.

IP Packet Format :

An IP datagram consists of a header part and a data part. The header has a 20-byte fixed part and a variable length optional part. The header format is shown in Fig. 6.1.

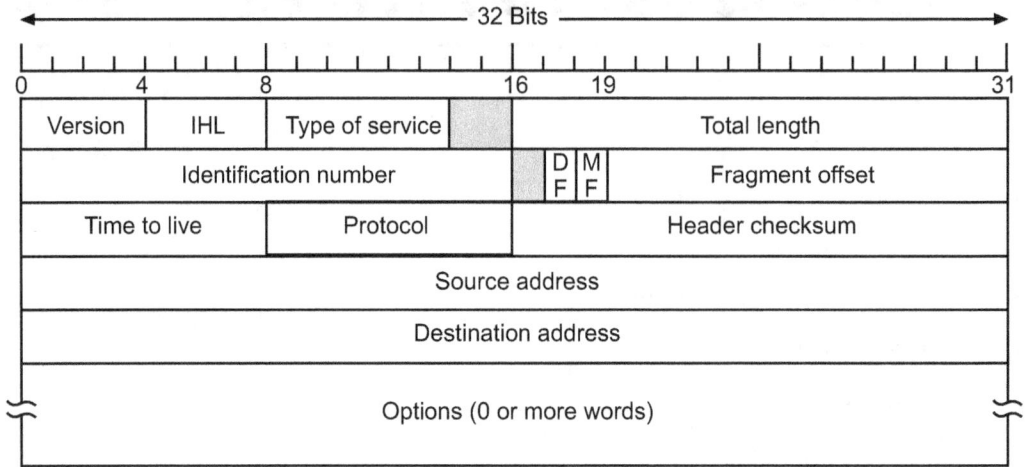

Fig. 6.1: IP header

Various fields of IP header are as follows:

1. **Version:** The *Version* field keeps track of which version of the protocol the datagram belongs to. Currently there are two versions of IP protocol, IPV4 and IPV6.

2. **Internet Header Length (IHL) :** This is 4 bit field. It contains the length of the header expressed in 4 bytes. The size of header without including the Options field is 20 bytes.

3. **Type of Service:** This is 8 bit field contains a combination of 1-bit flags that can be used to request delay, throughput and reliability parameters. It requests what priority the packet should have.

4. **Total Length:** This 16 bit field contains the total length of IP datagram. The total length includes the length of header as well as the data field. The maximum length is 65535 bytes.

5. **Identifier:** It helps the destination host to determine, to which datagram the newly arrived fragment belongs to. All the fragments of the datagram contain the same identification number. This helps packet reconstruct from several fragments.

6. **DF flag (Don't Fragment):** It is 1 bit field. DF stands for Do Not Fragment.
   If destination is incapable of putting the fragments of the datagram, back together that time DF flag is set to 1. It instructs the router for not doing fragments of the datagram.

7. **MF (More Fragments):** This is 1 bit field. MF stands for More Fragments. All fragments except the last one has this bit set. It is needed to know the destination that all fragments of the datagram are arrived.

8. **Fragment Offset:** This is 13 bit field, shows the relative position of this fragment with respect to the whole datagram. It is the offset of the data in the original datagram measured in units of 8 bytes.

9. **Time to live (TTL) :** This field is used as counter (number of HOPs), which is used to limit packet lifetimes. If the maximum lifetime is 255, the counter is decremented on visiting each hop. When the counter becomes zero, the packet is discarded from the network.

10. **Protocol:** This 8 bit field defines the higher-level protocol that uses the service of the IP layer. An IP datagram can encapsulate the data from several higher level protocols such as TCP, UDP, ICMP and IGMP. This field specifies the final destination protocol to which the IP datagram should be delivered. The value of this field for different higher level protocols (in network as well as transport layer protocols) is shown in the following Table 6.1.

Table 6.1: Protocols

Value	Protocol
1	ICMP
2	IGMP
6	TCP
17	UDP
89	OSPF

11. **Header Checksum:** This field verifies the header only. This field is used to detect the error in the header.

12. **Source address:** This 32 bit field defines the IP address of the source. This field must remain unchanged during the time the IP datagram travels from the source host to the destination host.

13. **Destination Address:** This 32 bit field defines the IP address of the destination. This field must remain unchanged during the time the IP datagram travels from the source host to the destination host.

14. **Options:** Allows IP to support various options, such as security.

6.2 IP Addresses

An IP address is a binary number that uniquely identifies computers and other devices on a TCP/IP network. Every computer on network requires an IP address to communicate with other computer. An IP is a 32-bit number comprised of a host number and a network prefix, both of which are used to uniquely identify each node within a network.

To make these addresses more readable, they are broken up into 4 bytes, or octets, where any 2 bytes are separated by a period. This is commonly referred to as dotted decimal notation. The first part of an Internet address identifies the network on which the host resides, while the second part identifies the particular host on the given network. This creates the two-level addressing hierarchy.

All hosts on a given network share the same network prefix but must have a unique host number. Similarly, any two hosts on different networks must have different network prefixes but may have the same host number. Here is a simple example of an IP address: 192.168.1.1

An additional value, called a subnet mask, determines the boundary between the network and host components of an address. Subnet masks are 32 bits long and are typically represented in dotted-decimal (such as 255.255.255.0) or the number of networking bits (such as /24). The networking bits in a mask must be contiguous and the host bits in the subnet mask must be contiguous. 255.0.255.0 is an invalid mask. A subnet mask is used to mask a portion of the IP address, so that TCP/IP can tell the difference between the network ID and the host ID. TCP/IP uses the subnet mask to determine whether the destination is on a local or remote network.

- Class A subnet mask 255.0.0.0

- Class B subnet mask 255.255.0.0

- Class C subnet mask 255.255.255.0

The bytes of an IP address can be further classified into two parts: the Network Part and the Host Part. The example below shows the components of the Class B network 192.168.1.100.

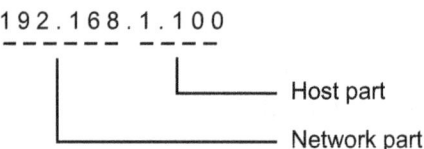

Fig. 6.2 : IP address

1. Network Part:

This part specifies the unique number assigned to the particular network. It is also the part that identifies the class of network assigned. In the above example, the network part takes up two bytes of the IP address, namely 192.168.

2. Host Part:

This is the part of the IP address that you assign to each host, and uniquely identifies each host on your network. Note that for each host on network, the network part of the address will be the same, but the host part must be different.

IP addresses can be displayed in three typical formats:

Binary Notation Binary notation is the format that systems on the network use to process the address. An example of binary notation is 11000000.10101000.00000001. 01100100.

Hexadecimal Notation Hexadecimal notation is the format typically used when identifying IPv6 addresses. An example of hexadecimal notation of an IPv4 address is C0.A8.01.64

Dotted-decimal Notation Dotted-decimal notation is the format that is typically used for displaying the IP address in a human-readable format. An example of dotted-decimal notation is 192.168.1.100.

The IP addressing scheme is integral to the process of routing IP datagram through an internetwork. There are two kinds of IP addresses, Public (also called globally unique IP addresses) and Private.

1. Public IP addresses are assigned by the Internet Assigned Numbers Authority (IANA). The addresses are guaranteed to be globally unique and reachable on the Internet. This assures that multiple computers do not have the same IP address.

An Internet service provider (ISP) obtains a range of public IP addresses from IANA, and then the ISP assigns the addresses to customers to use when they connect to the Internet through the ISP. Public IP addresses are routable on the Internet, which means that a computer with a public IP address is visible to other computers on the Internet.

2. Private IP addresses cannot be used on the Internet. IANA has set aside three blocks of IP addresses that cannot be used on the global Internet. These three blocks of addresses are private IP addresses, and they are used for networks that do not directly connect to the Internet.

A Private IP address is within one of the following blocks or range of addresses:

- 192.168.0.0/16: This block allows valid IP addresses within the range 192.168.0.1 to 192.168.255.254.
- 172.16.0.0/12: This block allows valid IP addresses within the range 172.16.0.1 to 172.31.255.254.
- 10.0.0.0/8: This block allows valid IP addresses within the range 10.0.0.1 to 10.255.255.254.

Fig. 4.4 shows IDs of IP address.

Network ID is used to identify the subnet upon which the host resides. The host ID is used to identify the host itself within the given subnet.

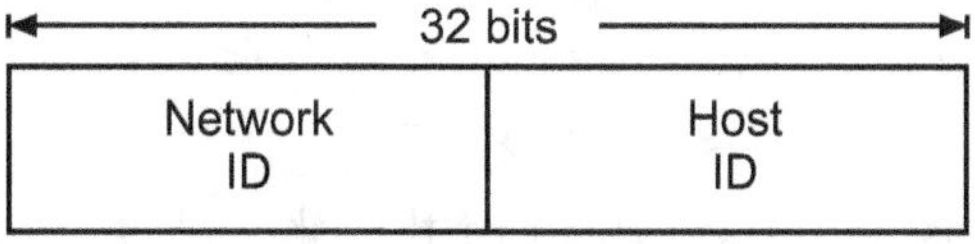

Fig. 6.3 : IDs of IP address

Parts of an IP AddressP:

Any TCP/IP network will require a unique network number and every host on a TCP/IP network will require a unique IP address. Before registering the networking and obtaining a network number, it is critical that understand how IP addresses are constructed.

Addressing :

A network address serves as a unique identifier for a computer on a network. When set up correctly, computers can determine the addresses of other computers on the network and use these addresses to send messages to each other.

Physical, Logical and Port Addresses :

In TCP/IP three different levels of addresses are used, (See Fig. 6.4).

1. **Physical Address (Hardware Address or Link Address):** Physical address is basically a part of Data Link Layer.

2. **Logical Address (IP Address):** Logical address is a part of Network Layer.

3. **Port Address:** Port address is a part of Transport Layer.

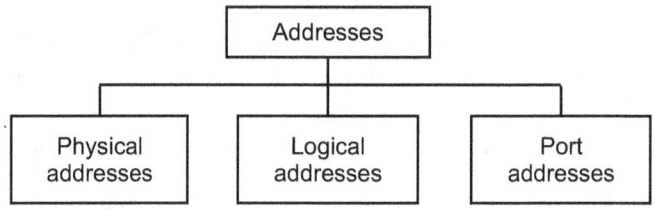

Fig. 6.4: Addresses in TCP/IP

Data link addresses sometimes are referred to as Physical or Hardware addresses. Data link addresses usually exist within a flat address space and have a pre-established and typically fixed relationship to a specific device.

Network addresses usually exist within a hierarchical address space and sometimes are called Virtual or Logical addresses.

Physical Address

Physical addresses are used to identify the specific host that data is being transmitted to. Physical addresses have a local significance only. This means that the physical address can only be used to communicate between hosts that share a common subnet or network segment. This is a legacy that goes back to the early days of networking where all hosts on a network received the electric signal that contained the data (such as how Ethernet functions). To ensure that only the host that the data belongs to processes the data, physical addresses were used to distinguish between hosts.

MAC address is the most common form of the physical address that is used for TCP/IP communications. This address is a vendor-assigned value that is supposed to be globally unique and that identifies the actual network card. MAC addresses are 6 bytes in length and typically consist of a 3-byte vendor identifier (known as the Organizationally Unique Identifier or OUI) followed by a 3-byte unique identifier that is assigned by the vendor.

The use of physical addresses allows for network communications between two hosts on the same subnet regardless of logical address and is a key element to how routing works. For example, when two hosts on different networks want to communicate with each other, they use their logical addresses to identify each other from a global perspective. When they transmit the data to each other, each host physically addresses the frames to the hardware address of their corresponding router interface. This allows the routers to receive and process the frames directly, while still being able to use the logical addresses to determine the original source and final destination of the data.

Fig. 6.5 illustrate how this process works.

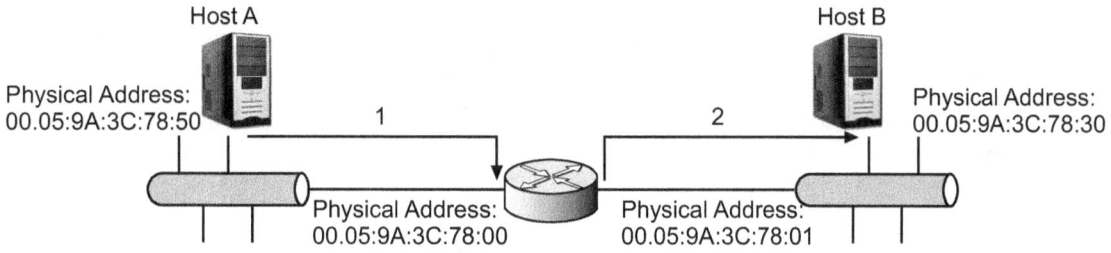

Fig. 6.5: Physical Addressing of data between hosts

The process is as follows:

1. Host A logically addresses the data for Host B but physically addresses it to 00:05:9A:3C:78:00, the router interface physical address.

2. The router receives the data, because it is physically addressed to it, but realizes that logically it must be delivered to Host B. Therefore, it rebuilds the frame, using the physical address of the interface on the same network as Host B (00:05:9A:3C:78:01) and physically addresses it to 00:05:9A:3C:78:30.

Logical addresses

Logical addresses are the counterpart to physical addresses and allow for the identification of hosts and the delivery of data to hosts regardless of physical location or proximity to each other. So, logical addresses must have a true global significance, and must be unique within all interconnected network segments. TCP/IP uses IP addresses as the logical addressing method.

Port addresses

Port address is a feature of a network device that translates TCP or UDP communications made between a host and port on an outside network. It allows a single IP address to be used for many internal hosts. Port address can automatically modify the IP packets' destination or source host IP and port fields belonging to its internal hosts.

Subnetting

Subnetting is a process of dividing large network into the smaller networks based on layer 3 IP address.

Subnetting allows you to create multiple logical networks that exist within a single Class A, B, or C network. If you do not subnet, you are only able to use one network from your Class A, B, or C network, which is unrealistic.

Each data link on a network must have a unique network ID, with every node on that link being a member of the same network. If you break a major network (Class A, B, or C) into smaller subnetworks, it allows you to create a network of interconnecting subnetworks. Each data link on this network would then have a unique network/subnetwork ID. Any device, or gateway, connecting n networks/subnetworks has n distinct IP addresses, one for each network / subnetwork that it interconnects.

In order to subnet a network, extend the natural mask using some of the bits from the host ID portion of the address to create a subnetwork ID. For example, given a Class C network of 204.17.5.0 which has a natural mask of 255.255.255.0, you can create subnets in this manner:

```
204.17.5.0 -        11001100.00010001.00000101.00000000
255.255.255.224 -   11111111.11111111.11111111.11100000
                    -------------------------|sub|----
```

By extending the mask to be 255.255.255.224, you have taken three bits (indicated by "sub") from the original host portion of the address and used them to make subnets. With these three bits, it is possible to create eight subnets. With the remaining five host ID bits, each subnet can have up to 32 host addresses, 30 of which can actually be assigned to a device since host ids of all zeros or all ones are not allowed (it is very important to remember this). So, with this in mind, these subnets have been created.

```
204.17.5.0 255.255.255.224        host address range 1 to 30
204.17.5.32 255.255.255.224       host address range 33 to 62
204.17.5.64 255.255.255.224       host address range 65 to 94
204.17.5.96 255.255.255.224       host address range 97 to 126
204.17.5.128 255.255.255.224      host address range 129 to 158
204.17.5.160 255.255.255.224      host address range 161 to 190
204.17.5.192 255.255.255.224      host address range 193 to 222
204.17.5.224 255.255.255.224      host address range 225 to 254
```

The network subnetting scheme in this section allows for eight subnets, and the network might appear as:

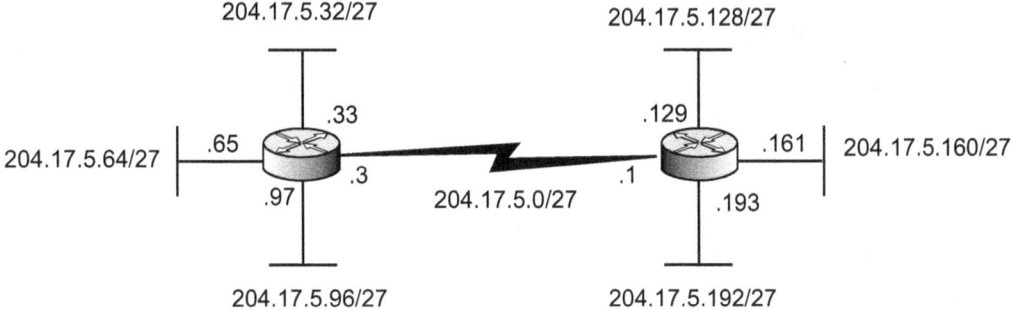

Fig. 6.6 : Network sunetting

Notice that each of the routers in Fig. 6.6, is attached to four subnetworks, one subnetwork is common to both routers. Also, each router has an IP address for each subnetwork to which it is attached. Each subnetwork could potentially support up to 30 host addresses.

Advantage of Subnetting :

1. Subnetting breaks large network in smaller networks and smaller networks are easier to manage.

2. Subnetting reduces network traffic by removing collision and broadcast traffic, that overall improve performance.

3. Subnetting allows you to apply network security polices at the interconnection between subnets.

4. Subnetting allows you to save money by reducing requirement for IP range.

Supernetting:

The inverse of subnetting is supernetting. Instead of moving mask bits to the right of the default mask for subnetting, we move mask bits to the left for supernetting. With subnetting we create more network address at the host expense of host address. With supernetting we create more host address at the expenses of network addresses.

Supernetting is not for users, it is only for Internet Service Providers who are attempting to obtain the most efficient allocation of IP address using the A,B,C class scheme. In this method networks bits are convert into host bits.

Supernetting combines two smaller blocks of contiguous IP addresses together into a continuous range of addresses that form a larger super-net. You create a supernet whenever you need to aggregate blocks of IP addresses together. The two most common situation where you would create and use a supernet are:

- Expanding the number of hosts in a local area network
- Aggregating several routes to a contiguous block of IP addresses, into a single route announcement

6.3 Network Masks

A mask used to determine which subnet an IP address belongs to. An IP address has two components, the Network Address and the Host Address.

For example, consider the IP address 150.215.017.009. Assuming this is part of a Class B network, the first two numbers (150.215) represent the Class B network address, and the second two numbers (017.009) identify a particular host on this network.

Subnet Masks:

A subnet is simply a subdivision of a network address that can be used to represent one LAN on an internetwork or the network of one of an ISP's clients. Thus, a large ISP might have a Class A address registered to it and it might farm out pieces of the address to its clients in the form of subnets. In many cases, a large ISP's clients are smaller ISPs, which in turn supply addresses to their own clients.

Subnetting is the process of breaking down a main class A, B, or C network into subnets for routing purposes. A subnet mask is the same basic thing as a netmask with the only real difference being that breaking a larger organizational network into smaller parts, and each smaller section will use a different set of address numbers.

This will allow network packets to be routed between subnetworks. When doing subnetting, the number of bits in the subnet mask determine the number of available subnets.

Two to the power of the number of bits minus two is the number of available subnets.

$$\text{Number of available subnets} = 2^n - 2$$

where, n : Number of bits

When setting up subnets the following must be determined:

- Number of segments, and
- Hosts per segment.

Subnetting provides the following advantages:

- **Network traffic isolation:** There is less network traffic on each subnet.
- **Simplified Administration:** Networks may be managed independently.
- **Improved security:** Subnets can isolate internal networks so they are not visible from external networks.

A 14 bit subnet mask on a class B network only allows 2 node addresses for WAN links. A routing algorithm like OSPF (Open Shortest Path First) must be used for this approach.These protocols allow the Variable Length Subnet Masks (VLSM). RIP (Routing Information Protocol) and IGRP (Interior Gateway Routing Protocol) don't support this. Subnet mask information must be transmitted on the update packets for dynamic routing protocols for this to work. The router subnet mask is different than the WAN interface subnet mask.

One network ID is required by each of:

* Subnet,
* WAN connection.

One host ID is required by each of:

* Each NIC on each host.
* Each router interface

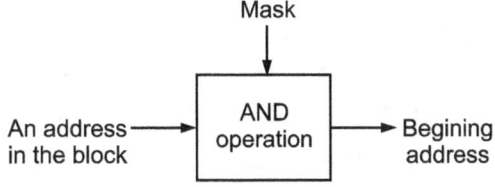

Fig. 6.7: Masking Concept

Types of subnet masks:

o **Default:** Fits into a Class A, B, or C network category.

o **Custom:** Used to break a default network such as a Class A, B, or C network into subnets.

Fig. 6.8: AND operation

Default Masks

Class	Mask in Binary	Mask in dotted-decimal
A	11111111 00000000 00000000 00000000	255.0.0.0
B	11111111 11111111 00000000 00000000	255.255.0.0
C	11111111 11111111 11111111 00000000	255.255.255.0

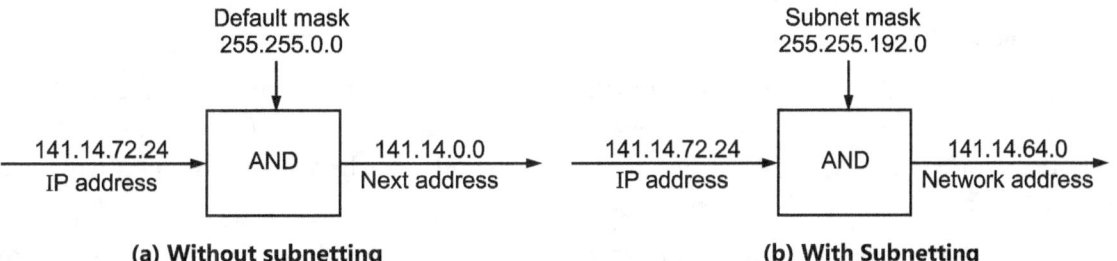

(a) Without subnetting   **(b) With Subnetting**

Fig. 6.9 : Default mask and Subnet mask

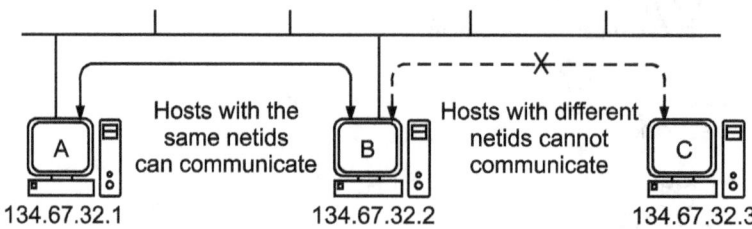

Fig. 6.10 : Host communication on a local network

A subnet is defined by applying a bitmask, the subnet mask, to the IP address. If a bit is on the mask, the equivalent bit in the address is interpreted as a network bit. If the bit in the mask is off, the bit belongs to the host part of the address. The subnet is only known locally.

To the rest of the Internet, the address is still interpreted as a standard IP address.

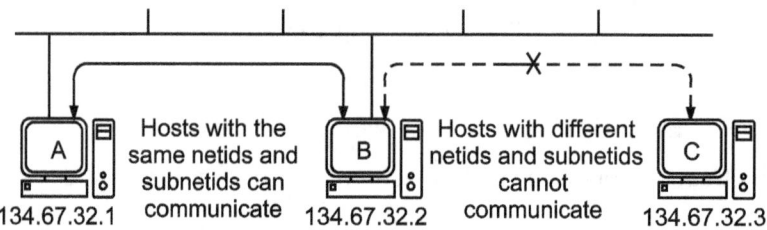

Fig. 6.11 : Host communication with sub netting

6.4 Network and Broadcast Addresses

Network Address

A network address serves as a unique identifier for a computer on a network. When set up correctly, computers can determine the addresses of other computers on the network and use these addresses to send messages to each other. One of the best known form of network addressing is the Internet Protocol (IP) address. IP addresses consist of four bytes (32 bits) that uniquely identify all computers on the public Internet.

Another popular form of address is the Media Access Control (MAC) address. MAC addresses are six bytes (48 bits) that manufacturers of network adapters burn into their products to uniquely identify them.

Broadcast Address

A broadcast address is a logical address at which all devices connected to a multiple-access communications network are enabled to receive datagrams. A message sent to a broadcast address is typically received by all network-attached hosts, rather than by a specific host.

This address is an IP address that targets all systems on a specific subnet instead of single hosts.

The broadcast address of any IP address can be calculated by taking the bit complement of the subnet mask, sometimes referred to as the **reverse mask**, and then applying it with a bitwise OR calculation to the IP address in question.

Some systems that are derived from BSD (Berkeley Software Distribution) use zeros-broadcasts instead of ones-broadcasts. This means that when a broadcast address is created, the host area of the IP address is filled while displayed using binary values with zeros instead of ones.

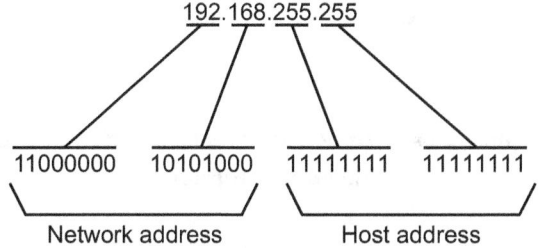

Fig. 6.12: Broadcast address

Most operating systems use ones-broadcasts. Changing systems to use zeros-broadcasts will break some communications in the wrong environments, so the user should understand needs before changing the broadcast address or type.

Math Example:

If a system has the IP address 192.168.12.220 and a network mask of 255.255.255.128, what should the broadcast address for the system be? To do this calculation, convert all numbers to binary values. For bitwise, remember that any two values where at least one value is 1, the result will be 1, otherwise the result is 0.

IP Address:	11000000.10101000.00001100.11011100
Reverse Mask:	00000000.00000000.00000000.01111111
bitwise OR:	————————————————————
Broadcast:	11000000.10101000.00001100.11111111

Convert the binary value back to octal and the resulting value is 192.168.12.255.

6.5 Address Classes

The most complicated part of an IP address is that the division between the network identifier and the host identifier is not always in the same place. IP addresses can have various numbers of bits assigned to the network identifier, depending on the size of the network. For example: A hardware address, , consists of 3 bytes assigned to the manufacturer of the network adapter and 3 bytes that the manufacturer itself assigns to each card.

The IANA defines several different classes of IP addresses, which provide support for networks of different sizes, as shown in Fig. 6.13 (a).

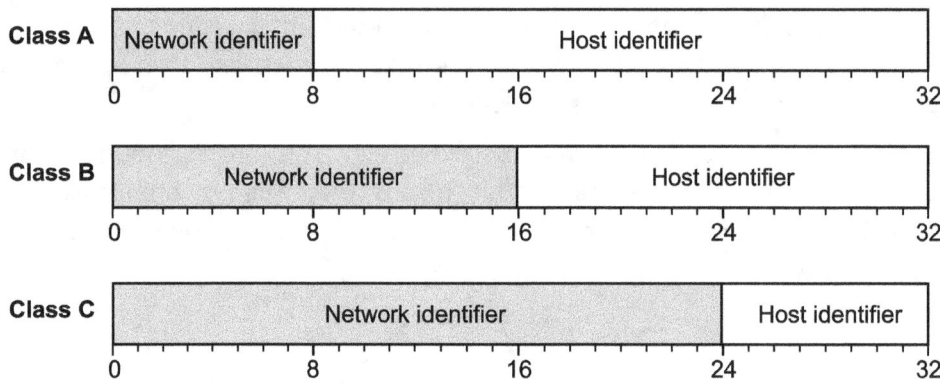

Fig. 6.13 (a): Three Classes of IP addresses have different sized network and host identifiers

IP Network Address :

IP addresses are broken into 4 octets (IPv4) separated by dots called dotted decimal notation. An octet is a byte consisting of 8 bits. The Ipv4 addresses are in the following form:

192.168.10.1

There are two parts of an IP address:

- Network ID
- Host ID

The various classes of networks specify additional or fewer octets to designate the network ID versus the host ID.

Class	1st Octet	2nd Octet	3rd Octet	4th Octet
	Net ID		Host ID	
A				
	Net ID		Host ID	
B				
		Net ID		Host ID
C				

Fig. 6.13 (b) : Classes of Network ID vs Host ID

A network address is an identifier for a node or network interface of a telecommunications network. The addressing scheme for class A through E networks is shown below.

Note: We use the 'x' character here to denote don't care situations which includes all possible numbers at the location. It is many times used to denote networks.

Table 6.2 : Addressing scheme for classes in Network ID

Network Type	Address Range	Normal Netmask	Comments
Class A	001.x.x.x to 126.x.x.x	255.0.0.0	For very large networks
Class B	128.1.x.x to 191.254.x.x	255.255.0.0	For medium size networks
Class C	192.0.1.x to 223.255.254.x	255.255.255.0	For small networks
Class D	224.x.x.x to 239.255.255.255		Used to support multicasting
Class E	240.x.x.x to 247.255.255.255		Reserved for future use

1. Class A Addressing:

- First byte specifies the network portion (8 bits).
- Remaining bytes specify the host portion (24 bits).
- The highest order bit of the network byte is always 0.
- Network values of 0 and 127 are reserved.
- This class is used for large addressing networks.
- There are 126 class A networks.
- There are more than 16 million host values for each class A network.

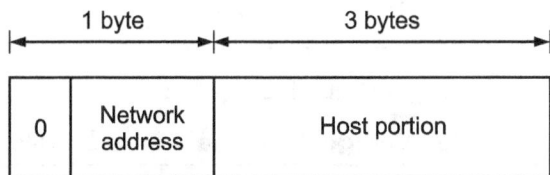

Fig. 6.14: Class A IP Addresses

2. Class B Addressing:

- The first two bytes specify the network portion (16 bits).
- The last two bytes specify the host portion (16 bits).
- The highest order bits 6 and 7 of the network portion are 10.
- This class is used for medium sized addressing networks.
- There are more than 16 thousand class B networks.
- There are 65 thousand nodes in each class B network.

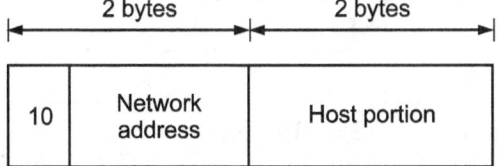

Fig. 6.15 : Class B IP addresses

3. Class C Addressing:

*   The first three bytes specify the network portion (24 bits).

*   The last byte specifies the host portion (8 bits).

*   The highest order bits 5, 6 and 7 of the network portion are 110.

*   This class is used for addressing small sized networks.

*   There are more than 2 million class C networks.

*   There are 254 nodes in each class C network.

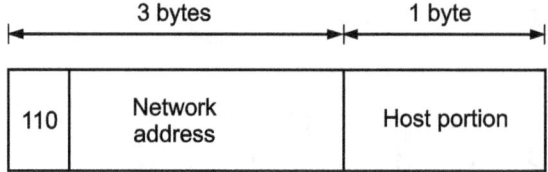

Fig. 6.16 : Class C IP addresses

4. Class D Addressing:

*   Class D address defines a group-ID and used for multicasting.Internet authorities have designated some multicast addresses to specific groups.

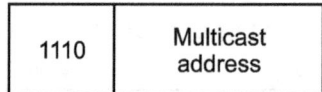

Fig. 6.17 : Class D IP addresses

Table 6.3 : Categories of class D addresses

Address	Group
224.0.0.0	Reserved
224.0.0.1	ALL SYSTEMS on this SUBNET
224.0.0.2	ALL ROUTERS on this SUBNET
224.0.0.4	DVMRP ROUTERS
224.0.0.5	OFPFIGP ALL ROUTERS
224.0.0.6	OSPFIGP Designated ROUTERS
224.0.0.7	ST Routers
224.0.0.8	ST Hosts
224.0.0.9	RIP2 Routers
224.0.0.10	IGRP Routers
224.0.0.11	Mobile Agents

5. Class E Addressing:

- Fig. 6.18 shows address format of class E addressing. This format begins with 1110 that shows it is reversed for the future use.

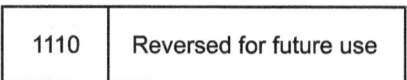

1110	Reversed for future use

Fig. 6.18: Class E IP addresses

6.6 Loopback Address

Loopback address is a special IP number (127.0.0.1) that is designated for the software loopback interface of a machine. The loopback interface has no hardware associated with it, and it is not physically connected to a network. The loopback interface allows IT professionals to test network applications. IP defines a loopback address used to test.

Programmers often use loopback testing for preliminary debugging after a network application has been created. To perform a loopback test, a programmer must have two application programs that are intended to communicate across a network. Each application includes the code needed to interact with TCP/IP protocol software. Instead of executing each program on a separate computer, the programmer runs both the programs on a single computer and instructs them to use a loopback IP address when communicating.

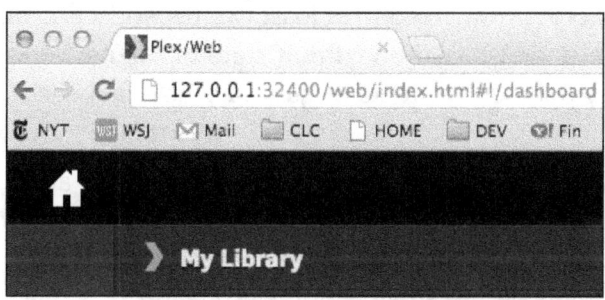

Fig. 6.19 : Loopback Address

When one application sends data to another, data travels from the protocol stack to the IP software, which forwards it back up through the protocol stack to the second program. Thus, the programmer can test the program logic quickly without needing two computers and without sending packets across a network. IP reserves the network prefix 127/8 for use with loopback. In above fig., the host address used with 127 is irrelevant that means all host addresses are treated the same. By convention, programmers often use host number 1, making 127.0.0.1 the most popular form of loopback address. The 32400 is the port number.

During loopback testing, no packets ever leave a computer that means the IP software forwards packets from one application program to another. Consequently, the loopback address never appears in packet traveling across a network. A loopback address tells the computer not to test its connections to another computer, but to test its own basic network setup.

6.7 IP Routing Concepts

Routing is the process of taking a packet from one device sending it through the network to another device in a different network, performed at Network Layer of OSI model. It is the act of moving information across an internetwork from a source to a destination.

Routing schemes differ in their delivery semantics:

- **Unicast** delivers a message to a single specific node.
- **Broadcast** delivers a message to all nodes in the network.
- **Multicast** delivers a message to a group of nodes that have expressed interest in receiving the message.
- **Anycast** delivers a message to any one out of a group of nodes, typically the one nearest to the source.
- **Geocast** delivers a message to a geographic area.

The routing function is performed by Internet Protocol (IP) on networks running TCP/IP. Routing is a way to get one packet from one destination to the next. Routers or software in a computer determines the next network point to which a packet should be forwarded towards its final destination.

The router or software is connected to at least two networks and makes a decision which way to send each data packet based on current state of the networks it is connected to. A router is located at any point of networks or gateway, including each Internet POP (Point of Presence).

A router or software creates or maintains a table of the available routes and their conditions and uses this information along with distance and cost algorithms to determine the best route for a given packet. Typically, a packet may travel through a number of network points with routers before arriving at its destination.

Routing Components:

Routing involves two basic activities: determining optimal routing paths and transporting information groups (typically called packets) through an internet work. In the context of the routing process, the latter of these is referred to as packet switching. Although packet switching is relatively straightforward, path determination can be very complex.

Path Determination:

Routing protocols use metrics to evaluate what path will be the best for a packet to travel. A metric is a standard of measurement, such as path bandwidth, that is used by routing algorithms to determine the optimal path to a destination. To aid the process of path determination, routing algorithms initialize and maintain routing tables, which contain route information. Route information varies depending on the routing algorithm used.

Routing algorithms fill routing tables with a variety of information. Destination/next hop associations tell a router that a particular destination can be reached optimally by sending the packet to a particular router representing the "next hop" on the way to the final destination. When a router receives an incoming packet, it checks the destination address and attempts to associate this address with a next hop. Fig. 6.20 depicts a sample destination/next hop routing table.

Routing tables also can contain other information, such as data about the desirability of a path. Routers compare metrics to determine optimal routes, and these metrics differ depending on the design of the routing algorithm used.

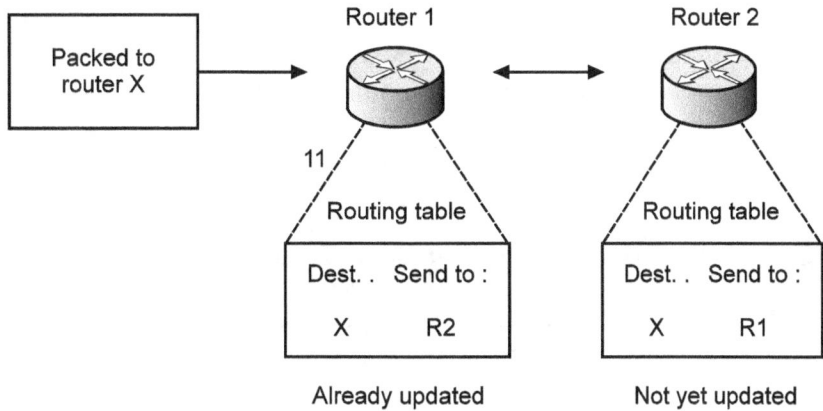

Fig. 6.20 : Destination/next hop routing table

Routers communicate with one another and maintain their routing tables through the transmission of a variety of messages. The routing update message is one such message that generally consists of all or a portion of a routing table. By analyzing routing updates from all other routers, a router can build a detailed picture of network topology.

A link-state advertisement, another example of a message sent between routers, informs other routers of the state of the sender's links. Link information also can be used to build a complete picture of network topology to enable routers to determine optimal routes to network destinations.

(ii) Packet Switching:

Packet switching algorithm is relatively simple; it is the same for most routing protocols. In most cases, a host determines that it must send a packet to another host. Having acquired a router's address by some means, the source host sends a packet addressed specifically to a router's physical (Media Access Control [MAC]-layer) address, this time with the protocol (network layer) address of the destination host.

As it examines the packet's destination protocol address, the router determines that it either knows or does not know how to forward the packet to the next hop. If the router does not know how to forward the packet, it typically drops the packet. If the router knows how to forward the packet, however, it changes the destination physical address to that of the next hop and transmits the packet. The next hop may be the ultimate destination host. If not, the next hop is usually another router, which executes the same switching decision process. As the packet moves through the internetwork, its physical address changes, but its protocol address remains constant.

The preceding discussion describes switching between a source and a destination end system. The International Organization for Standardization (ISO) has developed a hierarchical terminology that is useful in describing this process. Using this terminology, network devices without the capability to forward packets between subnetworks are called end systems (ESs), whereas network devices with these capabilities are called intermediate systems (ISs). ISs are further divided into those that can communicate within routing domains (Intradomain ISs) and those that communicate both within and between routing domains (Interdomain ISs).

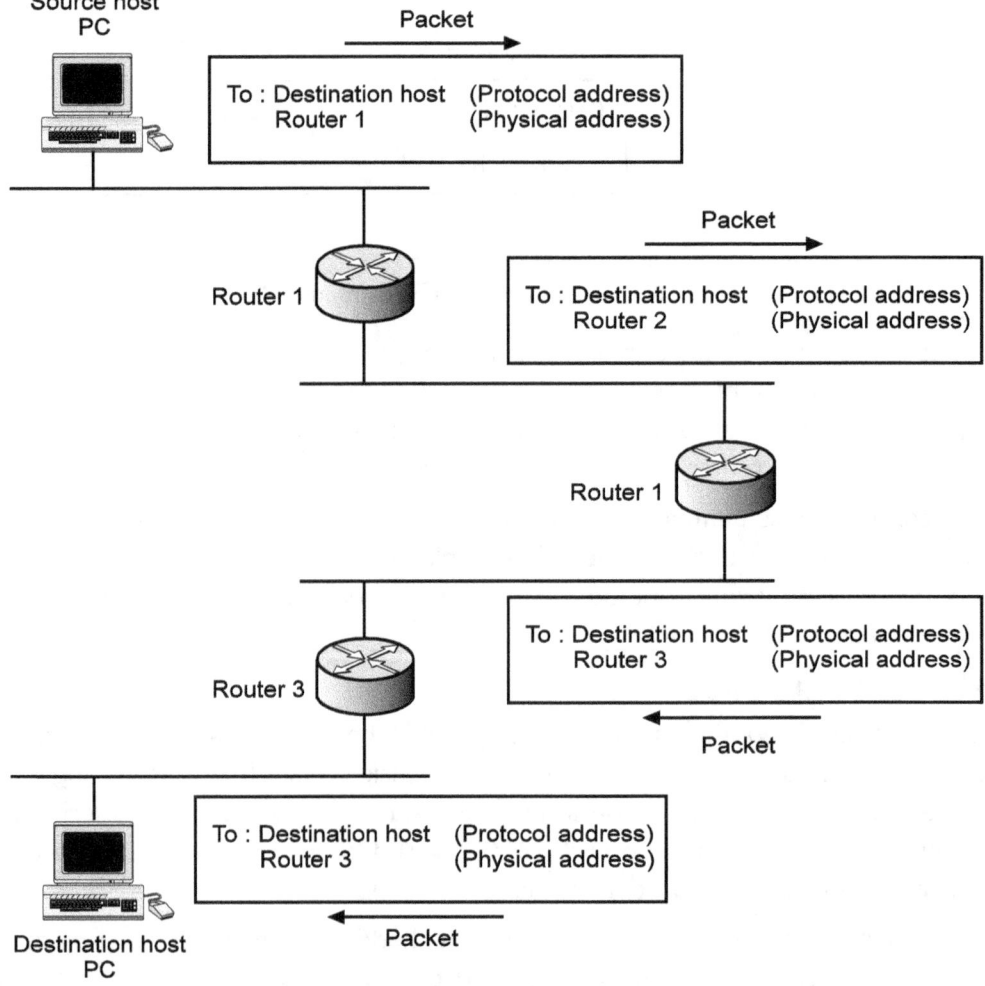

Fig. 6.21: Packet switching in Routing

A routing domain generally is considered a portion of an internetwork under common administrative authority that is regulated by a particular set of administrative guidelines. Routing domains are also called **autonomous systems**. With certain protocols, routing domains can be divided into routing areas, but inter domain routing protocols are still used for switching both within and between areas.

IP Routing Concepts :

IP Routing is the process of forwarding a packet based on the destination IP address. Routing occurs at a sending TCP/IP host and at an IP Router. In each case, the IP layer at the sending host or router must decide where to forward the packet. For IPv4, routers are also commonly referred to as "gateways".

To make these decisions, the IP layer consults a routing table stored in memory. Routing table entries are created by default when TCP/IP initializes, and entries can be added either manually or automatically.

What is IP Routing?

The movement of data from your computer to a known destination (computer) is known as Routing. IP Routing is a summed up process for the set of protocols (IP/TCP) that determine the path that data follows in order to travel across different networks from its source to its destination.

The moving of data from source to destination across multiple networks is controlled by routers. The series of routers makes use of IP routing protocols to build up a routing table consisting of remote network addresses. Following example shows how a network router connects other networks and also shows IP routing process.

For example:

```
R2#show IP route
[Output omitted]
Gateway of last resort is not set
C    192.168.1.32/27 is directly connected, fastEthernet0/1
C    192.168.1.0/27 is directly connected, fastEthernet0/2
C    10.10.1.0/30 is directly connected, serial 0/0/0
```

The Network C in the routing table means the networks are directly connected. Remote networks are not found and displayed in the routine table because, we have not added a routing protocol – such as RIP, EIGRP (Enhanced Interior Gateway Routing Protocol), OSPF etc. etc or configured Static routes.

Looking at the above output, when the network router receive a packet with the destination address of 192.168.1.10, the router will send the packet to interface fast Ethernet 0/2, and this interface will frame the packet and then send it out on the network segment to Network B.

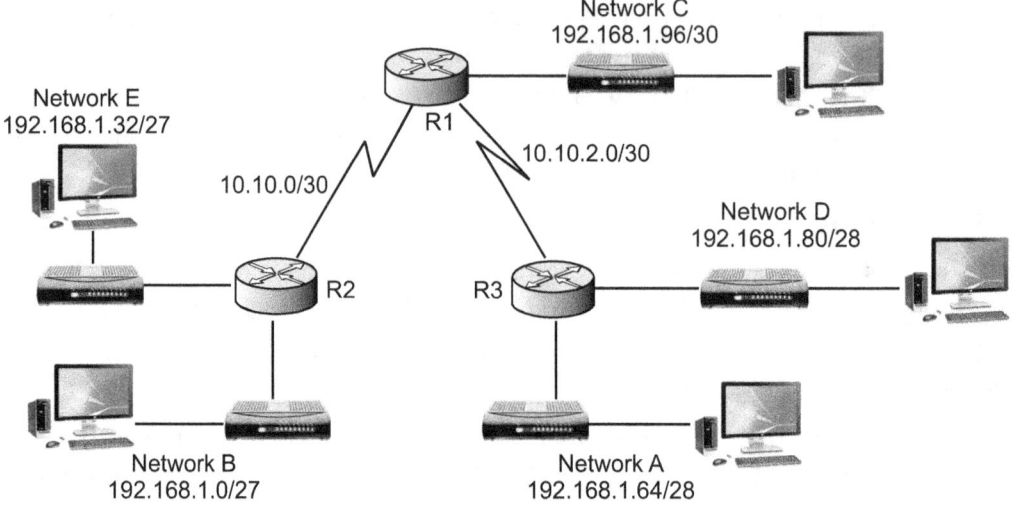

Fig. 6.22: IP Routing Process

Direct and Indirect Delivery:

Forwarded IP packets use at least one of two types of delivery based on whether the IP packet is forwarded to the final destination or whether it is forwarded to an IP router. These two types of delivery are known as direct and indirect delivery.

Direct delivery occurs when the IP node (either the sending host or an IP router) forwards a packet to the final destination on a directly attached subnet. The IP node encapsulates the IP datagram in a frame for the Network Interface layer. For a LAN technology such as Ethernet or Institute of Electrical and Electronic Engineers (IEEE) 802.11, the IP node addresses the frame to the destination's Media Access Control (MAC) address.

Indirect delivery occurs when the IP node (either the sending host or an IP router) forwards a packet to an intermediate node (an IP router) because the final destination is not on a directly attached subnet. For a LAN technology such as Ethernet or IEEE 802.11, the IP node addresses the frame to the IP router's MAC address.

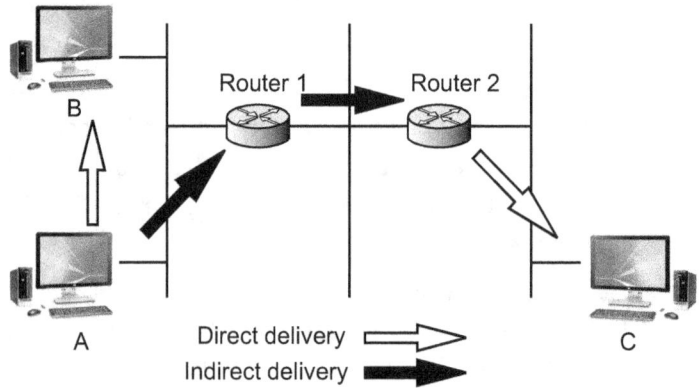

Fig. 6.23 : Direct and indirect delivery

End-to-end IP routing across an IP network combines direct and indirect deliveries. In Fig. 6.23, when sending packets to Host B, Host A performs a direct delivery.

When sending packets to Host C, Host A performs an indirect delivery to Router 1, Router 1 performs an indirect delivery to Router 2, and then Router 2 performs a direct delivery to Host C.

Types of Routing:

1. Static Routing:

Static routing is performed using a preconfigured routing table which remains in effect indefinitely, unless it is changed manually by the user. This is the most basic form of routing, and it usually requires that all machines remain on their respective networks.

For IP packets to be efficiently routed between routers on the IP network, routers must either have explicit knowledge of remote subnet routes or be properly configured with a default route.

On large IP networks, one of the challenges that you face as a network administrator is how to maintain the routing tables on your IP routers so that IP traffic travels along the best path and is fault tolerant.

Routing table entries on IP routers are maintained in two ways:

(i) Manually: Static IP routers have routing tables that do not change unless a network administrator manually changes them. Static routing requires manual maintenance of routing tables by network administrators. Static routers do not discover remote routes and are not fault tolerant. If a static router fails, neighbouring routers do not detect the fault and inform other routers.

(ii) Automatically: Dynamic IP routers have routing tables that change automatically when the routers exchange routing information. Dynamic routing uses routing protocols, such as Routing Information Protocol (RIP) and Open Shortest Path First (OSPF), to dynamically update routing tables. Dynamic routers discover remote routes and are fault tolerant. If a dynamic router fails, neighbouring routers detect the fault and propagate the changed routing information to the other routers on the network.

2. Dynamic Routing:

Dynamic routing is the automatic updating of routing table entries to reflect changes in network topology. A Router with dynamically configured routing tables is known as a dynamic router. Dynamic routers build and maintain their routing tables automatically by using a routing protocol, a series of periodic or on-demand messages that contain routing information.

Except for their initial configuration, typical dynamic routers require little ongoing maintenance and, therefore, can scale to larger networks. The ability to scale and recover from network faults makes dynamic routing the better choice for medium, large, and very large networks. Some widely used routing protocols for IPv4 are RIP, OSPF, and Border Gateway Protocol 4 (BGP-4).

Routing protocols are used between routers and represent additional network traffic overhead on the network. You should consider this additional traffic if you must plan WAN link usage. When choosing a routing protocol, you should pay particular attention to its ability to sense and recover from network faults.

How quickly a routing protocol can recover depends on the type of fault, how it is sensed, and how routers propagate information through the network. When all the routers on the network have the correct routing information in their routing tables, the network has converged. When convergence is achieved, the network is in a stable state, and all packets are routed along optimal paths.

When a link or router fails, the network must reconfigure itself to reflect the new topology by updating routing tables, possibly across the entire network. Until the network re-converges, it is in an unstable state. The time it takes for the network to re-converge is known as the 'convergence time'. The convergence time varies based on the routing protocol and the type of failure, such as a downed link or a downed router.

Types of Routing Protocols

Routing protocols are the software that allows routers to dynamically advertise and learn routes, determine which routes are available and which are the most efficient routes to a destination. Actually routing protocols are different types of algorithms or functions that are running in routers to find the paths.

Figure 6.24 displays a hierarchical view of Dynamic Routing Protocol classification.

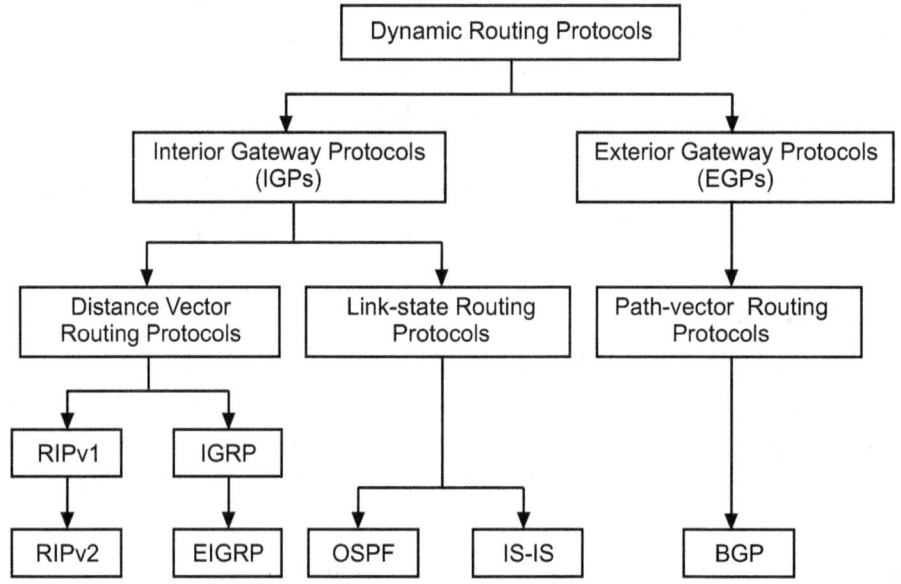

Fig. 6.24 : Classification of dynamic routing protocols

An autonomous system (AS) is a collection of routers under a common administration such as a company or an organization. An AS is also known as a routing domain. Typical examples of an AS are a company's internal network and an ISP's network.

The Internet is based on the AS concept; therefore, two types of routing protocols are required:

Interior Gateway Protocols (IGP): Used for routing within an AS. It is also referred to as intra-AS routing. Companies, organizations, and even service providers use an IGP on their internal networks. IGPs include RIP, EIGRP, OSPF, and IS-IS.

Exterior Gateway Protocols (EGP): Used for routing between autonomous systems. It is also referred to as inter-AS routing. Service providers and large companies may interconnect using an EGP. The Border Gateway Protocol (BGP) is the only currently viable EGP and is the official routing protocol used by the Internet.

Distance Vector Routing Protocols (3.1.4.3) :

Distance vector means that routes are advertised by providing two characteristics:

Distance: Identifies how far it is to the destination network and is based on a metric such as the hop count, cost, bandwidth, delay, and more

Vector: Specifies the direction of the next-hop router or exit interface to reach the destination

There are four distance vector IPv4 IGPs:

1. **RIPv1:** First generation legacy protocol
2. **RIPv2:** Simple distance vector routing protocol
3. **IGRP:** First generation Cisco proprietary protocol (obsolete and replaced by EIGRP)
4. **EIGRP:** Advanced version of distance vector routing

Link-State Routing Protocol :

In contrast to distance vector routing protocol operation, a router configured with a *link-state routing protocol* can create a complete view or topology of the network by gathering information from all of the other routers. To continue our analogy of sign posts, using a Link-State Routing Protocol is like having a complete map of the network topology. The sign posts along the way from source to destination are not necessary, because all Link-State routers are using an identical map of the network. A link-state router uses the link-state information to create a topology map and to select the best path to all destination networks in the topology.

RIP-enabled routers send periodic updates of their routing information to their neighbors. Link-state Routing Protocols do not use periodic updates. After the network has converged, a Link-State update is only sent when there is a change in the topology.

Link-state protocols work best in situations where:

- The network design is hierarchical, usually occurring in large networks.

- Fast convergence of the network is crucial.

- The administrators have good knowledge of the implemented link-state routing protocol.

There are two link-state IPv4 IGPs:

OSPF: Popular standards-based routing protocol

IS-IS: Popular in provider networks

Path Vector Routing Protocol :

A routing protocol, sometimes known as a Policy Routing Protocol, that is used to span different autonomous systems. Examples are EGP and BGP. A path vector routing protocol is more recent concept compared to both a distance vector protocol and the Link-State Protocol. In this vector protocol, a node does not just receive the distance vector for a particular destination from its neighbor; instead, a node receives the distance as well as the entire path to the destination from its neighbor. This path information is helpful in detecting loops.

Border Gateway Protocol (BGP) :

BGP is an exterior/interdomain protocol. The purpose of this protocol is to enable two different Autonomous Systems (AS) to exchange routing information so that IP traffic can flow across the autonomous system border. This protocol was developed to use in conjunction with internets that employ the TCP/IP protocol suite thats is based on the routing method called as "Vector Path Routing".

BGP is interdomain routing protocol that is used to exchange network reachability information among BGP routers (BGP speakers). Each BGP speaker establishes a connection with one or more BGP speakers (routers).Two routers are considered to be neighbours, if they are attached to the same subnetwork. If two routers are in different autonomous systems, they may wish to exchange routing information.

Boarder Gateway Protocol is used to exchange routing information for the Internet and is the protocol used between Internet Service Providers (ISP). It performs three functional procedures:

1. Neighbour Acquisition:

This procedure is used to exchange the routing information between two routers in different autonomous systems. To perform neighbour acquisition, one router sends an open message to another. If target router accepts the message, it returns a keep-alive message in response.

2. Neighbour Reachability:

Once a neighbour relationship is established, the neighbour reachability procedure is used to maintain the relationship. Both sides need to be assured that the other side still exists and is still engaged in the neighbour relationship. For this purpose both routers send keep-alive messages to each other.

3. Network Reachability:

Both sides routers maintain a database of the subnetworks that can be reached and the preferred route for reaching the subnetworks. If the database changes, router issues an update message that is broadcast to all other routers implementing BGP. By broadcasting this update message, all the BGP routers can build up and maintain routing information.

BGP connections inside an autonomous system are called as Internal BGP and BGP connections between different autonomous systems are called as External BGP.

BGP Messages:

BGP has four different types of messages: Open, Update, Keep-alive and Notification (Refer Fig. 6.25).

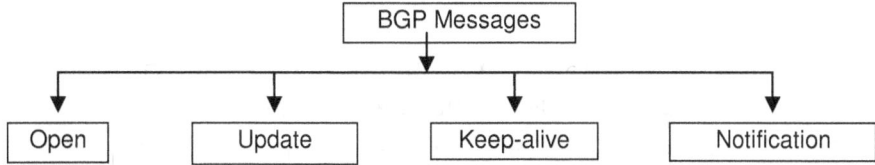

Fig. 6.25: Types of BGP messages

1. **Open Message:** To create a neighbourhood relationship, a router running BGP opens a connection with a neighbour and sends an open message. If neighbour accepts the neighbourhood relationship, it responds with a keep-alive message, which means that a relationship has been established between the two routers.

2. **Update Message:** The update message is the heart of BGP protocol. It is used by a router to withdraw destinations that have been advertised previously, announce a route to a new destination, or do both. Note that BGP can withdraw several destinations that were advertised before, but it can only advertise one new destination in a single update message.

3. **Keep-alive Message:** Routers running BGP protocols exchange keep-alive messages regularly to tell each other that they are alive.

4. **Notification Message:** A notification message is sent by a router whenever an error condition is detected or a router wants to close a connection.

Packet Format:

All the BGP packets (messages) share the same common header. The fields of this header are as follows, (Refer Fig. 6.26).

1. **Marker:** The 16 byte marker field is reserved for authentication. The sender may insert value in this field that would be used as part of an authentication mechanism to enable the recipient to verify the identity of the sender.

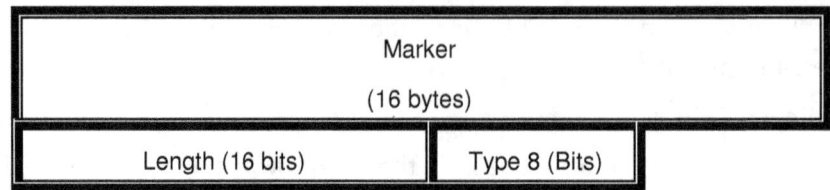

Fig. 6.26: BGP header format

2. **Length:** This 2 byte field defines the length of the total message including the header.

3. **Type:** This 8 bit (1 byte) field indicates the type of the message, which we have already seen.

BGP Operation:

To acquire a neighbor, a router first opens a TCP connection to the neighbor router of interest.Then it sends the OPEN message. The message identifies the AS to which the sender belongs and provides the IP address of the router. This message includes a hold timer parameter. The hold timer defines the maximum number of seconds that can elapse until one of the parties receives a keep-alive or update message from the other. If a router does not receive one of these messages during the hold time period, it considers the other party is dead. The KEEP-ALIVE messages are exchanged often enough as to not cause the hold timer to expire.

The recommended time between successive KEEP-ALIVE messages is one-third of the hold time interval. This value ensures that, the KEEP-ALIVE message arrive at the receiving router almost always before the hold timer expires, even if the transmission delay of TCP is variable. If hold time is zero, then KEEP-ALIVE messages will not be sent. When a BGP router detects an error, the router sends a NOTIFICATION message and then closes the TCP connection. After the connection is established, BGP peers exchange routing information by using the UPDATE message. The UPDATE message may contain three pieces of information:

1) Unfeasible Routes

2) Path Attributes and

3) Network Layer Reachability Information (NLRI).

An UPDATE message can advertise a single route and withdraw a list of routes. UPDATE messages are used to construct a graph of AS connectivity. It also withdraws multiple unfeasible routes.A BGP router uses Network Layer Reachability Information (NLRI), the total path attribute length and the path attributes to advertise a route. The NLRI field contains a list of IP address prefixed that can be reached by the router.

Routing Information Protocol (RIP)

The Routing Information Protocol, or RIP, as it is more commonly called, is one of the most enduring of all routing protocols. RIP used for smaller networks with a maximum of 15 routers. Today's open standard version of RIP, sometimes referred to as IP RIP, is formally defined in two documents: Request For Comments (RFC) 1058 and Internet Standard (STD) 56.

RIP is an Intradomain (interior) routing protocol used inside an Autonomous System (AS).This is very simple protocol based on Distance Vector Routing mechanism.

RIP Message Format (RIPv1):

The format of RIP version 1 message is shown in the Fig. 6.27.

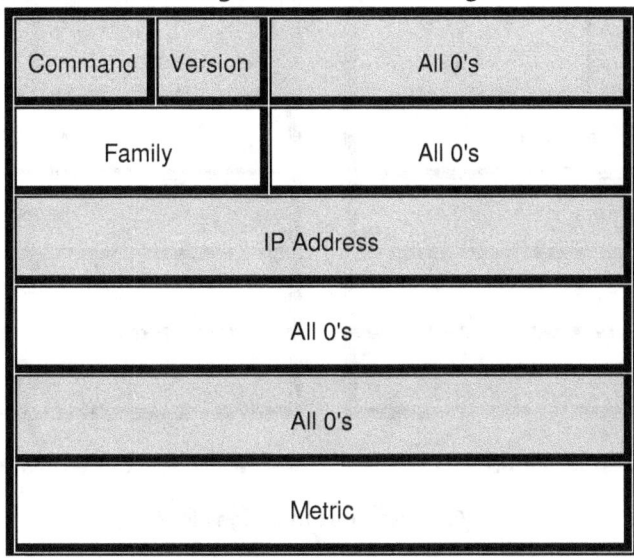

Fig. 6.27: RIP message format (RIPv1)

Following are the fields of RIP message:

o   Command: This is 8 bit field. It specifies the type of the message: Request and Response.

o   Version: This 8 bit field defines a version. There are two versions of RIP message. (RIPv1 and RIPv2)

o   Family: This 16 bit field defines the family of the protocol used. For TCP/IP protocol the value is 2.

o   IP Address: The address field defines the IP address of the specific entry.

o   Metric: This 32-bit field defines the hop count from the advertising router to the destination network. This value is between 1 to 15 for valid route and 16 for unreachable route.

RIP Messages:

1. Request Message:

A Request Message is sent by a router that has just come up or by a router that has some timeout entries. A request can ask about specific entries or all entries, (See Fig. 6.28).

2. Response Message:

Response can be either solicited or unsolicited. A solicited response is sent only in answer to a request. An unsolicited response, on the other hand, is sent periodically, every 30 seconds or when there is a change in the routing table.

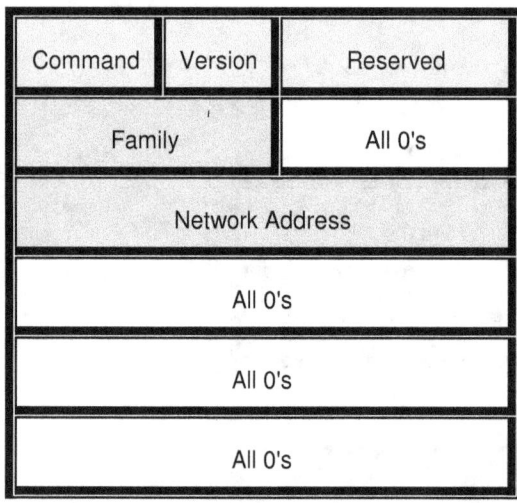
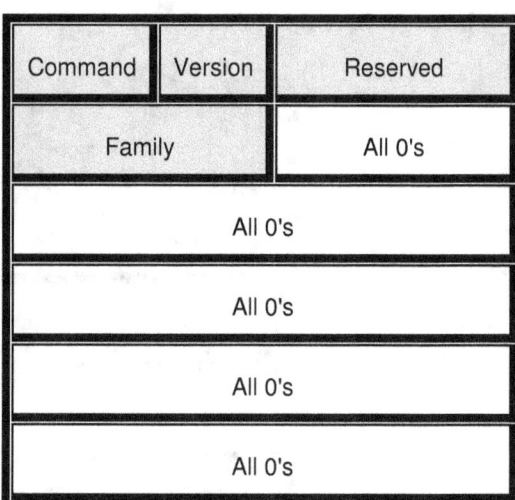

(a) Request for some   **(b) Request for all**

Fig. 6.28: Request messages in RIP

Timers in RIP:

1. Periodic Timer:

It controls advertising and regular update messages. Although the protocol specifies that this timer must be set to 30 seconds, the working model uses a random number between 25 and 35 seconds. It is countdown timer; when 0 is reached, the update message is sent, and the timer is randomly set once again.

2. Expiration Timer:

It governs the validity of the route.When router receives update information for a route, expiration timer is set to 180 sec for that particular route.Every time a new update for a particular route is received, the timer is reset.In normal situations, it occurs after every 30 seconds. If there is a problem on an internet and no update is received within the allotted 180 seconds, the route is considered as expired which means the destination is unreachable. Every route has its own expiration timer.

3. Garbage Collection Timer:

This timer is used to remove the routing information from the table when the route becomes invalid. When this timer becomes zero, the route is washed out from the routing table.

RIP Version 2:

RIPv2 was designed to overcome some of the shortcomings of RIPv1. The designers of version 2 have only replaced those fields in version 1 that were filled with 0s by some new fields. The message format is shown in the Fig. 6.29.

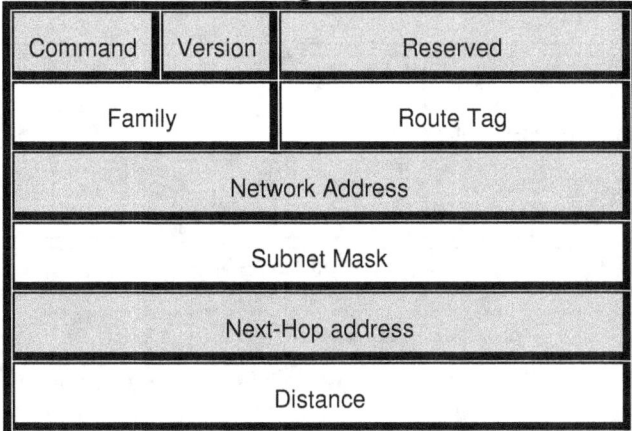

Fig. 6.29: RIPv2 message format

The new fields that are not present in RIPv1 are:

○ **Route Tag:** This field carries information such as autonomous system number.

○ **Subnet Mask:** It is 4 byte field that carries the subnet mask. This means that RIPv2 supports classless addressing and CIDR (Classes Inter-Domain Routing).

○ **Next-Hop Address:** This field shows the address of the next hop.

Open Shortest Path First (OSPF)

OSPF is an intradomain/interior routing protocol based on link state routing. Its domain is an autonomous system. For handling routing efficiently, OSPF divides an autonomous system into 'Areas'.

○ An Area is a collection of networks, hosts and routers within a specific autonomous system.

○ An autonomous system can be divided into many different areas.
   All the networks inside an area must be connected.

Open Shortest Path First is used for larger enterprise level network consisting of multiple router installations. Normally two types of routers are used in the autonomous system:

1. Area Border Routers:

These are the special routers used at the border of the area. These routers summarize the information about its area and send it to other areas.

2. Backbone Routers inside backbone area:

Among the areas inside the autonomous system, there is a special area called as Backbone Area. All of the areas inside an autonomous system must be connected to the backbone. In short, backbone works as primary area and the other areas work as secondary areas. The routers inside the backbone area are called as backbone routers that can be an Area Border Router.

In case, if some problem occurs and the connectivity between the backbone and the area is broken, virtual link between the routers must be created by the administrator to allow continuity of functions of the backbone as the primary area. Each area has area identification. The area identification of backbone is zero. Following figure shows an Autonomous System and its areas.

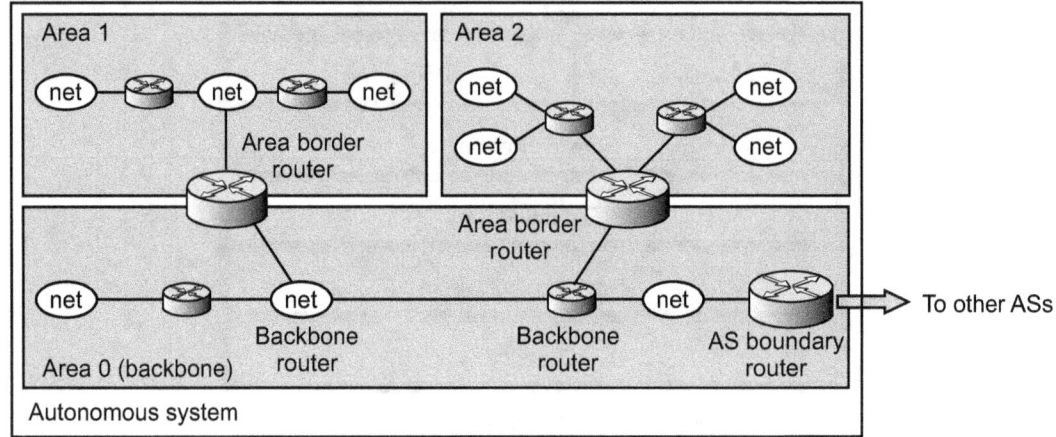

Fig. 6.30: Areas in Autonomous System

Features of OSPF:

1. **Type of service:** Depending on the requirement and the nature of the application, it can provide different services to different routes. e.g. high throughput can be selected for one class of service, while minimum delivery delay is more critical for some other applications.

2. **Load balancing:** When multiple routes are available to a particular destination, traffic can be distributed on the routes so as to balance the traffic load. No path will carry a very high traffic and no path will carry very low traffic. Traffic will be distributed evenly.

3. **Subdivision of Autonomous system:** Autonomous systems are further divided into smaller areas, which is always better from network administration point of view.

4. **Security:** Routing information is exchanged between the authenticated routers. Malicious transmissions from foreign routers are discarded.

5. **Special features to support LAN environment:** Although the relationships between routers are maintained on a logical link basis, link state transmissions are minimized by the architecture.

6. **OSPF is an open specification:** It means, anyone can implement this standard without paying royalties.

7. **OSPF area:** An area is a collection of networks, hosts and routers within a specific autonomous system. The topology of area is hidden from rest of the autonomous system. This technique reduces the storage of routing traffic information on a specific router.

Metric:

OSPF protocol allows the administrator to assign a cost, called the metric, to each route. A metric can be based on type of service such as minimum delay, maximum throughput, and so on. As a matter of fact a router can have multiple routing tables, each based on different type of service.

Types of Links:

In OSPF terminology, a connection is called as link. There are four types of links/ connections available in OSPF.

1. Point to Point Link:

A Point To Point Link connects two routers without any other host or router in between. Graphically, routers are represented by nodes and the link is represented by bidirectional edge connecting the nodes (Refer Fig. 6.31).

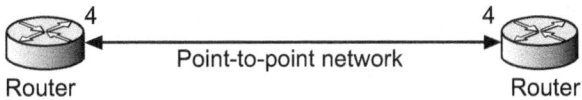

Fig. 6.31 : Point to point link

2. Transient Link:

Transient link is a network with several routers attached to it. The data can enter and exit through any of the router. All LANs and some WANs with two or more routers are of this type (refer Fig. 6.32).

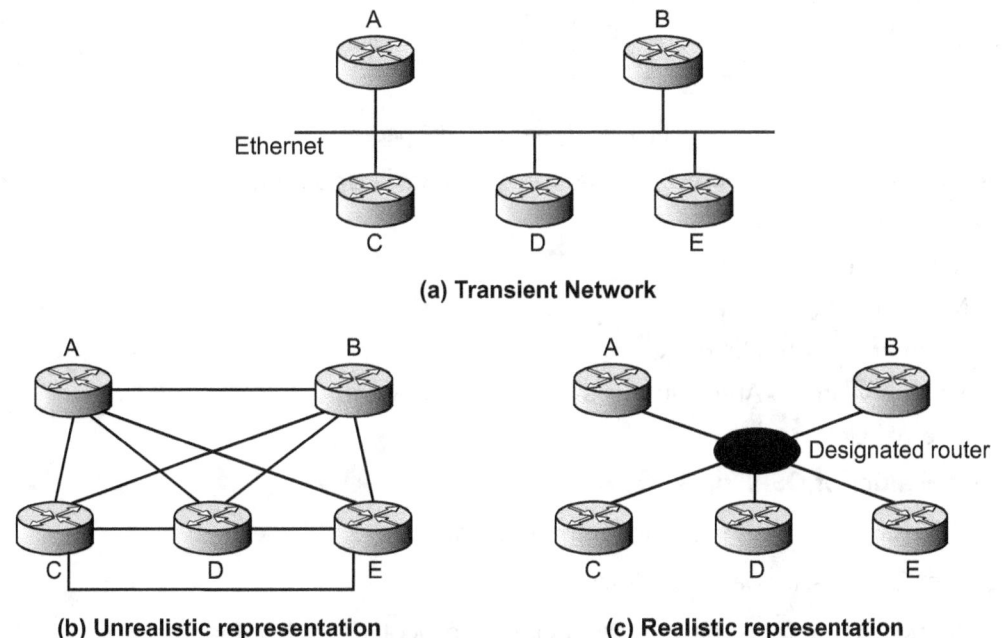

Fig. 6.32: Transient Link

3. **Stub Link:**

A Stub Link is a network that is connected to only one router.Data packets enter and exit the network through this single router.This is a special case of transient network. (Refer Fig. 6.33).

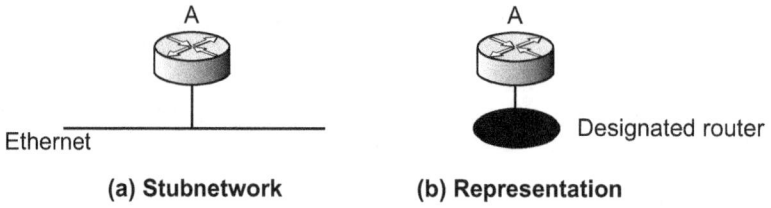

(a) **Stubnetwork**   (b) **Representation**

Fig. 6.33: Stub Link

4. **Virtual Link:**

When the link between two routers is broken, the administration may create a Virtual Link between them using a longer path that probably goes through several routers.

OSPF Packets:

OSPF uses five different types of packets as shown in the Fig. 6.34.

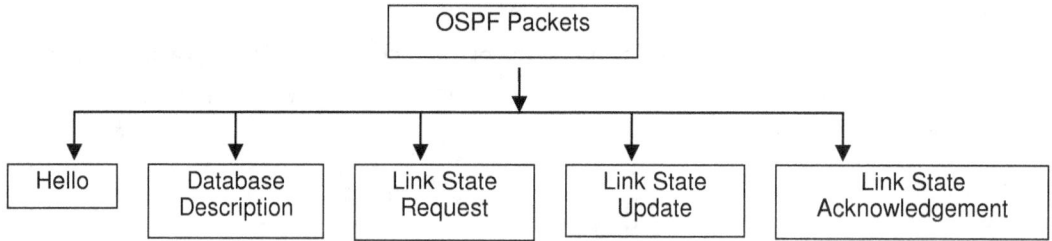

Fig. 6.34: Types of OSPF packets

The most important type of OSPF packet is Link State Update that itself has five different kinds which are as follows:

1. Router Link,
2. Network Link,
3. Summary Link to Network,
4. Summary Link to Autonomous System boundary router, and
5. External Link.

Common Header of OSPF packet:

All OSPF packets have the same common header.

Fields of OSPF Header are as follows:

1. **Version:** It defines the version of OSPF protocol. Currently it is version 2.

2. **Type:** It defines the type of the packet. We have five types as defined earlier.

3. **Message Length:** It defines the total length of the message including header.

4. **Source Router IP address:** It defines an IP address of the router that sends the packet (sender router).

5. **Area Identification:** It defines the area within which the routing takes place.

6. **Checksum:** This field is used for error detection on the entire packet excluding the authentication type and authentication data field.

7. **Authentication Type:** It defines the authentication protocol used in this area. At this time, two types of authentication are defined: 0 for none and 1 for password.

8. **Authentication:** This 64-bit field is the actual value of the authentication data. If authentication type is 0, this field is filled with 0s. If authentication type is 1, this field carries an eight-character password.

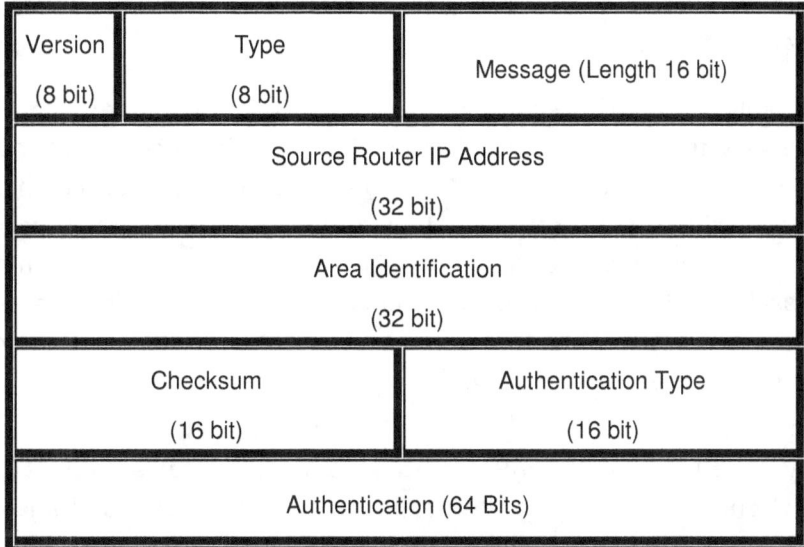

Fig. 6.35: OSPF header

Link State Update Packet:

It is the most important type of OSPF packet.It is used by the router to advertise the states of its links.

Characteristics of Routing protocol

Routing protocols can be compared based on the following characteristics:

1. Speed of convergence: Speed of convergence defines how quickly the routers in the network topology share routing information and reach a state of consistent knowledge. The faster the convergence, the more preferable the protocol.

2. Scalability: Scalability defines how large a network can become, based on the routing protocol that is deployed. The larger the network is, the more scalable the routing protocol needs to be.

3. **Classful or classless (use of VLSM):** Classful routing protocols do not include the subnet mask and cannot support *variable-length subnet mask (VLSM)*. Classless routing protocols include the subnet mask in the updates. Classless routing protocols support VLSM and better route summarization.

4. **Implementation and maintenance:** Implementation and maintenance describes the level of knowledge that is required for a network administrator to implement and maintain the network based on the routing protocol deployed.

5. **Resource usage:** Resource usage includes the requirements of a routing protocol such as memory space (RAM), CPU utilization, and link bandwidth utilization. Higher resource requirements necessitate more powerful hardware to support the routing protocol operation, in addition to the packet forwarding processes.

6.8 IP Routing Tables

A Routing Table is a set of rules, often viewed in table format, that is used to determine where data packets traveling over an Internet Protocol (IP) network will be directed. A routing table is present on all IP nodes. This table contains the information necessary to forward a packet along the best path toward its destination. Each packet contains information about its origin and destination. When a packet is received, a network device examines the packet and matches it to the routing table entry providing the best match for its destination. Then the table provides the device with instructions for sending the packet to the next hop on its route across the network.

Because all IP nodes perform some form of IP routing, routing tables are not exclusive to IP routers. Any node using the TCP/IP protocol has a routing table. Each table contains a series of default entries according to the configuration of the node, and additional entries can be added manually, for example, by administrators that use TCP/IP tools, or automatically, when nodes listen for routing information messages sent by routers. When IP forwards a packet, it uses the routing table to determine:

1. **The Next-Hop IP address:** For a direct delivery, the next-hop IP address is the destination address in the IP packet. For an indirect delivery, the next-hop IP address is the IP address of a router.

2. **The Next-Hop interface:** The interface identifies the physical or logical interface that forwards the packet.

Routing Table Entries :

A typical IP routing table entry includes the following fields:

o   **Destination:** Either an IP address or an IP address prefix.

o   **Prefix Length:** The prefix length corresponding to the address or range of addresses in the destination.

o   **Next-Hop:** The IP address to which the packet is forwarded.

○ **Interface:** The network interface that forwards the IP packet.

○ **Metric:** A number that indicates the cost of the route so that IP can select the best route, among potentially multiple routes to the same destination. The metric sometimes indicates the number of hops (the number of links to cross) in the path to the destination.

Routing Table entries can store the following types of routes:

1. **Directly-attached subnet routes:** Routes for subnets to which the node is directly attached. For directly-attached subnet routes, the Next-Hop field can either be blank or contain the IP address of the interface on that subnet.

2. **Remote subnet routes:** Routes for subnets that are available across routers and are not directly attached to the node. For remote subnet routes, the Next-Hop field is the IP address of a neighbouring router.

3. **Host routes:** A route to a specific IP address. Host routes allow routing to occur on a per-IP address basis.

4. **Default route:** Used when a more specific subnet or host route is not present. The next-hop address of the default route is typically the default gateway or default router of the node.

Table 6.4 : Windows 2000 Routing Table

Network Destination	Netmask	Gateway	Interface	Metric	Purpose
0.0.0.0	0.0.0.0	157.55.16.1	157.55.27.90	1	Default Route
127.0.0.0	255.0.0.0	127.0.0.1	127.0.0.1	1	Loopback Network
157.55.16.0	255.255.240.0	157.55.27.90	157.55.27.90	1	Directly Attached Network
157.55.27.90	255.255.255.255	127.0.0.1	127.0.0.1	1	Local Host
157.55.255.255	255.255.255.255	157.55.27.90	157.55.27.90	1	Network Broadcast
224.0.0.0	224.0.0.0	157.55.27.90	157.55.27.90	1	Multicast Address
255.255.255.255	255.255.255.255	157.55.27.90	157.55.27.90	1	Limited Broadcas

6.9 Stream and Packets

Stream is an abstraction of a connection to a communication channel, (TCP/IP network, the memory, file, a terminal, etc.).When a computer sends a stream of data to another computer, that stream fundamentally consists of:

1. Source IP,
2. Destination IP, and
3. Data.

The source IP is the IP address of the originating computer. The destination IP is the IP address of the destination computer.

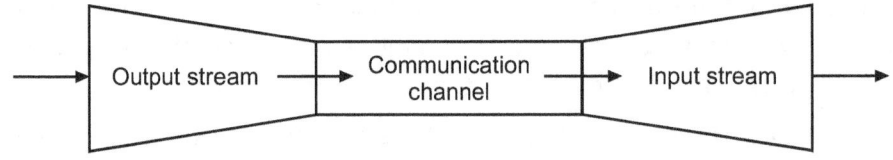

Fig. 6.36: Streams in TCP

Properties of Streams:

1. **FIFO:** The first thing written to the OutputStream will be the first thing read from the corresponding InputStream.

2. **Sequential Access:** Allows to read/write bytes only one after the other. (There are several exceptions.)

3. **Read-only or Write-only:** A stream supports only writing to a channel or only reading from the channel.

4. **Blocking:** A thread that reads/writes data blocks while no data is yet available to read, or when the write operation is in progress. Very little support for non-blocking I/O in Java.

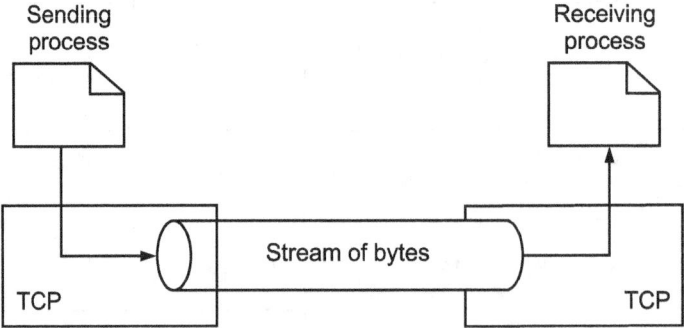

Fig. 6.37: Stream delivery in TCP

TCP is a stream oriented protocol. TCP allows the sending process to deliver data as a stream of bytes. TCP creates an environment in which the two processes seem to be connected by an imaginary "tube". This tube carries data across the Internet. This imaginary environment is shown in Fig. 6.37. The sending process produces the stream of bytes and the receiving process reads data from it.

Packets: A packet consists of control information and user data, which is also known as the Payload. Control information provides data for delivering the payload, for example: source and destination network addresses, error detection codes, and sequencing information. Typically, control information is found in Packet headers and trailers.

A Packet has the following components.

Addresses: The routing of network packets requires two network addresses, the source address of the sending host, and the destination address of the receiving host.

Error detection and correction: Error detection and correction is performed at various layers in the protocol stack. Network packets may contain a checksum, parity bits or cyclic redundancy checks to detect errors that occur during transmission.

At the transmitter, the calculation is performed before the packet is sent. When received at the destination, the checksum is recalculated, and compared with the one in the packet. If discrepancies are found, the packet may be corrected or discarded. Any packet loss is dealt with by the network protocol. In some cases modifications of the network packet may be necessary while routing, in which cases checksums are recalculated.

Hop counts: Under fault conditions packets can end up traversing a closed circuit. If nothing was done, eventually the number of packets circulating would build up until the network was congested to the point of failure. A time to live is a field that is decreased by one each time a packet goes through a network node. If the field reaches zero, routing has failed, and the packet is discarded.

Ethernet packets have no time-to-live field and so are subject to broadcast radiation in the presence of a switch loop.

Packet length: There may be a field to identify the overall packet length. In some protocols, the length is implied by the duration of transmission.

Class/priority: Some networks implement quality of service which can prioritize some types of packets above others. This field indicates which packet queue should be used; a high priority queue is emptied more quickly than lower priority queues at points in the network where congestion is occurring.

Payload: In general, Payload is the data that is carried on behalf of an application. It is usually of variable length, up to a maximum that is set by the network protocol and sometimes the equipment on the route. Some networks can break a larger packet into smaller packets when necessary.

IP Packets : IP packets are composed of a header and payload. The IPv4 packet header consists of field version, Header length, Types of service, Total length, Identifier, flags, fragment offset, TTL, protocol, Header checksum, Source and destination address [For more information see section 6.1].

Optional flags can be added of varied length, which can change based on the protocol used, then the data that packet carries is added. An IP packet has no trailer. However, an IP packet is often carried as the payload inside an Ethernet frame, which has its own header and trailer.

6.10 Sliding windows

Sliding windows, a technique also known as *windowing*, is used by the Internet's Transmission Control Protocol (TCP) as a method of controlling the flow of packets between two computers or network hosts. TCP requires that all transmitted data be acknowledged by the receiving host. Sliding windows is a method by which multiple frames are sent by sender at a time before needing an acknowledgment. Multiple frames sent by source are acknowledged by receiver using a single ACK frame.

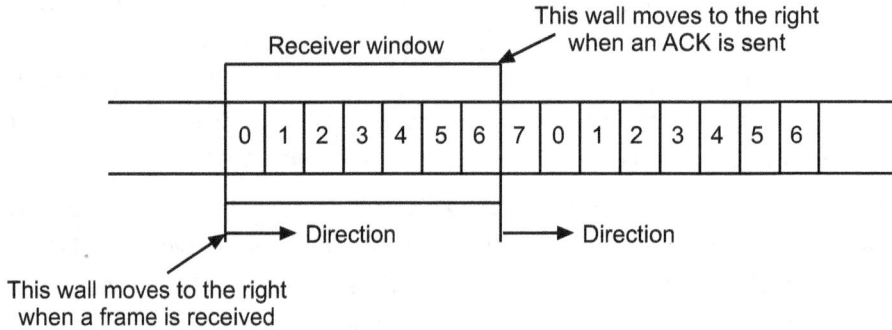

(a) Sliding window with size = 7

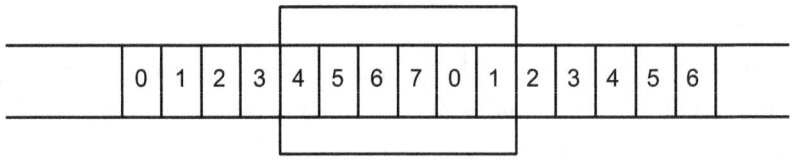

(a) Sliding window containing 6 frames

Fig. 6.38 : Sliding window on sender side

Sliding Window on Sender Side

At the beginning of a transmission, the sender's window contains n-1 frames.

Step 1 : As the frames are sent by source, the left boundary of the window moves inward, shrinking the size of window. If window size is w, and if four frames are sent by source after the last acknowledgment, then the number of frames left in window is w-4.

Step 2 : When the receiver sends an ACK, the source's window expand i.e. (right boundary moves outward) to allow in a number of new frames equal to the number of frames acknowledged by that ACK.

Step 3 : For example, Let the window size is 7 (see Fig 6.38), if frames 0 through 3 have been sent and no acknowledgment has been received, then the sender's window contains three frames - 4,5,6.

Step 4 : Now, if an ACK numbered 3 is received by source, three frames (0, 1, 2) have been received by receiver and are undamaged.

Step 5 : Then sender's window will now expand to include the next three frames in its buffer. At this point, the sender's window will contain six frames (4, 5, 6, 7, 0, 1).

Sliding Window on Receiver Side

At the beginning of transmission, the receiver's window contains n-1 spaces for frame but not the frames. As the new frames come in, the size of window shrinks.

Step 1 : The receiver window represents not the number of frames received but the number of frames that may still be received without an acknowledgment ACK must be sent.

Step 2 : Given a window of size w, if three frames are received without an ACK being returned, the number of spaces in a window is w-3.

Step 3 : As soon as acknowledgment is sent, window expands to include the number of frames equal to the number of frames acknowledged. For example, let the size of receiver's window is 7. It means window contains spaces for 7 frames. (See Fig. 6.39).

Step 4 : With the arrival of the first frame, the receiving window shrinks, moving the boundary from space 0 to 1. Then, window has shrunk by one, so the receiver may accept six more frame before it is required to send an ACK.

Step 5 : If frames 0 through 3 have arrived but have DOC been acknowledged, the window will contain three frame spaces.

Step 6 : As receiver sends an ACK, the window of the receiver expands to include as many new placeholders as newly acknowledged frames.

Step 7 : The window expands to include a number of new frame spaces equal to the number of the most recently acknowledged frame minus the number of previously acknowledged frame. For example; If window size is 7 and if prior ACK was for frame 2 and the current ACK is for frame 5 the window expands by three.

Therefore, the sliding window of sender shrinks from left when frames of data are sending. The sliding window of the sender expands to right when acknowledgments are received.

Step 8 : The sliding window of the receiver shrinks from left when frames of data are received. The sliding window of the receiver expands to the right when acknowledgement is sent.

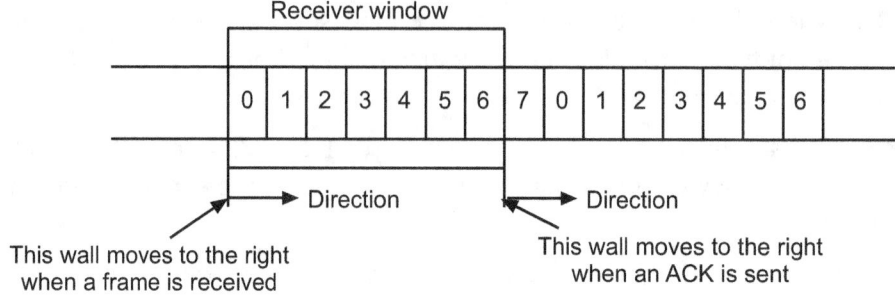

Fig. 6.39 : Sliding window on receiver side

6.11 Roles and Features of TCP/IP

TCP (Transmission Control Protocol) was specifically designed to provide a reliable end-to-end delivery of data over an unreliable internetwork. TCP is a Connection-Oriented, reliable transport protocol. It lies between Application Layer and Network Layer and serves as intermediary between application programs and network operation. TCP provides a way for applications to send encapsulated IP packets by establishing a connection. It uses flow and error control mechanisms in the transport layer. It helps in process to process communication that uses port numbers to accomplish this task.

It is a full duplex protocol, meaning that each TCP connection supports a pair of byte streams, one flowing in each direction. In number of ways, it is more interesting to look at how TCP does its job than the functions of the job itself. By examining the most important attributes of TCP and its operation, we can get a better handle on the way TCP works.

Features of TCP/IP:

1. **Connection-Oriented:** TCP requires that devices first establish a connection with each other before they send data.

2. **Multiply-connected and Endpoint-identified:** TCP connections are identified by the pair of sockets used by the two devices in the connection. This approach allows each device to have multiple connections opened, either to the same IP device or different IP devices, and to handle each connection independently without conflicts.

3. **Bidirectional:** Once, a connection is established, TCP devices send data bidirectionally i.e. both devices on the connection can send and receive, regardless of which of them initiated the connection.

4. **Reliable:** TCP is a reliable protocol because it uses acknowledgement to check the arrival of data.

5. **Data-unstructured:** An important consequence of TCP's stream orientation is that there are no natural divisions between data elements in the application's data stream. When multiple messages are sent over TCP, applications must provide a way of differentiating one message, data element, record, etc. from the next.

6. **Acknowledged:** A key to provide reliability is that all transmissions in TCP are acknowledged. The recipient must tell the sender "yes, I got that" for each piece of data transferred. This is in contrast to typical messaging protocols where the sender never knows what happened to its transmission.

7. **Stream-oriented:** TCP allows the sending process to deliver data as a stream of bytes.

8. **Flow control:** TCP provides flow control mechanism. The receiver of data controls the amount of data that are to be sent by the sender. By doing this, receiver is not swamped by data sent by the sender. The numbering system allows TCP to use a byte oriented flow control.

9. **Error control:** For providing reliable service, TCP uses error control mechanism. Error control is byte oriented.

10. **Congestion control:** TCP also provides congestion control. Receiver not only control the amount of data sent by the sender (flow control), but it is also determined by the level of congestion in the network.

Roles of TCP/IP :

The following are main tasks that TCP performs:

1. **Addressing/Multiplexing:** TCP is used by many different applications as their transport protocol. Therefore, like its simpler sibling UDP, an important job for TCP is multiplexing the data received from these different processes so they can be sent out using the underlying network layer protocol. At the same time, these higher-layer application processes are identified using TCP ports. The section on TCP/IP transport layer addressing contains a great deal of detail on how this addressing works.

2. **Connection Establishment, Management and Termination:** TCP provides a set of procedures that devices follow to negotiate and establish a TCP connection over which data can travel. Once opened, TCP includes logic for managing connections and handling problems that may result with them. When a device is done with a TCP connection, a special process is followed to terminate it.

3. **Data Handling and Packaging:** TCP defines a mechanism by which applications are able to send data to it from higher layers. This data is then packaged into messages to be sent to the destination TCP software. The destination software unpackages the data and gives it to the application on the destination machine.

4. **Data Transfer:** Conceptually, the TCP implementation on a transmitting device is responsible for the transfer of packaged data to the TCP process on the other device. Following the principle of layering, this is done by having the TCP software on the sending machine, pass the data packets to the underlying Network Layer Protocol.

5. **Providing Reliability and Transmission Quality Services:** TCP includes a set of services and features that allow an application to consider the sending of data using the protocol

to be "reliable". This means that normally, a TCP application doesn't have to worry about data being sent and never showing up, or arriving in the wrong order. It also means other common problems that might arise if IP were used directly are avoided.

6. **Providing Flow Control and Congestion Avoidance Features:** TCP allows the flow of data between two devices to be controlled and managed. It also includes features to deal with congestion that may be experienced during communication between devices.

TCP Header:

A packet in TCP is called as a segment. The format is shown in Fig. 6.40. The segment consists of a 20 to 60 byte header, followed by data from application layer. The header is of 20 bytes if no options are used and upto 60 bytes if it contains options.

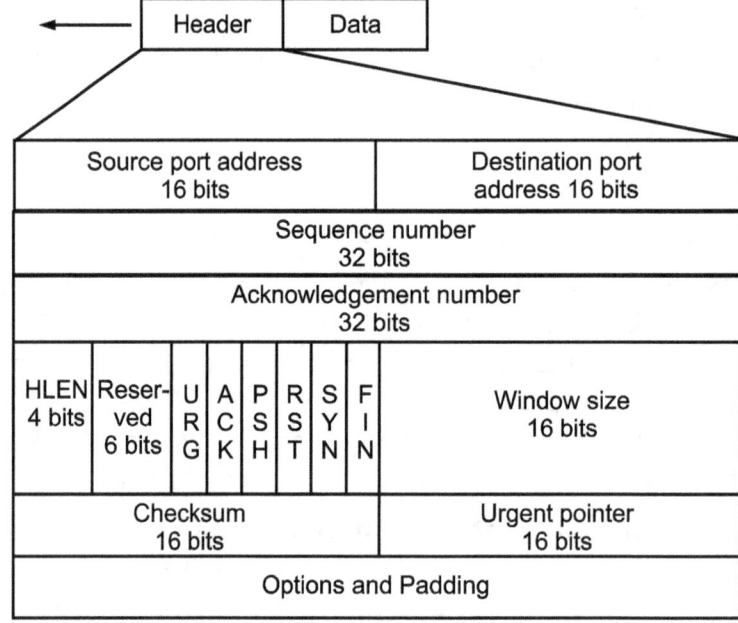

Fig. 6.40: TCP segment Format

Fields of TCP Segment:

- **Source Port Address:** This 16 bit field defines the port number of the application program in the host that is sending the segment.

- **Destination Port Address:** This 16 bit field defines the port number of the application program in the host who is receiving the segment.

- **Sequence Number:** This 32 bit field defines the number assigned to the first byte of data contained in the segment.

- **Acknowledgement Number:** This 32 bit field defines the byte number that the receiver of the segment is expecting to receive from other party.

- **Header Length:** This 4 bit field defines length of the header. The length of the header can range between 20 to 60 bytes.

- **Reserved:** This 6 bit field is reserved for future use.

- **Control:** This field defines 6 different control bits or flags as shown in Fig. 6.41. One or more flags can be set at a time.

URG	ACK	PSH	RST	SYN	FIN

URG   : Urgent pointer is valid   RST   : Reset the connection

ACK   : Acknowledgement is valid   SYN   : Synchronize sequence no.

PSH   : Request for push   FIN   : Terminate the connection

Fig. 6.41: Control Field

Table 6. 5: Control with descriptions

Flag	Description
URG	The value of the urgent pointer field is valid.
ACK	The value of the acknowledgement field is valid.
PSH	Push the data.
RST	Reset the connection.
SYN	Synchronize sequence number during connection.
FIN	Terminate the connection.

- **Window Size:** This 16 bit field defines the size of the window in bytes, that the other party must maintain.

- **Checksum:** This 16 bit field contains the checksum used for error control.

- **Urgent Pointer:** This 16 bit field is valid only if the urgent flag is set, it is used when the segment contains urgent data.

- **Options:** There can be upto 40 bytes of optional information in the TCP header.

TCP – A Reliable Pipe

TCP provides for the recovery of segments that are lost, damaged, duplicated or received out of their correct order. TCP is described as a 'reliable' protocol because it attempts to recover from these errors. TCP functions by opening connections to a remote computer called connection-oriented communication and it maintains status information regarding the connections.

A single TCP connection is identified by combination of IP addresses and virtual port numbers used by both the ends. During communication, additional numbers are used to keep track of the order or sequence in which the data segments are transmitted. The sequence number indicates what order the segments of data should be reassembled. Finally, a maximum transmission size is constantly being negotiated via a fallback mechanism called Windowing (As discussed in section 6.10). The combination of port numbers, sequence numbers and window sizes constitutes a connection, or pipe.

Communication using TCP is said to be reliable because TCP keeps a track of data that has been sent and received to ensure that all gets to its destination. TCP provides basic reliability using Positive Acknowledgement with Retransmission (PAR). Basic reliability in a protocol running over an unreliable protocol like IP can be implemented by closing the loop so the recipient provides feedback to the sender. This is most easily done with a simple acknowledgement system.

Device X sends a piece of data to Device Y. Device Y, receiving the data, sends back an acknowledgement saying, "Device X, I received your message". Device X then knows its transmission was successful.

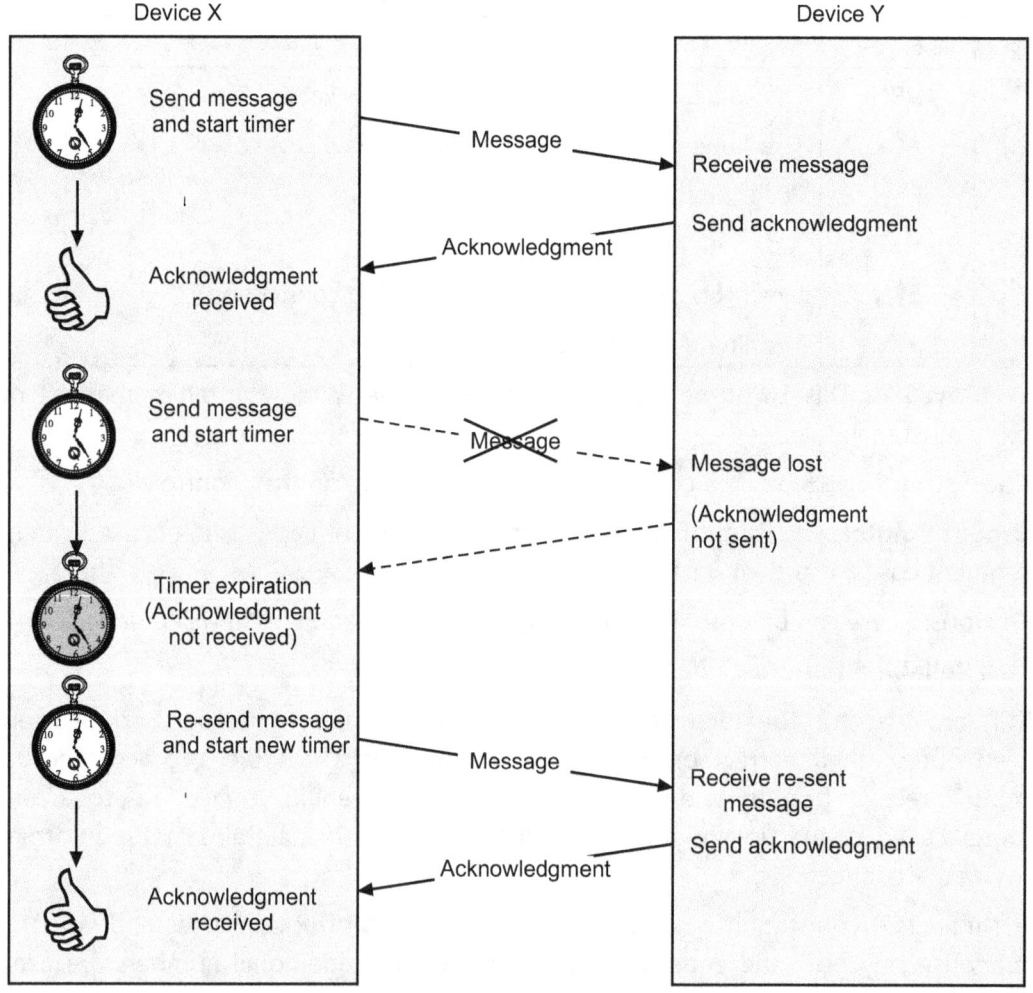

Fig. 6.42 : Basic reliability (Positive Acknowledgment with Retransmission (PAR))

Of course, since IP is unreliable, that message may in fact never get to where it is going. Device X will sit waiting for the acknowledgement and never receive it. Conversely, it is also possible that Device Y gets the message from Device X, but the acknowledgement itself vanishes somehow. In either case, we do not want Device X to sit forever waiting for an acknowledgement that is never going to ever arrive.

To prevent this from happening, Device X starts a timer when it first sends the message to Device Y, which allows sufficient time for the message to get to Y and the acknowledgement to travel back, plus some reasonable time to allow for possible delays.If the timer expires before the acknowledgment is received, X assumes there was a problem and retransmits its original message.

Since, this method involves positive acknowledgments ("yes, I got your message") and a facility for retransmission when needed, it is commonly called (ta-da!) positive acknowledgement with retransmission (PAR), as shown in Fig. 6.42.

Fig. 6.42 shows one of the most common simple techniques for ensuring reliability. Each time a message is sent by Device X, it starts a timer, Device Y sends an acknowledgment back to X when it receives a message so X know it was successfully transmitted. If a message is lost and the timer goes off then X retransmits the data. Note that only one message can be outstanding at any time, making this system rather slow.

6.12 TCP Connections types and working

A TCP connection is managed by an operating system through a programming interface that represents the local end-point for communications called as the Internet socket.

TCP 3-Way Handshake

The TCP three-way handshake in Transmission Control Protocol (also called the TCP-handshake; three message handshake and/or SYN-SYN-ACK) is the method used by TCP set up a TCP/IP connection over an Internet Protocol based network. TCP's three way handshaking technique is often referred to as "SYN-SYN-ACK" (or more accurately SYN, SYN-ACK, ACK) because there are three messages transmitted by TCP to negotiate and start a TCP session between two computers. The TCP handshaking mechanism is designed so that two computers attempting to communicate can negotiate the parameters of the network TCP socket connection before transmitting data such as SSH and HTTP web browser requests.

This 3-Way Handshake process is also designed so that both ends can initiate and negotiate separate TCP socket connections at the same time. Being able to negotiate multiple TCP socket connections in both directions at the same time allows a single physical network interface, such as Ethernet, to be multiplexed to transfer multiple streams of TCP data simultaneously.

- For establishing a connection, the server, passively waits for an incoming connection by executing the LISTEN and ACCEPT primitives.

- The other side, the client executes a CONNECT primitive, specifying the IP address and port to which it wants to connect. The CONNECT primitive sends a TCP segment with the SYN= 1 and ACK= 0 and SEQ=x and waits for a response.

- If the connection is rejected (there is no host listening or the server is too busy, a segment with RST=1 is returned.

- If the connection is accepted, an acknowledgment segment with SEQ=y and ACK=x+1 is returned.

- The "third" handshake is then made establishing the connection.

- This still works even if both ends try to establish the connection independently.

The sequence of TCP segments sent in normal is shown in Fig. 6.43 (a).

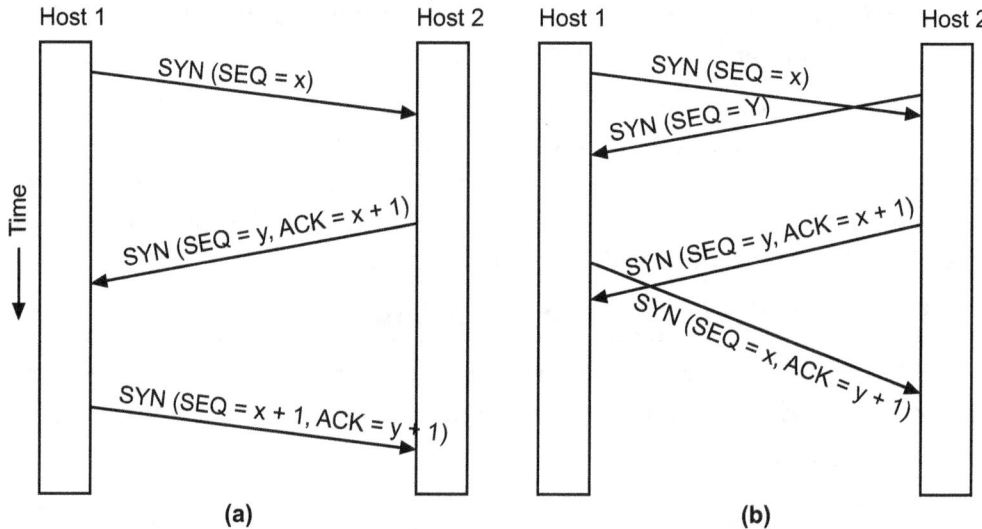

Fig. 6.43: (a) TCP connection establishment in the normal case, (b) Call collision

In Fig. 6.43 (b), TCP uses symmetric disconnects along with timers to avoid the two-array problem.

- At the end of its transmission, each side sends a segment with FIN=1 which must be acknowledged. When both sides have done that, the connection is released.

- If there is no response to the FIN, after two packet lifetimes (2T) the sender releases its connection. Eventually, the other host times out as well since no one is out there.

Four TCP segments are needed to release the connection: one FIN and one ACK for each direction.

TCP Multiplexing :

Multiplexing is the process of combining two or more data streams into a single physical connection. TCP provides multiplexing facilities by using source and destination port numbers. These port numbers allow TCP to set up a number of virtual connections over a physical connection and multiplex the data stream through that connection. -

TCP Port Numbers :

A port number is a way to identify a specific process to which an Internet or other network message is to be forwarded when it arrives at a server. For the Transmission Control Protocol (TCP) and the User Datagram Protocol (UDP), a port number is a 16-bit integer that is put in the header appended to a message unit. This port number is passed logically between client and server transport layers and physically between the transport layer and the Internet Protocol layer and forwarded on.

For example, a request from a client (perhaps on behalf of you at your PC) to a server on the Internet may request a file be served from that host's File Transfer Protocol (FTP) server or process. In order to pass your request to the FTP process in the remote server, the Transmission Control Protocol (TCP) software layer in your computer identifies the port number of 21 (which by convention is associated with an FTP request) in the 16-bit port number integer that is appended to your request. At the server, the TCP layer will read the port number of 21 and forward your request to the FTP program at the server.

A host may have many TCP and UDP connections at any time. Connections to a host are distinguished by a port number, which serves as a sort of mailbox number for incoming datagrams. There may be many processes using TCP and UDP on a single machine, and the port numbers distinguish these processes for incoming packets. When a user program opens a TCP or UDP socket, it gets connected to a port on the local host.

The application may specify the port, usually when trying to reach some service with a well-defined port number, or it may allow the operating system to fill in the port number with the next available free port number. After IP passes incoming data to the transport protocol which passes data to the correct application process. Application processes are identified by port numbers(16-bit values). The source port number identifies the process that send the data. The destination port number which identifies the process that is to receive the data. These two port numbers are contained in the header of each TCP segment and UDP packet. Port numbers are not unique between transport layer protocols but they are unique within a specific transport protocol. It is the combination of protocol and port numbers that uniquely identify the specific process the data should be delivered to.

In Fig. 6.44, if a data packet arrives specifying a transport protocol of 6, it is forwarded to the TCP implementation. If the packet specifies 17 as the required protocol, the IP layer would forward the packet to the programs implementing UDP.

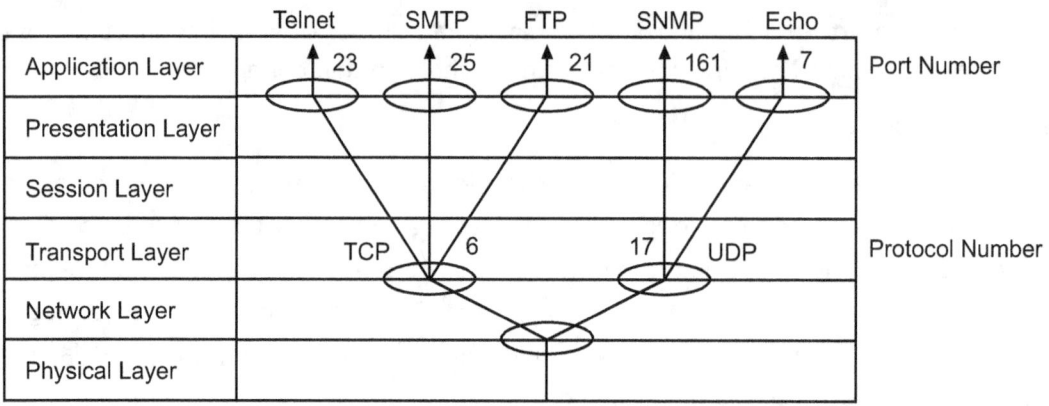

Fig. 6.44: TCP Multiplexing

In Fig. 6.45, the source host randomly generates a source port, in this example 3044. It sends out a segment with a source port of 3044 and a destination port of 23. The destination host receives the segment, and responds back using 23 as its source port and 3044 as its destination port.

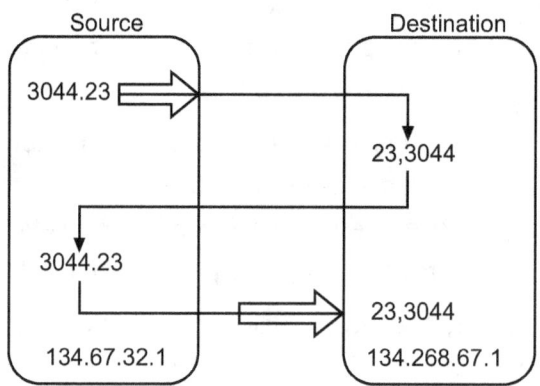

Fig. 6.45: Exchange of port numbers during the TCP handshake

Table 6.6 : Well-known Ports used by TCP

Port	Protocol	Description
7	Echo	Echoes a received datagram back to the sender.
9	Discard	Discards any datagram that is received.
11	Users	Active users.
13	Daytime	Returns the date and the time.
17	Quote	Returns a quote of the day.
19	Chargen	Returns a string of characters.

Contd...

20	FTP. Data	File Transfer Protocol (data connection).
21	FTP. Control	File Transfer Protocol (control connection).
23	TELNET	Terminal Network.
25	SMTP	Simple Mail Transfer Protocol.
53	DNS	Domain Name Server.
67	BOOTP	Bootstrap Protocol.
79	Finger	Finger.
80	HTTP	Hypertext Transfer Protocol.
111	RPC	Remote Procedure Call.

Table 6.7: Well-known Ports used with UDP

Port	Protocol	Description
7	Echo	Echoes a received datagram back to the sender.
9	Discard	Discards any datagram that is received.
11	Users	Active users.
13	Daytime	Returns the date and the time.
17	Quote	Returns a quote of the day.
19	Chargen	Returns a string of characters.
53	Nameserver	Domain Name Service
67	Bootps	Server port to download bootstrap information.
68	BOOTPE	Client port to download bootstrap information.
69	TFTP	Trivial File Transfer Protocol.
111	RPC	Remote Procedure Call
123	NTP	Network Time Protocol.
161	SNMP	Simple Network Management Protocol.
162	SNMP	Simple Network Management Protocol (trap).

6.13 IPv6 : The Next Generation Protocol

IPv6 is short for "Internet Protocol Version 6". It is also called IPng (**I**nternet **P**rotocol **n**ext **g**eneration) protocol designed by the IETF (The Internet Engineering Task Force) to replace the current version Internet Protocol, Version 4 (IPv4). Most of today's Internet uses IPv4, which is now nearly twenty years old. IPv6 fixes a number of problems in IPv4, such as the limited number of available IPv4 addresses. It also adds many improvements to IPv4 in areas such as routing and network auto configuration.

IPv6 is expected to gradually replace IPv4, with the two coexisting for a number of years during a transition period. IPv6 is a connectionless, unreliable datagram protocol used primarily for addressing and routing packets between hosts. Connectionless means that a session is not established before exchanging data. Unreliable means that delivery is not guaranteed. IPv6 always makes a best-effort attempt to deliver a packet.

Advantages of IPv6:

Due to the limitations of IPv4, IPv6 comes into existence. This is next-generation internet protocol and had many advantages on the previously existing version of Internet protocol (IPv4).

Advantages of IPv6 are listed below:

1. **Larger address space:** An IPv6 address is 128 bits long (compared to IPv4, IPv6 address is very long because IPv4 address was only of 32 bits). So total number of addresses generated using IPv6 is 2^{128}.

2. **Better Header Format:** IPv6 uses a new header format in which options are separated from the base header and inserted when needed, between base header and upper layer data. This simplifies and speeds up the routing process because most of the options do not need to be checked by routers.

3. **New options:** IPv6 has new options to allow additional functionalities.

4. **Allowance for extension:** IPv6 is designed to allow the extension of the protocol if required by new technologies or applications.

5. **Support for resource allocation:** In IPv6, the type of service field has been removed, but a mechanism (called Flow Label) has been added to enable the source to request special handling of packet. This mechanism can be used to support traffic such as real time audio and video.

6. **Support for more security:** The encryption and authentication options in IPv6 provide confidentiality and integrity of the packet.

7. **Plug and Play:** IPv6 includes plug and play in the standard specification. It therefore must be easier for novice user to connect their machines to network, it will be done automatically.

8. **Clearer specification:** IPv6 follows good practices of IPv4, and rejects its minor problems.

IPv6 Packet Format :

An IPv6 packet, also known as an IPv6 datagram, consists of an IPv6 header and an IPv6 payload, as shown in Fig. 6.46.

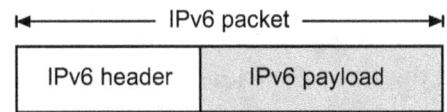

Fig. 6.46 : IPv6 packet

The IPv6 header no longer contains the Header length, Identification, Flags, Fragment Offset and Header Checksum fields. Some of these options have been placed in extension headers. The 'Time To Live' field has been replaced with a 'Hop Limit', and the IPv4 'Type of Service field' is now replaced with a Traffic Class field.

Fig. 6.47 shows Header format of IPv6.

```
                     1                   2                   3
 0 1 2 3 4 5 6 7 8 9 0 1 2 3 4 5 6 7 8 9 0 1 2 3 4 5 6 7 8 9 0 1
+-----+---------------+---------------------------------------+
| Ver | Traffic Class |              Flow Label               |
+-----+---------------+-----------------+---------------------+
|      Payload Length  |   Next Header   |      Hop Limit      |
+----------------------+-----------------+---------------------+
|                                                             |
|                  128-bit source IP address                  |
|                                                             |
|                                                             |
+-------------------------------------------------------------+
|                                                             |
|               128-bit destination IP address                |
|                                                             |
|                                                             |
+-------------------------------------------------------------+
|                                                             |
|               Optional extension headers                    |
+-------------------------------------------------------------+
|                       User data                             |
|                                                             |
+-------------------------------------------------------------+
```

Fig. 6.47 : IPv6 Header Format

Table 6.8 : Field description of IPv6 packet format

Field	Function
Ver	The version of the IP protocol that created the packet. For IPv6, this field has a value of 6.
Traffic class	An 8-bit value which indicates the priority that a packet should be given.
Flow label	A 20-bit value which indicates the data flow to which this packet belongs. This flow may be handled in a particular way.
Payload length	The length of user data portion of the packet. If the data payload is larger than 64 kB, the length is given in the optional "Jumbo Payload" header and the Payload length header is given a value of zero.

Next header	A number which indicates the type of header that immediately follows the basic IP header. This header type may be an optional IPv6 extension header, a relevant IPv4 option header, or another protocol, such as TCP or ICMPv6.
	The IPv6 extension header values are:
	0 (Hop-by-Hop Options Header)
	43 (IPv6 Routing Header)
	44 (IPv6 Fragment Header)
	50 (Encapsulating Security Payload)
	59 (IPv6 Authentication Header)
	60 (Destination Options Header)
Hop limit	A field which is the equivalent of the IPv4 Time To Live field, measured in hops.
Source IP address	The 128-bit IPv6 address of the sender.
Destination IP address	The 128-bit IPv6 address of the receiver.
Optional extension headers	The optional headers, which give less-frequently used information.

IPv6 Addressing

An IPv6 address consists of 8 sets of 16-bit hexadecimal values separated by (:), totaling 128 bits in length. For example: 2001:0db8:1234:5678:9abc:def0:1234:5678.

Leading zeros can be omitted, and consecutive zeros in contiguous blocks can be represented by a double colon (::). Double colons can appear only once in the address.

For example: 2001:0db8:0000:130F:0000:0000:087C:140B can be abbreviated as

2001:0db8:0:130F::87C:140B.

As with the IPv4 Classless Inter-Domain Routing (CIDR) network prefix representation (such as 10.1.1.0/24), an IPv6 address network prefix is represented the same way:

2001:db8:12::/64.

An IPv6 address consists of 16 bytes (octets); it is 128 bits long as shown in Fig. 6.48.

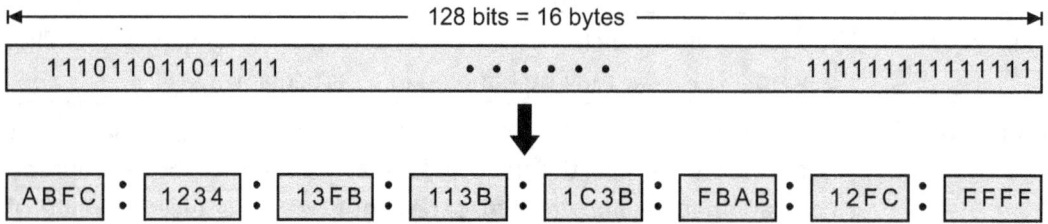

Fig. 6.48: IPv6 address

Hexadecimal Colon Notation:

- IPv6 specifies hexadecimal colon notation to make addresses more readable

- In this notation, 128 bits are divided into eight sections, each of 2 bytes in length.

- Two bytes in hexadecimal notation require four hexadecimal digits.

- Therefore, the address consists of 32 hexadecimal digits, with every four digits separated by a colon.

Abbreviation:

Although, IP addresses in hexadecimal format are very long, many of the digits are zeros, in this case we can abbreviate the address. The leading zeros of the section can be omitted. Only leading zeros can be dropped, not the trailing zeros, (Refer Fig. 6.49).

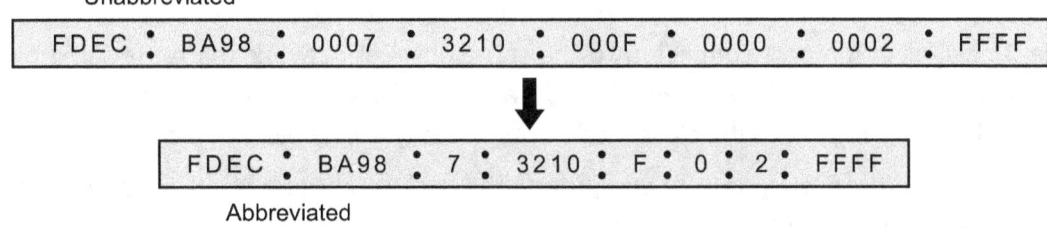

Fig. 6.49: Abbreviated address

Using this form of abbreviation, 0074 can be written as 74, 000F as F, and 0000 as 0. Note that 3200 can not be abbreviated. Further abbreviation is possible, if there are consecutive sections consisting of zeros only, we can remove the zeros altogether and replace them with double colon, (Refer Fig. 6.50). Note that this type of abbreviation is allowed only once per address. If there are two runs of zero sections, only one of them can be abbreviated.

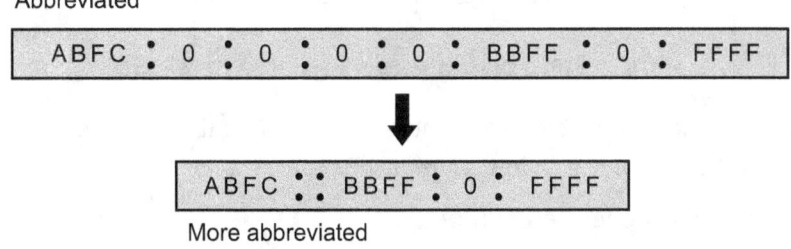

Fig. 6.50: Abbreviated address with consecutive zeros

Re-expansion of the abbreviated address is very simple: align the unabbreviated portions and insert zeros to get the original expanded address.

CIDR Notations:

IPv6 allows classless addressing and CIDR notation. For example, Fig. 6.51 shows how we can define a prefix of 60 bits using CIDR.

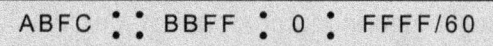

ABFC :: BBFF : 0 : FFFF/60

Fig. 6.51: CIDR address

Categories of IPv6 Addresses:

IPv6 defines three types of addresses:

1. **Unicast:** A unicast address defines a single computer. The packet sent to unicast address must be delivered to that specific computer.

2. **Anycast:** It defines a group of computers with addresses that have the same prefix. For example, all computers connected to the same physical network share the same prefix address. A packet sent to an anycast address must be delivered to exactly one of the members of the group – the closest or the most easily accessible.

3. **Multicast:** It defines a group of computers. The packet sent to a multicast address must be delivered to each member of the group.

Lets see above addresses in detail.

1. IPv6 Unicast Addresses:

IPv6 unicast address generally use 64 bits for the network ID and 64 bits for the host ID as shown in Fig. 6.52.

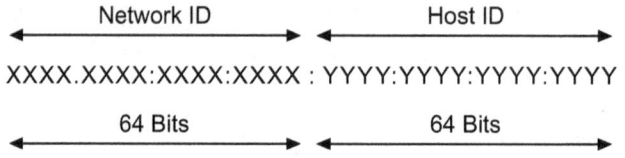

Network ID   Host ID

XXXX.XXXX:XXXX:XXXX : YYYY:YYYY:YYYY:YYYY

64 Bits   64 Bits

Fig. 6.52 : IPv6 Unicast network and host ID format

The network ID is administratively assigned, and the host ID can be configured manually or auto-configured by any of the following methods.

1. Using a randomly generated number.

2. Using DHCPv6.

3. Using the Extended Unique Identifier (EUI-64) format. This format expands the device interface 48-bit MAC address to 64-bits by inserting FFFE into the middle 16 bits, (See Fig. 6.53).

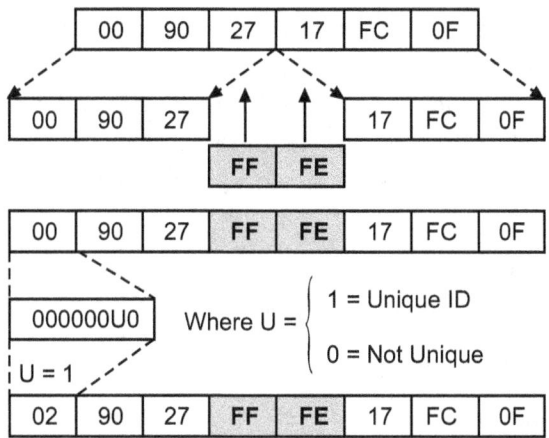

Fig. 6.53: Conversion of EUI-64 MAC address to IPv6 host address Format

Address Scopes:

An address scope defines the region where an address can be defined as a unique identifier of an interface. These scope or region are the link, the site network and the global network, corresponding to link-local, unique local unicast and global address (See Fig. 6.54).

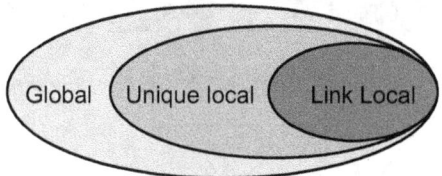

Fig. 6.54: IPv6 address Scopes

(i) Global Unicast Addresses:

Global unicast address are:

- Routable and reachable across the internet.
- IPv6 addresses for widespread use.
- Structured as a hierarchy to allow address aggregation.
- Identified by their three high-level bits set to 001 (2000::/3).

Fig. 6.55 illustrates the format of a global unicast address.

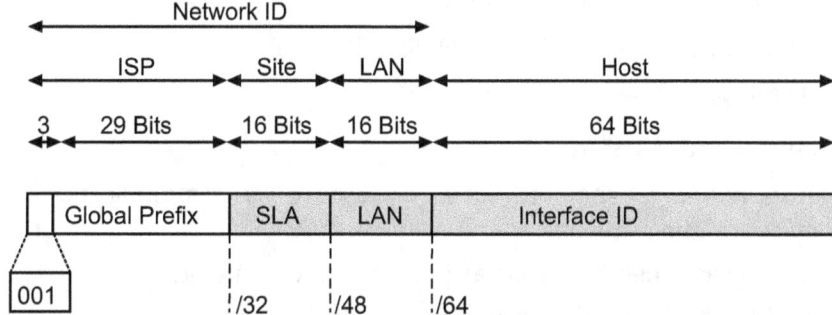

Fig. 6.55: Global Unicast address format

The global routing prefix is assigned to a service provider by the Internet Assigned Numbers Authority (IANA). The site level aggregator (SLA) or subnet ID is assigned to a customer by their service provider. The LAN ID represent individual networks within the customer site and is administered by the customer. The Host of Interface ID has the same meaning for all unicast addresses. It is 64 bits long and is typically created by using the EUI-64 format.

Example of a global unicast address.

2001:0DB8:BBBB:CCCC:0987:65FF:FE01:2345

(ii) Unique Local Unicast Addresses:

Unique local Unicast addresses are:

- Analogous to private IPv4 addresses, for example 10.1.1.254.
- Used for local communications, inter-site VPNs and so forth.
- Not routable on the internet routing would required IPv6 NAT.

Fig. 6.56 illustrates the format of a unique local Unicast address:

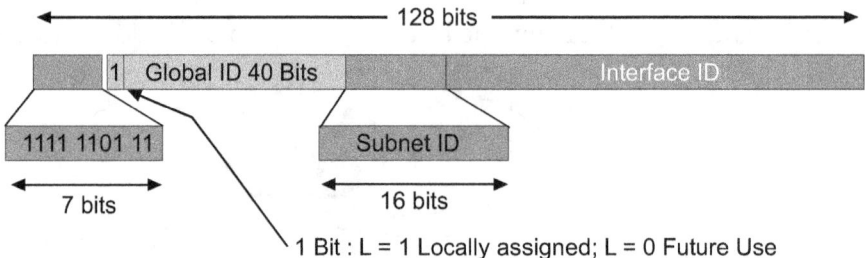

Fig. 6.56: Unique local Unicast address Format

Global IDs do not have to be aggregated and are defined by the administrator of the local domain. Subnet IDs are also defined by the administrator of the local domain. Subnet IDs are typically defined using a hierarchical addressing plan to allow for route summarization.

The Host of Interface ID has the same meaning for all unicast addresses. It is 64 bits long and is typically created by using the EUI-64 format.

Example of a unique local unicast address:

FD00:aaaa:bbbb:CCCC:0987:65FF:FE01:2345.

(iii) Link Local Unicast Addresses:

Link local unicast addresses are:

- Mandatory addresses that are used exclusively for communication between two IPv6 devices on the same link.
- Automatically assigned by device as soon as IPvc6 is enabled.
- Not routable addresses (Their scope is link-specific only).
- Identified by the first 10 bits (FE80).

Fig. 6.57 illustrates the format of a link local unicast address.

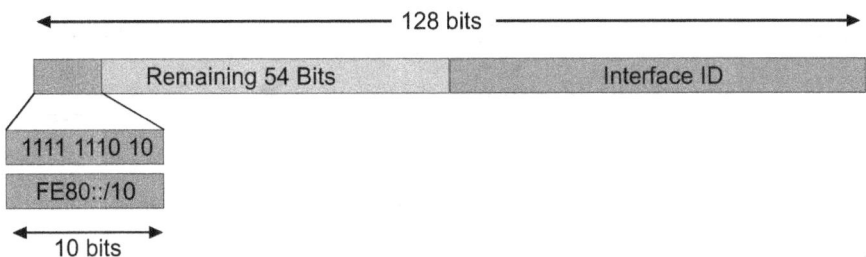

Fig. 6.57: Link local Unicast address Format

The remaining 54 bits of the network ID could be zero or any manually configured value.

The interface ID has the same meaning for all unicast addresses. It is 64 bit long and is typically created by using EUI-64 format.

Example of a link local unicast address:

FE80:0000:0000:0000:0987:65FF:FE01:2345

This address would generally by represented in shorthand notation as:

FE80::987:65FF:FE01:2345

2. IPv6 Multicast Addresses:

A Multicast Address identifies multiple interfaces. With the appropriate multicast routing topology packets addressed to a multicast address are delivered to all interfaces that are identified by the address. IPv6 Multicast Addresses have an 8-bit prefix, FF00::/8 (1111 1111). The second octet defines the lifetime and scope of the multicast address, (See Fig. 6.58).

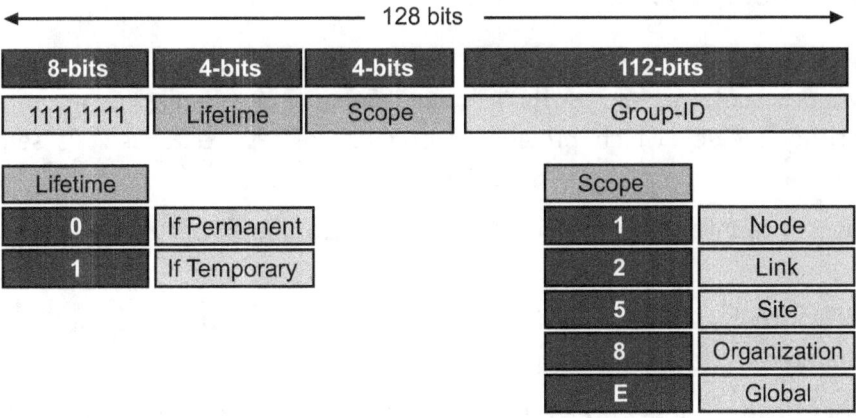

Fig. 6.58: Multicast Address Format

Multicast addresses are always destination addresses. Multicast addresses are used for Router Solicitations (RS), Router Advertisements (RA), DHCPv6 (Dynamic Host Configuration Protocol Version 6), multicast applications and so forth.

Table 6.9 : Well known Multicast Addresses.

Address	Scope	Meaning
FF01::1	Node-local/interface local	Same node/interface local node
FF02::1	Link-local	All nodes on a link
FF01::2	Node-local/interface local	Same router
FF02::2	Link-local	All routers on a link
FF05::2	Site-local	All routers on the internet
FF02::1:FFxx:xxxx	Link-local	Solicited node

3. Anycast Addresses:

An anycast address is a unicast address that is attached to more than one interface. If a packet is sent to an anycast address it will be delivered to the nearest interface with that address, with the definition of "nearest" depending on the protocol used for routing. If the protocol is RIPv6, the nearest interface will be the one which is the shortest number of hops away.

Anycast addresses can only be assigned to routers, and packets cannot originate from an anycast address. A router must be configured to know if it is using an anycast address, because the address format cannot be distinguished from that of a unicast address. Only one anycast address has been predefined, the subnet-router address. The subnet-router address is used to send messages to the nearest router on a subnet, and consists of the subnet's prefix followed by zeros.

Security :

The IPv6 protocol for Microsoft®Windows Server 2003 family incorporates Internet Protocol security (IPSec), which provides protection of IPv6 data as it is sent over the network.

IPSec is a set of Internet standards that uses cryptographic security services to provide the following:

1. **Confidentiality:** IPSec traffic is encrypted. Captured IPSec traffic cannot be deciphered without the encryption key.

2. **Authentication:** IPSec traffic is digitally signed with the shared encryption key so that the receiver can verify that it was sent by the IPSec peer.

3. **Data integrity:** IPSec traffic contains a cryptographic checksum that incorporates the encryption key. The receiver can verify that the packet was not modified in transit.

IPv6 Applications :

The Windows Server 2003 family includes the following IPv6-enabled applications and components:

1. **FTP client:** The File Transfer Protocol (FTP) client, 'Ftp.exe', can be used to establish FTP sessions with IPv4 and IPv6 FTP servers.

2. **Telnet client :** The Telnet client, 'Telnet.exe', can be used to establish Telnet sessions with IPv4 and IPv6 Telnet servers.

3. **Internet Explorer:** The new Internet extensions dynamic link library, 'Wininet.dll', enables Web browsers to access IPv6-enabled Web servers. For example, Wininet.dll is used by Microsoft Internet Explorer to make connections with a Web server to view Web pages. Internet Explorer uses IPv6 to download Web pages when the Domain Name System (DNS) query for the name of the Web server in the URL returns an IPv6 address.

Disadvantages :

1. IPv6 will be much harder to remember IP addresses compared to the addresses of IPv4.
2. Creating a smooth transition from IPv4 to IPv6.
3. IPv6 is not available to machines that run IPv4.
4. Any consumer costs in having to replace an IPv4 machine.
5. Time to convert over to IPv6.
6. Most experts classify network security threats in two major categories: logic attacks and resource attacks.

Logic attacks are known to exploit existing software bugs and vulnerabilities with the intent of crashing a system. Some use this attack to purposely degrade network performance or grant an intruder access to a system.

Table 6.10 : Difference between IPv4 and IPv6

IPv4	IPv6
1. It is 32 bit source and destination addresses.	1. It is 128 bit source and destination addresses.
2. There are maximum 2^{32} IP addresses.	2. There are maximum 2^{128} IP addresses.
3. IPv4 addresses are written by dotted decimal notation. For example, 10.15.11.23	3. IPv6 addresses are written in hexadecimal colon notation. For example, FADB:A2B2:A453:1212:AAB3: ADBD:BBCC:1234
4. Basic length of IPv4 header is 20 bytes (excluding option field).	4. Length of IPv6 header is 40 bytes.

5. IPv4 header has a checksum.	5. It has no header checksum.
6. Security is optional parameter.	6. It has been designed to satisfy the growing and expanded need for network security.
7. Headers include option field.	7. No option field is present in the basic header. All optional data is moved to extension header.
8. IPsec support is optional.	8. IPsec support is compulsory.
9. Manual or DHCP configuration is required.	9. Gets automatically configured, no need of manual and DHCP configuration.
10. Fragmentation is done by sender and forwarding routers.	10. Fragmentation is done by only sender.
11. Address Resolution Protocol (ARP) is available to map IPv4 address to MAC address.	11. Address Resolution Protocol (ARP) is replaced with Neighbour Discovery Protocol.
12. It does not support packet flow identification.	12. Supports packet flow identification within IPv6 header using flow label field.
13. Broadcast messages are available.	13. Broadcast messages are not available.

Practice Questions

1. What is IP Addressing?
2. Define IP Routing.
3. Write short notes on:
   (a) Physical address, (b) Broadcast address, (c) Loopback address.
4. Explain IP Protocol and its types.
5. What is addressing ? Explain address classes in detail.
6. With the help of diagram describe IP packet format.
7. Write short note on: 'Border Gateway Protocol'.
8. Explain the term 'routing table' in detail.
9. What is meant by loopback address ?
10. Describe RIP protocol with packet format.
11. What is IPv6 ? and its addressing ?
12. Explain IPv6 packet format with diagram.
13. What are the disadvantages of IPv6 ?
14. Write difference between IPv6 and IPv4 Addresses.
15. Define terms : Unicast Address, Anycast Address.

Chapter 7 ...

APPLICATION LAYER

Contents ...

7.1 Application Layer

    7.1.1 Domain Name System (DNS)

    7.1.2 DNS servers

7.2 Electronic Mail

    7.2.1 Architecture and Services

    7.2.2 Message Formats

    7.2.3 MIME

    7.2.4 Message Transfer

    7.2.5 SMTP

    7.2.6 Mail Gateways

    7.2.7 Relays

    7.2.8 Configuring Mail Servers

    7.2.9 File Transfer Protocol

        7.2.9.1 General Model

        7.2.9.2 Commands

7.3 World Wide Web

    7.3.1 Introduction

    7.3.2 Architectural Overview

    7.3.3 Static and Dynamic Web Pages

    7.3.4 WWW pages and Browsing

    7.3.5 HTTP

   • Practice Questions

7.1 Application Layer

It is the top most layer in OSI and TCP/IP layered model. This layer exists in both layered Models because of its significance, of interacting with user and user applications. This layer is for applications which are involved in communication system.

There are several protocols which work for users in Application Layer. Application layer protocols can be broadly divided into two categories:

- Protocols which are used by users. For example, E-Mail.

- Protocols which help and support protocols used by users. For example DNS.

Few of Application layer protocols are described below:

7.1.1 Domain Name System (DNS)

DNS stands for Domain Name System. or Domain Network Service. DNS is the way in which computers can contact each other and do things such as exchange electronic mail, or display Web pages. A domain name is the unique name that is assigned to a website.

The Internet Protocol (IP) uses Internet address information and the DNS to deliver mail and other information from computer to computer. DNS is used mostly to translate between domain names (www.domainname.com) and IP addresses (123.123.123.123), and to control Internet email delivery.

DNS has two independent aspects:

1. It specifies the name syntax and rules for delegating authority over names. The basic syntax is: `local.group.site`

2. It specifies the implementation of a distributed computing system that efficiently maps names to addresses.

The job that DNS performs is very simple: it takes the IP addresses that computers connected to the Internet, use to communicate with each other and it maps them to hostnames.

The Domain Name System (DNS) provides:

1. A method for identifying hosts with friendly names instead of IP addresses.

2. A distributed mechanism for storing and maintaining lists of names and IP addresses of hosts.

3. A method for locating hosts by resolving their names into their associated IP addresses so that network communication can be initiated with the host.

Domain Name Space

Name space is the abstract space or collection of all possible addresses, names, or identifiers of objects on a network, internetwork, or the Internet. The name in the DNS database form a hierarchical tree structure called the domain name space. Domain name space is hierarchical, which is similar to UNIX file system. Domain names are case insensitive (i.e. com and COM are same).

In this design, names are defined in an inverted tree structure with the root at the top. Every node has a label of maximum 63 characters long. The root label is NULL string.

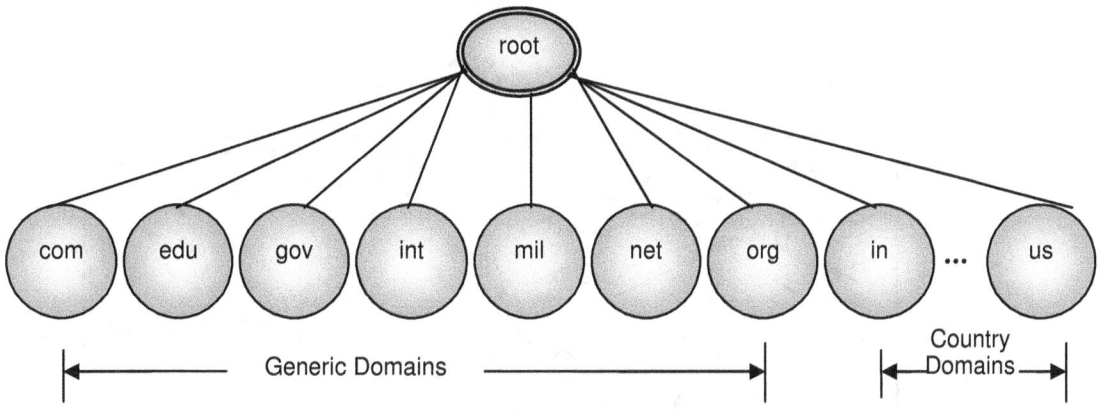

Fig. 7.1: Hierarchical organization of DNS

The domains name space (tree) is divided into two sections i.e. Generic Domains and Country Domain.

1. The **Generic Domains** define registered hosts according to their generic behavior. Each node in the tree defines a domain, which is an index to the domain name space database.

Table 7.1: Example of Generic Domains

Label	Description
com	Commercial organization, such as Hewlett-Packard (*hp.com*), Sun Microsystems (*sun.com*), and IBM (*ibm.com*).
edu	Educational institute, such as U.C. Berkeley (*berkeley.edu*) and Purdue University (*purdue.edu*).
gov	Government institute, such as NASA (*nasa.gov*) and the National Science Foundation (*nsf.gov*).
int	International Organization, such as NATO (*nato.int*).
mil	Military groups, such as the U.S. Army (*army.mil*) and Navy (*navy.mil*).
net	Network support engineers, such as NSFNET (*nsf.net*).
org	Nonprofit organization, such as the Electronic Frontier Foundation (*eff.org*).

Fig. 7.2 shows generic domains.

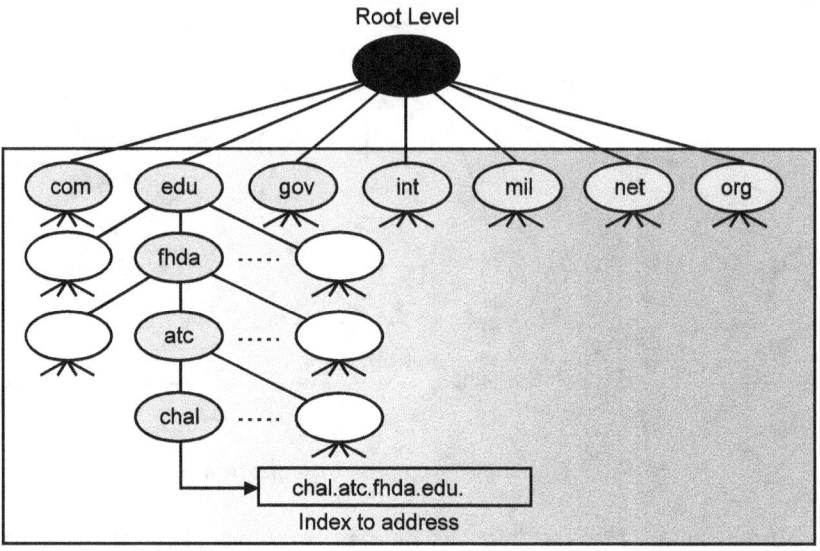

Fig. 7.2: Generic Domain

Recently, a few more Generic Domains have been approved.

Table 7.2: New Generic Domains

Label	Description
aero	Airlines and aerospace companies
biz	Business or firms
coop	Cooperative business organizations
info	Information service provider
museum	Museums and other nonprofit organizations
name	Personal name (individuals)
pro	Professional individual organization
arts	Cultural organization
nom	Personal nomenclatures
rec	Recreation/entertainment organization
store	Businesses offering goods to purchase
web	Web-related organization

2. The **Country Domain** section follows the same format as the generic domains but uses two-character country abbreviations in place of three character organizational abbreviations at the first level.

Table 7.3: Example of Country Domains

Label	Description
au	Australia
ca	Canada
in	India
uk	United Kingdom
fr	France
th	Thailand
us	United States
zw	Zimbabwe

Fig. 7.3 shows Country Domains.

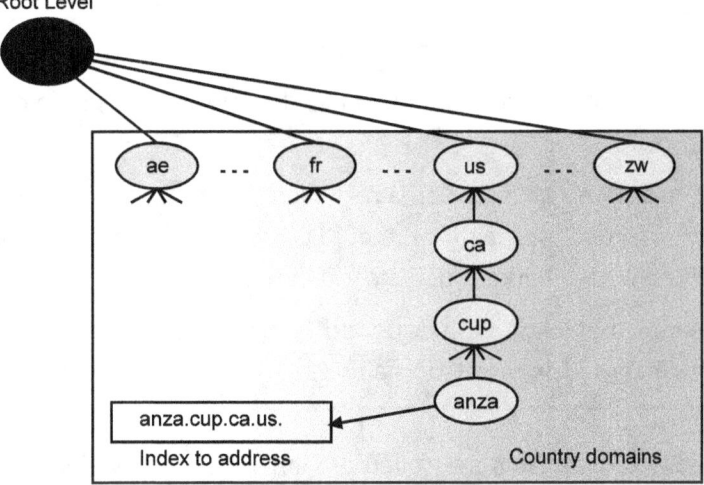

Fig. 7.3: Country Domains

Domain : A domain is a subtree of domain name space. (Refer Fig. 7.4). The name of the domain is the domain name of the node at the top of the subtree. Fig. 7.4 shows .com and .edu domains

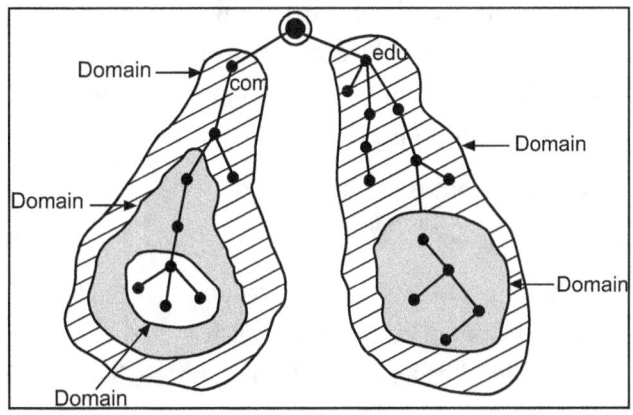

Fig. 7.4: Domains

Domain Name: Domains are the building blocks of DNS. This consists of a group of nodes in the DNS namespace. These are organized hierarchically in the DNS namespace, with the topmost domain called the root domain. The DNS creates a hierarchy of domains or groups of computers and it establishes a domain name (also known as an Internet address) for each computer on an intranet or the Internet, using easily recognizable letters and words instead of numbers.

Major domains also have the responsibility for maintaining lists and addresses of the domains that are underneath them. That next level of domains is responsible for the following level down and so on. Domain name within the Domain Name System (DNS), usually registered with the Internet Network Information Center (InterNIC) for example, the Microsoft.com domain owned by Microsoft Corporation. Domain names can include only the characters a–z, A–Z, and 0–9, the dash (-), and the period.

DNS domains can be classified as one of the following:

1. **A Parent domain**, which contains other domains. An example of a parent domain is microsoft.com.

2. **A Child domain**, or sub-domain, which is contained within a parent domain. Examples of child domains in the Microsoft.com parent domain are northwind. microsoft.com and marketing.microsoft.com.

A domain name that ends with a period is called as absolute domain name or fully qualified domain name. Top level domains are divided into two areas; i.e. generic and countries as shown in Fig. 7.1.

- Three character domains are called as Generic Domains. The generic domains '.gov' and '.mil' are restricted to the United States only.

- Two character domains are called as Country Domains (e.g. in for India, us for United States, nz for New Zealand).

Each domain is named by the path upward from it to the root. The components are separated by periods. This is called as **Hierarchical Routing**. As we know that root label is null, this means that a full domain name always ends in null label; this means the last character is dot because the null string is nothing.

Fig. 7.5 shows some domain names and labels.

1. **Fully Qualified Domain Names:**

   If a label is terminated by a null string, it is called as a Fully Qualified Domain Name (FQDN).A fully qualified domain name contains full name of the host. For example, mail.yahoo.com.It is also called as absolute domain name. It always ends with a period '.' (a dot).

2. Partially Qualified Domain Names:

If a label is not terminated by a null string, it is called as a Partially Qualified Domain Name (PQDN). It starts from a node but never reach to the root node. e.g. mail.yahoo.com. It is also called as relative domain name. It never ends with a period ' . ' (a dot).

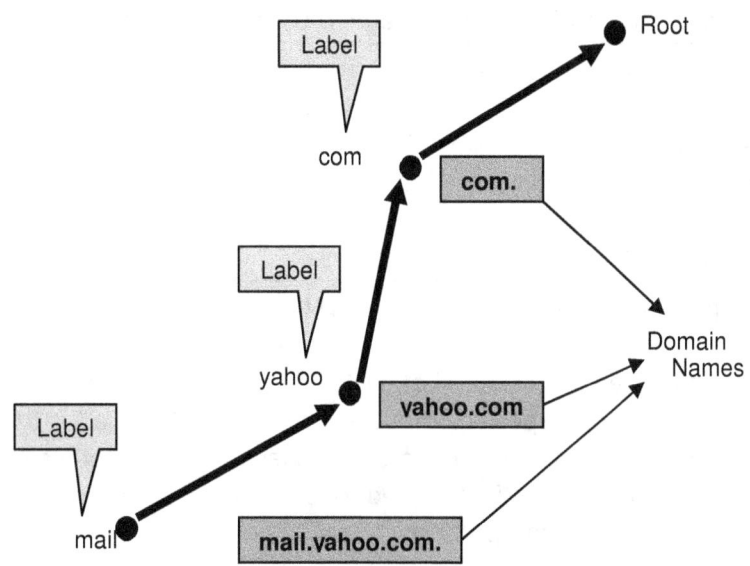

Fig. 7.5: Domain Names and Labels

Table 7.4: Summary of domain names

Name Type	Description	Example
1. Root domain	This is the top of the tree, representing an unnamed level; it is sometimes shown as two empty quotation marks (" "), indicating a null value. When used in a DNS domain name, it is stated by a trailing period (.) to designate that the name is located at the root or highest level of the domain hierarchy. In this instance, the DNS domain name is considered to be complete and points to an exact location in the tree of names. Names stated this way are called FQDN.	A single period (.) or a period used at the end of a name, such as "example. microsoft. com."
2. Top level domain	A name used to indicate a country/region or the type of organization using a name.	".com", which indicates a name registered to a business for commercial use on the Internet.

Contd...

3. Second level domain	Variable-length names registered to an individual or organization for use on the Internet. These names are always based upon an appropriate top-level domain, depending on the type of organization or geographic location where a name is used.	"microsoft.com.", which is the second-level domain name registered to Microsoft by the Internet DNS domain name registrar.
4. Subdomain	Additional names that an organization can create that are derived from the registered second-level domain name. These include names added to grow the DNS tree of names in an organization and divide it into departments or geographic locations.	"example.microsoft.com. ", which is a fictitious subdomain assigned by Microsoft to use in documentation example names.
5. Host or resource name	Names that represent a leaf in the DNS tree of names and identify a specific resource. Typically, the leftmost label of a DNS domain name identifies a specific computer on the network. For example, if a name at this level is used in a host (A) RR, it is used to look up the IP address of computer based on its host name.	"host-a.example.microsoft.com." , where the first label ("host-a") is the DNS host name for a specific computer on the network.

7.1.2 DNS Servers

1. Name Server and DNS Server:

Name server is a host on the Internet or on a TCP/IP internetwork that can be used to resolve host names into IP addresses. These servers are an essential component of the Domain Name System (DNS), which provides the namespace of all hosts on the Internet or on a private TCP/IP internetwork.

Because of name servers, when you want to access or reference a host on a TCP/IP network, you can use its friendly DNS name instead of its IP address, which is generally harder to remember. A DNS server provides 'name resolution service' which means that DNS servers resolve names into IP addresses or vice-versa. DNS servers are also called name servers. Every computer on the Internet has a unique IP addresses (a series of four decimal numbers from 0 to 255 separated by dots).

A DNS server is usually located on the network to which you are attached. If you are using an Internet Service Provider (ISP), your DNS server is at your ISP. If you are using the network at college or office, you probably have a local DNS server somewhere near you.

When user use the web browser to connect to a website, the computer uses the DNS system to find the numerical address of the server on which the website is contained. Within the website address is a portion that is called the 'Domain Name'. The system designed to look this domain up and find the correct server address is called the Domain Name System.

The DNS is a system which allows computers to turn domain names into the unique numerical addresses of the sites and systems you wish to connect to.

When you type "http://www.yahoo.com" into your web browser, your browser sends a DNS query to request that the DNS system look up the exact IP address of Yahoo's web server. The Domain Name System consists of a centralized database that maps domain names to servers that can provide resolution for that domain.

2. Zone:

Since the complete domain name hierarchy can not be stored on a single server, it is divided among many servers. Server is responsible for a zone. We can define a zone as a contiguous part of the entire tree.

If a server accepts responsibility of a domain and does not divide the domain into smaller domains, the domain and the zone refer to the same thing. A server makes a database called a "zone file" and keeps all the information for every node under that domain.

However, if the server divides its domain into subdomains and pass on a part of its authority to other servers then domain and zone will be different from each other. This is shown in the Fig. 7.6.

The information about the nodes in the subdomains is stored in the servers at the lower levels, with the original server keeping some sort of reference to these lower-level servers.

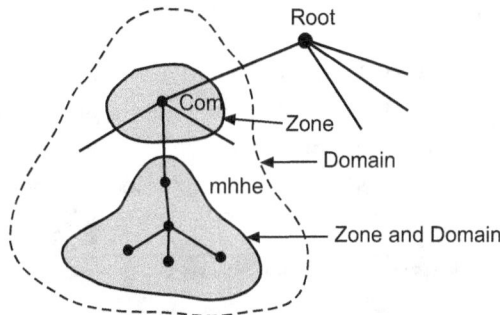

Fig. 7.6: Zones and Domains

3. Root Server:

Root server is a server whose zone consists of the whole tree. Root server does not store any information about domains but pass on its authority to other servers. There are several root servers distributed all over the world.

4. Primary and Secondary Servers:

There are two types of DNS servers:

(a) Primary server: Primary server stores a file about the zone for which it is an authority. Primary server is responsible for creating, maintaining and updating a zone file. It stores the zone file on a local disk.

(b) Secondary server.: A Secondary server is a server that transfers the complete information about a zone from another server (primary and secondary) and stores the file on its local disk.

The Secondary server neither create nor update the zone files, updating is done only by the Primary server, which further sends the updated zone file to the secondary.

A Primary server loads all information from the disk file; the Secondary server loads all information from the Primary server.

5. Zone Transfer:

When the Secondary server, downloads the information from the primary server, it is called as zone transfer. In other words "the process of replicating a zone file to multiple DNS servers is called zone transfer".

Zone transfer is achieved by copying the zone file from one DNS server (primary) to a second DNS server (secondary). It can be made from both primary and secondary DNS servers.

A master DNS server is the source of the zone information during a transfer. The master DNS server can be a primary or secondary DNS server. If the master DNS server is a primary DNS server, then the zone transfer comes directly from the DNS server hosting the primary zone. If the master server is a secondary DNS server, then the zone file received from the master DNS server by means of a zone transfer is a copy of the read-only secondary zone file.

As shown in the Fig. 7.7 zone transfers between servers follow an ordered process. This process varies depending on whether a zone has been previously replicated, or if initial replication of a new zone is being performed.

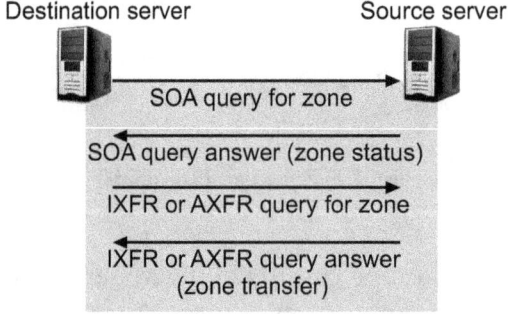

Fig. 7.7: Zone transfer process

1. During new configuration, the destination server sends an initial "all zone" transfer (AXFR – Asynchronous Full Transfer Zone) request to the master DNS server configured as its source for the zone.

2. The master (source) server responds and fully transfers the zone to the secondary (destination) server. The zone is delivered to the destination server requesting the

transfer with its version established by use of a Serial number field in the properties for the Start Of Authority (SOA) RR (Resource Record). The SOA RR also contains a stated refresh interval in seconds (by default, 900 seconds or 15 minutes) to indicate when the destination server should next request to renew the zone with the source server.

3. When the refresh interval expires, an SOA query is used by the destination server to request renewal of the zone from the source server.

4. The source server answers the query for its SOA record. This response contains the serial number for the zone in its current state at the source server. The destination server checks the serial number of the SOA record in the response and determines how to renew the zone. If the value of the serial number in the SOA response is equal to its current local serial number, it concludes that the zone is the same at both servers and that a zone transfer is not needed. The destination server then renews the zone by resetting its refresh interval based on the value of this field in the SOA response from its source server.

5. If the value of the serial number in the SOA response is higher than its current local serial number, it concludes that the zone has been updated and that a transfer is needed. If the destination server concludes that the zone has changed, it sends an IXFR (Incremental Zone Transfer) query to the source server, containing its current local value for the serial number in the SOA record for the zone.

6. The source server responds with either an incremental or full transfer of the zone. If the source server supports incremental transfer by maintaining a history of recent incremental zone changes for modified resource records, it can answer with an Incremental Zone Transfer (IXFR) of the zone. If the source server does not support incremental transfer, or does not have a history of zone changes, it can answer with a full (AXFR) transfer of the zone instead.

Authoritative servers:

DNS servers can be configured to host more than one domain. A server can be primary for one domain, and secondary for another. The term authoritative refers to any DNS servers that has a complete copy of the domain's information, whether it was entered by an administrator or transferred from a primary server. Thus, a secondary server can and should be authoritative for any domain for which it performs secondary authoritative resolution.

DNS server that contains a complete copy of the domain's zone file is considered to be authoritative for that domain only.

A complete copy of a zone file must have:

*   A valid Start Of Authority (SOA) record,
*   Valid Name Server (NS) records for the domain.

The listed records i.e. NS should match the servers listed in the sort record. Servers listed in the zone file, but not in the sort record are called lame servers. The term authoritative Only is normally used to describe two concepts:

- The server will deliver Authoritative Responses – it is a zone master or slave for one or more domains.
- The server will not cache.

There are two configurations in which Authoritative Only servers are typically used.

1. As the public or external sever in a Stealth (DMZ or Hidden Master) DNS used to provide perimeter security.

2. In high performance DNS servers, the DNS servers such as BIND may not provide an ideal solution and there are a number of Open Source. Alternatives some of which specialise in high performance authorities only solution.

It is considered standard practice to have a primary authoritative DNS server and secondary authoritative DNS server. When registering your domain with an accredited domain name registrar, the primary authoritative DNS server is the server you list first, all other DNS servers you list will be secondary. The secondary server and the primary server should be on different IP subnets and the hardware should be located in different physical locations.

By putting the two DNS servers on different subnets and placing them geographically apart, you greatly reduce the risk that a single catastrophe will take down the entire system of DNS servers for your domain. Having more than one secondary DNS server for your domain is also good practice, but you can only designate one primary DNS server with your registrar because DNS can only point to a single primary DNS server for your domain.

1. **Authoritative responses:** Any response to a DNS query that originates from a DNS server with a complete copy of the zone file is said to be an 'authoritative response'.

2. **Non-authoritative responses:** It is a response that comes from DNS servers that have cached an answer for a given host, but received that information from a server that is not authoritative for the domain.

1. Delegation:

Delegation is a process of assigning responsibility for a portion of a DNS namespace to a separate entity. This separate entity could be another organization, department or workgroup within your company. In technical terms, delegating means assigning authority over portions of DNS namespace to other zones.

Such delegation is represented by the NS (Name Server) record that specifies the delegated zone and the DNS name of the server authoritative for that zone. Delegating domains works a lot like delegating tasks at work. A manager may break up a large project into smaller tasks and delegate responsibility for each of these tasks to different employees.

Delegation is the process of distributing the responsibility for resolving names or IP addresses across multiple DNS servers maintained by different organizations. The delegation process is how DNS names, domain names, are resolved.

Likewise, an organization administering a domain can divide it into subdomains. Each of those subdomains can be delegated to other organizations. This means that an organization becomes responsible for maintaining all the data in that subdomain. It can freely change the data and even divide its subdomain up into more subdomains and delegate those.

The parent domain contains only pointers to sources of the subdomain's data so that it can refer queriers there. The domain stanford.edu, for example, is delegated to the folks at Stanford who run the university's networks, (See Fig. 7.8).

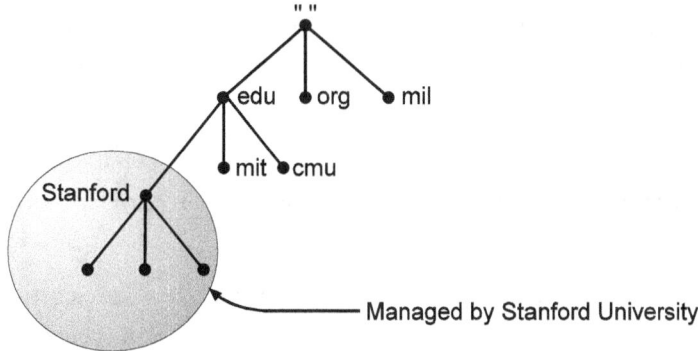

Fig. 7.8: stanford.edu is delegated to Stanford University

Delegating across multiple zones was part of the original design goal of DNS. Following are the main reasons for the delegation of a DNS namespace:

o   A need to delegate management of a DNS domain to a number of organizations or departments within an organization.

o   A need to distribute the load of maintaining one large DNS database among multiple name servers to improve the name resolution performance as well as create a DNS fault tolerant environment.

o   A need to allow for host's organizational affiliation by including them in appropriate domains.

2.   Delegation of Authority:

The concepts of Delegation and Authority lies at the core of domain name system hierarchy. The Authority for the root domain lies with Internet Corporation for Assigned Numbers and Names (ICANN). Since, 1998 ICANN, a non-profit organization, has assumed this responsibility from the US government. The gTLDs (Generic Top Level Domains) are authoritatively administered by ICANN and delegated to a series of accredited registrars. The ccTLDs (Country-Code Top Level Domains) are delegated to the individual countries for administration purposes.

Delegation within any domain may be almost limitless and is decided by the delegated authority, for example, the US and Canada both delegate city within province/state domains thus the address (or URL) tennisshoes.nb.us is the town of Tennis Shoes in the State of Nebraska in the United States and we could even have "mycompany. tennisshoes.nb.us".

By reading a domain name from right to left you can track its delegation. This unit of delegation can also be referred to as a zone in standards documentation.

"www.example.com" is built up from www and example.com. The domain-name example.com part was delegated from a gTLD registrar which in turn was delegated from ICANN. The www part was chosen by the owner of the domain. Since they are new the delegated authority for the example.com name, they own everything to the left to the delegated domain name. The leftmost part, www in this case, is called a host name. By convention (but only convention) web sites have the 'host' name of www, (World Wide Web) but you can have a web site whose name is fred.example.com.

Equally you may have a web site whose access address (URL) is www.example.com running on a server whose real name is mary.example.com. Again this is perfectly permissible.

In short, the host part may refer to a real host name or a service name such as www. Since, the domain owner controls this process it's all allowed. Every computer, or service, that is addressable (has a URL) via the Internet or an internal network has a host name part, here are some more illustrative examples:

`www.example.com:` the company web service

`ftp.example.com:` the company file transfer

3. Authority Records:

Zones are based on a concept of server authority. When a DNS server is configured to load a zone, it uses two types of resource records to determine the authoritative properties of the zone:

(i) First, the Start Of Authority (SOA), Resource Record (RR) indicates the name of origin for the zone and contains the name of the server that is the primary source for information about the zone. It also indicates other basic properties of the zone.

(ii) Next, the Name Server (NS), Resource Record (RR) is used to notate which DNS servers are designated as authoritative for the zone. By listing a server in the NS RR, it becomes known to others as an authoritative server for the zone. This means that any server specified in the NS RR is to be considered an authoritative source by others, and is able to answer with certainty any queries made for names included in the zone.

Resource Records (RR) :

A DNS database consists of Resource Records (RRs).Each RR identifies a particular resource within the database. Resource records for a domain are stored in a standardized format an ASCII text file often called as a Zone file.

DNS resource records are the data that is associated with DNS names in the DNS namespace. Each domain name of the DNS namespace tree contains a set of resource records, and each resource record in the set contains different types of information relating to the domain name.

Resource records have the following syntax:

```
Owner TTL Class Type RDATA
```

Table 7.5 : Fields of Resource Record

Name	Description
Owner	It is the name of the host or the DNS domain to which this resource record belongs.
Time To Live (TTL)	It is a 32-bit integer that represents, in seconds, the length of time that a DNS server or resolver should cache this entry before it is discarded. This field is optional, and if it is not specified, the client uses the Minimum TTL in the SOA record. Value zero indicates entry should not be cached.
Class	It is 16 bit value which defines the protocol family in use. Class is almost always IN (Internet Protocol) for the Internet system.
Type	It is identifies the type of resource record.
RDATA	It is the resource record data and is a variable type that represents the information being described by the type.

Resource records (RRs) are represented in binary form in packets when lookups and responses are made using DNS. Different types of resource records can be used to provide DNS based data about computers on a TCP/IP network. These are listed below:

1. Address Records (A):

Address, or A records, map the name of a machine to its numeric IP address. In clearer terms, this record states the hostname and IP address of a certain machine. To resolve a hostname means to find its matching IP address. This is the record that A name server would send another name server to answer a resolution query.

The record below is an example of how an A record should look:

eric.pict.com. IN A 36.36.1.6

The first column contains the machine's hostname. The second column lists which class the record is of. For most basic DNS work, all you will need is the IN designation, which stands for InterNet. The next column denotes the type of record the entry is actually, and the last column is the IP address itself.

It is possible to map more than one IP address to a given hostname. This often happens for people who run a firewall and have two ethernet cards in one machine. All you must do is add a second A record, with every column the same save for the IP address.

It is also possible to map more than one host name to one IP address. This is not recommended, however, since DNS has a special record for allowing machines to have aliases, called a canonical name, or CNAME record.

2. Canonical Name Records (CNAME):

CNAME records simply allow a machine to be known by more than one hostname. There must always be an A record for the machine before aliases can be added. The host name of a machine that is stated in an A record is called the canonical, or official name of the machine. Other records should point to the canonical name.

Here is an example of a CNAME:

www.pict.com. IN CNAME eric.pict.com.

You can see the similarities to the previous record. Records always read from left to right, with the subject to be queried about on the left and the answer to the query on the right. A machine can have an unlimited number of CNAME aliases. A new record must be entered for each alias.

3. Mail Exchange Records (MX):

MX records are far more important than they sound. They allow all mail for a domain to be routed to one host. This is exceedingly useful. It abates the load on your internal hosts since they do not have to route incoming mail, and it allows your mail to be sent to any address in your domain even if that particular address does not have a computer associated with it. For example, we have a mail server running on the fictitious machine eric.pict.com. For convenience sake, however, we want our email address to be "user@pict.com" rather than "user@eric.pict.com".

This is accomplished by the record shown below:

pict.com. IN MX 10 eric.pict.com.

The column on the far left signifies the address that you want to use as an Internet email address. The next two entries have been explained thoroughly in previous records. The next column, the number 10, is different from the normal DNS record format. It is a signifier of priority. Often larger systems will have backup mail servers, perhaps more than one. Obviously, you will only want the backups receiving mail if something goes wrong with the primary mail server. You can indicate this with your MX records. A lower number in an MX record means a higher priority, and mail will be sent to the server with the lowest number (the lowest possible being 0). If something happens so that this server becomes unreachable, the computer delivering the mail will attempt every other server listed in the DNS tables, in order of priority.

Obviously, you can have as many MX records as you would like. It is also a good idea to include an MX record even if you are having mail sent directly to a machine with an A record. Some sendmail programs only look for MX records.

It is also possible to include wildcards in MX records. If you have a domain where your users each have their own machine running mail clients on them, mail could be sent directly to each machine. Rather than clutter your DNS entry, you can add an MX record like this one:

*.pict.com. IN MX 10 eric.pict.com.

This would make any mail set to any individual workstation in the pict.com domain go through the server eric.pict.com. One should use caution with wildcards; specific records will be given precedence over ones containing wildcards.

4. Pointer Records (PTR):

Although there are different ways to set up PTR records, we will be explaining only the most frequently used method, called "in-addr.arpa".

In-addr.arpa PTR records are the exact inverse of Address records. They allow your machine to be recognized by its IP address. Resolving a machine in this fashion is called a "reverse lookup". It is becoming more and more common that a machine will do a reverse lookup on your machine before allowing you to access a service (such as a World Wide Web page). Reverse lookups are a good security measure, verifying that your machine is exactly who it claims to be. In-addr.arpa records look as such:

6.1.36.36.in-addr.arpa. IN PTR eric.pict.com.

The Address record   simply has the IP address in reverse for the host name in the last column.

A note for those who run their own name servers: although Internet is capable of pulling zones from your name server, we cannot pull the inverse zones (these in-addr.arpa records) unless you have been assigned a full class C network. If you would like us to put PTR records in our name servers for you, you will have to fill out the online web form on the support.allegianceinternet.com page.

5. SOA records:

Every zone must begin with a Start Of Authority (SOA) record, which names the zone and provides default information for the zone. It lists the fields that appear in the RDATA section of an SOA record. Note that these fields are positional, so you should include a value for all of them and list them in the order specified. Because the SOA record has so many RDATA fields, you'll probably need to use parentheses to continue the SOA record onto multiple lines.

The SOA record controls how fast updated zones propagate from the master to the slave servers, and how long resource records (RRs) are cached in caching servers before they are flushed. Both of these affect your ability to effectuate "instant" changes in the zones you maintain.

6. Name Server Records (NS):

NS records are imperative to functioning DNS entries. They are very simple; they merely state the authoritative name servers for the given domain. There must be at least two NS records in every DNS entry. NS records look like this:

pict.com. IN NS draven.pict.com.

There also must be an A record in your DNS for each machine you enter as A NAME server in your domain.

If Internet is doing primary and secondary names service, we will set up these records for you automatically, with "nse.algx.net" and "nsf.algx.net" as your two authoritative name servers.

SOA Records

An SOA (Start of Authority) record is the most essential part of a zone file. The SOA record is a way for the Domain Administrator to give out simple information about the domain like, how often it is updated, when it was last updated, when to check back for more information, what is the admin's email address and so on. A zone file can contain only one SOA Record.

A properly optimized and updated SOA record can reduce bandwidth between name servers, increase the speed of website access and ensure the site is alive even when the primary DNS server is down. SOA indicates the DNS server that either is originally created it or is now the primary server for the zone.

It is also used to store other properties such as version information and timings that affect zone renewal or expiration. These properties affect how often transfers of the zone are done between servers authoritative for the zone.

The SOA resource record contains the information on the next page:

Field	Description
Primary server (owner)	The host name for the primary DNS server for the zone where the file was created.
Responsible person Contact email	The e-mail address of the person responsible for administering the zone. A period (.) is used instead of an at sign (@) in this e-mail name.
Serial number	The revision number of the zone file. This number increases each time a resource record in the zone changes. It is important that this value increases each time the zone is changed, so that either partial zone changes or the fully revised zone can be replicated to other secondary servers during subsequent transfers.

contd...

Refresh interval	The time, in seconds, that a secondary DNS server waits before querying its source for the zone to attempt renewal of the zone. When the refresh interval expires, the secondary DNS server requests a copy of the current SOA record for the zone from its source, which answers this request. The secondary DNS server then compares the serial number of the source server's current SOA record (as indicated in the response) with the serial number in its own local SOA record. If they are different, the secondary DNS server requests a zone transfer from the primary DNS server. The default for this field is 3600 seconds (15 minutes).
Retry interval	The time, in seconds, a secondary server waits before retrying a failed zone transfer. Normally, this time is less than the refresh interval. The default value is 600 seconds (10 minutes).
Expire interval	The time, in seconds, before a secondary server stops responding to queries after a lapsed refresh interval where the zone was not refreshed or updated. Expiration occurs because at this point in time, the secondary server must consider its local data unreliable. The default value is 86,400 seconds, (24 hours).
Minimum (default) TTL	The default Time-To-Live (TTL) of the zone and the maximum interval for caching negative answers to name queries. The default value is 3,600 seconds (1 hour).

The following is an example of a default SOA resource record:

```
@    IN  SOA      nameserver.example.microsoft.com.
postmaster.example.microsoft.com. (
; serial number
             3600           ; refresh   [1h]
             600            ; retry     [10m]
             86400          ; expire    [1d]
             3600 )         ; min TTL   [1h]
```

In the above example SOA record shown above, the primary or originating server for the zone is shown as nameserver.example.microsoft.com. The e-mail address for the person to contact regarding questions about this zone is postmaster.example.microsoft.com.

Periods are used to represent e-mail addresses when writing and storing DNS domain names in a zone. In an e-mail application, the previous example address would instead likely appear as "postmaster@example.microsoft.com".

The parentheses used in the SOA resource record as it appears in a zone file are used to enable wrapping of the record over multiple lines of text. If an individual TTL value is assigned and applied to a specified resource record used in the zone, it overrides the minimum (default) TTL set in the SOA record.

DNS Protocol

The DNS protocol consists of different types of DNS messages that are processed according to the information in their message fields. DNS protocols consist of message type which consists of queries; updates, and responses, DNS (Domain Name System) query message format has fixed length which is 12 bytes. DNS Header has fixed length and all other such as Question Entries, Answer Resource Records, Authority Resource Records, Additional Resource Records have variable length.

There are many other type of DNS messages or protocol such as DNS query message header, DNS query question entries, DNS resource records, Name query message, Name query response, Reverse name query message, DNS update message format, DNS update message flags, Dynamic update response message.

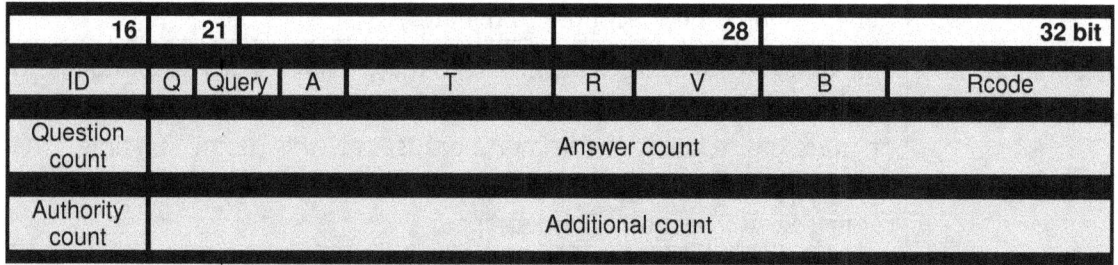

Fig. 7.9: DNS Protocol Message

Various fields of DNS protocol messages are:

ID: Identification field used to correlate queries and responses.

Q: Identifies the message as a query or response.

Query: Describes the type of message: 0 Standard query (name to address); 1 Inverse query; 2 Server status request.

A (Authoritative Answer): When set to 1, identifies the response is one made by an authoritative name server.

T (Truncation): When set to 1, indicates the message has been truncated.

R: Set to 1 by the resolve to request recursive service by the name server.

V: Signals the availability of recursive service by the name server.

B: Reserved for future use. Must be set to 0.

Rcode: Response Code, that is set by the name server to identify the status of the query.

Question count: Defines the number of entries in the question section.

Answer count: Defines the number of resource records in the answer section.

Authority count: Defines the number of name server resource records in the authority section.

Additional count: Defines the number of resource records in the additional records section.

7.2 Electronic Mail

Email, e-mail or electronic mail is the transmission of messages (emails or email messages) over electronic networks like the internet. It is a computer based method of sending message from one computer user to another. E-mail originated in the early 1970s with ARPANET and is now the primary method of business communication today.

The use of a network to transmit text messages, memos, and reports; usually referred to as e-mail. Users can send a message to one or more individuals, to a predefined group, or to all users on the system. When you receive a message, you can read, print, forward, answer, or delete it.

Electronic mail (e-mail) is probably the most widely used TCP/IP application. The basic Internet mail protocols provide mail (note) and message exchange between TCP/IP hosts; facilities have been added for the transmission of data that cannot be represented as 7-bit ASCII text.

7.2.1 Architecture and Services

E-mails travel across the Internet between the source and destination via servers, in the same way that traditional paper mail travels the world via post offices .On the Internet, the role of post offices or sorting offices are assumed by Mail Transfer Agents or MTAs. The concept of E-mail varies slightly from a traditional post office in that a Mail Server stores E-mails for an E-mail client. The E-mail client retrieves and delivers them. Traditional mail is usually delivered, not retrieved. Mail Servers are sometimes called Delivery Agents and Mail Clients are sometimes referred to as Mail User Agents (MUAs), e.g. MS Outlook.

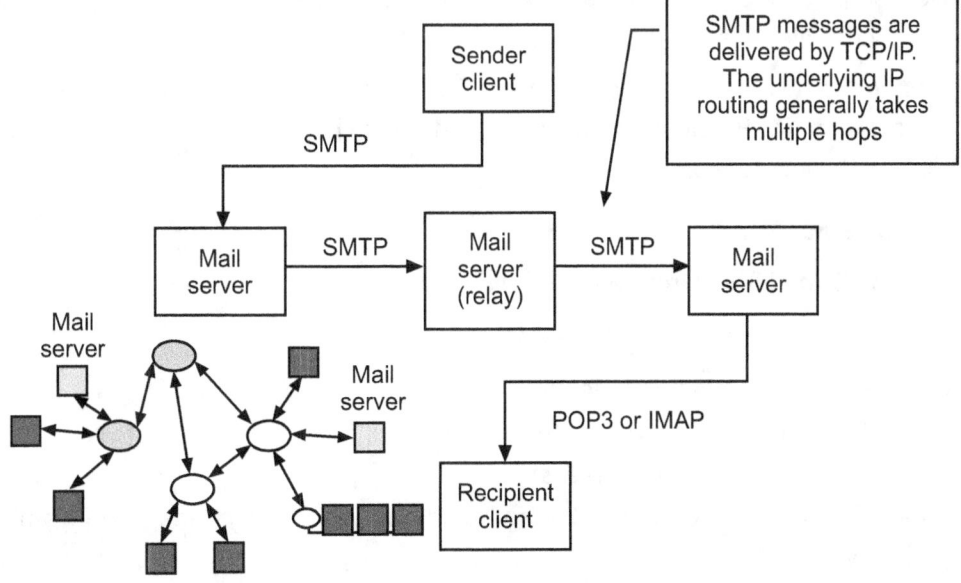

Fig. 7.10: Basic Email Architecture

E-mails can either be stored locally on the AXS GUARD mail server or on a dedicated server, e.g. in the AXS GUARD LAN. Mail servers are sometimes also referred to as Delivery Agents.

Typically, E-mail systems support following 5 basic functions:

(i)   **Composition** refers to the process of creating messages and answers. Although any text editor can be used for the body of the message, the system itself can provide assistance with addressing and the numerous header fields attached to each message.

For example, when answering a message, the e-mail system can extract the originator's address from the incoming e-mail and automatically insert it into the proper place in the reply.

(ii)   **Transfer** refers to moving messages from the originator to the recipient. This requires establishing a direct connection with the destination MTA or some intermediate MTA, outputting the message, and releasing the connection. The e-mail system should do this automatically, without user interaction. At this stage, security checks are performed. By default, the transfer of messages is unencrypted. However, message traffic can be encrypted, as the AXS GUARD MTA supports the Transport Layer Security Protocol or TLS.

(iii) **Storage** is the process of saving new messages in the appropriate folders, archiving, etc.

(iv) **Reporting** refers to communicating to the originator and system administrators what happened to a message, For example: the delivery status.

(v)   **Displaying** incoming messages is needed so people can read their e-mail. Sometimes conversion is required or a special viewer must be invoked, For Example: if the message is a PostScript file.

(vi) **Disposition** is the final step and refers to what the recipient does with the message after receiving it. Possibilities include deleting it before reading, deleting it after reading, archiving, forwarding, etc.

7.2.2 Message Formats

Starting a New E-mail Message: (For MS-Outlook)

Following are ways to start a new message.

- Choose File → New → Mail Message.
- Press Ctrl + n (Windows) or Cmd + N (Macintosh).
- Choose Actions → New Mail Message.
- Choose Actions → New Mail Message Using and then select an option from the list (Windows only)
- With the e-mail folder (Inbox) or Outlook Today open click

- If you want to start a new e-mail message with a folder other then Inbox or Outlook Today open (the New button changes depending upon what outlook folder is open).
  - o Click on the triangle in the new button to open the drop-down list.
  - o Choose New Mail Message.

1. The E-mail Message Window:

- From field (not shown)
  - o If Outlook automatically enters your e-mail address for you, 'From field' box is not shown by default.
  - o If you want to see it manually, choose 'View → From field' option.

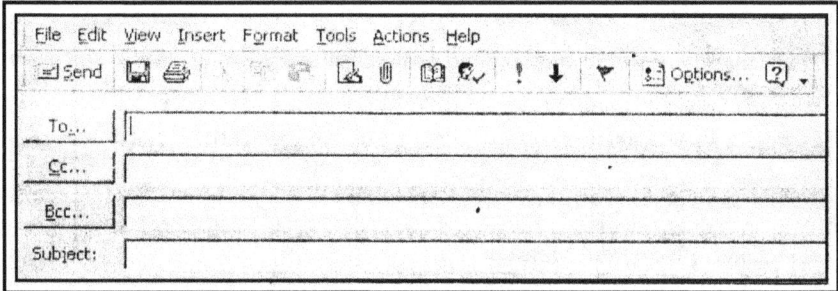

Fig. 7.11 : Addressing E-mail

- **To field:**
  - o This field contains the addresses of the primary recipients of this e-mail.
  - o To enter multiple addresses, separate them by semicolons, or by pressing the < **Enter** > or < **Returns** > key after each address.

- **Cc field:**
  - o Cc Stands for "Carbon copy" or "Courtesy copy".
  - o This field constants the addresses of the secondary recipients of this e-mail.
  - o Anyone whose address is listed here is known to all primary recipients and to all other secondary recipients.

- **Bcc field:**
  - o If this field is not visible choose View → Bcc field .
  - o Bcc stands for "Blind carbon copy" or "Blind courtesy copy".
  - o This field contains the addresses of any person that must receive the message without any primary or secondary recipient knowing that fact furthermore, if there are multiple Bcc recipients, none of them know of the other Bcc recipients.

- **Subject field:**
  - o All e-mail messages should have a subject.

2. E-mail Address:

Any of several types of addresses that ensure an e-mail message reaches its intended recipient. An e-mail address must contain sufficient information so that the message can be routed to its specific recipient. There are various kinds of e-mail address formats depending on the e-mail system in use. Address formats typically include at least two parts:

(i) A User Portion indicates the name or alias of the user to whom the mail is directed.

(ii) A Routing Portion indicates the information needed to route the message to the particular mail system on which the user has his or her mailbox

An e-mail system may be implemented on a Peer-to-Peer network, Client/Server architecture, a Mainframe computer, or on a Dial-up service, such as America Online. Email is by far the most popular Internet application, with well over 80 percent of Internet users taking advantage of the service.

E-mail has several advantages over conventional mail systems, including:

1. E-mail is fast - very fast when compared with conventional mail.

2. If something exists on your computer as a file - text, graphical images, even program files and video segments - you can usually send it as e-mail.

3. E-mail is very extensive. You can now send e-mail to well over half the countries in the world.

The problems associated with e-mail are similar to those associated with online communications in general, such as security, privacy (always assume that your e-mail is not private), and the legal status of documents exchanged via e-mail.

- To deliver mail, a mail handling system must use an addressing system with unique address. The addressing system used by SMTP consists of two parts: a local part and a domain name, separated by an @ sign.

- The local part defines name of user mailbox, where all the mail received for a user is stored for retrieval by the mail reader (user agent).

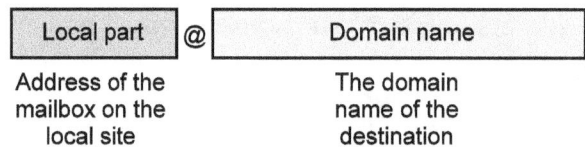

Fig. 7.12: E-mail Address

An organization usually selects one or more hosts to receive and send mail; they are called as mail exchangers. The domain name assigned to each mail exchanger either comes from the DNS database or is a logical name (e.g., the name of the organization).

Example of email address: abc@gmail.com

3. Mailbox:

In e-mail systems, an area of hard-disk space used to store e-mail messages until users can access them. An onscreen or audio message often tells users that they have mail. Before email can be sent to an individual, the person must be assigned an electronic mailbox. The mailbox consists of passive storage area. An electronic mailbox is private, the permissions are set to allow the mail software to add an incoming message to an arbitrary mailbox, but to deny anyone except owner to examine or remove message.

The email system periodically checks the mailboxes. If a user has mail, it informs the user with a notice. If the user is ready to read the mail, a list is displayed in which each line contains summary of the info about a particular message in the mailbox. The summary usually includes the sender mail address and the subject. The user can select any of the messages and display its contents on the screen.

4. E-Mail Structure:

To send mail, the user creates mail that looks very similar to postal mail.

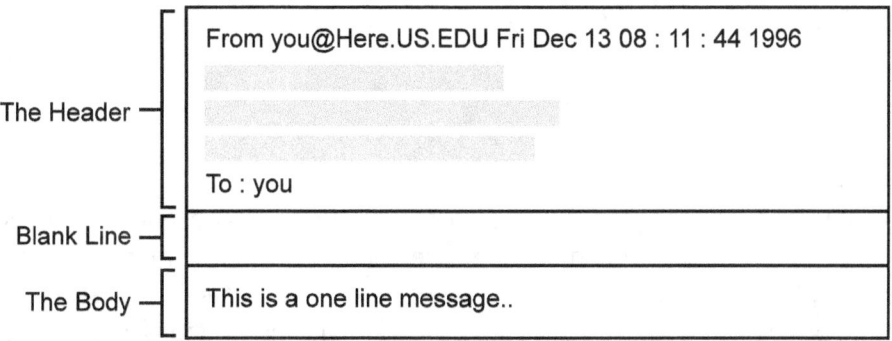

Fig. 7.13: Every mail message is composed of the header and the body

A email message consists of the text of the message (called the body) and a chunk of information at the beginning of the message that contains information about who sent the message, where it is going, and so on(called the header). Usually the header and body of the mail message are separated by a blank line.

Many messages also include a chunk of data at the end of the message that is called the Signature. The signature is a bit of ASCII data written by the sender to be included in every message; it gives information about the sender and may contain a pithy saying.

The header is made up of two parts. The first part contains information about the sender and recipient and includes their addresses. This portion is often called the envelope. The second part of the header has information specific to the handling of the mail message, including the subject, the transport used to send the message, recipients on a copy list, the date, and similar information.

The header of a mail message consists of a number of lines separated by new line characters. Each line has a field name followed by a colon and the contents of the field. The mail header is terminated by a null line (that is, a line with nothing preceding the <CRLF> (Carriage Return Line Feed) sequence).

The following is an extract from a header file:

From brutus-bignet.com Thu Sep 21 17:40:32 1995
Received: from bignet.com by tpci.tpci.com id aa00184; 21 Sep 95 17:39 EDT
Received: from mailserv.biggernet.com ([147.77.1.1]) by bignet.com with
SMTP id <250079-4>; Thu, 21 Sep 1995 20:48:04 -0400
Received: by biggernet.com (4.1/SMI-4.1)
id AA00266; Thu, 21 Sep 95 17:39:03 PDT
Date: Thu, 21 Sep 1995 20:39:03 -0400
From: Yvonne <yvonne@chatton.bignet.com>
Message-Id: <9509220039.AA00266@yvonne@chatton.bignet.com>
To: tparker@tpci.com
Subject: Important stuff
Cc: prudie@bignet.com

The first few lines of the header show who sent the message and how it got to its destination. The rest of the header shows the date, message ID (each message has a unique identification number), the subject line, and any users copied on the message. Each line has the field:value format, although the exact layout of each line changes depending on the field.

5. Sending Messages:

To send e-mail immediately, simply click .

6. Receiving New Messages:

When you receive new mail, Outlook will alert you with a sound. Outlook Windows users will also see a picture of an envelope in the Systray of the Task Bar.

By default:

- All new messages are deposited in the Inbox folder
- Unread messages are displayed in bold type; read message in normal type
- Messages are listed in Received order

Double-click on a message to open and read it

Choose View → Auto Preview to display the first few lines of the message in the Inbox folder window.

Advantages of E-mails:

1. **E-mails are easy to use:** You can organize your daily correspondence, send and receive electronic messages and save them on computers.

2. **E-mails are fast:** They are delivered at once around the world. No other form of written communication is as fast as an email.

3. **Language:** The language used in emails is simple and informal.

4. When you reply to an email you can attach the original message so that when you answer the recipient knows what you are talking about. This is important if you get hundreds of emails a day.

5. **Auto Responders:** It is possible to send automated emails with a certain text. In such a way it is possible to tell the sender that you are on vacation. These emails are called Auto Responders.

6. **Emails do not use paper:** They are environment friendly and save a lot of trees from being cut down.

7. **Images/Pictures:** Emails can also have pictures in them. You can send birthday cards or newsletters as emails.

8. Products can be **advertised** with e-mails. Companies can reach a lot of people and inform them in a short time.

Disadvantages of E-mails:

1. E-mails may carry viruses. These are small programs that harm your computer system. They can read out your email address book and send themselves to a number of people around the world.

2. Many people send unwanted emails to others. These are called spam mails. It takes a lot of time to filter out the unwanted emails from those that are really important.

3. Emails cannot really be used for official business documents. They may be lost and you cannot sign them.

4. Your mailbox may get flooded with emails after a certain time so you have to empty it from time to time.

7.2.3 MIME

MIME stands for "Multipurpose Internet Mail Extensions". MIME is a widely used Internet standard for encoding binary files to send them as e-mail attachments over the Internet.

MIME is an Internet specification that allows users to send multiple-part and multimedia messages, rather than simple text messages. A MIME-enabled e-mail application can send PostScript images, binary files, audio messages, and digital video over the Internet. Email can send message only in NVT (Network Virtual Terminal) 7-bit ASCII format.

In MIME, email has some limitations e.g. one cannot use it for writing the mail in the languages which are not supported by 7-bit ASCII characters. (French, German, Russian are some of the languages that can't be represented by 7-bit ASCII format). Also, MIME can not be used to send binary files or video or audio data. It allows non ASCII data to be sent through email.

MIME transforms non-ASCII data at the sender site to NVT-ASCII data & delivers it to the client MTA (Message Transfer Agent) to be sent through the internet. The message at the receiving side is transformed back to the original data (Non-ASCII). From the point of normal user, MIME is a set of software functions that transforms non-ASCII data to ASCII data and vice versa as shown in Fig. 7.14.

Fig. 7.14: MIME

MIME defines five headers that can be added to the original e-mail header.

1. **MIME Version:** This field defines the version of MIME used. Current version of MIME is 1.1.

2. **Content-Type:** This field defines the type of the data used in the message body. The data can be of different types such as text, image, audio, video multipart or application data. These data types are further divided into subtypes. For example, text data type is further divided into plain text and HTML, Image data type is further divided into JPG images, GIF images etc.

3. **Content-Transfer-Encoding:** This field gives information about the encoding type of the message. Five types of encoding methods are listed below:

   (a) **7 Bit**: used for NVT ASCII characters and short lines

   (b) **8 Bit:** used for Non ASCII characters and short lines

   (c) **Binary:** used for Non ASCII characters with unlimited length lines

   (d) **Base 64:** 6 bits block of data are encoded into 8 bit ASCII characters.

   (e) **Quoted Printable:** Non-ASCII characters are encoded as an equal sign followed by an ASCII code.

4. **Content-Id:** This header uniquely identifies the whole message in a multiple message environment.

5. **Content-Description:** This header defines whether the body is image, audio or video (non textual).

Fig. 7.15 shows MIMI header.

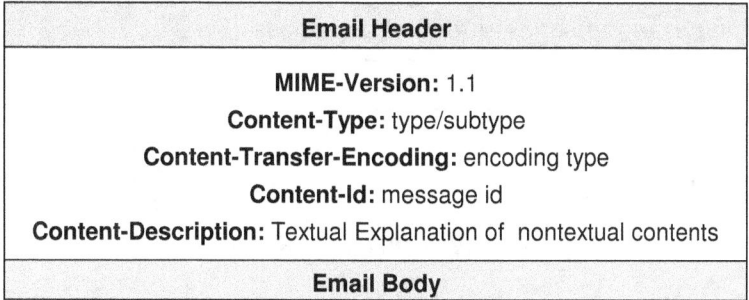

Email Header
MIME-Version: 1.1
Content-Type: type/subtype
Content-Transfer-Encoding: encoding type
Content-Id: message id
Content-Description: Textual Explanation of nontextual contents
Email Body

Fig. 7.15 : MIME header

Advantages of MIME:

1. Multiple mail is possible in MIME.
2. MIME is a very flexible format, permitting one to include virtually any type of file or document in an email message.
    *   Multiple objects in a single message.
    *   Text having unlimited line length or overall length.
    *   Character sets other than ASCII, allowing non-English language messages.
    *   Binary or application specific files.
    *   Images, audio, video and multi-media messages.

Disadvantage of MIME:

1. At a time we can see only one mail.

DNS Message:

There is one DNS message defined for both queries and responses. Fig. 7.16 shows the overall format of the DNS message.

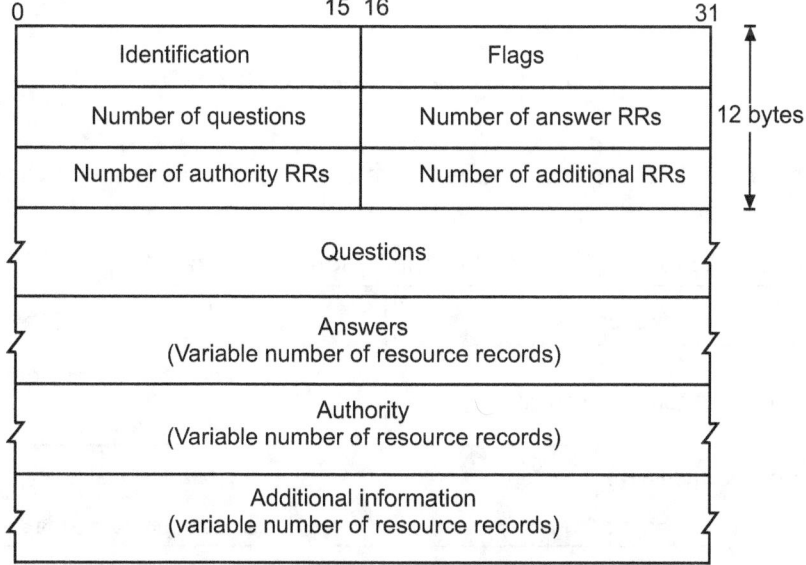

Fig. 7.16 : General format of DNS queries and responses

The message has a fixed 12-byte header followed by four variable-length fields.

DNS has two types of messages: query and response, (See Fig. 7.17).

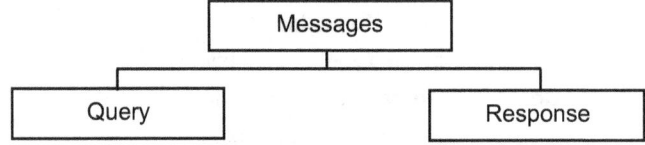

Fig. 7.17 : DNS message types

Both types have same format. The query message consists of a header and question record; the response message consists of a header, question records answer records, authoritative records and additional records, (Refer Fig. 7.18).

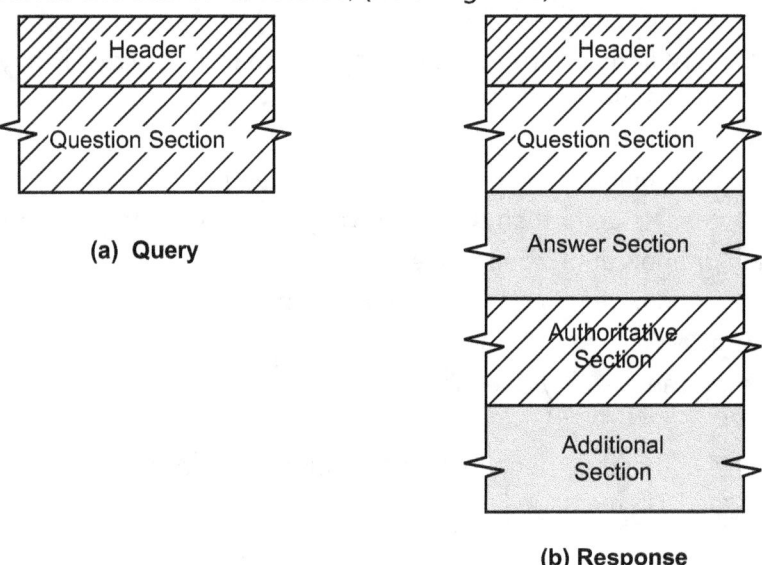

Fig. 7.18: Query and Response Messages

DNS Message Header:

Both the query and response messages have the same header format with some fields set to zero for the query message.

The header is of 12 bytes. The format of the header is shown in the Fig. 7.19.

Identification	Flags
Number of question records	Number of answer records (all 0s in query message)
No. of authoritative records (all 0s in query message)	No. of additional records (all 0s in query message)

Fig. 7.19: Header format

The header fields are as follows:

- **Identification:** This is 16 bit field used by the client to match the response with the query.
- **Flags:** This is 16 bit field, which is a collection of subfields that defines the type of the message, type of the answers requested, type of the desired resolution and so on.

The 16-bit flags field is divided into numerous pieces, as shown in Fig. 7.20.

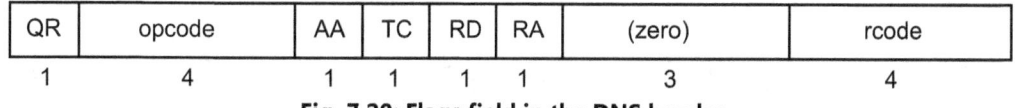

QR	opcode	AA	TC	RD	RA	(zero)	rcode
1	4	1	1	1	1	3	4

Fig. 7.20: Flags field in the DNS header

We will start at the leftmost bit and describe each field.

1. **QR** is a 1-bit field, 0 means the message is a Query, 1 means it's a Response.

2. **opcode** is a 4-bit field. The normal value is 0 (a standard query). Other values are 1 (an inverse query) and 2 (server status request).

3. **AA** is a 1-bit flag that means "Authoritative Answer." The name server is authoritative for the domain in the question section.

4. **TC** is a 1-bit field that means "Truncated." With UDP this means the total size of the reply exceeded 512 bytes, and only the first 512 bytes of the reply was returned.

5. **RD** is a 1-bit field that means "Recursion Desired." This bit can be set in a query and is then returned in the response. This flag tells the name server to handle the query itself, called a Recursive Query. If the bit is not set, and the requested name server doesn't have an authoritative answer, the requested name server returns a list of other name servers to contact for the answer. This is called an Iterative Query.

6. **RA** is a 1-bit field that means "recursion available." This bit is set to 1 in the response if the server supports recursion. We'll see in our examples that most name servers provide recursion, except for some root servers.

7. **rcode** is a 4-bit field with the Return Code. The common values are 0 (no error) and 3 (name error). A name error is returned only from an authoritative name server means the domain name specified in the query does not exist.

- **Number of question records:** It contains the number of queries in the question section of the message.
- **Number of answer records:** It contains the number of answer records in the answer section of the response message. Its value is zero in the query message.
- **Number of authoritative records:** It contains the number of authoritative records in the authoritative section of the response message. Its value is zero in the query message.

- **Number of additional records:** It contains the number of additional records in the additional section of the response message. Its value is zero in the query message.
- **Question section:** This section consists of one or more question records. It is present on both query and response messages.
- The format of each question in the *question* section is shown in Fig. 7.20. There is normally just one question.
- The query name is the name being looked up. It is a sequence of one or more labels. Each *label* begins with a 1-byte count that specifies the number of bytes that follow. The name is terminated with a byte of 0, which is a label with a length of 0, which is the label of the root. Each count byte must be in the range of 0 to 63, since labels are limited.

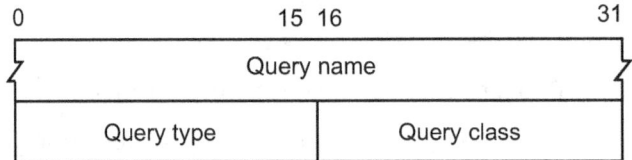

Fig. 7.21: Format of question portion of DNS query message

The final three fields in the DNS message, the answers, authority, and additional information fields, share a common format called a Resource Record or RR.

- **Answer Section:** This is a section consisting of one or more resource records. It is present only in response message.
- **Authoritative Section:** This section consists of one or more resource records. It is present only on response message. This section gives information about one or more authoritative servers for the query.
- **Additional Information Section:** This is a section consisting of one or more resource records. It is present only on response message. This section provides additional information that may help the resolver.

Resource Record:

Fig. 7.22 shows the Format of a Resource record.

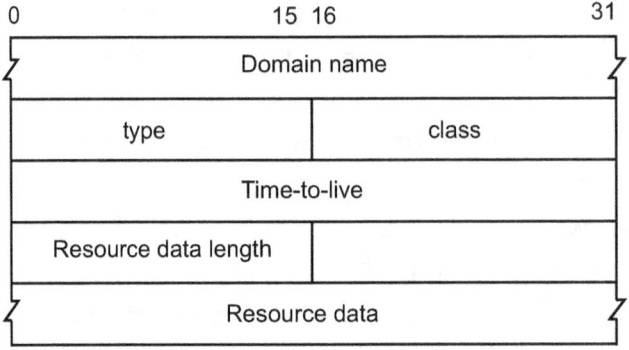

Fig. 7.22: Format of DNS resource record

- The **domain name** is the name to which the following resource data corresponds.
- The **type** specifies one of the RR type codes. These are the same as the query type values that we described earlier.
- The **class** is normally 1 for Internet data.
- The **Time-To-Live (TTL)** field is the number of seconds that the RR can be cached by the client. RRs often have a TTL of 2 days.
- The **Resource data length** specifies the amount of resource data. The format of this data depends on the type. For a type of 1 (an A record) the **resource data** is a 4-byte IP address.

Resolution:

Resolution is the process of turning a name into an IP address or an IP address back into a name. The mechanism of mapping a name to an address or an address to a name is called as Name-Address Resolution.

1. Resolver:

DNS is a Client-Server application. A resolver program is called by the client when a host wants to map an address to a name or a name to address. For this purpose, the nearest DNS server is accessed by the resolver.

If this server has information, it satisfies the resolver; otherwise, it refers the resolver to other servers or asks other servers to provide the information. After receiving the correct mapping, resolver delivers the result to the process that requested it.

2. Mapping Names to addresses:

Many times, the resolver gives a domain name to the DNS server and asks for the corresponding address. Here, server checks the generic or country domains to find mapping. If the domain name is from the generic domain area, the resolver receives the domain name such as "mail.viit.edu". The query is sent by the resolver to the local DNS for resolution. If the local DNS server seems unable to solve the query, it either refers the resolver to other servers or it itself contact to other DNS servers.

3. Mapping addresses to names:

In this case, client sends an IP address to a server to be mapped to a domain name. This type of query is called as PTR (POINTER) query. To solve such queries, DNS uses the inverse domain.

For example, if the resolver receives an IP address 129.132.12.37, the resolver first inverts the address and then adds the two labels before sending. The domain name sent is "129.132.12.37.in-addr.arpa", which is received by the local DNS and resolved.

Recursive Resolution:

The client can ask for a recursive answer from a name server. This means that the resolver expects the server to supply the final answer. If the server is the authority for the domain name, it checks its database and responds. If the server is not the authority, it sends the request to another server and waits for the response. If the parent is the authority, it responds; otherwise it sends the query to yet another server. When the query is finally resolved, the response travels back until it finally reaches the requesting client, (See Fig. 7.23).

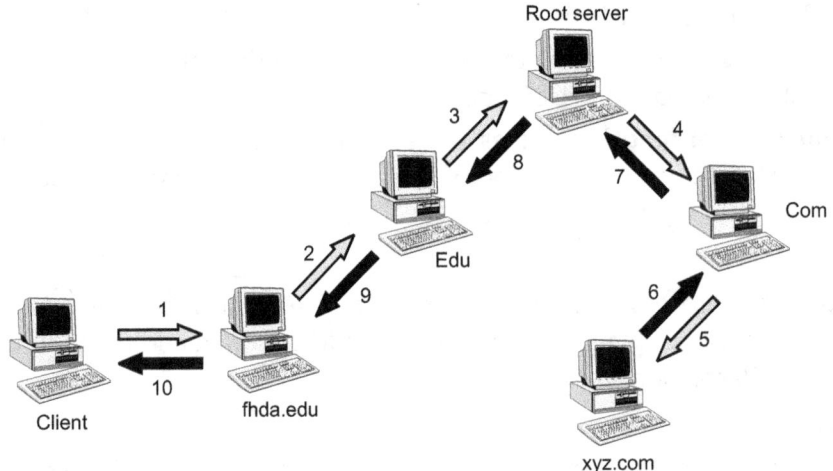

Fig. 7.23: Recursive Resolution

Iterative Resolution:

If the client does not ask for a recursive answer, the mapping can be done iteratively. If the server is an authority for the name, it sends the answer. If it is not, it returns the IP address of the server that it thinks can resolve the query.

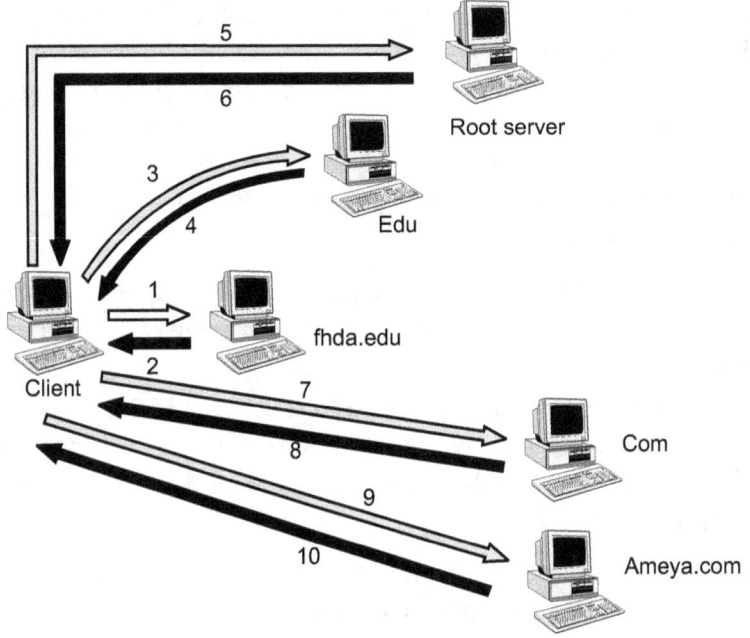

Fig. 7.24: Iterative Resolution

The client has to repeat the query to the second server. If the new server can resolve the problem, it answers the query with the IP address: otherwise it returns the IP address of the new server to the client. Now the client once again repeats the query to the third server. The process becomes iterative as the client is repeating the same query to multiple servers.

Fig. 7.24 shows Iterative Resolution.

Caching:

After getting the query, server does searching in the database. Searching mechanism requires some time. Reduction of this search time can increase the server efficiency. For reducing the search time, DNS uses a mechanism known as Caching.

When a server asks for mapping from another server and receives the response, it stores this information in its cache memory before sending it to client. If the same or another client asks for the same mapping, it can check the cache memory and resolve the problem, so it reduces the time that is required for searching in the database.

Caching speeds up the resolution, but it can also be problematic. If the server caches a mapping for a long time, it may send outdated mapping to the client. There are two solutions on this problem.

- First, the authority server always adds information to the mapping called Time-To-Live (TTL). It defines the time in seconds that the receiving server can cache the information. After that time, the mapping is invalid and any query must be sent again to the authority server.

- In the second solution, DNS server requires that each server keep a TTL counter for each mapping it caches. The cache memory must be searched periodically and those mapping with an expired TTL must be washed out.

7.2.4 Message Transfer

A Mail-Server (also known as a mail transfer agent or MTA, a mail transport agent, a mail router or an Internet mailer) is an application that receives incoming e-mail from local users (people within the same domain) and remote senders and forwards outgoing e-mail for delivery. A computer dedicated to running such applications is also called a Mail-Server. Microsoft Exchange, sendmail are common mail server programs.

The Mail-Server works in conjunction with other programs to make up what is sometimes referred to as a messaging system. A messaging system includes all the applications necessary to keep e-mail moving as it should. When you send an e-mail message, your e-mail program, such as Outlook or Eudora, forwards the message to your mail server, which in turn forwards it either to another mail server or to a holding area on the same server called a message store to be forwarded later. As a rule, the system uses SMTP (Simple Mail Transfer Protocol) or ESMTP (extended SMTP) for sending e-mail, and either POP3 (Post Office Protocol 3) or IMAP (Internet Message Access Protocol) for receiving e-mail.

The major functions of an MTA are:

- Accepting messages originating from the user agent and forwarding them to their destination (other user agents)

- Receiving all messages that are transmitted from other user agents for further transmission

- Keeping track of each and every activity and analyzing and storing the recipient list to perform future routing functions

- Sending auto-responses about non-delivery when a message does not reach its intended destination

The computing terms MX, mail exchanger and mail server may be used to refer to the system that is engaged in MTA functions.

7.2.5 SMTP

Simple Mail Transfer Protocol (SMTP) is an Internet standard for electronic mail (e-mail) transmission across Internet Protocol (IP) networks. SMTP is a connection oriented, text based protocol in which a mail sender communicates with a mail receiver by issuing command strings and supplying necessary data over a reliable ordered data stream channel, typically a Transmission Control Protocol (TCP) connection. This is standard application layer protocol for delivery of e-mail over a TCP/IP internetwork such as the Internet.

E-mail system is implemented with the help of Message Transfer Agents (MTA).There are normally two MTA's in each mailing system: One for sending emails and another for receiving e-mails. The formal protocol that defines the MTA client and server in the internet is called Simple Mail Transfer Protocol (SMTP). Fig. 7.25 shows the range of SMTP protocol.

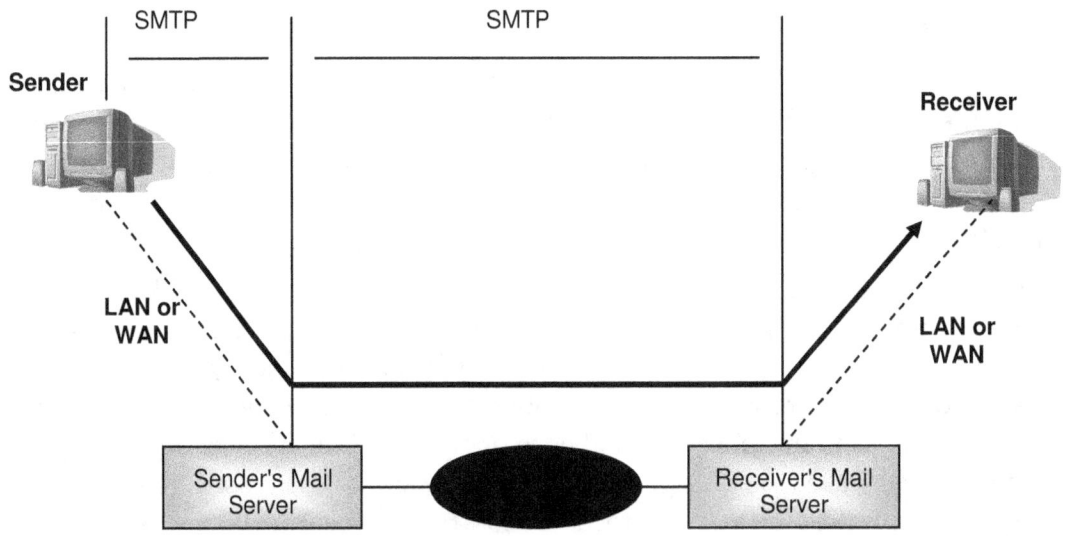

Fig. 7.25: SMTP Range

By referring the above diagram, we can say that SMTP is used two times. That is between the sender and sender's mail server and between the sender's mail server and receiver's mail server. Another protocol is used between the receiver's mail server and receiver. SMTP simply defines how commands and responses must be sent back and forth. This is a simple ASCII protocol. It establishes a TCP connection between a sender and port number 25 of the receiver.

No checksums are generally required because TCP provides a reliable byte stream. After exchanging all the e-mail, the connection is released.

1. Commands and Responses:

SMTP uses commands and responses to transfer messages between an MTA client and MTA server. Each command or reply is terminated by a two character (carriage return and line feed) End-Of-Line (EOF) token.

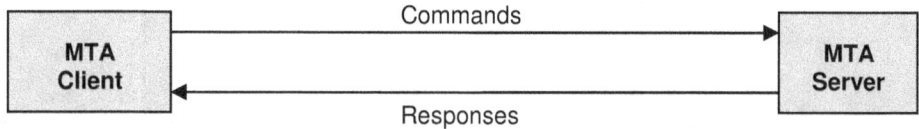

Fig. 7.26: Commands and Responses

Commands:

Client sends commands to the server. SMTP defines 14 commands. Out of that first 5 commands are mandatory; every implementation must support these commands. The next three commands are often used and are highly recommended. Last six commands are hardly used.

Table 7.6 : FTP commands

Keyword	Description
HELO	Used by the client to identify itself. The argument is domain name of the client host. The format is: **HELO:** mail.pragati.ac.in
MAIL FROM	Used by the client to identify the sender of the message. The argument is email address of the sender. Format is: **MAIL FROM:** niralipune@yahoo.co.in
RCPT TO	Used by the client to identify the intended recipient of the message. The argument is the email address of the recipient. The format is: **RCPT TO:** niralimumbai@yahoo.co.in

Contd...

DATA	This command is used to send the actual message. The lines following DATA command are treated as mail message. Format is: **DATA** There is an important meeting on this Sunday. So please be present for it. Regards; Nirali Prakashan
QUIT	It terminates the message. The format is: **QUIT**
RSET	It aborts the current email transaction. The stored information of the sender and receiver is deleted after executing the command. The connection gets reset. The format is: **RSET**
VRFY	This command is used to verify the address of the recipient. In this sender asks the receiver to confirm that a name identifies a valid recipient. Its format is: [**VRFY: nirali**@puneatoz.net]
NOOP	By using this command the client checks the status of the recipient. It requires an answer from recipient. Its format is: **NOOP**
TURN	It reverses the role of sender and receiver.
EXPN	It asks the receiving host to expand the mailing list.
HELP	It sends system specific documentation. The format is: **HELP:** mail
SEND FROM	This command specifies that the mail is to be delivered to the terminal of the recipient, and not the mailbox. If the recipient is not logged in, the mail is bounced back. The argument is the address of the sender. The format is: **SEND FROM:** niralipune@gmail.com
SMOL FROM	This command specifies to send the mail to the terminal if possible, otherwise to the mailbox.
SMAL FROM	It sends mail to the terminal and mail box.

2. Working of SMTP:

SMTP works in the following three stages:

(i) Connection Establishment:

Once, the TCP connection is made on port no. 25, SMTP server starts the connection phase. This phase involves following three steps which are explained in the following figure. The server tells the client that it is ready to receive mail by using the code 220. If the server is not ready, it sends code 421 which tells that service is not available. Once, the server becomes ready to receive the mails, client sends HELO message to identify itself using the domain name address. This is important step which informs the server of the domain name of the client. Remember that during TCP connection establishment, the sender and receiver know each other through their IP addresses. Server responds with code 250 which tells that the request command is completed.

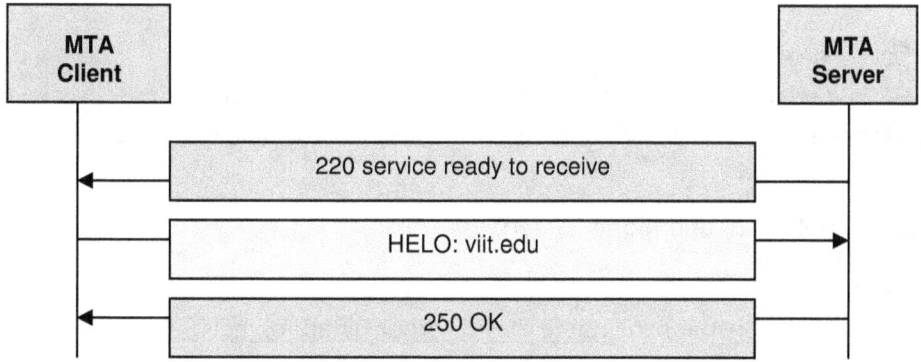

Fig. 7.27: Connection establishment

(ii) Message Transfer:

Once, the connection has been established, SMTP server sends messages to SMTP receiver. The messages are transferred in three stages:

(a) A MAIL command identifies the message originator.

(b) RCPT command identifies the receiver of the message.

(c) DATA command transfers the message text.

(iii) Connection Closing:

After the message is transferred successfully, the client terminates the connection. The connection is terminated in two steps:

(a) The client sends the quit command.

(b) The server responds with code 221 or some other appropriate code.

After the connection termination phase, the TCP connection must be closed.

3. Mail Exchange:

The SMTP design is based on the model of communication shown in Fig. 7.28. As a result of a user mail request, the sender SMTP establishes a two-way connection with a receiver SMTP. The receiver SMTP can be either the ultimate destination or an intermediate (mail gateway). The sender SMTP will generate commands that are replied to by the receiver SMTP.

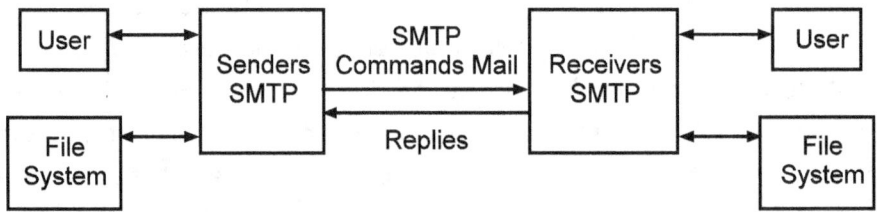

Fig. 7.28: SMTP design

Advantages:

1. SMTP is a relatively simple, text-based protocol, in which one or more recipients of a message are specified along with the message text and possibly other encoded objects.

2. Easy to implement and higher speed.

Disadvantages:

1. SMTP cannot transmit executable files or other binary objects.

2. SMTP servers may reject mail messages over a certain size.

3. SMTP gateways that translate from ASCII to EBCDIC and vice versa do not use a consistent set of code page mappings, resulting in translation problems.

Post Office Protocol (POP) :

The Post Office Protocol (POP) is an application layer Internet standard protocol used by local e-mail clients to retrieve e-mail from a remote server over a TCP/IP connection. POP defines an email server and a way to retrieve mail from it. Incoming messages are stored at a POP server until the user logs in and downloads the messages to their computer. Things that can be done via the POP include:

1. Retrieve mail from an ISP and delete it on the server.

2. Retrieve mail from an ISP but not delete it on the server.

3. Ask whether new mail has arrived but not retrieve it.

4. Peek at a few lines of a message to see whether it is worth retrieving.

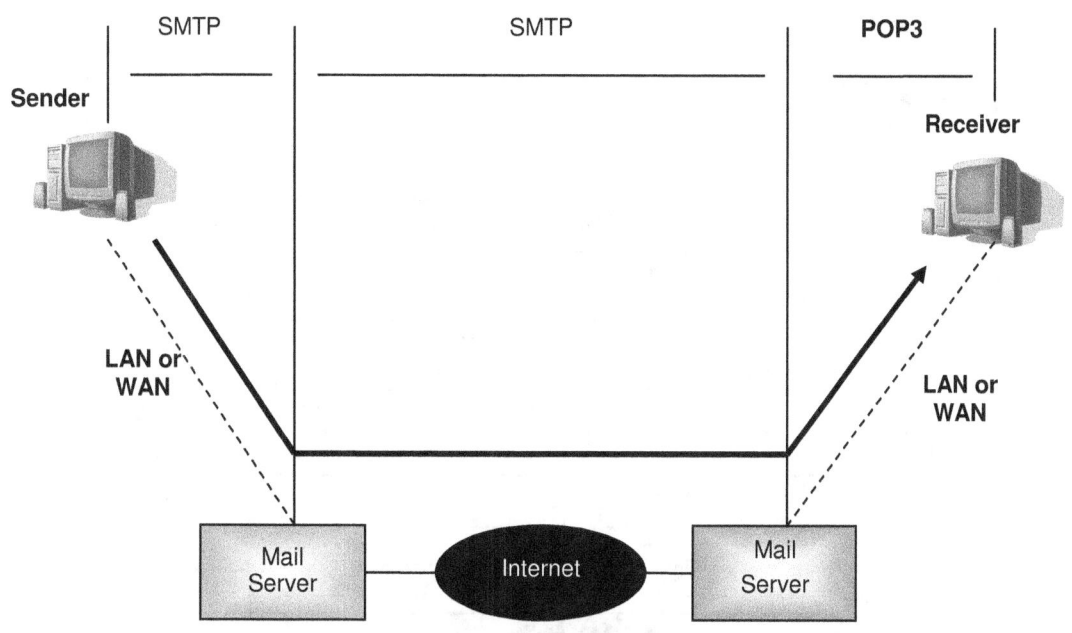

Fig. 7.29 : Mail/Data pulling

POP version 3 of the Post Office Protocol (POP-3), documented in RFC 1725, is designed for user-to-mailbox access and is the latest version of POP. In the first and second stage of mail delivery, SMTP protocol is used. As SMTP is a push protocol, it is not used into the third stage of mailing system. SMTP is called as push protocol because it pushes the messages from the client to the server. On the other hand, the third stage needs a pull protocol; the client must pull messages from the server.

The direction of the bulk of data is from server to the client, where client pulls the messages from the server, [Refer Fig. 7.30].

POP3 version of post office protocol is simple and is having limited functionality. The client's POP3 software is installed on the recipient computer and server's POP3 software is installed on mail server. When the user wants to read its mail, the user downloads mails from the mailbox on the mail server.

7.2.6 Mail Gateways

For downloading the mails from the mail server, the client opens a TCP connection with the mail server on port no. 110. By giving appropriate username and password, the user does its authentication. The user can then retrieve the mail messages one by one.

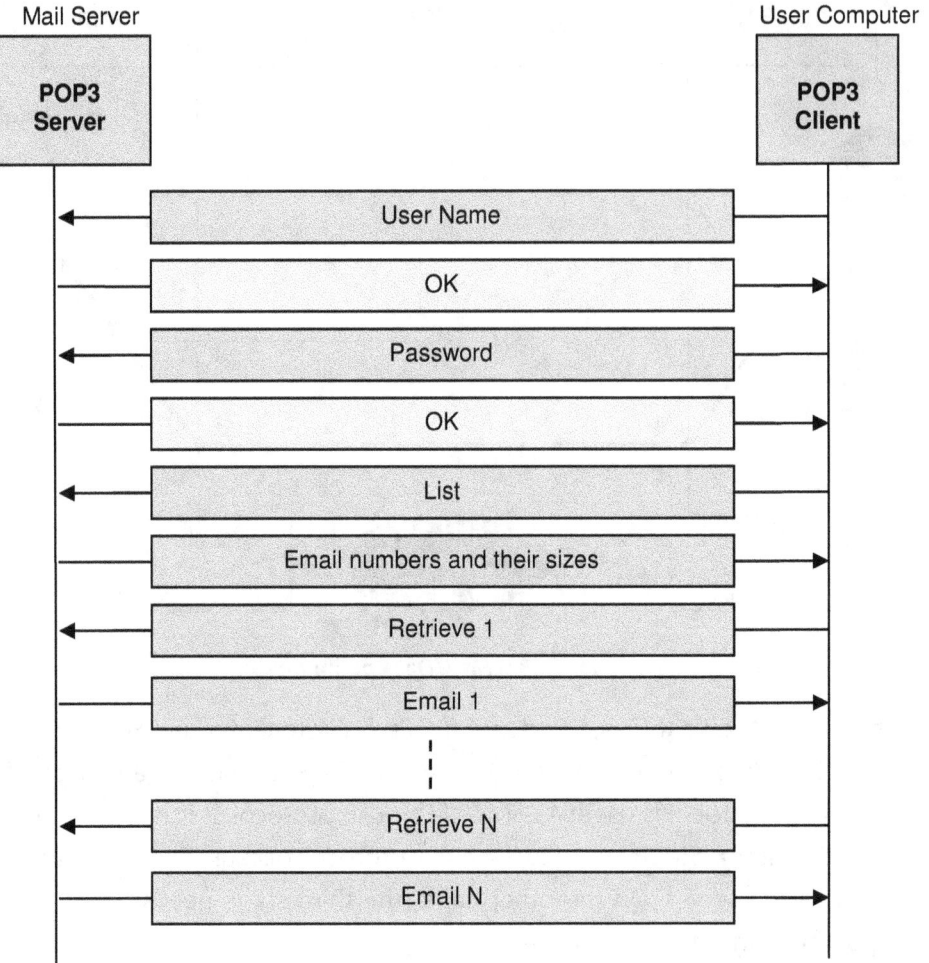

Fig. 7.30 : Working of POP3

Fig. 7.30 (b) shows the working of POP3 protocol. POP3 is a mail protocol used by a client to access and download messages that are held temporarily by the server. POP3 works in two modes:

1. Delete Mode, and

2. Keep Mode.

1. **Delete Mode:** The mail is deleted from the mailbox after each retrieval. This mode is normally used when the user is working at her own computer, and can save and organize received mails after reading and replying.

2. **Keep Mode:** The mail remains in the mailbox after retrieval. The keep mode is normally used when the user accesses the mail away from his/her primary computer. The mail is read but kept in the system for later retrieval and organizing.

Advantages of POP3:

1. A local copy of your email.

2. Very little remote server storage space overhead required (if emails are deleted from the server as they are retrieved).

3. Consolidation of many email accounts and servers to deliver to one inbox.

Limitations of POP3:

1. POP3 does not allow organization of email on the server.

2. The user cannot have different folders on the server.

3. The user cannot partially check the content of email before downloading.

7.2.7 Relays

What is Mail Relay?

Mail relay is the process of transferring an email from one server to another for delivery. An example of this is if you work for Company A and send an email to someone at Company B. You connect to your company's SMTP server which then relays your email to the server owned by Company B. One server accepting an email from another server is called "relaying."

If you were to send an email to a person with an email address at the same domain as yours, there would not be a second server involved, so it is not considered relaying. It's much like sending a paper letter to someone in your town – your local post office receives and delivers the letter without involving another post office.

SMTP Relay Service:

A Simple Mail Transfer Protocol relay (SMTP Relay) is a service that is used as a means to transport email messages in between different email hosting services, servers and/or domains. It most often specializes in sending large batches of emails (newsletters) or for automatic transactional emails (delivery confirmations, password resets, etc). Many internet providers put a cap on how many SMTP relays it can conduct per day to combat spam. Businesses often exceed this limit and need enterprise level email sending features. An STMP Relay provider can help businesses deliver large volumes of email without getting mislabeled as spam.

SMTP relays are essential to send out transactional emails, newsletters, and all other forms of bulk mailing: to deal with such an amount of messages and deliver them correctly, SMTP servers route them through a trusted third party.

Open Relay

Your server is said to be an Open Relay if it accepts messages on behalf of other domains and does NOT require user authentication. In the case of an Open Relay, a person sitting in Singapore can send an email to California through your server, which could be in

London. Open relay servers are frequently misused by spammers sending unsolicited emails. Once a malicious user finds out about an open relay server on the Internet, he/she can send millions of messages all over the world, potentially bringing your network to its knees. Several organizations have setup databases of IP Addresses that list and track open relay servers. If you have an open relay server you run the risk of having your IP listed in one of these databases. As a result many SMTP servers may not accept emails from you.

7.2.8 Configuring Mail Servers

Configure this computer as a Mail Server to install E-mail Services, which provides e-mail transfer and retrieval services. E-mail Services includes the POP3 service, which provides e-mail retrieval, and the SMTP service, which provides e-mail transfer. Administrators can use the POP3 service to store and manage e-mail accounts on the mail server. After configuring this computer as a mail server, users can connect to the mail server and retrieve e-mail to their local computer using an e-mail client that supports the POP3 protocol, such as Microsoft Outlook.

After you have completed the Configure Your Server Wizard, you must perform additional required steps to create mailboxes. After you have completed the Configure Your Server Wizard and created the appropriate mailboxes, you will have a fully-functioning mail server. You can configure both member servers and stand-alone servers to be a mail server. However, the default authentication method and the available authentication methods will vary.

Configure an Internal Mail Server

To configure a mail server, start the Configure Your Server Wizard by doing either of the following:

- From Manage Your Server, click **Add or remove a role**. By default, Manage Your Server starts automatically when you log on. To open Manage Your Server, click **Start**, click **Control Panel**, double-click **Administrative Tools**, and then double-click **Manage Your Server**.

- To open the Configure Your Server Wizard, click **Start**, click **Control Panel**, double-click **Administrative Tools**, and then double-click **Configure Your Server Wizard**.

On the **Server Role** page, click **Mail server (POP3, SMTP)**, and then click **Next**.

7.2.9 File Transfer Protocol

FTP stands for File Transfer Protocol. It's the concept of moving a file from your storage space to your server so others can look at it. This protocol allows you to connect to a remote computer (host) using an FTP program on your machine, browse a list of files available, retrieve files, and navigate the directory structure of the host system. FTP is the simplest and most secure way to exchange files over the Internet. The most common use for FTP is to download files from the Internet.

7.2.9.1 General Model

FTP is an example of a Client-Server *system*. You use a *client* program on your system to connect to the server running on the remote host. The server coordinates activity between the client and the host operating system. Clients developed for PCs move us away from the cryptic world of workstation operating systems by providing interactive browsers that operated on a point-and-click strategy to navigate the directory space.

In the basic model of FTP, the FTP client has three components: user interface, client control process and the client data transfer process. The FTP server has two components: the server control process and the server data transfer process. The control connection is made between the control processes. The data connection is made between the data transfer processes. Control connection is maintained during the entire FTP session.

The data connection is opened and then closed for each file transferred. It opens each time commands that involve transferring files are used, and it closes when the file is transferred.

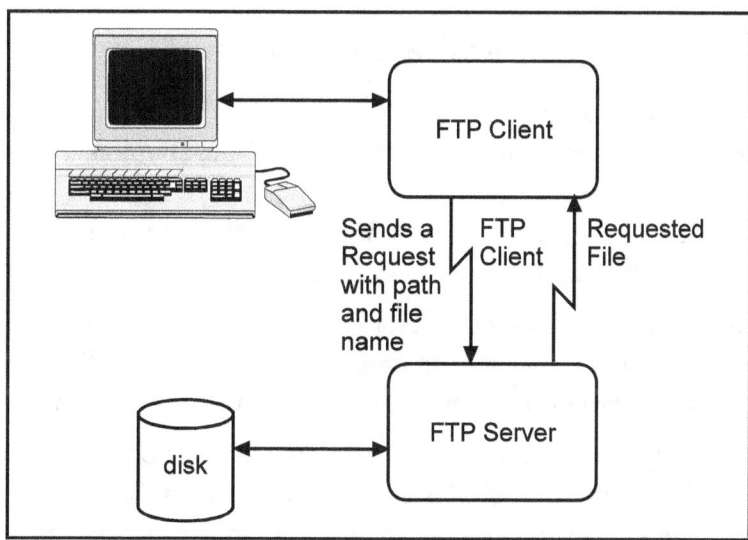

Fig. 7.31: FTP Model

Working of FTP :

File Transfer Protocol is one of the earliest Internet protocols, and is still used for uploading and downloading files between clients and servers. An FTP client is an application that can issue FTP commands to an FTP server, while an FTP server is a service or daemon running on a server that responds to FTP commands from a client.

FTP commands can be used to change directories, change transfer modes between binary and ASCII, upload files, and download files.

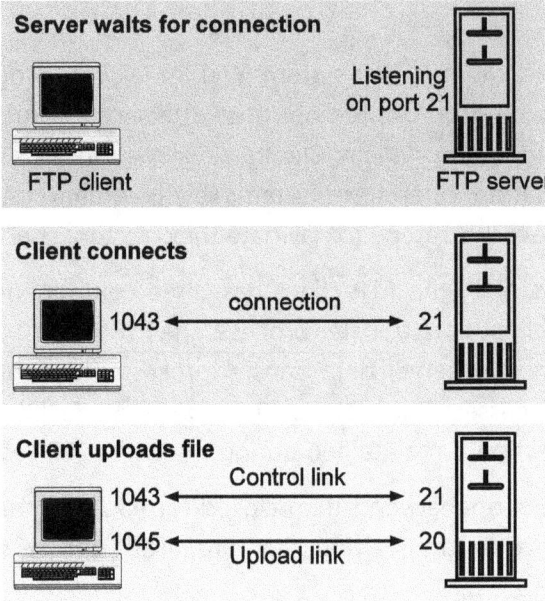

Fig. 7.32: File Transfer Protocol (FTP)

FTP uses Transmission Control Protocol (TCP) for reliable network communication by establishing a session before initiating data transfer. TCP port number 21 on the FTP server listens for connection attempts from an FTP client and is used as a control port for establishing a connection between the client and server, for allowing the client to send an FTP command to the server, and for returning the server's response to the command.

Once, a control connection has been established, the server opens port number 20 to form a new connection with the client for transferring the actual data during uploads and downloads. File transfer is a very common operation on the computer network.

We require two types of protocols for transferring the files on the network: 1) FTP and 2) TFTP (Trivial File Transfer Protocol). FTP is a standard mechanism provided by TCP/IP for copying a file from one host to another. There are some problems associated with file transfer mechanism from one machine to another, which can be as follows:

- Two systems may have different ways to represent text and data.

- These systems may have different directory structure.

It is necessary for the FTP to solve all such sort of problems for transferring a file. For transferring a file, FTP establishes two connections between the hosts. One connection is used for data transfer, and other for control information (commands and responses). Separation of commands and data transfer makes FTP more efficient. Data connection uses very complex rules for transmission of data (due to variety of data types transferred); on the other hand control connection uses very simple rules of communication.

Points to be remembered:

- FTP uses the service of TCP.
- It needs two TCP connections.
- Port 21 is used for control connection and Port 20 is used for data connection.

The server has two major components and the client has two major components as given in Fig. 7.33. The control connection is made between the control processes at server and client side while the data connection is made between the data transfer processes.

One more thing that is very important about the control and data connection is that, the control connection remains open during the entire FTP interactive session, while the data connection is opened when the user wants to transmit a file and then it is closed after the file transfer. In short the data connection is opened and closed for each file transferred.

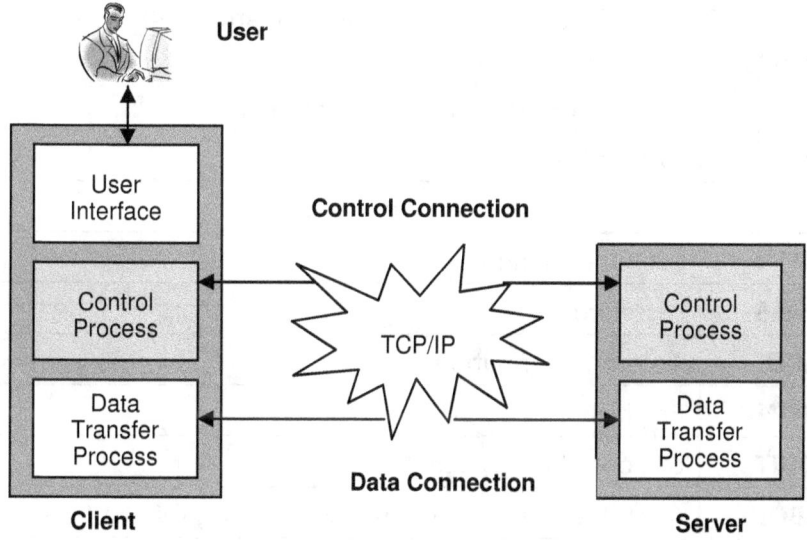

Fig. 7.33: Basic architecture of FTP

File Transfer:

File transfer takes place over the data connection in association with the control connection. File transfer in FTP means one of the following:

(i) Retrieving a file: A file is copied from server to the client.

(ii) Storing a file: A file can be copied from client to the server.

(iii) A Server sends a list of directory or file names to the client. FTP treats such a list of directory as a file.

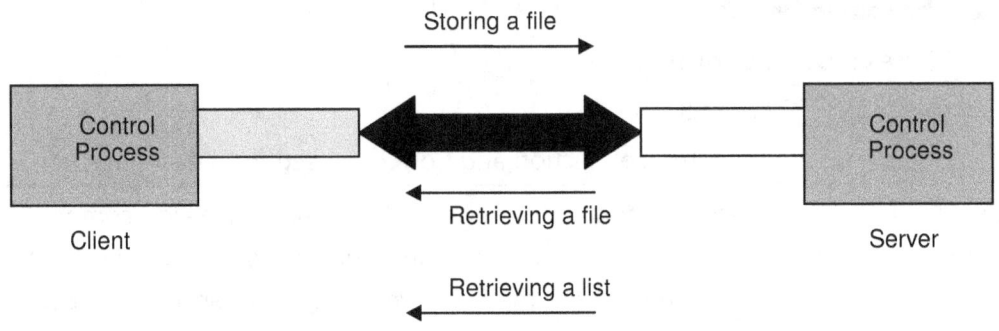

Fig. 7.34: File transfer

7.2.9.2 FTP Commands

FTP creates a control connection between a client control process and server control process. During this communication, commands are sent from the client to the server and responses are sent from the server to the client. FTP commands are roughly divided into six groups: 1) Access, 2) File Management, 3) Data Formatting, 4) Port Defining, 5) File Transferring and 6) Miscellaneous Commands.

Table 7.7 : FTP Commands

No.	Command	Description
Access Commands		
1.	**USER**	User Information
2.	**PASS**	Password
3.	**ACCT**	Account Information
4.	**REIN**	Reinitialize
5.	**QUIT**	Log out of the system
6.	**ABOR**	Abort the previous command
Data Formatting Commands		
1.	**TYPE**	Defines the file type and if necessary the print format
2.	**STRU**	Defines the organization of data
3.	**MODE**	Defines the transmission mode
File Management Commands		
1.	**CWD**	Change to another directory
2.	**CDUP**	Change to parent directory
3.	**DELE**	Delete a File
4.	**LIST**	List subdirectories or files

5.	**MKD**	Create (make) new directory
6.	**PWD**	Display name of current (present working) directory
7.	**RMD**	Delete (remove) directory
8.	**RNFR**	Identify a file to be renamed (rename from)
9.	**RNTO**	Rename the file (rename to)
Port Defining Commands		
1.	**PORT**	Client chooses a port
2.	**PASV**	Server chooses a port
File Transfer Commands		
1.	**RETR**	Retrieve files
2.	**STOR**	Store files: files are transferred from client to server
3.	**APPE**	Similar to STOR except if file exists, data must be appended to it
4.	**STOU**	Similar to STOR except that the file name will be unique in the directory
5.	**ALLO**	Allocate the storage space for the files at the server
6.	**REST**	Position a file marker at a specified data point
7.	**STAT**	Return the status of the files
Miscellaneous Commands		
1.	**HELP**	Ask information about the server
2.	**NOOP**	Check if server is alive
3.	**SITE**	Specify the site specific commands
4.	**SYST**	Ask about the operating system used by the server

7.3 World Wide Web

7.3.1 Introduction

WWW Stands for "World Wide Web." is a subset of the Internet. The Web consists of pages that can be accessed using a Web browser. The Internet is the actual network of networks where all the information resides. Things like Telnet, FTP (File Transfer Protocol), Internet gaming, Internet Relay Chat (IRC), and e-mail are all part of the Internet, but are not part of the World Wide Web. The Hyper-Text Transfer Protocol (HTTP) is the method used to transfer Web pages to your computer. With hypertext, a word or phrase can contain a link to another Web site. All Web pages are written in the hyper-text markup language (HTML), which works in conjunction with HTTP.

7.3.2 Architectural Overview

Today www is a distributed Client/Server Service, in which a Client using a browser can access a service using a Server. However, the service provided is distributed over many and different locations called sites, as shown in Fig. 7.35.

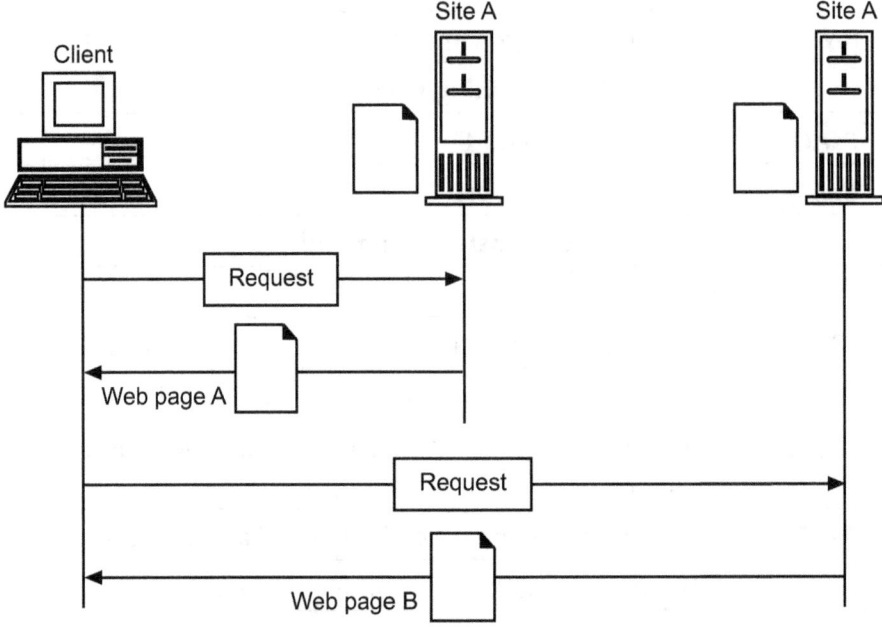

Fig. 7.35 : Architecture of WWW

Each and every site holds one or more web documents, referred to as Web pages. Each Web page contain a link to other web pages in the same site or at other sites. The web pages can be retrieved and viewed by using browsers. The client needs to see some information that it knows belongs to site A. It sends a request through its browser, a program that is designed to fetch Web documents. The request among other information, includes the address of the site and the Web page, called the URL (Uniform Research Locator). The server at site A finds the document and sends to the client. When the user views the document, she finds some references to other documents, such as a Web page at site B. The reference has the URL for the new site. The user is also interested in seeing this web document. The client sends another request to the new site, and the new page is retrieved.

1. Server :

The web page is stored at the server. Each and every time a client request arrives, the corresponding web document is sent to the client. Servers normally store requested files/information in a cache in memory. A server can also become more efficient through multiprocessing or multithreading. In such conditions, a server can answer more than one request at a time.

2. Client (Browser) :

Each and every browser usually consists of the following parts :

(i) A Controller,

(ii) Client protocol, and

(iii) Interpreters.

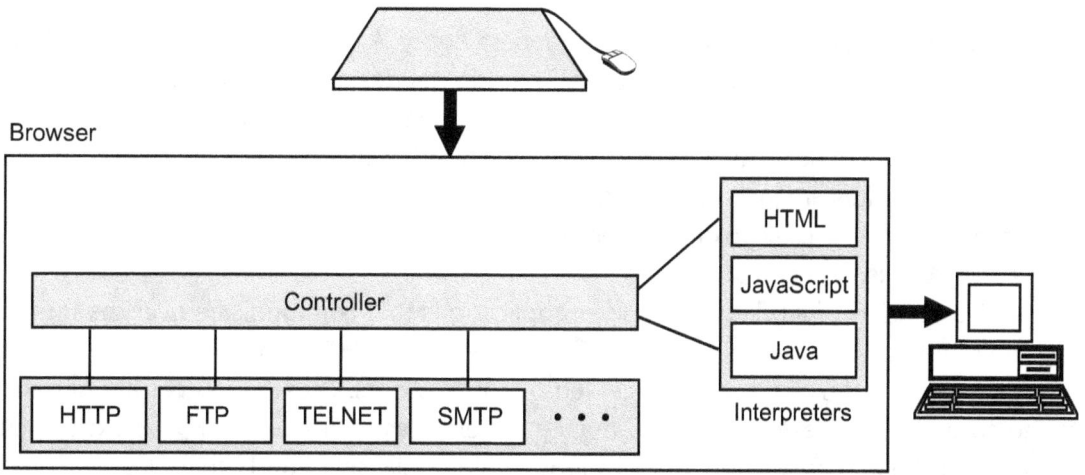

Fig. 7.36 : Browser

The Controller receives input from the keyboard or any input device and uses the client programs to access the document. Fig. 7.36 shows a browser and its parts. When the document has been accessed, the Controller uses one of the interpreters to display the document on the screen. The client protocol can be one of the protocols described previously such as HTTP or FTP. The interpreter can be Java, HTML or JavaScript, depending on the type of web document.

3. Uniform Resource Locator (URL) :

A client that wants to access a web page needs the address of the web page. To facilitate the access of documents distributed throughout the world, HTTP uses locators. The Uniform Resource Locator (URL) is a standard for specifying any kind of information on the Internet. It defines four things: Protocol, Host computer, Port and Path shown in Fig. 7.37.

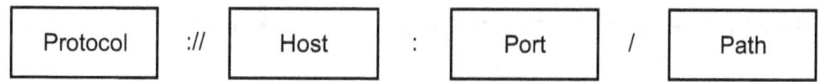

Fig. 7.37 : URL

(i) **Protocol :** It is the client/server program used to retrieve the web document. Variety of protocols can retrieve a web document; among them are FTP or HTTP. The most commonly today is HTTP.

(ii) **Host :** It is the computer on which the information is located. Basically, web pages are stored in computers and computers are given alias names that usually begin with the characters www.

(iii) Port : The URL can contain the port number of the server. If the port is included, it is inserted between the host and the path. Ports is separated from the host by a colon.

(iv) Path : It is the pathname of the file where the information is located.

4. Cookies :

The www was originally developed as a stateless entity. A client sends a request and then a server responds. Their relationship is over. The original design of www, retrieving publicly available web documents, exactly fits this purpose. Some functions of web are given below :

1. Some websites need to allow access to registered clients only.
2. Some websites are just advertising.

For these purposes, the cookie mechanism was devised.

How WWW Works ?

The Web consists of all client and server applications that communicate over the Internet using the client/server protocol Hypertext Transfer Protocol (HTTP), as well as the resources that reside on those servers and are accessed by those clients. These resources are generally referred to as "Web sites" and consist mainly of text files formatted in Hypertext Markup Language (HTML) and associated image, sound, multimedia, script and other files.

Each HTML file is called a Web page, Web document or page, and pages in a site are generally linked in a hierarchical fashion, starting with the home or top page, using anchor tags. Web sites are stored on Web servers, which run software that handles the server side of HTTP, such as Internet Information Services (IIS) for Microsoft Windows 2000. Users access Web sites on the Internet by using client software, typically called a Web browser such as Microsoft Internet Explorer.

The Web browser is the client component. Examples of Web browsers include Mosaic, Netscape Navigator, Microsoft Internet Explorer, or Sun HotJava browser. Web browsers are responsible for formatting and displaying information, interacting with the user, and invoking external functions, such as telnet, or external viewers for data types that Web browsers do not directly support.

7.3.3 Static and Dynamic Web Pages

The documents in the www can be grouped into three categories :

1. Static,
2. Dynamic, and
3. Active.

The category is based on the time at which the contents of the document are determined.

1. Static Documents :

They are fixed-content documents. Static document are created and stored in a server. The client can get only a copy of the document. The contents of the file are determined when the file is created, not when it is used. The contents in the server can be changed, but the user cannot change them. When a client accesses the document, a copy of the document is sent. The user can then use a browsing program to display the document, (see Fig. 7.38).

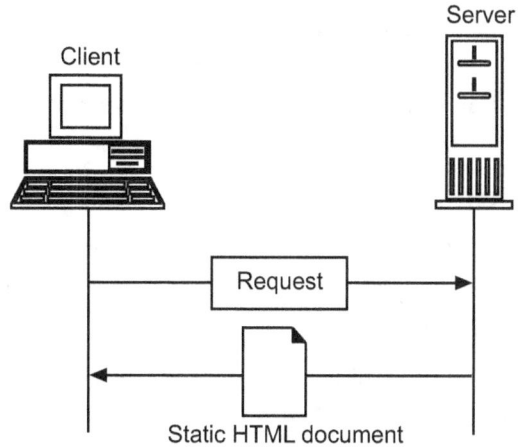

Fig. 7.38 : Static document

HTML : Hyptertext Markup Language is a language for creating web page. A markup language allows us to embed formatting instructions in the file itself. The instructions are included with the text. In this way, any browser can read the instructions and format the text according to the specific workstation.

For example : To make part of a text displayed in Italic face with HTML, we put beginning and ending italicface tags (marks) in the text, as shown in Fig. 7.39.

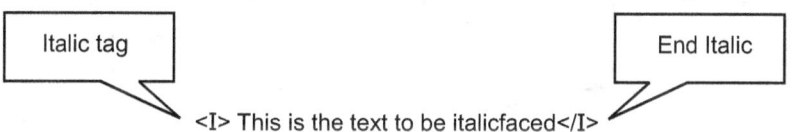

Fig. 7.39 : Italicface tags

The two tags <I> and <\I> are instructions for the browser. When the browser sees these two marks, it knows that the text must be italicface (See Fig. 7.40)

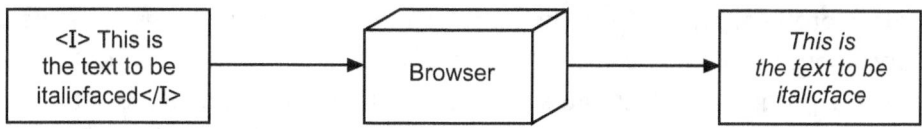

Fig. 7.40 : Effect of Italicfaced tags

A web page is make up of two parts :

1.   Head and   2.   Body.

The head is the first part of a web page. The head contains the title of the web page and other parameters that the browser will use. The actual contents of a web page are in the body, which includes the text and the tags.

2.   Dynamic Documents :

It is created by a web server whenever, a browser requests the document. When a client request arrives, the web server runs an application program which creates the dynamic document. The server returns the output of the program as a response to the browser which requested the document. Because a fresh document is created for each request, the contents of a dynamic document can vary from one request to another request. A very simple example of a dynamic document is the retrieval of the time and data from a server.

(i)   Common Gateway Interface (CGI) :

CGI is a technology that creates and handles dynamic documents. It is a set of standards which defines how a dynamic document is written, how data are input to the program and how the output result is used.

CGI is not a new language. CGI allows progmmers to use any of server languages such as C, Bourne Shell, C Shell, C++, Korn Shell, Tel, or Perl etc. Fig. 7.41 shows the step in creating a dynamic program using CGI technology.

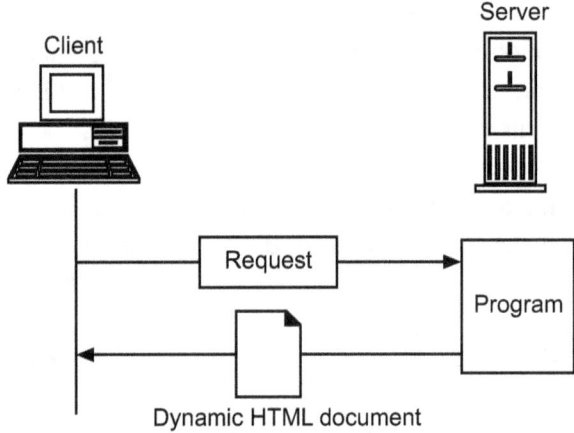

Fig. 7.41 : Dynamic document using CGI

Scripting technologies for Dynamic Documents :

The main problem with CGI technology is the inefficiency. It results if part of the dynamic document i.e. to be created is fixed and not changing from request to request. If you use CGI, the program must create an entire document each time a request is made. The solution of these problem is to create a file containing the fixed part of the document using HTML and embedded a script, a source code, that can be run by the server to provide the varying availability and price section. Fig. 7.42 shows the idea.

A few technologies have been involved in creating dynamic documents using scripts, among the most common are Active Server pages (ASP), a Microsoft product which uses Visual Basic language for scripting Hypertext Preprocessor (PHP), which uses the Perl language; etc.

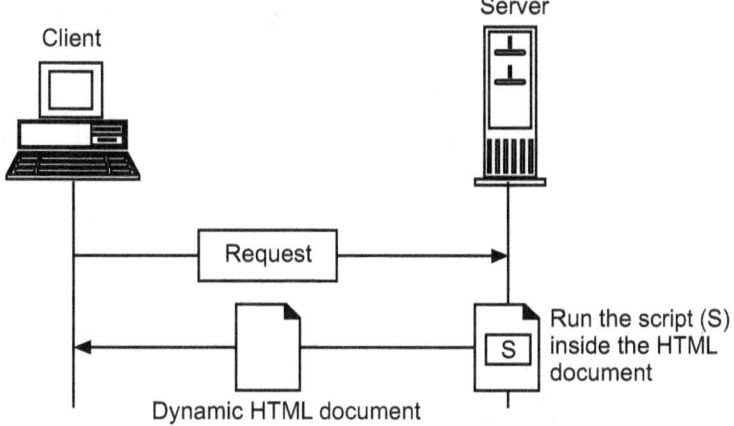

Fig. 7.42 : Dynamic document using server-site script

3. Active Documents :

For number of applications, you need a program or a script to be run at the client site, these are called active documents. For example, suppose you want to run a program which creates animated graphics on the screen that interacts with the user. The program definitely needs to be run at the client site where the animation takes place. When a browser requests an active document, the server sends a copy of the document. The document is then run at the client browser site.

(i) JavaScript : The basic idea of script in dynamic documents can also be used for active documents. JavaScript, which bears a small resemblance to Java JavaScript is a very high level scripting language developed for this purpose. Fig. 7.43 shows how JavaScript is used to create an active document.

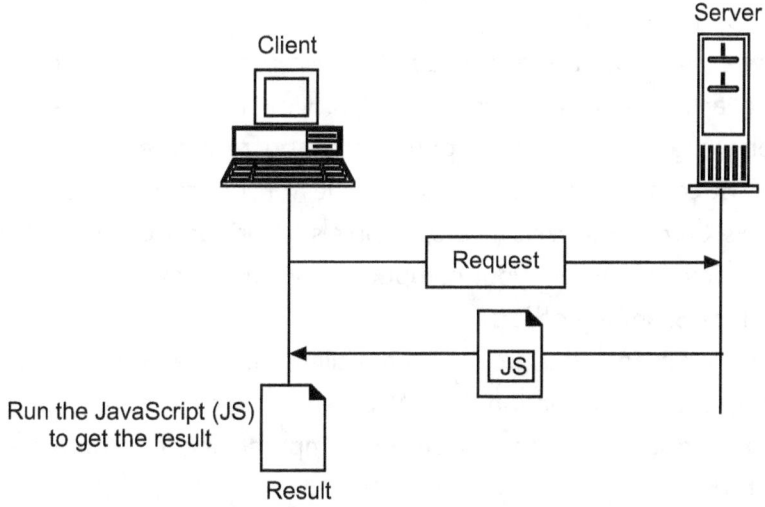

Fig. 7.43 : Active document using client-site script

(ii) Java Applets : One common way to create an active document is to use Java Applets. An Java applet is a program written in Java on the server. A Java Applet can be run by the browser in two ways. In the first way, the browser can directly request the Java applet program in the URL and receive the Applet in binary form. In second way the browser can retrieve and run an HTML file that has embedded the address of the applet as a tag. Fig. 7.44 shows how Java applets are used in the first way; the second way is similar but needs two transactions.

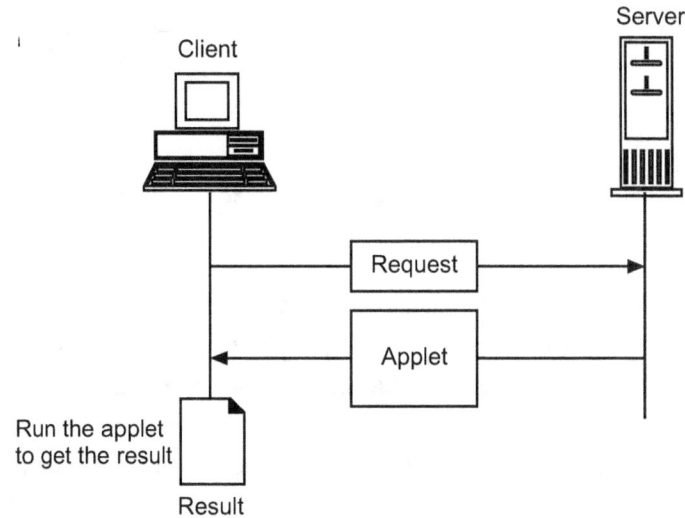

Fig. 7.44 : Active document using Java applet

7.3.4 WWW Pages and Browsing

Web Page is a document on the World Wide Web. Every Web page is identified by a unique URL (Uniform Resource Locator).

A Web browser is software that is used to access the internet. A browser lets you visit websites and do activities within them like login, view multimedia, link from one site to another, visit one page from another, print, send and receive email, among many other activities. The most common browser software titles on the market are: Microsoft Internet Explorer, Google's Chrome, Mozilla Firefox, Apple's Safari, and Opera. Browser availability depends on the operating system your computer is using (for example: Microsoft Windows, Linux, Ubuntu, Mac OS, among others).

As a Client/Server model, the browser is the client run on a computer that contacts the Web server and requests information. The Web server sends the information back to the Web browser which displays the results on the computer or other Internet-enabled device that supports a browser.

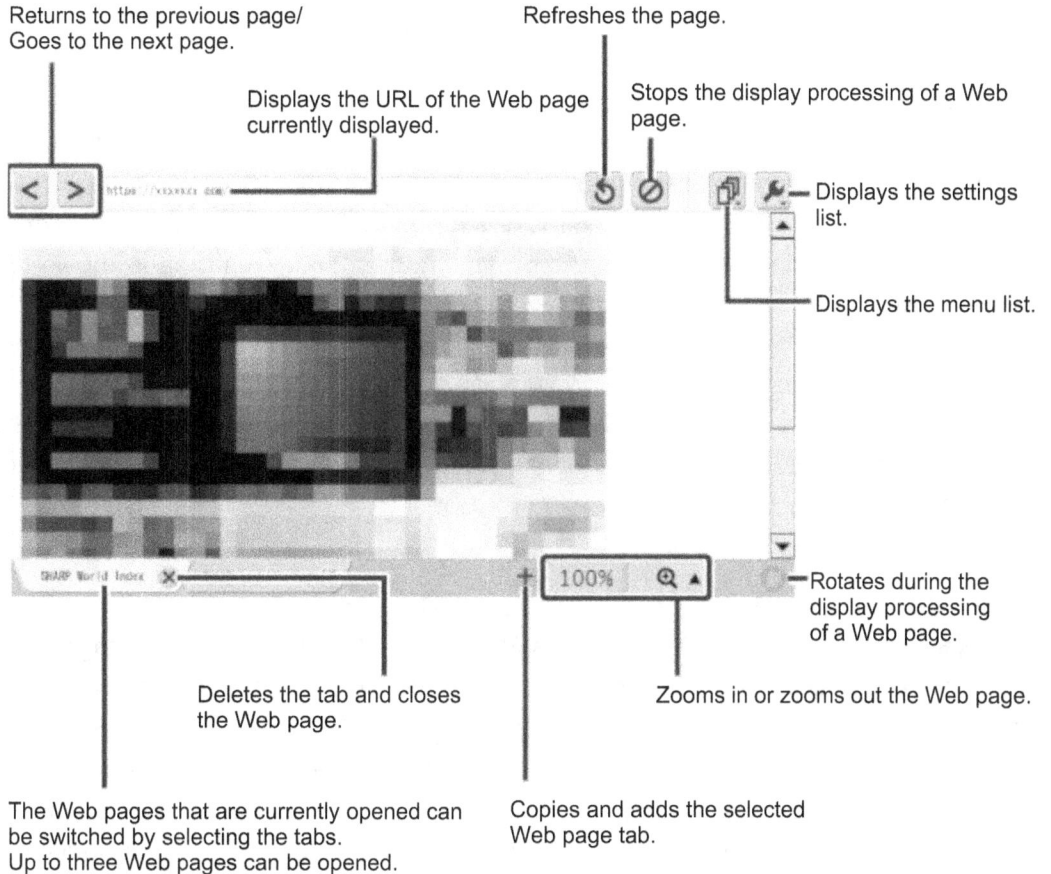

Returns to the previous page/ Goes to the next page.

Refreshes the page.

Displays the URL of the Web page currently displayed.

Stops the display processing of a Web page.

Displays the settings list.

Displays the menu list.

Rotates during the display processing of a Web page.

Deletes the tab and closes the Web page.

Zooms in or zooms out the Web page.

The Web pages that are currently opened can be switched by selecting the tabs. Up to three Web pages can be opened.

Copies and adds the selected Web page tab.

Fig. 7.45: A Web Page

User interface

Most major web browsers have following user interface elements in common:[27]

- *Back* and *forward* buttons to go back to the previous resource and forward respectively.
- A *refresh* or *reload* button to reload the current resource.
- A *stop* button to cancel loading the resource. In some browsers, the stop button is merged with the reload button.
- A *home* button to return to the user's home page.
- An address bar to input the Uniform Resource Identifier (URI) of the desired resource and display it.
- A search bar to input terms into a search engine. In some browsers, the search bar is merged with the address bar.
- A status bar to display progress in loading the resource and also the URI of links when the cursor hovers over them, and page zooming capability.
- The viewport, the visible area of the webpage within the browser window.
- The ability to view the HTML source for a page.

There are four leading web browsers – Explorer, Firefox, Netscape, and Safari, but there are many others browsers available.

1. Internet Explorer (IE) is a product from software giant Microsoft. This is the most commonly used browser in the universe. This was introduced in 1995 along with Windows 95 launch and it has passed Netscape popularity in 1998.

2. Google Chrome : This web browser is developed by Google and its beta version was first released on September 2, 2008 for Microsoft Windows. Today, chrome is known to be one of the most popular web browser with its global share of more than 50%.

3. Mozilla Firefox : Firefox is a new browser derived from Mozilla. It was released in 2004 and has grown to be the second most popular browser on the Internet.

4. Safari : Safari is a web browser developed by Apple Inc. and included in Mac OS X. It was first released as a public beta in January 2003. Safari has very good support for latest technologies like XHTML, CSS2 etc.

7.3.5 HTTP

HTTP is an application layer network protocol built on top of TCP. HTTP clients (such as Web browsers) and servers communicate via HTTP request and response messages. It is a set of standards that allow users of the World Wide Web to exchange information found on web pages. This protocol is used to access the data on World Wide Web.This protocol normally transfers the data in the form of plain text, hypertext, audio, video and so on.

HTTP is called as Hypertext Transfer Protocol because it is used in an environment where there are rapid jumps from one document to another.HTTP functions like a combination of FTP and SMTP. It is said to be similar to FTP because it transfers files. It is said to be similar to SMTP because the data transferred between the client and server are similar to the SMTP messages. However, HTTP differs from SMTP in the way the messages are sent from client to server and from server to client. In case of SMTP, messages are only transferred from server to client.

There are three important properties of HTTP:

1. **HTTP is connectionless:** After a request is made, the client disconnects from the server and waits for a response. The server must re-establish the connection after it process the request.

2. **HTTP is media independent:** Any type of data can be sent by HTTP as long as both the client and server know how to handle the data content. How content is handled is determined by the MIME specification.

3. **HTTP is stateless:** This is a direct result of HTTP's being connectionless. The server and client are aware of each other only during a request. Afterwards, each forgets the other. For this reason neither the client nor the browser can retain information between different request across the web pages reducing the memory overhead of server.

HTTP Communications

The working of HTTP is very simple. A client sends a request and server sends a reply (response) to the client, HTTP uses the services of TCP on well known port 80. Although HTTP uses the services of TCP, HTTP itself is a **"stateless protocol"**. The client initializes the transaction by sending a request message. The server replies by sending a response.

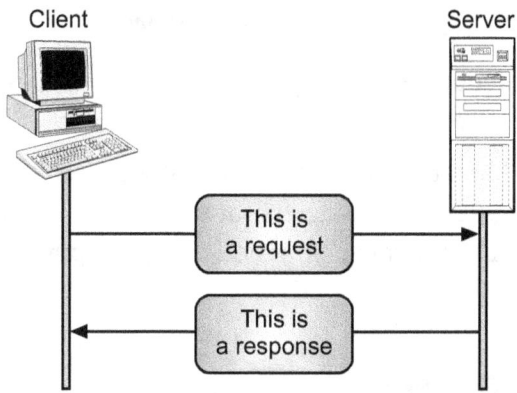

Fig. 7.46 : HTTP Transaction

There are two types of HTTP messages:

1. Request Message, and

2. Response Message.

1. Request Message:

Request message consists of a request line, headers and sometimes a body,

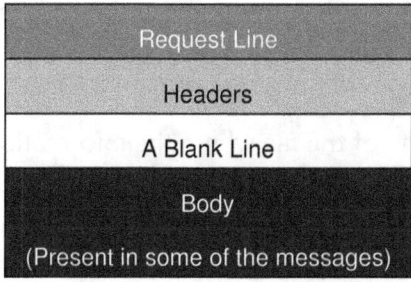

Fig. 7.47: Request message

Fields of request message are described as below:

Request Line:

The request line defines the request type, Uniform resource locator (URL) and HTTP version as shown in Fig. 7.48.

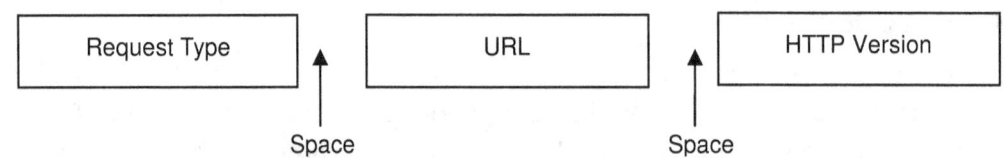

GET http:/www.w3.org/pub/www/sample.html HTTP/1.1

Fig. 7.48: Request line

o **Request Type:** It categorizes the request message into several methods, which will be discussed later.

o **Uniform Resource Locator (URL):** A client that wants to access a web page needs an address. HTTP uses URL to facilitate the access of any document distributed over the world. The URL defines four things: method, host computer, port and path as shown in Fig. 7.49.

URL

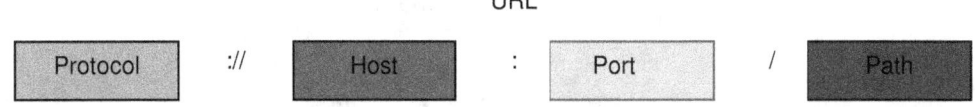

Fig. 7.49: URL

(a) Protocol: A protocol such as FTP, HTTPs, TELNET, etc. that is used to retrieve the document from the web.

(b) Host: Host is a computer where the URL specific information is located. This information can be in terms of webpages or audio video files or other types of files such as doc files or pdf files etc.

(c) Port: URL can originally contain the port number of the server. If the port number is included, it is inserted between the host and the path, and it should be separated from the host by a colon.

(d) Path: It is the pathname of the file where the information is located.

(e) Version: The latest version of HTTP is 1.1 but the versions 0.9 and 1 are also used.

Request Types in the Request Line:

The request method is the actual request that a client issues to the server. Following are some of the important methods:

1. **GET:** The GET method is used when the client wants to retrieve a document from the server. The address of the document is defined in the URL; this is the main method for retrieving a document. The server usually responds with the contents of the document in the body of the response message unless there is an error. The request data that client sends is sent through URL directly.

2. **HEAD:** The HEAD method is used when the client wants some information about a document but not the document itself. It is similar to GET, but the response from the server does not contain a body.

3. **POST:** The POST method is used by the client to provide some information to the server through request message body instead of through URL. For example, it can be used to send input to a server.

4. **PUT:** The PUT method is used by the client to provide a new or replacement document to be stored on the server. The document is included in the body of the request and stored in the location defined by the URL.

5. **PATCH:** PATCH is similar to PUT, except that the request contains a list of differences that should be implemented in the existing file.

6. **COPY:** The COPY method copies a file to another location. The location of the source file is given in the request line (URL). The location of the destination is given in the entity header.

7. **MOVE:** The MOVE method moves a file to another location. The location of the source file is given in the request line (URL); the location of the destination is given in the entity header.

8. **DELETE:** The DELETE method removes a document on the server.

9. **LINK:** The LINK method creates a link or links from a document to another location. The location of the file is given in the request line (URL); the location of the destination is given in the entity header.

10. **UNLINK:** The UNLINK method deletes links created by the LINK method.

11. **OPTION:** The OPTION method is used by the client to ask the server about the available options which the server supports.

2. **Response Message:**

A response message consists of a status line, a header and sometimes a body. (Refer Fig. 7.50)

Status Line: The status line defines the status of the response message. It consists of the HTTP version, a status code and a status phrase.

(i) **HTTP Version:** This field is the same as the corresponding field in the request line.

(ii) **Status Code:** The status code field is similar to those in the FTP and the SMTP protocol. It consists of three digits.

(iii) **Status Phrase:** This field explains the status code in text form.

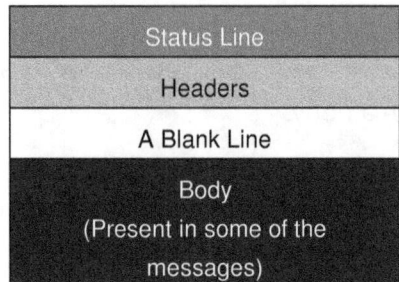

Fig. 7.50: Response message

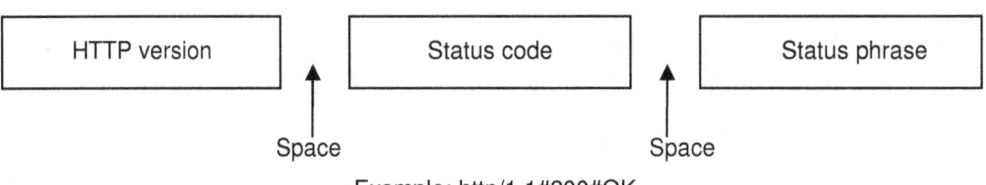

Example: http/1.1#200#OK

Fig. 7.51 Status line

Headers:

The headers exchange additional information between the client and the server. The header can be of one or more lines. Each header line is made of a header name, a colon, a space and a header value as shown in the Fig. 7.52.

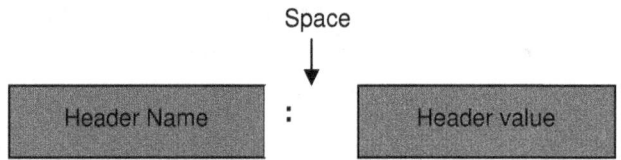

Fig. 7.52: Header format

The header lines can be of four categories:

1. General header,

2. Request header,

3. Response header,

4. Entity header

A request message can contain general request and entity headers while response message can contain general response and entity headers.

1. **General Header:** It gives general information about the message. It is present in request as well as response message.

2. **Request Header:** It can be present only in request message, which is used to specify client's configuration and client's preferred file format.

3. **Response Header:** It can be present only in the response message. It is used for specifying the server's configuration.

4. **Entity Header:** It is used for giving the information about the body of the document. It is mostly present in the request message and some response message.

Message Body:

An HTTP message may have a body of data sent after a blank line after the header lines. In a response, this is where the requested resource is returned to the client (the most common use of the message body), or perhaps explanatory text if there's an error. In a request, this is user-entered data or uploaded files are sent to the server.

If an HTTP message includes a body, there are usually header lines in the message that describe the body. In particular:

1. **The Content-Type:** header gives the MIME-type of the data in the body, such as text/html or image/gif.

2. **The Content-Length:** header gives the number of bytes in the body.

A comparison of request message and response message is shown in Fig. 7.53.

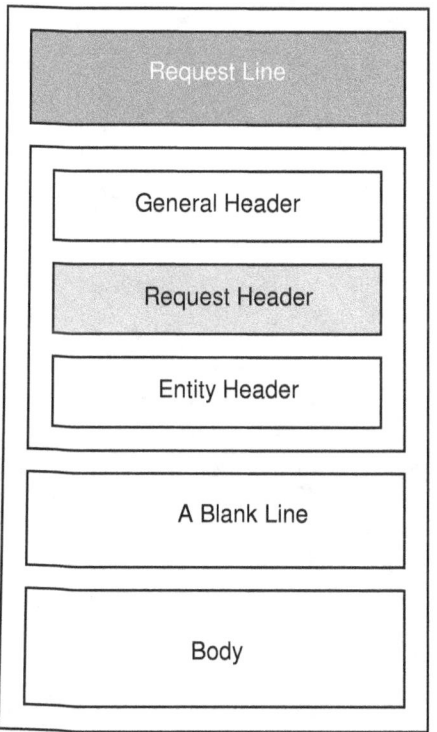

Request Message

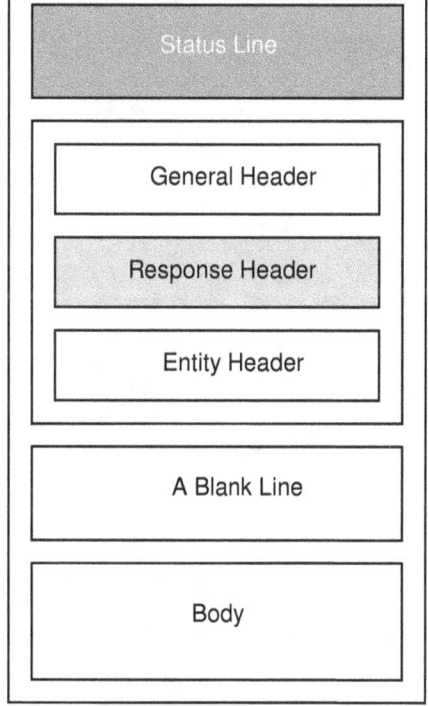

Response Message

Fig. 7.53 : Request and Response Message Headers

Practice Questions

1. What is Domain Name system? Explain with diagram.

2. Which are types of DNS?

3. Write a short note on DNS server.

4. Which are types of Resource records.

5. Describe Message format of DNS.

6. Explain concept of E-mail and its Architecture.

7. What is MIME?

8. Explain terms: SMTP, Mail gateways, Relays.

9. Write a short note on HTTP.

10. What are Static and Dynamic Web Pages?

www.ingramcontent.com/pod-product-compliance
Lightning Source LLC
Chambersburg PA
CBHW081146020726
47504CB00009B/2022